Estelle Ryan

DISCARDED FROM THE
NASHVILLE PUBLIC LIBRARY

The

Courbet Connection

D0967739

The Courbet Connection

The Courbet Connection
A Genevieve Lenard Novel
By Estelle Ryan

All rights reserved. No part of this book may be reproduced in any manner whatsoever, including internet usage, without written permission from the author except in the case of brief quotations embodied in critical articles and reviews.

First published 2014
Copyright © 2014 by Estelle Ryan

This is a work of fiction. Names, characters, places and incidents are either a product of the author's imagination or are used fictitiously. Any resemblance to actual persons, living or dead, business establishments, events, or locales is purely incidental.

The Courbet Connection

Acknowledgements

I want to take up this space by acknowledging my readers. You guys have no idea how much I appreciate every like on Facebook, every comment, every newsletter subscriber, every email and every review.

Frequently, I find myself staring at my computer screen in amazement, simultaneously humbled, deeply touched and grateful that so many truly wonderful people take the time to connect with me. Please know that not once do I take any of your communication for granted.

To my amazing support system: I would not be here without you and this journey would not be half as much fun if I couldn't share it with you.

A shout-out to all those readers who so graciously allowed me to use their names.

The Courbet Connection

Dedication

To Jane.

Chapter ONE

"Doctor Lenard! I want to speak to Doctor Genevieve Lenard! Where is she? The Red Sea is the warmest sea in the world! Doctor Lenard!"

I looked away from the computer monitors to glare at the glass doors to my left. The doors separating my viewing room from the team room had been sealed. Now they were slightly ajar, allowing the yelling to distract me.

"Doctor Lenard! You need me! Doctor Lenard!" The loud voice belonged to a young person. That much was clear to me. I rolled my shoulders to stretch the taut *trapezius* muscles in my neck.

My room was set up for maximum comfort and efficiency when viewing video footage. The glass doors had been specially fitted to seal so I could work in a soundproof—and uninterrupted—environment. I only went into the team room for meetings, which I often experienced to be chaotic, the constant digression a vexing waste of time.

More yelling ensued, but it was the lack of emotion, and the increase in volume of the young voice that completely drew my attention away from my work. I sighed and shook my head angrily. This disturbance was most unwelcome. The case I was working on was much more pressing than a stranger seeking me out and reciting strange geographical facts.

In front of me, ten monitors were arranged in a curve, filled with information we had gathered on Dukwicz. The notorious international assassin had evaded capture for more than a year. Not only had he killed people without remorse, he had terrorised me inside my own apartment and had stolen three clocks I had highly valued until he'd touched them.

It didn't matter that he had returned those clocks to my apartment. I had seen that action for what it was—an intimidation technique. It hadn't worked. If anything, it had made us more determined to find him.

His weakness for timepieces might very well be the key to catching him. Two days ago, Vinnie had heard from one of his contacts about a man offering to beat up non-paying clients for a fee or for a valuable timepiece. It was the latter form of payment that made me take notice.

Vinnie, the most intimidating member of our team, had convinced his contact to divulge information on how he had heard of this service, and how to get in touch with the service provider we suspected was Dukwicz. I had learned early on to never question Vinnie's methods in gaining information. It caused me much less mental distress not knowing.

"Doctor Lenard! I want to speak to you! Japan has six thousand eight hundred and fifty-two islands!" The yelling was much closer now, possibly in the hallway outside my viewing room. Movement in the team room drew my attention. Through the glass doors, I watched Vinnie get up from the round table used for our meetings and walk towards the hallway.

Manny, an Interpol agent and the only law enforcement individual on our team, followed Vinnie to the hallway. Manny was the oldest and was in constant conflict with the other team members who were not known to be law-abiding citizens. Yet he was the first to defend us. Aggressively, if needed.

I turned back to my computer and ten monitors. I had full confidence in Manny and Vinnie handling this situation. I also knew that Phillip, my boss and the owner of Rousseau & Rousseau, the insurance company I worked for, would keep away the person shouting out random facts.

No sooner had I started looking into the phone records of Vinnie's contact than the glass doors opened fully, allowing the panicked yelling from further down the hallway to reach me.

"Jen-girl, I think you're going to have to come out and deal with this." Vinnie stood in the open doorway, his usual place. The *depressor anguli oris* muscles turned the corners of his mouth down.

"You know I don't handle things. Why would you even ask? Can't Phillip handle this?"

"He asked me to call you." Vinnie lifted one shoulder in a half-shrug. A gesture employed when we weren't convinced of our thoughts or statements. "Phillip and the old man reckon the kid is like you."

"Like me?" Did the young person have an exceptionally high IQ? Was he a world-renowned expert at reading and interpreting nonverbal communication?

"They think he might be on the autistic spectrum."

"How did they become experts to make such a diagnosis?" My eyebrows raised and I leaned away from Vinnie. I didn't want to admit that the quality in the young man's tone of voice and his odd recitation of geographical facts could confirm their suspicions.

Vinnie tilted his head to the side. "Please? Colin isn't here and they don't know what else to do."

Colin was my romantic partner. I refused to call him my boyfriend. We were both in our mid-thirties, far too mature to be girlfriend and boyfriend. Colin had an uncanny ability in dealing with me. He knew what to say and how to say it. More importantly, he knew when not to say anything. I wished he was here. He would know to leave me alone. And he would've handled the situation.

"Jen-girl?"

I pushed myself out of my chair, making sure Vinnie saw my disapproving expression. "I don't know what you expect me to do."

"Not just me. Phillip and the old man too." Vinnie followed me through the team room to the hallway. "I wanted to throw the whining little shit out. Phillip wouldn't let me."

"Where are they?" We were in the hallway. Alone.

Before Vinnie could answer, screaming came from the conference room. It was the yelling not to be touched that had me increasing my pace to the large conference room. Having high-functioning autism, I couldn't bear being touched. My personal space was particularly wide, much to Manny's annoyance. The only person who'd broken through my intense dislike of close personal contact was Colin.

Vinnie and I walked into the conference room and immediately I smelled it. A body that had not been washed for an extended period. On the far side of the conference table stood a teenager. His eyes were wide in his dark-skinned face, giving him a wild, out-of-control look, and he continued screaming not to be touched. I had never been good with estimating ages, but he looked no older than sixteen. An adolescent. An extremely challenging stage to work through for an autistic individual, especially without any guidance.

Looking a bit more closely at him, I was sure he'd been wearing the same outfit for the last week or so. His long-sleeved t-shirt had a few holes, many stains and hung loosely on his body. Not only did this teenager look in desperate need of a shower, he looked severely underfed. His pallor could be attributed to emotions, but I wondered if it wasn't because of a lack of care, a lack of nutrition.

Manny and Phillip were both standing close to the door, their body language completely non-threatening. Not that the young man noticed it. Like many other autistic individuals, he probably had never learned to read the subtle cues we give with our body language, helping others understand our intentions. If he'd been able to read Manny and Phillip's cues, he might have calmed down by now.

"Doctor Lenard! You're here! I want to speak to you! In February 1979 and March 2012, it snowed in the Sahara. Tell them to go away!" Staring at my shoulder, he pushed his back against the wall, his voice echoing in the large room.

"No." I kept my voice low. I wanted him to strain to hear me.

"What do you mean, 'no'?" Instead of imitating my lowered voice, he raised his even more.

"I mean that I refuse to speak to you if you are screaming. Or if you are rude to my friends."

Typical of people on the spectrum, he didn't respond immediately. People with autism were each unique, as was their processing time. Some needed a few seconds to work through the information presented to them before they responded. Others needed minutes. It appeared this young man needed minutes. His lips were moving in a silent monologue. We waited in silence while he bounced his back against the wall in a semi-rocking motion.

"I cannot guarantee that I will not be rude." His tone was appropriately low for an indoor conversation, albeit without much inflection. "I can, however, refrain from shouting. As long as you speak to me. As long as they don't come close to me. As long as…"

"Stop." I raised my hand, palm towards him. "You are a guest in our conference room. You have no right to make any demands."

"Oh, but I do. I have information that gives me the right."

Immediately, Manny's body language changed from non-threatening to alert. The change in his slouched posture was subtle, but after working with him for almost two years, it was easy to spot. Vinnie took a step closer to me.

"What do you mean, you have information?" Manny asked.

"I won't speak to you. You are not intelligent enough."

I turned around and walked to the door. I stopped just outside the room and looked back. "You seem to be an intelligent young man. Ponder upon this. No matter how softly you speak, I refuse to listen to you if you insist on being rude to the people in this room. Either you treat them with respect or you can find someone else to speak to."

I didn't wait for an answer. I had numerous degrees, most of those in psychology, but I was not a therapist. I didn't know how to sensitively work with neurotypical or non-neurotypical people. I was not going to act as this young man's counsellor or confessor. Very likely, he could benefit greatly from cognitive therapy, but I had zero interest in providing it. I returned to my viewing room, fully intending to continue my search for more information on Dukwicz. We needed to find him and make sure that he could no longer kill or beat people up for payment—be it cash or timepieces.

When the glass door to my viewing room silently slid open a few minutes later, I sighed heavily and swivelled my chair to face Phillip. As usual, my boss was dressed in a bespoke suit, his appearance immaculate and appropriate for the CEO of a high-end insurance company. He walked closer and looked down at me. "He's ready to talk."

"I don't want to talk to him. He's rude and abrasive."

Phillip raised one eyebrow and just looked at me. I knew that look. This man had become the father I'd never had. After working together for eight years, he had my respect. When he looked at me like he did now, I paid attention. It was his way of telling me to reconsider the position I'd taken on a topic. For a few seconds I did just that.

My shoulders dropped a little and I briefly closed my eyes. "I try really hard not to be rude and abrasive."

"And you succeed more and more every day." He lowered his chin to give me his serious look. "Of all people, you should empathise with Caelan."

"Who's Caelan?"

"The young man wanting to speak to you. He refused to give us his surname, and is now waiting for you in the conference room."

"Why do you want me to speak to him?" I lifted both shoulders. "I'm not the people person here. You have a natural ability to put people at ease. Francine will quickly connect with him on some level. I'm sure Tim would also do much better than I would."

I'd watched Francine, our IT specialist and my only female friend, gain the trust of waiters, shop assistants and complete strangers on the street. Tim was Phillip's assistant and it was his job to build rapport with strangers.

"I don't have your ability to read people. I also don't have your personal understanding of what Caelan is experiencing. He needs care, Genevieve. I'm sure you saw that." Phillip pulled his shoulders back, the posture he employed when he was finalising his negotiations with clients. "At some point in our lives, everyone needs to be given a chance. I'm asking you to give Caelan one. Listen to what he has to say, please."

Phillip was the one who'd given me a chance. Despite my lack of interpersonal skills, he had employed me, giving me the first opportunity to be completely independent. I thought about affording people chances some more. "Did someone give you a chance?"

"Yes. Many years ago. I'll tell you about it one day. Right now, we have a young man who needs you."

I nodded once and followed Phillip to the conference room. Vinnie was standing by the door, his irritation clear in his lowered brows, his hands on his hips, and his broadened chest. Manny sat slumped in a chair as if he didn't care. I knew this to merely be an illusion.

Caelan was sitting in the chair furthest from the door, hugging his knees to his chest and gently rocking. It took him a few seconds to stop rocking and straighten when he saw me enter the room.

He looked at my shoulder. "You'll listen to me?"

"Yes." I walked deeper into the room and sat down three chairs away from him. I studied him for a few seconds. I needed that time to decide on my approach. "What is your IQ?"

"Hundred and forty-three."

"Lower than mine."

"I know. You are considered the most proficient in nonverbal communication analysis. Every paper you've ever written on the topic is an academic achievement and used in most universities in the world. There are also three Facebook pages dedicated to your lectures and articles."

"I have Facebook pages?"

"Three."

"Oh."

It was silent in the conference room for a while.

"It is because of your achievements that I'm here. I know that you are working in a team supervised by the president of France. I know that the old guy is Colonel Manfred Millard, an Interpol agent. The big, scarred dude is your criminal liaison, and you have a thief and a hacker working for you as well."

Manny's muscle tension increased significantly, Vinnie's posture became more threatening. After two years, I no longer noticed the long, ragged scar running down the left side of Vinnie's face. Francine had told me it made Vinnie look more dangerous and intimidating to most people.

"How do you know this?" I kept my tone low, even though tension tightened my vocal cords.

Caelan pressed his lips together. People on the spectrum were seldom good liars. Unless I used my in-depth knowledge on deception, I was a remarkably unsuccessful liar. Telling the truth was a strong compulsion I often had to control in order to not give offence.

I was watching these typical autistic traits in Caelan. The expression on his face led me to believe he was finding it hard not to give in to his need to tell the truth. For some reason he didn't want to share how he knew so much about us.

"If your IQ is what you claim it to be, you'll see the dilemma you're in." I ignored his quick intake of breath when I questioned his IQ. "You came to us for some reason. I can only assume that you want or need some help. Yet you insist on being rude, on not co-operating."

"I wasn't being rude. I just didn't answer."

"Which is rude." Vinnie folded his arms, his top lip slightly curled.

I pointed at Vinnie's bulging arms. "See his posture? Vinnie's nonverbal cues tell me that he doesn't trust you, he would like to get the truth from you in some aggressive manner, and he sees you as a threat to our team."

"You can't make me talk!" Caelan pulled his legs up and hugged his knees tightly against his chest. "I won't tell you anything."

Phillip lifted one hand when both Vinnie and Manny inhaled to question Caelan. He leaned forward, resting his hands on the table. "You came to us, Caelan. Unless you offer something worth our time and attention, your side of the negotiation doesn't carry much power."

Caelan looked at Phillip's shoulder for a few seconds. I watched his expression alter slightly to one of respect. As he inhaled to speak, Vinnie stepped forward. I was used to his tall, muscular frame and sometimes forgot how frightening he could appear. The fear flooding Caelan's face was a strong reminder of Vinnie's intimidation skills.

"Listen, you little twerp. You think you're so smart, but I'm beginning to think that you lied about your IQ." It wasn't only Vinnie's tone, but this outrageous statement that made me look at him in surprise. I registered his modified shrug and his hand rubbing his neck. Vinnie was lying. "I also think that you pretend to be older than you really are. I reckon you're a fourteen-year-old loser who's been kicked out of school for missing too many classes, not showering and failing a few exams. Your teachers know what you don't seem to accept. That you're average. An average little kid with average grades and a bad attitude."

My *masseter* muscles slackened, causing my bottom jaw to drop slightly. Vinnie was manipulating Caelan with worrying success. The young man's distress was reaching levels high enough to make him utter an involuntary keen. His eyes were growing wider, he was chewing his bottom lip and he was rocking in the chair.

It disturbed me greatly to watch someone so young in such emotional anguish. I was equally horrified that Manny and Phillip hadn't stepped in. Just as I leaned forward, Caelan jumped out of the chair. He took a step towards Vinnie, glaring at his shoulder. "It's not true, you... you... big man!

You only wish you had an IQ as high as mine. At least then you could see that I am at the very least sixteen years old, but because of my smaller build, you would know I am seventeen. But your average IQ is not allowing you to see this, is it?"

Vinnie shrugged. "I don't believe you. Your teachers will confirm my suspicions, I'm sure."

"Teachers! Hah!" Caelan wiped his mouth on his grimy sleeve. "My teachers were so scared of my intellect that they avoided me. I was teaching *them* math. They couldn't teach me anything else, so I left."

"And ran to Mommy?" Vinnie rolled his eyes. "Loser."

"My mom only cares about her gin, my dad about his football. I'm sure they didn't even notice I was gone until a week after I left."

"So you've been on your own for a whole week? Like I would believe that." Vinnie's method was becoming clear to me and I felt conflicted. It was commendable that he had managed to gain so much information from Caelan in such a short time. I just didn't feel comfortable with his technique.

"You really are stupid! I've been on my own for three years now. See! You don't know anything. I've been living alone, without parents and teachers who didn't care and knew nothing."

Vinnie leaned back, smirking. "Hey, at least I can switch on a computer. More than you can do, I'm sure."

"I can drain your bank account faster than you can write an SMS on your antiquated cell phone. How do you think I found you? I will agree that my hacking skills do not equal those of Francine, but I'm good enough to know her name. And to know that you should do an extra spell check when you send emails." Caelan turned to me. "How do you work with such imbeciles?"

I felt uncommon sympathy for this young man. "Take a moment and think about the last few minutes before you call Vinnie an imbecile. What has he achieved?"

For two minutes I observed Caelan processing his conversation with Vinnie. His nonverbal cues were not the same as neurotypical people's, but it was easy to see when realisation came to him. He looked up at Vinnie, his eyes large, this time with respect. "Brilliantly devious. Teach me to do that."

"Oh, no, bucko. You're a menace enough as it is." Vinnie pulled out a chair and sat down.

"Now that we know a little more about you, tell us why you are here, lad." Manny's tone was as relaxed as his slouched posture. Yet I saw the calculation around his eyes and mouth.

Caelan stared at the wall behind me for a few seconds before he sat down, his posture not as confident as before. "Promise you won't kick me out."

"I can promise you that," Phillip said. "We don't kick people out."

"You are the big boss who deals with stolen art, right?"

"Yes, I own this company."

"And you let a thief work for you."

"Don't be rude." Vinnie's fierce loyalty towards Colin elicited a gentle feeling in my chest. Colin didn't call himself a thief. He insisted that he merely reappropriated art and other objects. I maintained taking something that didn't belong to you was stealing.

I returned my focus to Caelan. "What do you want to tell me?"

Caelan pulled his shoulders back. "In the last fifteen months, I've seen fifteen paintings being sold on the dark net. I'm not as good an expert as Colin, but I feel confident that they are superior forgeries of paintings that are listed as stolen."

Phillip's body tensed. "What paintings?"

"If I tell you, you'll let me stay?"

"What do you mean by 'stay'?" Vinnie asked. I had explained to him about the literal thinking of those on the spectrum. Even I was concerned that Caelan intended to move in, either here at Rousseau & Rousseau or at one of our homes.

"Stay on the case." Caelan's expression showed he'd lost some respect for Vinnie because of the inane question. "I want to help you solve this case."

"No." It had taken me two years to be comfortable working with other people. I was not going to allow a stranger, a neglected young man, into my professional life.

Phillip looked at me until I paid attention to his expression. He respected my opinion, but was curious about Caelan's information. Phillip blinked to break eye contact with me and turned to Caelan. "If you can help Rousseau & Rousseau track down forged art, we might consider—"

"Yay! I'm part of the team." Caelan's expression lightened.

"Not yet, lad." Manny sat up, his expression distrustful. "What paintings were sold? And what is the dark net?"

"Ask Francine what the dark net is. She'll know. And she'll know how to explain it to old people. I'll just make you angry."

"You're making me angry now."

"Oh."

"What paintings?" Manny asked through his teeth.

"There was a Jean Désiré Gustave Courbet." Caelan looked at my shoulder. "Tell Colin it was the *Full Standing Figure of a Man*. He'll know what it implies."

Having limited insight into the workings of his mind, I studied his nonverbal cues for a few seconds. "You are proud of yourself."

"I'm part of a team."

"It's more than that. What are you so proud of?"

Caelan took his time to answer. He looked at my shoulder, biting his lips. "Normal people trade information."

I inhaled sharply at his unspoken desire to be normal. Had no one ever told him 'normal' is an undefinable concept? An ideal unattainable for most? Accepting one's uniqueness was the true art of living a fulfilled life. I brought my thoughts back to the last part of his statement. "What do you want to trade it for?"

"Time with you. Not just you. The whole team. I want to spend time with you."

I was about to immediately dispel that notion, but Phillip interrupted me. "As a team, we need to discuss this. Surely you can understand that. If you are going to help on this case, if you want to be part of the team, everyone will have to agree to this."

"And we need to check your information," Manny said. "You're going to have to give us more than the name of an artist and a dark net."

Caelan took plenty of time preparing an answer. After a minute, Manny became impatient, drumming his fingers on the arm of his chair.

Caelan looked up, his eyes bright. "Tell Francine that Silk Road has a repeat. Not Silk Road 2.0, 2.1 or even 3.0. It's a whole new place."

"What the bleeding hell does that mean?"

Caelan pressed his lips together, again staring at the far wall. The three men tried numerous methods of coaxing something else from him, but he simply sat in the chair rocking.

Three more minutes of this and I went to my viewing room. I planned to get another two hours of work in before I went home. Colin had said he would meet me at home for dinner. Hopefully, he would be able to give more insight into Caelan's scant revelations.

Chapter TWO

I opened the door to my apartment, stepped into my haven and stopped in horror. To the right of the door was a coat tree. Under the coat tree was a special mat I had bought for shoes. It was that space that sped up my heart rate and breathing. Three pairs of sneakers were thoughtlessly dropped there in disarray. One pair was larger than the other two, obviously a man's shoes. They were well worn and dirty in a way that sent a shudder through my whole body.

Chatter coming from deeper inside my apartment forced my eyes away from the disturbing lack of neat arrangement at the front door. Beyond the sitting area to my right, three young people were seated around my dining room table. They were involved in a passionate discussion. I closed the door behind me and walked deeper into the large open-space living area.

Three empty pizza boxes, open cans of cola and scattered papers and books made it impossible for me to pay any attention to the topic of discussion. I swallowed at the strong compulsion to snatch the greasy boxes from my solid wood table top and start an intensive cleaning session. I had planned on coming home and enjoying a cup of calming camomile tea. Not standing a few feet away from three students debating some issue while desecrating my immaculate apartment.

Sitting in my usual seat at the table, Nikki was pointing her finger at a young man. The young woman had come into our lives a year ago under difficult circumstances. Since then, she'd changed from an adolescent not sure of herself into a caring and confident young woman. She had surprised me by being quite an easy housemate. Generally.

When she'd chosen to study art out of all her other options, I'd supported and encouraged her. We had mutually agreed that I wouldn't enter her bedroom. She needed that space to express her artistic soul, she'd said. She also enjoyed using her 'artistic soul' as an excuse for being melodramatic. Like now. Only when I reached the table did they notice my presence.

"Oh, you're home!" Nikki sat up in her chair, her eyes widening briefly. That involuntary nonverbal cue happened not only when we were surprised, but also when we were pleased to see someone. I saw the exact moment she registered my expression and concluded the cause of it. She grabbed a pile of papers in front of her and tried to straighten them. "Oh, shit. Sorry, Doc G. We were studying and kinda lost track of time. I really meant to clean up before you came. How was your day?"

I could not answer her. The overpowering need to grab the papers from her ineffective shaking prevented me from forming any words.

"Doc G? These are my friends, Rebecca and Michael. I've told you about them before." Tension caused her voice to rise in pitch. Nikki frowned and glanced at the two young people staring at me with a combination of interest and discomfort. She dropped the papers in an untidy heap, stood up and walked around the table until she stood in front of me. She snapped her fingers in front of my face. "Doc G? Look at me?"

Her snapping fingers annoyed me. "Don't do that."

The *zygomaticus* muscles pulled her generous mouth into a wide smile. "At least I got your attention. We'll clean up in another two minutes. But first, please meet my friends."

It was clear on her face how much this meant to her. She was not the only one who had changed in the last year. Her presence in my life, in my apartment, had taught me that there were times when others' needs took precedence over my own. No matter how compulsive that desire was to put order to the many papers on the table. And to ensure there were no stains from the pizza boxes.

I closed my eyes and mentally played the first line of Mozart's Horn Concerto No.3 in E-Flat minor. There were times when Mozart was my closest link to serenity. Whether I mentally wrote a concerto or played it in my mind, it always succeeded in grounding me. The few seconds of perfect harmony were enough to put order to my thoughts and change my focus. I turned to the table and Nikki's two friends.

"This is Rebecca." Nikki waved her arm at the lanky girl, who straightened from her slouched position and wiped her hands on her lime-green skirt. Rubbing one's thighs was pacifying behaviour. Rebecca was uncomfortable. It was confirmed when she tugged at the hem of her multi-coloured shirt. Nikki took a step closer to her friend. "She's the one who made us all look bad with her amazeballs sculpture that won the Pierre DuPreez award."

The pride in Nikki's voice made me pay close attention to her friend. I looked at the awkward young woman and saw the intelligence in her eyes. "Good afternoon, Rebecca."

"Hi, Doc G. I've heard so much about you." Her hand flew to her throat. "Can I call you Doc G? Should I call you Doctor Genevieve? No! Doctor Lenard? Oh, God, I'm so sorry."

I blinked a few times at her nervous behaviour. "Doc G is acceptable."

"Phew. Thanks." Her genuine smile lifted her cheeks and crinkled the corners of her eyes. She turned to the young man next to her. "At least now you also know what to call her."

"This is—"

"I'm Michael Civitelli," the young man interrupted Nikki. "I'm very pleased to meet you, Doc G. Nikki talks about you all the time."

People blushed when they were embarrassed, excited, or in the throes of passion. The colour on Nikki's cheeks was from pleasure. More frequently I'd been seeing the accompanying expression of contentment. It affected me. She had brought many new challenges into my life. She'd also brought new emotions. An emotion that I'd come to associate with Nikki softened my annoyance.

"She only says good things about you, Doc G." Rebecca's quick addition was accompanied by concern.

"Why should she only say good things?" I looked at Nikki. "Did you lie to them?"

Nikki laughed. "No, I didn't. I told them that you're a pain in my butt. But I also told them how cool you are."

Tempted to go into yet another discussion about Nikki's vocabulary and incorrect descriptions, I reminded myself to remain socially aware of this situation. It was important to her. I nodded at the young man. "Good afternoon, Michael."

Amusement briefly lifted the corners of his mouth before he made an effort to neutralise his expression. I wondered why he had thought my polite greeting was humorous, but decided not to ask him. "What are you studying? Are you studying?"

"We were." Nikki glanced at the papers on the table. "We're taking a test on art history and Rebecca is making it much more interesting. She's smart, putting all the different events and dates together. We're the daft ones."

My eyes narrowed. "I don't know Michael, but you're not daft. Don't deprecate yourself."

"Okay." Nikki drew out the word while smiling sweetly. "Changing topics. Maybe you can settle an argument for us."

"I don't think that is wise." Only once had I tried to interfere in an argument between Vinnie and Francine. Siding with Vinnie regarding complementary spices to a dish had only heightened the tension and had given Francine more irrational points to add to her line of reasoning. After a lengthy discussion with Colin, I had concluded that staying neutral, but especially silent, was a judicious course of action.

"Bah!" Nikki waved one hand. "Michael doesn't think Pascal was kidnapped, but Rebecca and I are convinced that no one disappears out of the blue like this."

My eyes had strayed to the pizza boxes again, but Nikki's convoluted babbling had me turning to her with a frown pulling my brows together. "What are you talking about?"

"Pascal Brami," she said in a tone indicating that the name should be enough for me. I maintained my bemused expression until she threw her hands in the air. "You weren't listening last night, were you?"

"Did you address me directly? Was it a topic of interest?"

"No. Yes. I told Vinnie about this while he was cooking last night. You were sitting right here." She sighed dramatically. "You were writing Mozart in your head again, weren't you?"

"His Clarinet Concerto in A major."

Michael's expression was changing from entertained to perplexed. I shook my head to get away from this asinine discussion. "What did you tell Vinnie last night?" Nikki inhaled, but held her breath when I lifted my index finger. "Please keep it factual and in chronological order."

Michael leaned forward when Nikki exhaled on an unladylike snort. "Uhm, maybe I could tell this fairy tale?"

I studied the male student. Even though his hair was cut in

a neat style, it stood in all directions as if he hadn't combed it. His clothes looked clean enough, but possibly had been picked out of a pile of clean laundry. An interesting inconsistency was his thick textbook and the neat pile of papers on top of it. Several colourful tags serving as placeholders stuck out of the textbook, placed equidistant from each other.

I nodded to him. "Please tell me about Pascal."

Nikki fell into her chair. "He's going to make it sound silly."

"Because it *is* silly, Nikkidee." Michael rolled his eyes. "Pascal has a reputation around campus as a… party animal."

My eyes narrowed. "Your expression and the long pause tell me that there is some hidden meaning to 'party animal'. Please explain."

He glanced at Nikki. She nodded impatiently and waved him on.

"Okay then. Pascal experiments with everything. Drugs, girls, boys, everything. Even within the art student groups, he doesn't have a good reputation. He's a bit too wild."

"When he's on drugs, he's kinda okay, but alcohol makes him aggressive." Nikki's soft addition caused my throat to tighten.

I bit down on the insides of my lips to prevent myself from speaking before thinking it through. It took me ten seconds of awkward silence to organise my thoughts. I slowly turned to Nikki and schooled my nonverbal cues to communicate care, not the all-consuming concern I felt. "Please tell me you weren't around him when he was using drugs or drunk. Or that you were using."

"I didn't use. And I was only around him once when he was like that." Nikki tilted her head towards Rebecca. "We were all at a house party just after the holidays. As soon as Pascal started acting out, Rebecca and I left."

Nikki was telling the truth. The feeling of a vice tightening around my chest eased and I let out a shaky breath. "I need you to be careful, Nikki."

"I am, Doc G. Pascal is a really nice guy when he's not drinking or high. He's also really smart and we enjoy his company, but usually it's just the three of us hanging out." She leaned forward, exposing her face for my inspection. "We're careful and we look out for each other."

The other two responded with excessive verbal and nonverbal confirmation. Their truthfulness should've sufficed, but with Nikki, my emotions sometimes overrode all rationality. It took tremendous control not to pursue this topic any further. "I believe you. Now tell me why I needed to know about Pascal's narcotics use."

"Because I think that he's on a binge somewhere and the girls think that he's been abducted by aliens," Michael said.

"We don't think that, you dork." Rebecca pulled her shoulders back and looked at me. "Pascal parties really hard, but he never misses ceramics. He might miss any other class, but never this one. He rocks anything to do with ceramics and he tries to get in as much theory and practice as possible. When he wasn't in class today for the second day in a row, I asked our professor and he said that this week was the first time ever Pascal didn't show up for class."

"That is not enough reason to think he's been kidnapped." I pulled out a dining room chair and sat down, consciously keeping my eyes averted from the chaos on the table. "Do you have any evidence to support your suspicions?"

Nikki's shoulders pulled halfway up to her ears. "Uhm... Rebecca and I went to his flat this afternoon. His flatmate said that Pascal hasn't been home in three days. We went into his room and saw a half-eaten sandwich and a full mug of coffee next to his open laptop. It was as if he left in the middle of something. As if he was taken."

Michael blew through his lips and leaned back in his chair. "See, Doc G? Not enough to think that he was kidnapped. He could've just upped and left for a party when someone phoned him."

"I agree. Your suspicions don't have a solid base, Nikki."

"Aw, come on, Doc G." Nikki folded her arms. "Don't take Michael's side. He didn't read the articles about the other kidnappings."

"What other kidnappings?" This got my interest. And my concern.

"A week ago, another boy disappeared from a university in Paris. They knew he'd been kidnapped, because there were signs of a struggle in his flat, his door was broken and some other stuff the article talked about."

"And you allowed this article to influence you so strongly that you drew unsubstantiated conclusions about Pascal?" I lifted both eyebrows and stared at Nikki. "You are more intelligent than this."

Michael chuckled at the same time as Rebecca gasped. Nikki just rolled her eyes. "At this moment, I don't care how right your logic might sound. I'm going by my gut."

"Vinnie should never have encouraged you to start that silliness." No matter how I had tried to dissuade Nikki from being swayed by Vinnie's lack of rationality, she had decided to practice following her intuition. They preferred to call it 'following her gut'.

"Will you please check it out?" Nikki leaned towards me, her facial muscles contracted into an imploring expression. "Please, Doc G? Pascal might be an idiot at times, but I'm really worried about him."

I weighed up the time it would take to look into Nikki's suspicions. It didn't take me too long to conclude that my time would be better spent following leads to Dukwicz's whereabouts.

"Please, Doc G." Rebecca's quiet tone pulled me out of my thoughts. The concern on her face was as genuine as Nikki's. I was convinced they were misguided in their suspicions.

Why then did I feel an uncomfortable urge to give into their irrational request? I had never before been this concerned with someone else's happiness.

I shook my head and exhaled heavily. "I will not spend more than two hours on this undoubtedly fruitless search."

"Thank you!" Nikki jumped out her chair, ran around to where I was sitting and hugged me. I felt crowded and the need to push her away caused me to close my eyes tightly. I forced Mozart's Horn Concerto back into my mind until I could open my fists and pat her lightly on her back. Colin insisted that people appreciated a gesture of acceptance when they reached out. "Thank you, thank you, thank you!"

"Enough." I gently pried her arms from around my shoulders until she straightened. "I can't promise that I'll find anything. I'm only promising to look."

"That's all I'm asking."

The sound of keys in the front door thankfully interrupted the moment. I turned in my chair just as the door opened and Colin walked in. He was dressed in a pair of designer pants and a dark brown linen shirt. He never looked like the thief he was, but rather one of the old-moneyed art collectors he had stolen for or from. Sophistication, strength and intelligence were all clearly communicated in his posture and other nonverbal cues.

His eyebrows raised slightly when he noticed everyone around the table. He locked the door behind him and smiled at Nikki's friends. "Hi there. I didn't know we were entertaining."

"We're not," I said. "Nikki, Michael and Rebecca are supposed to be studying, but they're arguing and sullying my apartment."

"Our apartment." Colin winked at me as he stopped by my chair. He leaned down and kissed me. "Hi."

It had been very hard for me in the beginning to be comfortable with his spontaneous affections. I still found it disconcerting, but no longer wondered why he wanted to touch me or be close to me. I returned his soft kiss. "Hi."

He straightened and gave Nikki a sideways hug, looking at her friends. "You are the two Nikki always talks about. It's a real pleasure to meet you."

Rebecca blushed and Michael swallowed. I could understand their nervous behaviour. Many women considered Colin extremely handsome. Most men found themselves intimidated. The two young people mumbled their greetings.

"So, what are you arguing about?" Colin took an empty pizza box and stacked it on top of another without making it look like he was cleaning up. There was no agitation in his actions. I was not capable of that.

"We aren't arguing anymore. Doc G agreed to help us, so everything will be fine now." Nikki took the boxes from Colin. "We'll clean up. Please, leave this."

Rebecca grabbed piles of papers, shuffling them until they could fit into her shoulder bag. "We're done studying in any case. Right, Michael?"

Michael noticed Rebecca's exaggerated head tilt towards Colin and me, and reached for his books. "Yeah. Sure. We were leaving."

I slowly shook my head. "You are abysmal liars. Rebecca, your hand in front of your mouth when you are making a statement is a clear indication of your intention to hide what you are saying. Michael, shaking your head while saying 'yes' shows you do not agree with yourself. Why would you lie about leaving?"

"They're being polite, Doc G." Nikki walked back from the kitchen with a furniture wipe and started wiping down the table. "They don't want to overstay their welcome."

I was about to question the logic behind that, but Colin's hand on my forearm stopped me. He was smiling at the three young people cleaning up. "You don't have to leave, guys. You can stay for dinner."

"No!" Rebecca's hand flew to her throat, but then she became aware of her body language and hid her hands behind her back. "I mean, we already have dinner pl..."

"Don't even try, Rebecca." Nikki chuckled as she dropped the wipe in the bin. "Doc G will see right through you."

"I'm sorry, Doc G," Rebecca said softly. "I don't know how to act around you."

I nodded. "Understandable. People are so used to lying in order to maintain their standing in polite society. I don't take offence if you are uncomfortable and don't want to stay for dinner."

Colin put his hand on my shoulder. "You really are welcome to stay for dinner, but if you need to go, we understand. Maybe next time?"

"That will be nice," Nikki said. "Vinnie can cook for us."

"The big guy?" Rebecca's *procerus* muscle pulled her brow in and down. Fear. She glanced at Michael, who was watching us with increasing interest.

"Nikki, you shouldn't enjoy scaring your friends this much." It was hard to miss the constant muscle contractions around her mouth and eyes. She was teasing them. "Do not use us to scare them."

"We're not scared, Doc G," Michael said as he stood up. "Just uncomfortable and out of our depth. And Nikki is always teasing us. We know she means no harm."

"We'll come for dinner one night." Rebecca pulled her shoulders back. "With everyone here."

"That sounds great," Colin said, a warm smile crinkling the corners of his eyes. "And we'll try not to be too scary."

Nikki's friends responded positively to Colin's openness, the tension in their bodies and on their faces dissipating. Two minutes later and after promises from Michael and Rebecca to visit again soon, Nikki left with her friends to continue their studying in the library. I could barely wait for the front door to close behind them before I rushed to the kitchen to grab my cleaning supplies. There were pizza crumbs on the table and stains Nikki had not cleaned in her quick attempt.

Colin took the cleaning supplies from my gloved hands and put them on the floor. Leaning against the table, he pulled me closer until I stood stiffly between his legs. I'd come to know his expressions. The smile currently lifting his mouth meant he found me amusing.

"You find my cleaning funny?"

"No. I find it funny that anyone could be scared of you."

"Most people are." I hated that my voice dropped slightly at this admission.

"Nobody who is important." He kissed the tip of my nose. "Vinnie's not. Francine, Manny, Phillip, Nikki."

"And you." I relaxed slightly and put my latex-covered hands on his shoulders. He was right. It didn't matter that people were scared of that which they didn't understand. "You were never scared of me."

"Never." He pulled me a bit closer. "Now tell me what kind of promise Nikki managed to get out of you this time."

Colin understood the difficulty I experienced in my relationship with Nikki. He particularly enjoyed it when Nikki was able to get my unwilling agreement to something no one else would ever have been able to convince me to do.

"I'm going to investigate the disappearance of her friend. Her gut"—my tone indicated my derision of this notion—"tells her he has been kidnapped."

"Kidnapped?"

I glanced at a grease stain on the table. It motivated me to relate Nikki and Rebecca's suspicions in the most concise manner possible. Colin listened without interrupting. The moment I finished, I stepped out of his embrace and picked up the cleaning supplies.

"Do you think there's anything to Nikki's gut feeling?"

"Don't start calling it that too." I sprayed wood polish on the table and rubbed it in with a soft cloth. "And I don't know if there is anything to her ungrounded suspicions. I'll have to research it before I draw any conclusions."

For a few minutes I worked in silence, aware of Colin studying me. Eventually I looked at him. "What?"

"Something happened at the office today, didn't it?"

"Manny phoned you?"

Colin snorted. "Millard only phones me in dire situations, Jenny. No, he didn't phone me. I know your cleaning habits. This is not annoyance-at-students-eating-pizza cleaning. This is something-is-bothering-you cleaning."

"You study my cleaning habits?"

"No, I just observe you. That's what people do when they get to know each other. The same way you understand the deeper meaning behind most of my body language. It's more than just academic knowledge." Colin followed me to the kitchen and watched me put the cleaning products in their designated places. "So? What happened?"

I closed the cupboard door and leaned against it. "Caelan came in and insisted on speaking to only me. He wants to work with me on a case. He claims that there is a dark net that is selling forged masterpieces."

Colin held up both hands. "Who is Caelan?"

I inhaled deeply and took a moment to organise my thoughts. I relayed this afternoon's events to Colin. His expression went from interested to annoyed to worried, but the strongest emotion was when I mentioned the artist Caelan had told me to relay to Colin.

"Are you kidding me?" Excitement was all over his face. "And he said Gustave Courbet's *Full Standing Figure of a Man* was one of those paintings?"

"Yes."

"That painting was part of a huge discovery of Nazi-looted art two years ago. The authorities only recently revealed the full extent of the almost four thousand works of art discovered in a man's attic. Some amazing masterpieces were recovered. Including this Courbet."

I remembered the case Colin was talking about. Although I had only read one article about this shocking haul, it had been an in-depth report. "Those artworks are accounted for. Why would Caelan's mention of this artist be of such interest to you?"

The *orbicularis oris* muscles contracted Colin's mouth into a pout we adopted when we were contemplative or doubtful.

"Don't you dare say it."

Colin laughed as he took my hands and pulled me into his arms. "Okay, I won't say I have a gut feeling about this. A very strong gut feeling. I also won't say that I'm worried about Caelan and that we should make sure that he's okay."

"You don't make sense. You said it by saying that you won't say it." I pushed lightly against his chest. "Why are you worried about Caelan?"

"Because you said that he looked under-fed and uncared for. Do we know if he's eating? Does he have a safe place to sleep tonight?"

I blinked a few times. "I hadn't thought about this. Should I have?"

"No, love." Colin lowered his head until our noses touched. "You didn't have to think about that. You already gave him something much more important than a bed."

"What?"

"A sense of belonging."

Chapter THREE

As I had promised Nikki, the next morning I looked into the possibility of her friend being kidnapped. On three of the monitors were articles about the Paris kidnapping. On a fourth monitor was the police's case file. When I emailed the Parisian police department looking into the kidnapping, I had used an email Manny had made me promise to use as a template. It was an overly polite email, wasting a lot of time with platitudes. But the Paris investigator assigned to the case sent me everything he had on the kidnapping.

It had taken me fifteen minutes to read carefully through the whole file. The conclusion I had come to was the exact opposite of what the journalists implied with their articles. The police file had witnesses stating that the nineteen-year-old Matthieu Jean was a quiet student who'd kept to himself, studious and ambitious. He had no social media footprint and his professors had difficulty recalling him because he was so quiet.

The newspaper articles printed a photo of Matthieu in a pub with other young people. The table between them was laden with beers and shot glasses. Most of the students in the photo exhibited signs of inebriation. Matthieu sat with his back pushed deep against his chair, his arms folded and feet pointing to where I assumed the door was. He hadn't wanted to be there.

Yet the newspapers used that photo to create a profile of him as going on drinking binges that could last a week. Two anonymous sources said Matthieu frequently disappeared, and sometimes when he returned, he had no recollection of where he'd been.

It had been his landlady who'd phoned the police when she'd gone to collect Matthieu's rent and found the flat in disarray. When the police had found blood, they had decided to investigate. It had been eight days since Matthieu's disappearance and no one had heard from him.

Nikki had emailed me a description of Pascal, and I'd found very few similarities between the two young men. Pascal's reputation for abusing substances and for not being predictable in his routine directly contradicted Matthieu's. Pascal seemed to have a lot of friends, but no one really close. I would have to ask Nikki if anyone knew him on a level deeper than just socialising.

I closed the windows with the kidnapping information. I wasn't willing to spend more time on this, not until I could ask Nikki a few questions to focus my research. I would much rather spend that time going through the video footage I'd received this morning.

Two weeks ago, a prominent businessman had been murdered in the leafy suburbs of Salzburg. Nothing of note had been stolen, except for two antique clocks and a collection of watches. That report had caught my interest and Manny had contacted the Salzburg police.

I spent the next two hours studying the twenty-six minutes of footage frame by frame. The man caught on the cameras was unmistakably Dukwicz. It was of no consequence that he was wearing a ski mask. His posture and body language were easy to recognise, even in the dark shadows of the evening. As soon as he entered the house, he disabled the videos and the monitor went blank. However, the footage recorded prior to that moment had already been uploaded to the security company's server. That was what I was studying.

Secretly, I was grateful that I didn't have to watch him murder someone. A few months ago, I had seen the sick pleasure on his face as he'd garrotted and repeatedly stabbed a politician.

After going through the footage for the seventh time, I decided there was nothing of use to be gleaned from it. It was greatly disappointing that we were still no closer to stopping this man from continuing his murder-for-hire services.

I pushed myself away from my desk and stretched my arms above my head. My muscles were getting stiff. As I lowered my arms, movement in the team room caught my eye. Colin was standing in deep discussion with Manny. Colin hadn't come into the office with me this morning. He'd had to meet a contact about a forged painting, something he did from time to time to maintain his profile as an art thief.

I swivelled my chair to have a better view of the two men. Colin must have gone home to change out of one of his disguises he always wore when working as a thief. He was wearing light gray summer suit pants and a tailored black shirt with the top button undone. Juxtaposed with Colin's immaculate outfit, Manny looked even more rumpled than usual. He was wearing cheap brown pants, his cream shirt not crisp in colour or look, and his tie askew. Two days' stubble finished his unkempt look, an image he cultivated to ensure he was underestimated in intellect and competence.

It was not the men's attire that interested me. It was their nonverbal cues. The two men had been on opposite ends of the law when they'd first met. It had taken more than a year of working together before they were willing to show respect for each other. What I was witnessing now was not only respect, but trust. Their torsos slightly leaning forward and the openness of their other gestures made it very clear.

Colin said something that brought a jerk to Manny's body. Manny frowned deeply, leaned even closer and replied, his eyes never leaving Colin's face. The micro-expression of unease around Colin's eyes had me sitting up in my chair. The few times I'd seen Colin uneasy about something had been times he had been deeply concerned about something. Those times he'd usually predicted a negative outcome for a situation. And had been right.

I stood up and Colin looked in my direction. His expression softened and he waved me over. The glass doors slid open when I keyed in my code and I stepped into the other room.

"Hey, you." Colin's smile wasn't successful in erasing his concern. "Want some coffee? I was just about to go get some."

"What's wrong?" I walked closer and studied his face.

He closed his eyes and grunted. "Sometimes I really wish I could lie to you."

"Why?"

Manny camouflaged his reaction with a cough. "Morning, Doc."

Colin opened his eyes and his smile widened. I exhaled sharply and turned to Manny. "Tell me what is wrong. What were you talking about?"

"Frey was telling me about the artist Caelan mentioned yesterday."

"You might be a good liar, Manny, but I know you too well. You are not lying, but you are deflecting. Why? What won't you tell me? What is wrong?"

Colin rested his hand on my shoulder and I shook it off. The look I gave him communicated my ire.

"Jenny." Colin put his hand back on my shoulder and held on. "It's something I'm a bit concerned about, but since it's only a gut feeling at the moment, I didn't want to bother you with it."

"Your expression was much more than just a 'bit' concerned."

He lowered his chin to look me in the eyes. "It's still just a gut feeling. Allow Millard and me to check this out before we get everyone up in arms about this."

"You're using metaphors."

"Yes, I am." His smile was affectionate. Respecting my literal understanding of what people said, Colin seldom used figures of speech. Only when he felt the strong need to emphasise something did he give in to his need for a richer use of language. "If I promise to tell you everything the moment I have facts, can we talk about Caelan now?"

"I will remind you of your promise."

"I know."

I nodded. "What about Caelan?"

"Mornin', all y'all!" Vinnie's greeting boomed through the room as he stepped through the doorway. "How're y'all doin'?"

"Bloody hell." Manny shook his head in disgust and walked to his desk. "Again with the bleeding fake Texan accent."

"Don't get yer britches into a knot, old man." Vinnie fell into one of the chairs at the round table, groaned and then smiled. "It's a beautiful mornin'."

"I have to agree with Manny on the accent, Vinnie." I found it amusing that Vinnie felt the need to adopt a different accent depending on his mood. "You seem to be in pain, but at the same time you seem happy."

"I'm both, Jen-girl. But I'm more happy than sore."

"Why are you in pain?" I looked more closely, but couldn't see anything other than mild discomfort.

"I worked out with Daniel and the team yesterday."

"What has this world come to?" Manny didn't look away from his keyboard as he pressed a key unnecessarily hard. "The criminal working out with GIPN."

Vinnie's criminal past was still mostly unknown to me. Three years ago, I would have refused to even talk to him. Now I considered him one of my best friends. He was a kind and generous man, loyal to his friends and fiercely protective. I suspected his involvement with Interpol was on a level similar to Colin's, but I had never asked him and he hadn't volunteered that information.

In the last year and a half, we'd worked closely with GIPN, France's rapid response team, similar to SWAT teams. Daniel was the leader of the team we mostly worked with and had proven himself to be a reliable and trustworthy ally. Recently, he'd invited Vinnie to train with his team. Vinnie loved the challenge of showing the team they were not as good as they thought they were. Daniel enjoyed Vinnie's sense of humour and focus. They worked well as a team.

"Aw, old man." Vinnie leaned across the table. "You're just jealous that your puny little body would splinter if you had to train with us."

"Don't insult my hero's Michaelangelo body, Vin." Francine walked into the room, dropped her designer handbag on her desk and look at Manny. "I know you hide steel muscles under those messy clothes you wear, handsome."

Francine enjoyed pestering Manny. Today she was wearing a strappy sundress, hoop earrings and sandals. She looked like she should be on a beach holiday somewhere, not in a high-end insurance office as a member of an investigative team. With a natural elegance few women had, she walked to Manny and rested her derriere on his desk. She tilted her head and picked up his tie.

"If you let me, I'll dress you the way a man of your stature should look."

"Get off me, you evil woman." He pushed her hand away.

"You and I both know you don't want me off you, sexy." She ran a dark pink nail over his stubble and dropped her voice a bit. "I'm a patient woman, handsome. I can wait until you're ready to admit your animal attraction to me."

"Doc!" Manny looked around Francine. "Get your friend away from me."

"Why?"

Everyone except Manny laughed. I seldom knew how to respond to their teasing. Manny grunted and pushed Francine with his elbow. "Get off my table, woman. We have work to do."

"Have we found Dukwicz?" Francine gave Manny an exaggerated wink and walked to her desk. She turned on her powerful computers. "Girlfriend, did you get those vids?"

It took me three minutes to tell them my findings, or rather the lack thereof.

"You guys were talking about Caelan when I came in," Vinnie said.

"Who's Caelan? What did I miss?" Francine looked up from her computers. Her curiosity made her a good investigator.

I allowed Vinnie and Manny to relate the tale of yesterday's strange visitor. They gave a very general overview, leaving out many details—details I considered important. Manny often found my explanations too comprehensive and annoying.

"Poor baby." Francine pressed her hand to her sternum. "Is he okay? Did you take him for a meal?"

"You don't take a kid like that out to a restaurant, supermodel."

"But you did take care of him," I said. It wasn't hard to see the memory of it on Manny's face.

"It's nothing."

"It's not nothing, handsome. What did you do for him?"

Manny threw down the pen he was toying with. "I took him home. I don't know how he managed it, but the kid rents a studio apartment. It would be quite a big place if it wasn't stacked to the roof with crap. He's one of those hoarder people. One look inside and I knew he couldn't possibly have food in there."

"You bought him groceries? You really are a hero." The warmth in Francine's eyes was genuine.

"No, I didn't." Manny slumped deeper into his chair. "I took the little shit to the shops, but he was impossible to buy for. He only eats green food. No rice, potatoes, bread, pizza, normal stuff. Only green food."

"Some people on the spectrum have such food preferences." I felt fortunate that I didn't have that particular limitation.

"Why?" Vinnie's interest was sincere.

"You are the only person I know who likes Brussels sprouts. Why? What makes you like Brussels sprouts, but hate cabbage? There are different schools of thought explaining this. One is that it is connected to our body and brain chemistry. Since autism is a neurological disorder, Caelan's brain is probably telling him only green food is acceptable." Although a lot of people on the spectrum preferred white foods. I looked at Manny. "What did you buy him?"

"Broccoli." Manny spat out the word as if it tasted bad. "He also chose cucumbers, green peas and lentils. I don't know how the kid—how anyone—can live like that."

It was hard. I lived with mental limitations every day. Still, I considered myself less complicated than most neurotypicals. I didn't have to deal with their emotional complexities and nuance misunderstandings.

"But you did buy him food." Francine blinked away threatening tears. "You're the best, handsome."

Manny rubbed the back of his neck and turned his attention to Colin. "What were you going to say about the artists?"

"I mentioned to Jenny last night about the 2012 art haul in Munich and Salzburg. Do you know anything about this?"

"I vaguely remember it being in the headlines a few months ago. The paintings found were all from the Second World War. Nazi-looted art. The German authorities kept a lid on it for more than a year."

"Yes, they wanted to authenticate the works and determine provenance." Colin sat down at the round table. I was the only one still standing, so I joined Vinnie and Colin at the table.

"How did they find the paintings?" Vinnie asked.

"Very Al Capone-like. The old guy had a house in Salzburg and an apartment in Munich. That day he'd gone to his bank in Switzerland and was on his way home to Germany when customs officials did a routine inspection of the train. They searched him and found around nine thousand euros on him. It's below the legal limit of moving cash between countries, but it did raise their suspicions. So they started an investigation which led them to his flat in Munich. There they initially found more than one thousand two hundred works of art. "

"Holy Mother." Manny straightened. "How the bleeding hell did he manage to hide that many paintings for over six decades?"

"He lived modestly. No one ever suspected anything or had any reason to search his house." Disgust was clear around

Colin's mouth. "He had sales receipts for some of those paintings, but most of those were distress sales."

"What are distress sales?" Vinnie asked.

"The Nazis forced Jews and other specified groups of people to sell their art for a minimal amount. Sometimes it was to give them some cash to buy food, sometimes it was to spare the life of a loved one."

"It's horrible." Francine crossed her arms tightly against her chest. "That people can do such atrocious things to each other is beyond me."

"So what is the connection between the name Caelan gave us last night and this German guy?" Manny asked.

"I don't know if there's a connection. I told Jenny last night that the Courbet painting Caelan mentioned was among those found in the German haul."

"There's more, Frey. With you there is always more."

Colin's smile was unique to his satisfaction when he annoyed Manny. "In the last fifteen months, I've uncovered three Courbet forgeries. They were masterfully forged and had to be a few decades old, but they weren't the real thing. I started wondering who could create such perfect copies of Courbet's works without having the original painting. Which makes me wonder about those three originals hanging in museums and private collections. Maybe they're also forgeries."

"This is pure speculation." I didn't like it. I needed facts and Colin was not presenting us with any.

"Since it's Frey's speculation, he can follow up on that." Manny looked at me until I frowned.

"What?"

"Tell supermodel what the kid said."

"Is there anything specific you are referring to or should I recall all the geographical facts he shared with us?"

"Dear lord, no. Just tell her about the satin road thingie."

I pressed my lips together against the need to berate Manny for frequently misquoting people. I was convinced he did it on purpose. To what end, I didn't know.

"What satin road thingie?" Francine stopped swiping her tablet's touch screen and stared at me. "Genevieve, what satin road thingie?"

It was seldom that Francine called me by my name. I paid closer attention to her nonverbal cues as I continued. "Manny and Vinnie left out a lot of detail about yesterday. Firstly, Caelan knew that you are part of our team. He knew your name. He also knew Colin's name."

"How?" The word came out high-pitched and breathless.

"He said he's quite a good hacker, but not as good as you." I went back to the details that had been left out. "Secondly, Caelan didn't see the sale of those forgeries on the internet like Vinnie said earlier. Caelan called it the dark net. When Manny asked him what it is, he said to ask you."

"So, supermodel, what is the dark net?" Manny snapped his fingers in the air when Francine continued to stare at me without answering his question. "Hey, supermodel! Pay attention here. What is the dark net?"

"I'm so going over my security." She flicked her hair over her shoulder and lifted one eyebrow at Manny. "The dark net is a secret internet hidden within the internet, Mister Troglodyte."

"Can't call me a caveman if I know you're calling me one." Manny lowered his chin. "The dark net, supermodel."

"It's called Tor. At first it was an acronym for The Onion Router, but now it is simply called Tor—no acronym. Tor makes it impossible for flatfeet like you to trace my internet footprint. It's nigh on impossible to get my IP address when I'm on Tor."

"Who uses this dark place?"

"People who don't want to be seen by Big Brother, that's who. And it's the dark net." She huffed and looked at me. "What else did he say?"

"He said you would explain the dark net. And then he said to tell you that Silk Road has a repeat. Not Silk Road 2.0, 2.1 or even 3.0. It's a whole new place. Those were his exact words."

"Oh, my God." Francine's hand flew to her mouth. "It can't be. I would've known if there was a new Silk Road. Am I slipping? Working with the good guys all the time is making my skills go to the dogs. I used to be on top of my game. How long has this place been operating?"

"Supermodel!" The command in Manny's voice stopped Francine's self-castigation. "What is this Silk Road?"

"I need to find out what, where, how this new place is. I need to know everything." Ignoring Manny's question, she stood up, grabbed her handbag, sat down and stood up again. "I need to find out where this is. Why don't I know about this?"

"Wait!" Manny stood up, but was too late to catch Francine's arm as she rushed out the door.

"Where the hell is she going?"

"I reckon she's going to her basement." Vinnie stood up. "I'm going to make coffee. Can I bring some for everyone and that horrid tea for you, old man?"

We agreed and Vinnie left the team room.

"Do you know what Satin Road is, Doc? Or anything more about the dark place?"

"Not yet," I said. "I will research it and report back."

"Please keep it short, Doc. You know how much I hate tech speak." He looked at the door. "I hope supermodel isn't going to lock herself in that basement for days."

Six months ago, Francine's secret location, where she'd had an extensive computer setup, had been destroyed. From the large basement under an old apartment building she had done a lot of internet sleuthing, most likely all illegal. It had been while protecting the president and his wife that a gunfight had done extensive damage to her equipment.

The very next day, Phillip had presented Francine with an alternative. He owned the building that housed Rousseau & Rousseau and had kept the lowest level of this building confidential until he took Francine there. We had all thought there was only one level below the ground, but there was another. Phillip had offered it to Francine. She'd taken a week to consider it before she'd agreed.

In that week she had painstakingly located all the digital and paper plans of this building. Using her and Colin's contacts she had altered all the plans to only show one lower level. She'd presented it to Phillip as her condition for moving in below our offices. She didn't want anyone to know about the existence of that space and had renovated it with Vinnie's help. I'd been there on only three occasions. The chaotic arrangement of furniture and computer elements had brought on panic attacks that had needed a lot of soothing Mozart.

My thoughts were interrupted by Colin's cell phone. The glance he gave Manny after he looked at the screen reminded me of his worrying body language earlier on. We listened to his side of a short conversation. He disconnected the call and carefully put the phone on the round table.

"It's my fence."

"He has a new work for you to authenticate?" I asked. "Why is it worrying you?"

"My gut is telling me something is off, Jenny." Colin gently spun his phone on the smooth table top. "I wish I could tell you why I think there's something not right, but I can't. I don't know what it is."

"Is it your fence that is worrying you or the painting?"

"Not my fence." Colin had told me before about the triathlon athlete who acted as a mediator between the seller of illegal art and the buyer of illegal art. Apart from his obvious illicit activities, this man had proven himself reliable and trustworthy. "It's something about this art he's acquiring. I have a bad, bad feeling."

"Then don't go." Manny surprised me not only by suggesting this, but also by the sincerity of the concern on his face.

Colin considered this for a few seconds before shaking his head. "No. No, I'll go. I'll be careful, but I want to see what we can learn."

The genuine uneasiness I read in Colin's nonverbal cues caused my throat to constrict. I stood up when Colin got ready to leave, and walked to him. I stopped in front of him and awkwardly laid my hand on his chest. "Please be extra careful."

Chapter FOUR

"You're looking into Nazi-looted art?" Phillip's surprised question pulled me out of the last few hours' research. Finding it unproductive to fret about Colin, I had chosen to look into the cause of his unease. I had become so focussed on this task that I had lost myself in it and had not heard Phillip enter my viewing room.

I untucked my legs and winced as I straightened them. Whenever I became hyper-focussed, I often sat on my folded legs. Painful pins and needles accompanied the much-needed return of normal circulation and I groaned softly.

"Oh, Genevieve." Phillip sat down in the chair next to mine. "How long have you been at this?"

I glanced at one of the computer screens. "Four hours."

"Since Colin left?"

I nodded.

"I suppose you haven't stopped for lunch either, right?"

"I'll eat later. I had a large breakfast."

Phillip raised an eyebrow. "I'll ask Vinnie to get you something. But tell me first why you are looking into Nazi-looted art."

"I want to expand my knowledge on this topic."

When I didn't say anything else, Phillip sighed. "Please give me context. Did you suddenly develop an interest in this topic? Did you find something you haven't told me yet? Has Colin found an attic full of paintings?"

"No to all of your questions. Colin did, however, come across a few paintings in the last fifteen months that are causing him some concern." I told Phillip what Colin had said earlier. "And that is why I thought to inform myself on this topic."

"What have you found so far?"

"Are you sure you want to talk about this?"

"Why wouldn't I?" Phillip's head tilted slightly to the left.

"You'll become agitated." I knew my answer wasn't clear when his head tilted even more and his eyes narrowed. I sighed. "Whenever you talk about anything related to art looted during the Second World War, you become extremely agitated."

He nodded slowly. "So many wrongs were done to far too many people in that time. I suppose it is a trigger for me."

"Were you affected by this?"

"I'm not that old, Genevieve." His frown indicated he'd taken offence.

"I know. You were born shortly after the Second World War, but your parents must have been affected by the war."

"They were," he said softly after a few seconds. "They never suffered any of the atrocities so many other people did, but knowing what was going on around them and not being able to do anything killed them."

"Metaphorically?"

"Yes, it killed them metaphorically. They watched neighbours and friends they'd loved taken away to never be heard from again. My parents were newlyweds, my mom pregnant with my older sister. They were terrified of saying or doing anything that would've brought them into the sights of any of the authorities. And they hated themselves for being weak."

"That was not being weak. It was doing what they needed to in order to survive."

"They never saw it like that. From the first day I can remember, my parents carried that guilt with them." Phillip seldom shared personal information. I realised the importance of this moment and waited for him to continue. "Needless to say, it had an ugly effect on us as a family. My sister left home when she was seventeen."

"She died." I could see the grief on his face.

"Drug overdose. It was the sixties, the hippie era. Many other youngsters pursuing their freedom met with the same fate. My sister's death broke my parents." He fell quiet.

How was one expected to act in a situation like this? I was at a loss, so I tried to stay on topic. "And this is the reason for your strong feelings about Nazi-looted art?"

"I suppose it is." He shook his head and straightened. "So tell me what you've learned so far."

I turned to my monitors. "There are no specific numbers, only speculation that between six and seven hundred thousand works of art were looted from Europe by the Nazis. Many of those works have not been recovered. I'm finding it irritating that there are no exact lists of works not yet recovered."

"People didn't always keep such good records in those days. And a lot of the Jews who owned paintings were taken to concentration camps before they could report anything anywhere." Phillip's mouth and eyes conveyed increased tension. "The Nazis stored a lot of this art, but there were many people like this man in Germany who found ways to claim some of those artworks for themselves. A lot of cultural heritage is lost with every war. The Second World War resulted not only in the loss of millions of lives and destroyed families, but also in the loss of countless works of art, books and other items of cultural value."

"The paintings discovered in the Munich apartment were thought lost forever. Their estimated value is more than a billion dollars." I was trying to understand why someone would keep those paintings for six decades. How did one justify that level of theft?

"It is hard not to become outraged at such audacity."

The glass door to the team room whooshed open and Vinnie walked in, carrying a tray. "Hey, Jen-girl, I brought you food." He placed the tray next to me and looked from me to Phillip and back. "Everything all right in here? You two look mighty intense."

"We're talking about Nazi-looted art."

"Aha." His nod was exaggerated and slow. "And my man here is getting all hot under the collar about this. You should know better than to start a topic that's going to piss a man off, Jen-girl."

"He's not pissed off." The aroma of the food on the tray caught my attention. I lifted the lid on the plate. "Lasagne?"

"Yup. There was nothing to do here, so I went home to make some food for us." He looked at Phillip. "There's a plate for you in the team room as well."

"Thank you, Vinnie."

"It's really good," Manny said from the round table in the team room. He lifted a heaped fork. "At least the criminal is good for one thing."

"Aw, old man. You're just—"

"I'm never listening to you again!" Nikki stormed past Manny into my viewing room, pointing her finger at Vinnie. "Ever!"

"Why? What have—"

"You made me look stupid. Really, really stupid." She emphasised the last three words by pressing her index finger into Vinnie's chest. Even though Nikki was clearly at a height and weight disadvantage, she felt safe enough to confront him in a physical manner. Dressed in cream pants, a colourful top and flat sandals, she looked small and feminine against Vinnie's tall, muscular body in his usual dark fatigue pants and a black t-shirt. She pushed her finger hard into his pectoral muscle. "Doc G was right. You're a bad influence on me."

"I also said so," Manny called from the team room. He wiped his mouth, dropped the serviette on his plate and walked to my room. "You should never listen to this criminal. What did he tell you?"

"To listen to my gut." She turned to me. "I'm never listening to my gut again. Ever."

"It is not wise to make sweeping statements which include the words 'ever' or 'never'." I couldn't let her previous incorrect statements go. "I didn't say Vinnie is a bad influence on you. I said you shouldn't allow anyone to influence your own opinions or impressions of a person or situation."

Vinnie closed his hand over Nikki's and pressed it against his sternum. "What happened, little punk?"

She pulled her hand back, but Vinnie didn't let go. After a few seconds of senseless struggling against Vinnie's strength, she fell against him with a dramatic sigh and spoke into his chest. "Pascal is back in class."

"Who's Pascal?" Manny asked.

"Nikki thought he had been abducted when he didn't attend lessons." I leaned back from the growing crowd in my room. "She thought his kidnapping was connected to the one in Paris."

Manny grunted. "Can you people never make sense?"

"I can." Nikki pushed herself from Vinnie, but didn't move away. She liked physical closeness. It took her five minutes to relay her suspicions about Pascal's absence. Manny listened closely. "And then he walked into class this morning as if nothing was wrong. The dork had been partying for the last three days and didn't even thank me for being concerned. I'm taking him off my tea list."

"Tea list?" Manny asked.

Nikki smiled. "Francine talks about the people who you would invite for tea as being on your tea list. Well, Pascal is off. Out. Erased."

"Hmm." Manny's micro-expressions indicated there was something else on his mind. "You did good, Nikki."

"By looking like a doofus and thinking he's been sold into slavery?"

"No, by caring, by paying attention. There is a lot of human trafficking happening around us and most people don't even notice because they're absorbed in their own lives. You might have overreacted by asking Doc to investigate, but you shouldn't stop paying attention."

"What do I always tell you?" I asked.

She sighed, rolled her eyes and said in a bored voice, "Observe, assess, analyse and act. I know, I know. You've told me this like a million times already."

"Then you should listen to Doc. The criminal isn't as smart."

"And you are, old man?"

Manny ignored Vinnie. "We got updated stats on human trafficking last year. The report called human trafficking a modern form of slavery. It's estimated that there are at this very moment between twenty and thirty million people who are victims of slavery. The majority of these victims are eighteen to twenty-four years old. Your age."

"Thirty million people?" Nikki's eyes were wide. "That's like half the population of France."

"Less than half." France was home to an estimated sixty-five million people. "Or about two million more than the male population in France."

"Those poor girls can't all be from Russia, right? The movies always show trafficked girls coming from Russia."

I lowered my chin and glared at her. "Are you getting your facts from films?"

"Um. No. I just never really thought about this."

"Maybe you should." I'd read an in-depth report about this topic a few months ago. "There are around one and a half million people trafficked in the United States, which generates nine point five billion dollars a year."

Nikki pressed in closer to Vinnie and he put his arm around her shoulders. "That's horrible. People selling people. No. What's even worse is people *buying* people."

"In Europe there has also been an increase in human trafficking," Manny said. "The latest stats say that seventeen percent are men."

"So, according to statistics, the chances were really small that Pascal would've been kidnapped," Nikki said.

"For human trafficking, maybe." Vinnie patted her shoulder. "But kidnapping happens for many other reasons, punk. They could've wanted a ransom from his rich parents—"

"He's an orphan."

"—or it could've been his bookie beating up on him because he didn't pay his debts." Vinnie pulled away from her and crossed his arms. "You shouldn't hang around boys who get kidnapped, punk."

"Are you kidding me? How am I supposed to know who gets kidnapped and who doesn't?" Nikki looked at me. "Tell him he's being illogical, Doc G."

I pushed my back deeper into my chair. "I'm not getting involved in your argument, even if I agree with you."

"Hah! See? Doc G agrees with me."

"I would also like for you to take more care, Nikki." Manny took a step closer to Nikki. "You were smart taking note of this boy's absence. I want you to continue being smart."

"Oh, my God. You're serious." She pulled her arms closer to her body, rubbing her arms as if she was cold. "Do you think I'm in danger? What about Rebecca?"

I sighed. I understood the propensity young people had for overreacting, but it was tiresome to be a constant witness to Nikki's melodramatic reactions to situations. I lowered my voice in what Nikki called my trying-to-be-patient tone. "Think carefully about the situation, Nikki. Do you think you are in danger?"

She was about to respond, but held her breath when I lifted my index finger and stared at her with a raised eyebrow. I wanted her to consider her answer. She did. Her shoulders dropped and she rolled her eyes again. "Okay, fine. I suppose my life is not really in danger. Not any more than anyone else's. I'll just be extra careful."

"You do that, punk."

"That's my girl."

Manny and Vinnie glared at each other when they spoke at the same time, then turned away to stare at my monitors. The sound of Bach's Toccata and Fugue interrupted the awkward silence. Everyone, including me, looked at my smartphone in surprise. It was placed at an exact angle to the left of my keyboard, the screen flashing. The call was from an unknown number.

I grabbed my phone and swiped the screen. "Who is this?"

"It's me." Colin's voice sounded different than usual, but I was too annoyed with the dramatic ringtone to pay close attention.

"You really must stop changing my ringtones."

"Jenny, I have a situation." Only a few times had I heard that specific tone in Colin's voice. Adrenaline shot through my body, causing my fingertips to tingle.

I pressed the phone tighter against my ear. "What's wrong?"

"I've been arrested."

"Who caught you stealing what? Where are you? Are you hurt?"

"Jenny, I need you to focus."

I took a deep breath, ignoring the curious looks of everyone in the room. "I'm focussed."

"Good. Are you still in the office?"

"Yes."

"Is Millard there?"

"Yes. Why?"

"You must bring him with."

My eyebrows shot up. Colin never asked for Manny's help. "How bad is it?"

"I don't know. I can't talk much. They're only allowing me to make this one call."

"Who? The police?"

"No. Interpol."

"You've been arrested by Interpol?" My voice raised in pitch and volume. I shook my head when Manny stepped closer, holding out his hand towards my phone.

"Yes, Edward Taylor was arrested."

"Not you?"

"Yes, Jenny. I was arrested." His tone implied there was much more to his words. I hated that I couldn't see his nonverbal cues. I would've been more confident in my conclusion that he had been arrested under the alias of one of the seventeenth-century poets he so often disguised himself as.

I didn't know how to ask about his identity without saying the wrong thing. "What do you need me to do?"

"Bring Millard with you. There was some other situation during my arrest and Interpol brought me to the police station. I don't know how much longer I'll be here, so please hurry." He gave me the address of the police station where he was being held. I had been there before and had hoped to never go there again.

"I'll be there in ten minutes."

A strange voice coldly told Colin he had chatted enough and the call was disconnected. I lowered the phone and stared at it.

"Doc? What happened?"

I slowly looked up. "Interpol arrested Colin and he's being held at the police station. He said you must come with."

"Did he say anything else? Why he got arrested?" Not too long ago, Manny had still hoped to put Colin in prison. In the last few months, the dynamics had shifted and now I was witnessing exactly how much. The concern in Manny's nonverbal cues was genuine. There was not one hint of pleasure or triumph at the news of Colin's arrest.

"I think he got arrested as Edward Taylor. He wasn't very clear about that and didn't say anything else." I went to one of the three antique-looking filing cabinets against the wall behind my desk and took my handbag from the bottom drawer. "We have to go now."

"We'll take my car."

I froze mid-step and shook my head. "No. No. Definitely not. No. I'm not getting in your car. No."

"I'm a better driver than Frey." Manny's tone lost all its concern and warmth.

"It's not about your driving skills." Manny's car was not dirty. It was messy. Scraps of notepaper covered the backseat. On the passenger seat were numerous shopping lists that he never took into the shops with him. There was no way I was getting into that vehicle.

"I'll drive you, Jen-girl. I want to make sure my man is okay in any case." Vinnie took his car keys from one of the many side pockets on his cargo pants. "The old man can drive himself if he doesn't want to go with us."

"Let's go." I walked out of my viewing room, not caring how Manny was going to get to the police station. The tone in Colin's voice was making me increasingly concerned for his wellbeing. I barely registered Nikki calling out for us to be careful and Phillip telling Nikki to join him for lunch.

Manny got in the backseat of Vinnie's double-cab pickup truck without complaint. A trip that would usually take around ten minutes took Vinnie less than six minutes. I clung to the sides of the passenger seat and mentally wrote the first page of Mozart's Flute Concerto No.2 in D major, not paying attention to the scenery around me. By the time Vinnie double-parked in front of the police station, I'd gained a modicum of calm.

Manny and I exited the pickup truck. Vinnie had no desire to enter a police station. He was going to find legitimate parking and wait for us. I followed Manny to the few steps leading into the station. On the top step, he stopped, his expression serious. "Doc, you've got to let me handle this. I don't know what kind of delicate situation we're walking into."

"And I might say something inappropriate."

"Most likely something true and necessary, but it might work against us."

I thought back to earlier this morning and narrowed my eyes. "You weren't surprised when I told you Colin had been arrested. You know something. Is this what you and Colin were talking about this morning?"

Manny closed his eyes briefly. "We can't talk about this here, Doc. Let's get Frey out and we'll discuss it in full. Okay?"

I studied his expression and only when I could not detect any deception cues did I nod my agreement. I pressed my lips tightly together and followed Manny into the station. It took him less than a minute of professional and courteous inquiry to win the respect of the duty officer. It felt as if my skin was on fire from my impatience to get to Colin and assure myself he was well. Yet I continued to press my lips together and allowed Manny to take the lead in an environment he was more familiar with.

The duty officer told us the two Interpol agents would come to see us soon. I bit down harder on my jaw and leaned back to prevent myself from giving in to the strong compulsion to tell the young man to take me to Colin. Manny continued to talk about inconsequential things with the officer, making it even harder for me not to express my displeasure at wasting time with such frivolities.

Two minutes later three men came through a door towards the reception area. Two of those men looked like law enforcement officers. Even though they were dressed in slacks and long-sleeved shirts, their postures were unmistakable. Alert and ready to take aggressive action at any time. Between the two men was a man in his late forties. His arms were behind his back, his hands probably in cuffs.

The criminal's black leather pants were tucked into biker boots, his tight t-shirt untucked and his leather vest unbuttoned. His arms were covered in tattoos—intricate designs that disappeared into his sleeves. His long black hair framed his face, hanging down to below his chest. Something familiar about his face made me take a closer look. If I hadn't already been pressing my lips together, I might have uttered a loud gasp.

Even though his nose was thicker at the bridge, his cheekbones and lips were unmistakable. Colin was expertly disguised and was only a few feet away from me. He looked unharmed, but I could see it took him extra effort to hide his anger. Keeping Manny's warning in mind, I didn't know how to act. I had the ridiculous need to rush over to Colin and feel his arms around me. His touch would reassure me that he was well. I folded my arms tightly around my waist and swallowed a few times.

"Gentlemen." Manny stepped forward and held out his hand to the man on the left. "Manfred Millard. Thank you for bringing Mister Taylor to me."

The man shook Manny's hand, but there was no friendliness visible on his face. "We didn't bring him to you, Millard. We're about to transport him to Lyon."

"Ah, that won't do." Manny pointed at Colin. "He's mine, gents. Why don't we grab a phone and make a few calls? I'm sure we'll sort this out in no time."

"Who the hell do you think you are?" The other man pulled Colin closer to him, at the same time puffing out his chest.

"That, sonny, is what you'll find out when you phone your superior."

The first man was already dialling on his smartphone. "Taylor's ours, Millard."

"Make sure you speak to the Secretary-General," Manny said. "He'll set you straight."

The first man spoke into his smartphone, explaining the situation. As soon as he mentioned Manny, he was interrupted by the other person. The colour drained from his face as he nodded. "Yes, sir. I understand, sir. Immediately, sir."

He disconnected the call and uncuffed Colin while looking at his partner. "Gotta let him go."

"Fantastic." Manny's smile was not genuine. "Mister Taylor can go with my colleague while the three of us have ourselves a quick natter about this arrest."

Colin rubbed his wrists and walked to me. Fearing that I might give in to my need to touch him, I turned around and left the police station. Colin's soft footsteps followed me as I walked down the steps. A quick look around and I saw Vinnie's truck parked under the trees to the left.

"Jenny?" Colin fell into step next to me as we walked towards Vinnie. "Are you okay?"

I cleared my throat a few times, but still couldn't get myself to speak. Vinnie noticed us and straightened from where he was leaning against his truck. He looked Colin up and down, and nodded. "In one piece. You okay, dude?"

"I'm fine, thanks, Vin." Colin turned to me, lowered his head and waited until I looked at him. "Speak to me."

Much to my annoyance, tears gathered in my eyes. I shook my head, trying to clear it from the irrational concern I'd had. Colin's life had never been in danger. Why did I feel such intense relief at seeing him free?

"Hey." Colin took my hands and pulled me closer. His arms tightened around me and he spoke into my hair. "I'm okay, Jenny. It was just a stupid arrest. Nothing bad happened. You and Millard got here fast enough."

I gave in to this uncommon urge and wrapped my arms around his waist. I held on for a short while, trying very hard to steady my breathing. It took three bars of Mozart's Piano Concerto in E flat major before I could unlock my arms. I leaned back, still in his arms. "Don't tell me nothing bad happened. Something happened that made you sound extremely worried and stressed over the phone. That is not nothing."

He kissed the tip of my nose. "You were worried about me."

"Of course."

"Thank you."

"For what?" Why was he thanking me for being worried? "I don't understand."

He chuckled softly. "You don't have to understand everything, love."

"Okay, dude. Enough lovey-dovey shit. What happened?"

I stepped out of Colin's embrace, but allowed him to hold my hand. I stared in fascination at the tattoos. He hadn't had them this morning.

"We were set up, Vin."

"You sure Maurice didn't set you up?"

"No." Colin shook his head. "No, he was just as shocked as I was when we were arrested. And he's the reason I'm at the police station and not in some car on my way to Interpol's Headquarters."

"So what happened?"

"No," I said. "First tell me about this Maurice Dupin."

"I've been dealing with him for the last eight years, always as Edward Taylor. We have a good working relationship, one built on trust. I can't believe that he's part of this. He often brings me artwork to authenticate. A few times I've identified them as forgeries and his clients were very pleased that they weren't swindled. He phoned me last week, wanting to set up a meet. He had a painting he wanted me to look at. Said it was a masterpiece and would like for me to authenticate it."

"What was wrong with it?" I could see the evidence of it on Colin's face.

"It's Gustave Courbet's *Nude Reclining Woman.*"

"Courbet? The same dude who painted the painting the kid was shouting about?"

"The same." Colin rubbed his wrists where the cuffs had been.

"This new painting is causing you concern." It was clear in his body language.

"An understatement." He shook his head. "*The Nude Reclining Woman* has gone through some interesting legal battles. It was owned by a Hungarian collector before the Second World War. It vanished after it was looted by the Soviets in 1945 and turned up in 2000. It was offered for sale, but there was such a huge gap in its provenance that the Commission for Art Recovery got involved. It required five years of negotiations and three hundred thousand dollars before that painting was returned to the heirs of the original Hungarian owner."

"Why is the forgery such a problem, then?"

"Because it was as brilliant as the last three I'd seen. I would bet my bottom dollar that it was done by the same artist. It had the same techniques, the same brushstrokes... I'm convinced it's the same guy. Maurice said the owner had another five paintings he wanted me to look at. Apparently, this one needed to change hands quickly and we needed to meet today."

"Dude?"

"No, Vin. I'm not a hundred percent sure that he didn't set this up, but I really find it hard to believe."

"How did you land up in the cop house?" Vinnie nodded towards the police station.

"I had just picked up the painting when those two Interpol goons rushed into the back of Maurice's gallery and arrested us."

"Maurice Dupin owns a gallery?"

"It's called hiding in plain sight, Jenny. Anyway, they'd dragged us out of the gallery onto the street when Maurice made a run for it. Two patrol officers happened to be a few metres away and caught Maurice. I managed to convince them that I was not sure how real the Interpol agents were and that I would feel much safer if we all went to the police station." Colin's deception skills were exceptional, as were his persuasion skills.

"I'm glad you're a good liar."

Both Colin and Vinnie laughed at my honest statement. Siegfried's Funeral March by Wagner rang loudly from my handbag. I pulled my hand out of Colin's and glared at him while taking my smartphone from my bag. "Please stop changing my ringtones."

"This one is funny, Jenny." Colin smiled when Manny's face flashed on my smartphone screen. I huffed in annoyance.

I swiped the screen. "Is there a problem?"

"Well, hello to you too, Doc." When I didn't respond, Manny grunted loudly. "I'm going to be a while, Doc. You guys can go on home. I'll phone again in a bit to find out from Fr... Mister Taylor what happened."

"How long is a bit?"

"As long as it needs to be, missy." Manny disconnected the call.

I relayed his message to Colin and Vinnie, both happy to leave. The two men spent the whole trip to the office coming up with numerous unfounded hypotheses. By the time I was turning off my computer and preparing my office for tomorrow, I had lost count of the many improbable theories they'd come up with. When Colin hadn't been able to provide any more facts about the arrest, I'd stopped paying attention. I wondered when Manny was going to phone and what discoveries he would be able to share.

Chapter FIVE

"Courbet was revolutionary. He is known to be an innovator of Realism, his work not fitting into the Romantic or Neoclassical works prevalent at that time."

"When was that?" Vinnie asked from the kitchen. Colin and I were sitting in the living area, talking about my research earlier today. Vinnie had started cooking as soon as we'd arrived home. The aroma coming from the kitchen was highly appetising.

"Courbet died in 1877 at the age of fifty-eight."

"Let me guess." Vinnie dried his hands on a dishtowel. "Drinking too much?"

Colin smiled. "Like a lot of artists, yes. By that time, he'd established himself as a painter not scared of controversy. He took on social issues like the horrid working conditions of the poor and painted them. Later in life he painted a lot of erotic works, ruffling many feathers. One painting was banned from public display because it had two naked women on a bed in an embrace."

"Dirty old man." Vinnie chuckled. "Drunk, perverted artist. My kinda guy."

"He was also prolific. Around five hundred works are credited to him, most of those truly amazing pieces. I've seen few forgers able to do his work justice. With the exception of the paintings I've recently seen, of course."

"Dinner is ready." Vinnie placed a salad bowl on the dining room table. "The old man better not show up here like he always does around meal times. I didn't make enough to feed his face as well."

It had been four hours since we'd left the police station and Manny still hadn't phoned me. I planned to have a discussion with him about the exact meaning of 'in a bit'. More importantly though, I was truly curious about what he might have uncovered about Colin's arrest.

As soon as we'd arrived home, Colin had disappeared into our room. Ten minutes later he'd come out looking like Colin again. I had to give him credit for an expeditious skill at disguising himself.

We got up from the sofa and joined Vinnie at the table. Nikki had phoned him earlier to say she wouldn't be home for dinner. She was studying with Rebecca and Michael again. After a lifetime of living in isolation, in the last two years I had become used to the constant presence of people in my apartment. I had also become used to Nikki's infectious smile and light chatter. When she didn't join us for meals, I missed her presence.

I settled in my usual chair and reached for the salad bowl. The sound of keys in my front door stopped my hand mid-air and I turned to the door, wondering if it was Nikki or Francine. The melodic sound of Francine's voice reached us before the door opened wide enough to reveal her defensive posture. She was talking to someone out of view to the left of the door. All her nonverbal cues communicated discomfort.

"If you don't tell me who you are, I'll phone the police."

No sooner had Francine said those words than Colin and Vinnie were storming to the door, their postures aggressive. I followed them.

"Tonga is one of seventeen countries without any rivers!" a familiar young male voice shouted. "The Krubera cave in Abkhazia, Georgia is the deepest known cave on Earth!"

Vinnie's muscle tension decreased significantly when he also recognised Caelan's voice.

Francine looked at me as she walked past Vinnie and Colin into the apartment. "Do you know this kid?"

I looked into the hallway and recognised the slender, almost gaunt body. "It's Caelan."

"*The* Caelan?" Colin asked. The moment he stepped outside the apartment, Caelan started shouting geographical facts louder. "Hey, bud. My name is Colin."

"Annually, there are more than sixteen million thunderstorms around the globe!"

"Well, that's actually quite interesting." Colin's eyes narrowed as he took a moment to study Caelan. He walked back into the apartment. "You'll handle him better, Jenny. We'll be at the table."

"No." I grabbed his hand as he walked past me. "Just because I'm autistic doesn't mean I know how to deal with Caelan. You're good with me. Why don't you deal with him?"

"Did you not just see how he reacted to my presence?" Colin squeezed my hand. "Why don't you go outside, say hello and see what happens?"

I stared at him.

"I'll be right here, Jenny."

"Don't go to the table."

"Okay. I won't." He nodded to Vinnie, who grunted and joined Francine at the table.

I needed to mentally write four bars of Mozart's Quartet in G major before I could let go of Colin's hand and step outside my apartment. Caelan was pressing himself against the wall next to my front door, shaking his head repetitively. His breathing was ragged and shallow. "One million Earths could fit into the sun! The Earth is tilted at an angle of twenty-three and a half degrees towards the sun!"

"Hello, Caelan."

"The Baltic Sea is an average of fifty-five metres deep!" He took a deep breath. "Hello, Doctor Lenard. The Baltic Sea's water is much less salty than ocean water."

"Are you having a meltdown?" As I asked this, I realised how irrational it was to expect him to answer me. I'd had very few meltdowns, but remembered well how disconnected from reality I had been. "Okay. Um. You need to focus on something—something that makes you feel safe. Geography? Maybe the night sky makes you feel safe. Focus on that. Try to slow your breathing and just focus on the stars."

Nothing changed. He continued to shake his head, his breathing not slowing down. This was not working. I looked at Colin and shook my head. He moved his hand in a rolling motion, indicating I should continue. I felt deeply uncomfortable with this situation, but decided to try again. I lowered my voice like I did when Nikki was overreacting to some small situation. "I focus on Mozart to slow everything down. That's what works for me. You know best what works for you. If it is your geography, then you need to find something that will make you feel safe enough to slow down what is happening in your mind."

"Hydra is the largest constellation." He was clearly making an effort to lower his voice, although it still echoed through the hallway.

"So it is the stars?" I hated being in this situation, but kept my voice low and calm. "Tell me what fact you find interesting."

"The constellation Orion is best visible at twenty-one hundred hours during the month of January."

"Tell me something else about Orion, but try to first take a deep breath and then say it as slowly as you can."

Caelan's eyes locked onto the wall behind me. He shook his

head wildly a few times before he managed to take a deep, shuddering breath. "Orion appears differently in the southern latitudes. In South Africa, Orion's belt is formed by three bright stars known as the Three Kings or Three Sisters. In South America, they are known as the Three Marys." It came out in one breath. Very fast.

"That's not slow. You need to speak slower." I ignored Colin's disapproving sigh. "If you want to come inside my home, you have to take another deep breath and give me another fact. Slowly."

His breathing was marginally slower. He inhaled deeply, smoother this time, and on the exhale said, "The pyramids at Giza are an exact mirror of the three stars in Orion's belt."

"Good. That's better. Now would you like to come in or go home?"

He turned his head towards me, his eyes still on the wall behind me. "Come in."

"Do you have your control back?"

"Yes."

I tried to remember how I had felt as a child when I had an episode like this. Autism was so unique in each individual that I couldn't presume that Caelan was feeling the same. I decided to give him options. "Do you want to go in first or should I go first?"

"You."

I nodded and walked into my apartment. Colin walked halfway back to the dining room table, leaving enough space for Caelan not to feel crowded. The teenager followed me into my apartment and stopped next to the living area.

"I'm going to close and lock the door. Then I'm going to sit at the table. Do you want to join us?"

"Yes." Caelan's breathing was close to normal now, his body no longer folding into itself. He walked to the table and pulled out a chair at the far side, putting as much distance as possible between himself and Vinnie and Francine.

Colin and I took our seats. The tension around the table was uncommon and most disconcerting. Francine schooled her expression, but couldn't hide her discomfort. Vinnie's expression communicated distrust and dislike. Even though his relationship with Manny was contentious, he always offered the older man a meal. He didn't even offer Caelan a glass of water.

"Would you like to have dinner with us?" Colin asked.

"Too many colours. I'm not going to eat the disgusting colours. Only green. I only eat green food."

"Okay. Would you like to drink something?"

"Milk in a white glass."

"You must be shitting me." Vinnie leaned back in his chair and shook his head. "Are you for real?"

"Vinnie." Francine put her hand on his folded arms. "Don't."

I looked at the food that Vinnie must have dished onto my plate. It was an enormous serving. Surely he didn't expect me to eat it all.

I realised that thinking about the food was avoidance. I didn't want to deal with Caelan. I didn't like change. I didn't like situations I hadn't researched extensively. Caelan was not familiar. His behaviour made me feel deep discomfort on many different levels.

What surprised me more than Caelan's autistic behaviour was my friends' reaction to it. I took a moment to identify the other emotions that accompanied my shock. I was slightly disappointed by their antagonistic treatment of the young man. They had only been patient and kind towards me. Why would they treat Caelan any differently?

True, I'd learned to read people's nonverbal cues in order to adjust my approach, but I also knew I was far from neurotypical. I still didn't fully understand how and why Colin was so accepting and tolerant of me. Manny had an interesting mix of acceptance and impatience, but it was always accompanied by affection in his tone and expression. Vinnie frequently teased me, Francine too. I didn't see much of this at the moment.

"Tell me where you saw Courbet's *Full Standing Figure of a Man*." Colin took a bite of his food and waited for Caelan to answer. "I think it was more than just wanting to catch my attention. How and where did you see it?"

"I got…" Caelan sucked in a quick breath. "No! The Trans-Siberian railway is the longest railway in the world, around nine thousand kilometres long. I have another condition before I give you any answers. I want a girlfriend. Everyone has a girlfriend. I need a girlfriend. I want one. I want her."

Francine gasped when Caelan pointed his index finger straight at her. "Oh, I don't think so, kiddo."

"You're pretty. Your lips are so full and red. I want you. You must be my girlfriend."

"Just hold on now, you little shit." Vinnie straightened in his chair, his top lip curled, his nostrils flared. "You're in no position to make any demands."

"Then I say nothing." Caelan pressed his lips together for a few seconds. "Wait. Before I say nothing, I just want to say that I still want my milk. In a white glass."

Again he pressed his lips tightly together. Francine and Vinnie loudly protested Caelan's latest demand. They were addressing their arguments to me, as if I was in charge of this situation. My heart rate increased and darkness started creeping into my peripheral view. This was overwhelming me.

I mentally pulled up Mozart's Quartet in G major and wrote the next line of that exquisite masterpiece. It took only a few seconds for me to gather my thoughts. When I opened my eyes, Vinnie was still arguing. Caelan's lips were in a thin white line. I raised both hands, one palm towards Vinnie and one towards Caelan. "Please stop."

Vinnie stared at me for a few seconds before he leaned back in his chair, his arms folded across his chest. Caelan's expression didn't change.

"Caelan, would you consider a trade?" I ignored Francine's gasp. "I think it will be acceptable if you answer this question. You will not be giving away any of your information."

He thought about it for a few seconds. "What kind of trade?"

I might deeply regret this in the future, but I didn't know what else to do. "You are making enemies at the moment. Not friends. Nobody here likes you because of your behaviour."

"I don't care."

"I know. And that is the problem. If you want people to co-operate with you, you should treat them with respect." This might have been the most important lesson I had learned, especially in the last two years.

"So?"

"I can teach you how neurotypicals think and how they receive our communication. Then I can teach you how to communicate effectively with them and treat them with respect."

"You want me to lie?"

"No." This was a concept I grappled with frequently. Most neurotypical communication was based on polite diplomacies. In my mind those all qualified as lies. Through many unfortunate experiences, I had learned that people didn't want honesty.

"Jenny… Doctor Lenard has us." Colin waved his hand at Vinnie and Francine, who were both watching the discussion with increasing interest and decreasing aggression. "Not only do we love her, we also support her. If she has any problems, we're there for her. I don't think it's nice to go through life alone. It's hard. Wouldn't you also like to have friends? People who love and accept you for who you are?"

Caelan was looking up at the ceiling, appearing not to listen at all. I knew he was paying close attention. "I still want milk. And a girlfriend."

"If Genevieve is going to teach you how to be nice, I'll teach you how to find a girlfriend." Francine lowered her voice and muttered, "And keep her."

It took Caelan a few minutes to consider this offer. There was silence around the table except for the sound of cutlery on the plates. I didn't feel like eating, but took a few bites nonetheless. It was enough to reawaken my hunger. When Caelan shifted in his chair five minutes later, I'd eaten one third of Vinnie's generous serving.

"I want milk." Caelan didn't take his eyes off the ceiling.

"I need you to tell me if you agree to our trade, Caelan."

"I agree to your trade. Can I now have my milk?"

Vinnie grunted loudly and stood up. "I'll go find a white mug or something to serve his highness."

"Will you now please tell me about this painting?" Colin put his knife and fork down, watching Caelan.

"Courbet's *Full Standing Figure of a Man*."

Colin took a slow breath. "Yes. Where did you come across it?"

Vinnie put an unfamiliar white coffee mug in front of Caelan. He must have found it in his crockery collection. Even though we'd combined the two apartments, we only used my kitchen. Vinnie and I had agreed on one cupboard where he could keep his kitchen equipment. I never opened those doors.

Caelan drank his milk without taking a breath and placed the mug back on the table. He nodded a few times and got up. "I'll tell you tomorrow. Now I need to sleep. It is almost my reading time. I can't miss my reading time. I have to go home."

"Where is home? Can we give you a lift?"

Caelan ignored Colin's question and walked stiffly to the front door. He stopped a few feet from the door and stared at the locks. He didn't move, didn't asked for the door to be unlocked. He simply stood there.

Vinnie shook his head, picked up the serving dish and put a few more spoons of the stir-fry on his plate. Francine looked from me to Caelan and back to me. She lifted both shoulders and took another bite of her salad.

"He needs you, Jenny," Colin said softly.

I didn't want this young man to need my help. I wanted to tell Colin this, but knew it would affect Caelan. My parents and their friends had always thought I wasn't listening when they said hurtful things. Even though my mind had been occupied with something else or I'd appeared not to be listening, I'd heard it all. I remembered that pain and confusion. I wasn't going to subject Caelan to that.

I walked to the front door and unlocked all but the last lock. My hand lingered on it and I looked at Caelan. "You've given us nothing. We gave you milk. It is not a fair trade. Can you answer one question for me?"

He was staring at my hand, showing no indication that he'd heard me.

"I don't think you're interested in stopping the illegal sale of art. Why did you contact me?"

Caelan's jaw started moving, his head shaking a few times. I waited.

"I need help." His answer was so quiet I almost didn't hear him. But I did. I also understood the enormity of that statement.

"Okay." I unlocked the door. "We'll help you. You don't need to give us anything. You don't need to blackmail us with information. We'll help you. Unconditionally. All I ask in return is that you try to look past your fears and experiences, and see our actions. Look at it like you look at everything else—rationally, objectively. Maybe you could learn to trust us."

He didn't respond. His back was stiff and his head started shaking again. I opened the door and was glad he wasn't looking at me. I didn't want him to see the sadness on my face if by chance he registered the nonverbal cue. A few seconds later, he walked past me into the hallway, muttering geographical facts. I knew so little about him, but his reaction made me think that he didn't have a frame of reference for friendship or trust.

I locked all the locks and turned to find Colin, Vinnie and Francine staring at me, their food forgotten. The expressions on all three faces were notably similar. I saw affection, pride and a bit of sadness. I didn't know how to react to that, so I sat down as quickly as I could and pushed the cold food around on my plate.

"Jen-girl, you rock."

I'd learned that it was a compliment and nodded.

Colin took my hand in his and put my fork on my plate. "You did good, Jenny. We're proud of you."

"You were really good with him, girlfriend. I would never ha—"

I looked at them. "You would have. You have shown me kindness and understanding. Why can't you give it to Caelan?"

"He's a little shit, that's why," Vinnie said. "And you're prettier."

I ignored his attempt at humour. "Don't be rude to him. I was like that. I had to learn to pretend that I could function within social norms. It didn't come naturally or easily to me. Caelan is very young and it looks as if he's had no guidance."

"We'll try to be more patient, Jenny."

I pulled my hand back and looked at Francine. "What did you find out about Tor and the next Silk Road?"

"Oh, we're changing topics. Okay. Well, I didn't need to learn anything about Tor. I'm familiar with it. What I had to check was this new Silk Road. It took me some time since they hid it quite well. But then I quickly overrode their security and now I'm busy roaming around."

"What did you find?" I wished she would be more logical in her reports and treat it less like storytelling.

"No, no, no, my bestest BFF." Her smile was playful. "Since there are no lives on the line, I made the executive decision that I'll prepare a show and tell for tomorrow. We are not going to talk about work tonight."

"I want to talk about work. About Colin's arrest and your findings."

"I know and I don't care." She lifted her wine glass. "We're going to talk about travelling or books or maybe even watch a movie. No more work talk."

A few times Francine had taken control of our evenings. Without fail, the start of these evenings had been hard for me. To my surprise, spending time in such a manner had turned out to be quite enjoyable. But I truly wasn't feeling inclined to have a light-hearted conversation tonight. Too many things were pressing on my mind.

Francine didn't allow me to decline and, in her words, 'micro-micro-analyse' the current situation. She immediately started a lively debate about the benefits of romantic comedy movies. It was going to be a long night.

Chapter SIX

"Doc, I can reason with you, but that kid... He's something else." Manny stifled a yawn and stretched his neck. This morning he looked particularly rumpled, dark rings under his eyes. All of us had arrived early at the office, eager for updates. Everyone, including Phillip, was seated at the round table in the team room, coffee and fresh croissants in the centre. Manny took a sip of his milky tea and sighed. "Did the kid say when he would be coming in and sharing his oh-so-important information?"

"No, he didn't." Vinnie stirred another spoon of sugar into his coffee. "If he ever shows."

"He will." I knew Caelan wouldn't be able not to keep his word. It might just not be on our schedule. "What did you find out about Colin's arrest?"

"If you give me a chance to breathe, Doctor Face-reader, I'll tell you." Manny reached for another croissant. I didn't know how many breaths he needed before continuing, but knew from his nonverbal cues that he wasn't in good humour. I decided to wait for him to continue. He tore a large piece off the croissant, pushed all of it into his mouth and spoke around it. "Those two idiots at the police station were giving me the run-around. Doc, that means they weren't answering my questions and when they did, they lied. There's something off about them. So I went to Lyon."

"That's a four-hour drive." Francine pouted. "You should've taken me with, handsome. I would've kept you company."

Manny ignored her. "I took the train. Much less hassle and just as fast. And I slept on the way back. Came here directly from the station."

"I was wondering why you were wearing yesterday's clothes." Francine drew her dark red nail down Manny's sleeve. "I was just about to get jealous."

"Get off me, woman." Manny glared at her hand. "I'm too tired to deal with you."

"Lower resistance might mean victory for me." She gave him a seductive look, but leaned back in her chair.

"As I was saying before I was so rudely interrupted." He gave her another glare. "I met with a close contact I have at the Interpol headquarters. He asked around and found out that the art crimes unit has launched a full investigation into Edward Taylor. They have a file with all kinds of information at the moment."

"What information? What investigation?" Colin pushed his plate away. He breathed a bit louder through flared nostrils. "How the hell did they get onto Edward Taylor?"

"A reliable source not only gave them your name, but sat down with a sketch artist to create a physical description of you. I saw the sketch and it's exactly what you looked like yesterday."

"How the hell...?" Colin's lips thinned, his hands tightening into fists.

"I don't have all the answers yet, Frey." There was empathy in Manny's expression. "What I do have is a name."

"Who? I'll find that asswipe and sort him out." Vinnie looked ready to leave immediately.

"You're not going to do anything, criminal." Manny sighed heavily. "Would you please let me finish. I'm tired and not in the mood for stupidity."

He waited until Francine, Colin and Vinnie nodded, albeit reluctantly.

"Good. Laurence Gasquet is a private detective here in Strasbourg." Manny frowned when Francine grabbed her tablet and started tapping and swiping the screen. "He's currently in Amsterdam on an investigation that precludes him from any other contact but emails. I made an appointment to meet with him the moment he comes back."

"Because you want to see his reaction to your question."

"I might not be the expert you are, Doc, but having a face-to-face meeting, especially for the first time, often tells me much more than the answers they give me."

"Jenny won't assume anything, but I'm thinking that you would've emailed him if he'd been anyone else." Colin raised his eyebrows. "Is there a reason you don't trust him?"

"I don't trust anyone, Frey." Manny lifted his hand when I inhaled. "Anyone who hasn't proven themselves completely trustworthy. That being said, Laurence Gasquet has a brilliant record. I should have all the reasons in the world to just email my questions to him. He worked for MI5 for ten years before he joined Interpol. He stayed with the agency until he took an early retirement four years ago. Most of his clients are highly influential people who need someone who understands stealth and confidentiality. According to my friend, he takes on a limited number of clients, charges exorbitant fees, but is very good at what he does."

"He doesn't have a website." Francine shook her tablet in the air. "I looked everywhere. There is nothing anywhere on Laurence Gasquet, not even a high-school photo."

Manny pressed the heels of his hands against his eyes. "Are you not listening, supermodel? He's working on sensitive cases that don't need him to publicize himself. It's not like he's spying to see if some loser's wife is cheating on him. Apparently, his cases are industrial espionage, investigations into business partners suspected of skimming off the top, et cetera. I'm not surprised you can't find him living in that thing of yours."

"It's a tablet and you also have one."

"That you forced on me."

"Please stay on topic." I felt increasing disquiet because of the concern that Manny was trying very hard to conceal. "Do you think it is a good idea to visit him, Manny? What if he wants to get rid of Colin? What if—?"

"Don't go borrowing… looking for trouble, Doc. What I would like to know is why Edward Taylor has caught the interest of Laurence Gasquet. And why he made it the interest of Interpol."

"I can't even begin to guess." Colin lifted then dropped both hands onto the table. "Look, Edward Taylor is not one of my more frequently used personas. He only comes out when I'm dealing with Maurice. And that's not often."

Manny's eyes narrowed. "Tell me more about this Maurice Dupin. Where did you meet him?"

"In his art gallery." Colin proceeded to tell Manny what he had told us yesterday. He didn't add any more details or any more personal information about this man. Colin must also have observed the change in Manny's expression because he leaned forward and gave Manny a warning look. "Don't go and arrest him, Millard. He's helped me uncover a lot of forgeries and also a lot of war-looted art. He's not one of the bad guys. He's never moved a single work of art that had blood on it."

"Aah. An honourable thief. Well, that's all right then. My heart is going all gooey." The sweet tone of Manny's voice belied the visible annoyance on his face. He was being sarcastic again, and this time I agreed with his anger. It didn't matter that I'd learned not all criminals were bad people. In my opinion an illegal activity was exactly that. Illegal. Manny sat up. "I'm going to speak to your precious Maurice Dupin. I have a few questions for him."

Colin's head dropped back and he sighed at the ceiling. After a deep inhale, he faced Manny. "I know I can't stop you, but I would really appreciate it if you didn't interrogate him. He's not living under the radar and ninety percent of his sales are completely legit. His gallery is one of the better ones in Strasbourg. Don't destroy that."

"Hmm."

Manny's quiet response and his lack of usual annoyance, sarcasm and blustering caught not only my attention, but also Colin's. He narrowed his eyes and leaned forward. "You bastard. What have you done? Where is Maurice Dupin?"

Manny rolled his shoulders and cleared his throat. What could he have done that would embarrass him?

"Millard?" Colin's tone was hard.

"He's back at his gallery." It looked like it had pained Manny to speak. "I told those guys back at the station he was a confidential informant for me and that the two of you were working together with me on a case. That it had all been a huge misunderstanding and that they were interfering with an ongoing and very sensitive investigation."

"Aw, Millard. You smoothed things over for me?" Colin placed his open palm over his heart. "Little old me? You shouldn't have."

"Yeah, I'm thinking that too." Manny shifted in his seat, avoiding eye contact with anyone.

Francine reached over and gently cupped his cheek. "You're a good man, Manny. We all know you have our backs and you just proved it again."

He awkwardly patted her hand twice before pushing it away. I didn't know if anyone else noticed the slight puffing out of his chest and the *zygomaticus* muscles very briefly lifting the corners of his mouth. "Well, now you and your Maurice Dupin owe me, Frey."

"And you will collect. I know." Colin turned serious. "How bad is this going to get?"

"I don't know." Manny pinched the skin at his throat as he breathed heavily a few times. Classic nonverbal cues of concern. "My gut tells me this is not good. It's going to get worse before it gets better. But we're not going by gut feelings, right, Doc?"

"No." I forced conviction into my voice. I had not often seen Manny worried. "We should focus on finding more information before we draw any incorrect conclusions. Going on feelings will impede our reasoning skills and would not be helpful at all."

"What she said." Francine winked at me.

"Dude, I think you and I should be hanging out a bit closer over the next few days or so."

Colin's laugh was shocked, but genuine. "Vin? You're going to be my bodyguard?"

"Sure. Why not? And it'll give me time to convince you that *Die Hard* was the best action movie ever." When that particular argument had entered its third minute last night, I'd stopped paying attention.

Despite my initial resistance, the evening had turned out most enjoyable. Until the trivial action movie argument. It was fascinating to observe and listen to my three friends discuss topics I generally had no interest in. Their current argument, however, was boring me. That was why I interrupted Vinnie and Colin's rekindled debate. "Francine, you promised a presentation about Tor and Silk Road."

"Yes, supermodel. What can you tell us about this? And why did you run off when it was mentioned?"

"Firstly"—she raised an eyebrow and looked down her nose at Manny—"I didn't run off. I needed to find out if there was really another Silk Road."

"Is there?" Manny asked.

"Yes, there is." She got up while tapping on her tablet. The large screen against the wall came to life. Displayed on it was a website. "In order to understand Silk Road, you bunch of non-techy people first need a quick lesson on Tor." She pointed at the screen. "This is the big, bad, evil Tor."

"Why are you being hyperbolic?" I asked.

"Because most people think Tor is the dark net, the evil net."

"Isn't it?" Manny asked.

"No. It's just as evil as the internet you guys use every day. It is possibly much more helpful than the normal net. You see, Tor was initially sponsored by the US Navy. The original purpose of starting Tor was to create a safe place where crimes could be reported anonymously. Truly anonymously. It was also supposed to be a safe way for political dissidents, journalists and people living in politically unstable territories to report, connect and communicate with the rest of the world." She paused theatrically. "Of course, I believe the US just wanted to be first to catch anyone willing to come over to their side."

"Could you first give us the facts before your theories?" I realised my tone had been impatient and I added, "Please."

"Not as much fun, but okay. Tor is also useful for people living in the witness protection programme and for undercover cops to stay in touch with their families and team. See, it has a lot of fantastic uses."

"How does it work?" I had read up on it, but hoped Francine could add to my minimal knowledge.

"It's called The Onion Router for a reason. If I visit your website using Tor, it won't be a straight visit. My activity will be encrypted and then bounced through a network of relays around the globe before it reaches your website. The encryption is multi-layered like an onion and therefore the name. If anyone, and by anyone I mean the NSA, CIA or one of those places, wants to eavesdrop on my internet movement, they won't be able to—"

"Because the relays form too many layers between the original visitor and the end destination to identify either's IP addresses at the same time."

Francine pointed dramatically at me. "And that's why you're the genius. You're one hundred percent right."

"Why didn't I know about this earlier?" I considered myself rather well-informed about the internet.

"Are you hiding from someone?" Francine asked. "Want to communicate secretly, don't want anyone to know which sites you visit?"

"No."

"That's your answer. Unless you're an undercover cop, a journalist, or someone like Snowden—who, by the way, used Tor to send the initial files to the newspapers—you won't even think about needing a secret internet. Most people's internet use is boring. Emails, social networks, maybe the odd illegal movie download, but generally nothing interesting. They're also careless when using the internet. They use the same password for every single place they go to, never check their privacy settings and reveal details about their personal lives— all things that can be exploited by internet baddies. Even fewer people are paranoid enough not to have public profiles, not use social media and wipe their browsing histories frequently. Then there is the miniscule percentage that need to or want to use Tor."

"I'm waiting for the 'but', supermodel."

She sighed. "Unfortunately, it's also the perfect place for crooks to hide. As you can imagine, many child pornography sites have made their way to Tor. Since no one can trace the origins, you're quite safe uploading those awful videos as well as watching them." She folded her arms. "May they all burn in Hades."

"There is really no way at all to trace them?" I found that hard to believe.

"There's always some way to get into places, my bestest friend."

"Do you spend a lot of time there?" Colin asked.

"It's a safe place for hackers to communicate, so yes. But most of my time I spend on the normal internet. That's where the real secrets are. Companies think their systems are safe with the software and security they had specially designed, but often they're stupidly easy to get into. And there I find all the dirt." Her smile was genuine. "My favourite places are the financials. I'll never be as smart as our Genevieve, but even I can spot the ways they try to hide stuff. Silly little people."

"Tell them about Silk Road." Vinnie nodded at us, his body language clearly communicating that he knew about this topic.

"This is something our resident weapons expert would be familiar with." She winked at Vinnie. "Silk Road is, was, then is, then was the eBay or Amazon of Tor."

"You don't make sense." I hated when she did that. "Does Silk Road exist or not?"

"The site is still online, but not really functioning. It's had a lot of problems with its bitcoin protocols and millions were stolen."

"English, supermodel!" Manny slapped his hand on the table. "Speak the Queen's language, please."

"Should I speak slower too, handsome?" She laughed when he made a guttural sound similar to a growl. "Okay, let's first look at Silk Road. The first version of it was started as an online market, selling all kinds of things. It went live early 2011. What made it so very controversial was that it was not only selling books, clothes, art, computer equipment and other stuff. It was also trading in drugs, weapons and even assassinations."

"That is outrageous." It was the first time Phillip said anything. "If they were trading in those last three products and services, I have to wonder about the art that was sold there. Why didn't we know about this, Genevieve? We might have been able to locate numerous stolen artworks on there."

"We have." Colin's soft answer reminded me that his work for Interpol stretched further than the few investigations we handled. "Millard might not be familiar with Silk Road and all its functions, but every law enforcement agency's cyber-crimes division knows it very well. We've located many works through Silk Road."

"Are they still selling drugs, guns and murder?" Manny asked.

"No." Francine tapped on her tablet and an article came up on the screen. "In late 2013, the FBI managed to shut down Silk Road. They arrested a man who had only been known as Dread Pirate Roberts."

"What a ridiculous name," Manny muttered.

"Of course you would think that. I'm not even going to try and inform you about the poetic meaning of that name." She flipped her hair over her shoulder. "Well, Dread Pirate Roberts was arrested and charged for a gazillion crimes, including murder for hire, drug trafficking and money-laundering. That didn't seem to stop these guys. A month after the pirate's arrest, another, or maybe the same, Dread Pirate Roberts relaunched the site. The next month three more people were arrested in connection with Silk Road. Another person took over the site for a while until their bitcoin protocol showed vulnerabilities. Now it's pretty much dead."

"I suppose they received all their payments in bitcoins, right?" Phillip was rather well-informed for a man of his generation.

"Yes. In case someone doesn't know what bitcoins are, I'll explain quickly. They were created in 2009 by some fabulously mysterious person only known as Satoshi Nakomoto. If you have a powerful computer, you can mint the coins by using your computer to solve stupendously difficult math problems. These problems are progressively made more difficult to avoid the number of bitcoins from growing too fast. It's an online currency only and is the world's first decentralised online currency. A central bank is no longer needed to issue this currency." She winked at Manny. "Only you and your powerful equipment are needed."

"Where is it used?" I asked. "Only in this secret internet?"

"Oh, no, there are shops in the US that accept bitcoins for their products. It's not caught on much in Europe yet, but in some places in the US it's quite common. On the internet you use, there are marketplaces that also accept bitcoins, but on Tor it is the preferred currency."

I had so many questions, it was hard to choose just one. "How many other online markets are on Tor?"

"Quite a few, but not many are actually noteworthy. They start up, but are soon either shut down or close down on their own. The FBI is quite good at getting to the source and closing shop for them." She smirked. "There was one site that was stupid enough to make two amateur mistakes, one worse than the other. Firstly, the products they had on offer were not all legal. Secondly, and the worst mistake, they accepted not only bitcoins, but payment through PayPal and Western Union. That made it easy for law enforcement to trace payments. Stupid."

"What about Caelan's new site?" Vinnie asked. "Did you find it?"

"Did I ever." She tapped her tablet again and the screen displayed the storefront of an online store. "Lady and gentlemen, I present to you Sher Shah Suri."

Vinnie laughed. "Say what?"

"Sher Shah Suri." Colin tilted his head. "Hmm. That's smart and also very interesting."

"Maybe to you. To me it's impossible to pronounce. I bet no one can say that five times in a row." Vinnie chuckled again. "Why do you think it's interesting, dude?"

"The real Silk Road was also known as the Silk Route," Colin said. "It was actually a few routes that extended over more than six thousand kilometres connecting the East to the West—China to the Mediterranean Sea. It got its name from the lucrative trade in Chinese silk during a span of four centuries starting at two hundred BC. Nomads, monks, soldiers and obviously traders and merchants used this route."

"Well, that's all fine and dandy," Manny said. "What about this shitty sherry show?"

Colin smiled. "Sher Shah Suri was a man also known as the Lion King. He was the founder of the Sur Empire in North India early in the sixteenth century. In his attempt to grow his empire he rebuilt a major road going from his territory to the south. It was then known as the Great Road. Today it's known as the Grand Trunk Road, still a major north-south road."

"The owners of this new online store weren't very imaginative." People were inherently lazy and loved to copy rather than create something new. "Replacing one trade route with the name of someone connected to another. Not very original."

"Well, there's no way I'm saying that tongue-twister." Vinnie leaned back in his chair. "I'll stick with SSS."

"That's how it's referred to on Tor as well." Francine sat down. "It took me surprisingly long to find it. I must say these guys really hide themselves well. And you can enter by invitation only."

"That's not a good way to do business," Vinnie said. "Don't you want more people to find your online market?"

"One would think so. I suppose it's because SSS is pretty much doing what Silk Road was shut down for." Francine tapped on her tablet again. There were a few loud inhalations in the team room. On the screen was a page with different product photos, all in the same category. I counted twenty different handguns on display. Francine tapped again and another page came up, full of semi-automatic weapons.

"Those are illegal to own in most EU states," Manny said.

"That's another thing that sets SSS apart from Silk Road, who did most of their trade in the US. Since the Post Office in the US doesn't check packages sent within the country, it was the perfect way for drug dealers to mail heroin, cocaine or prescription pills to the recipient. If the buyer was smart, he would anonymously rent a mail box a town away from his own, collect his drugs and no one would ever suspect a thing."

"I hate to say it, but it *is* smart." Phillip shook his head.

"But that's the US." Francine changed windows and showed a map of Europe. "See those twenty-six countries that I highlighted?"

"The Schengen countries?"

"We know that nobody checks at the borders if you drive from Spain to France to Germany to Holland to Italy."

"Holland doesn't border Italy," I said.

"Ignore her." Manny waved his hand at me. "Tell us why you highlighted the countries."

"Because SSS offers a service to courier your drugs and guns for an extra fee. These guys smuggle these things from one country to the next. If I live in Hungary and want a semi-automatic gun that's for sale in France, it'll be delivered to a place of my choosing in Hungary." Again she changed windows to what looked like a forum. "Here are quite a few discussions about the fantastic service SSS offers. Some of the people here have bought drugs from SSS and had them delivered the next day. Same with the guns. I didn't have enough time to have a thorough look at the SSS site and to read through all the threads on the forum, but what I've found so far is quite shocking."

"Have you found Courbet's painting?"

"No. I plan to do that this morning." She looked at the door. "Unless Caelan arrives and generously shares with us what he was talking about."

Manny looked at his watch. "Doesn't look like he's an early bird. I suggest we all get on with what we're getting on with. If that little bugger shows up, we'll take it from there."

Chapter SEVEN

"Doctor Lenard! Doctor Lenard! I'm here! It's Caelan! I'm here!" The shouting came so suddenly that I jumped in my chair. I looked around Colin, who was sitting next to me in my viewing room. Through the glass door I saw Caelan peering around Vinnie, trying to see into my room.

Colin, Francine and I had been looking through the SSS online store for the last six hours. It was just after three in the afternoon and Francine had left to refill our coffee mugs. I was dealing with strong emotions as we worked our way through all the products SSS had on offer, outrage being the most prevalent. Colin and I had just found an authentic-looking Manet painting for sale when the shouting interrupted us.

"Doctor Lenard! Come out here! The largest desert in North America is the Great Basin Desert!"

"That kid knows the oddest things," Colin said.

"He's getting agitated." I stood up. "He's scared of Vinnie."

I could understand his fear. Vinnie was standing with his feet apart, his arms away from his sides, his hands in tight fists. There was no mistaking his aggression. Colin followed me to the door and we entered the team room.

"I'm here, Caelan." I kept my tone low and relaxed. I stopped next to Vinnie. "You are safe here."

Caelan looked at Vinnie's shoulder, then looked around the room. "Yes, this is safe. But I don't like this man. He's too big."

"But he's strong enough to protect us." I hoped this was the right thing to say. My life had been spent trying to understand neurotypical people—their psychology, their behaviour, their body language. I felt competent and therefore comfortable dealing with neurotypical people. I didn't know if I was saying or doing the right things when it came to Caelan. I pointed at the table. "Shall we sit down?"

He took a long time to consider my offer. After a while, he nodded and walked to the table. His dark green pants were at least ten centimetres too short, yet they hung loosely on his skinny hips. The pink t-shirt he had on today had a large hole in its left side and had stains all over it. His dark skin, especially his elbows, looked ashen from dryness. This young man was sorely neglected.

He pulled out a chair and stared at the seat for a few seconds before he sat down. My throat tightened with an unwelcome emotion when I noticed how small and vulnerable he looked. I turned away from the round table and walked back to my office. Seeing Colin's surprised expression made me realise how my action could be interpreted. I turned back to Caelan. "I need to confer with Colin. Please wait."

"How long do I have to wait?"

"I won't be longer than ten minutes."

He didn't respond, but he also didn't leave. I accepted that to be his agreement and walked into my viewing room. Colin was right behind me. The moment the doors sealed us in my soundproof room, he asked, "What's wrong?"

"We have to do something."

"About what?"

"Not what. Who." I rubbed my arms. "We have to help Caelan."

"I'm assuming you're talking about his clothes and underfed body, right?"

I nodded tightly. "Somebody needs to look after him. He's too young to be on his own."

"What if he doesn't want anyone to look after him?"

I thought about my own childhood and sighed. "Then someone needs to speak to him about personal hygiene."

"He does smell bad, doesn't he?" Colin smiled as he glanced at the glass doors. "Think about how you're going to tell him that."

"Me?" My hand flew up to cover my suprasternal notch, the hollow just above the breastbone.

"You're the best equipped... You know what? We've had this argument before and I won. This time is not going to be any different." He lowered his chin and stared at me until I put my fists on my hips.

"I don't want to."

"And I don't want to work with Millard, but I do it. We can't only do the things that come easy, Jenny."

I waved my arm at the ten monitors against the wall. "You think this came easy for me? None of this is easy for me, Colin. None."

"I know." His tone was softer, his expression contrite. "I know, love. I didn't mean for it to be understood like that."

I glared at him for a long time, my breathing eventually calming down. "Fine. But you had better be there to make sure I don't scar this young person for life. I don't want to cause him any more harm than he's already suffered at the hands of ignorant adults."

"Done."

The glass door slid open. Manny glared at us. "So? Are you going to stand here all day or is someone going to speak to the kid?"

"You're back." I grimaced at my inane observation. Manny had left to find out more about the file Interpol had on

Edward Taylor and I hadn't expected him back this soon. "Do you have any more information?"

"Nope. But I will have soon. Now let's get to the kid."

"I'm not a kid. A kid is a dependent young person, lacking responsibility. I'm independent and responsible." Caelan said all this in one breath while looking at the ceiling.

"How are you responsible?" Colin asked as we walked into the team room.

"I have my own place. I pay bills. I have clients."

Manny's eyes widened and then a deep frown pulled his eyebrows together. "What clients?"

"Clients are people who pay you to do work for them." Caelan's tone carried typical teenage condescension. "I don't like you."

"The feeling is mutual, lad. But you still have to explain your clients to me."

"I don't have to explain anything to you. Doctor Lenard said last night I don't have to tell you anything."

Manny's head swung towards me. "Did you now? Care to explain why you would say something like that, missy?"

"No." Knowing how hard it was for Caelan to admit he needed help, I didn't want to embarrass him in front of Manny.

"Then what is he doing here?"

I looked at Caelan. "You decided to tell us what you know, didn't you?"

"I did. But the old man is making me want to leave."

Vinnie snorted and I knew it was because Caelan had inadvertently used the moniker Vinnie had given Manny. I considered how to placate both Manny and Caelan. I needed Manny to treat Caelan with more patience and Caelan to stay. Before I could reach a workable plan, Caelan's body language shifted.

"No, no, no, no, no, no, no, no." He was staring at the large screen against the wall. An SSS page showing numerous weapons was on display. "Portugal is generally regarded as the warmest country in Europe. No."

I didn't know what was causing his distress. It could've been the weapons, one specific weapon, a word, the colour of the text, the screen itself. "Francine, could you please close that website?"

A second later the screen was blank, but Caelan was still shaking his head, muttering geographical facts in a monotone.

"Caelan." I put authority in my tone. "Focus on your geography and get control over yourself."

Vinnie snorted again and Colin frowned at me. I ignored them. "What is the estimated number of constellations?"

"There are eighty-eight officially recognised constellations covering the northern and southern hemispheres. That site was mine. It was mine. You weren't supposed to find it."

"What do you mean it's yours?" Again Manny was sitting up in his chair. "Are you running SSS? Are you selling illegal guns?"

Caelan made a loud sound similar to a buzzer. "Loser! The old man is a loser!"

This time Vinnie burst out laughing. Colin chuckled and pulled out a chair to sit next to Vinnie. I was pleased when they responded to my firm look and controlled their mirth.

"That is rude, Caelan. I told you that if you are rude to my friends, I will not work with you. Apologise to Manny." I remained standing, not knowing if my position would register with Caelan as authority.

Everyone around the table stared at me in shock. Everyone but Caelan. He was still looking at the screen. "I wasn't being rude. The old man was wrong. If he was on a quiz show, he would have been called a loser."

"He isn't on a quiz show. That behaviour is not acceptable. Apologise."

"Sorry," he said after a few seconds. He used the same monotone in which he'd given facts and arguments.

"Thank you. Also, his name is Manny. Not 'old man'." I paused, but wasn't surprised when Caelan didn't respond. He wouldn't see the need to acknowledge a fact. "Tell Manny why you said SSS is yours."

"It was my information. I was going to use it to trade."

"To get our further co-operation? I told you last night that we'd help you. You don't have to tell us anything."

"Doc." Manny's warning was low, an almost whisper.

"What if I want to?"

Manny's head swung back to Caelan. "Want to what? Tell us something? Then you can tell us anything you want to, lad."

It was an interesting experience, being an observer of someone on the spectrum. As Manny spoke to Caelan, I realised how I would've understood this. "You can tell us anything related to this case. I don't think Manny would like to hear more about constellations."

Manny pinched the bridge of his nose, but wasn't fast enough to hide the quick lift at the corners of his mouth. "Well, what do you know?"

"Your question is too generi... Oh, you were being rhetorical and sardonic." I pulled my shoulders back. "I pay attention and try to learn how to better communicate. You shouldn't mock."

"He wasn't mocking, Jenny." Colin put his hand over mine. "He was teasing."

"Oh." I struggled to differentiate. There were too many nuances.

"Okay, lad. Tell us what you want to about this case."

Caelan stared at the blank screen for a few more seconds before he looked at Vinnie's shoulder. "I want milk."

Vinnie looked at me. "Is he talking to me? Am I the milk man now?"

"Please, Vinnie."

Vinnie mumbled about having to find a white mug, but got up and left the team room. As soon as he left, Caelan inhaled deeply and held his breath for a few seconds.

"On SSS are three noteworthy art dealers selling real and fake art. The other art sellers are wannabe artists who think their work is much better than it really is, because they suck." All of this was delivered in one breath, in monotone.

"Tell us about the art dealers," Colin said.

"For some stuff, they make straightforward deals. Sell art for bitcoins. But for some of the real stuff, the better real stuff and also the fake stuff, they are only middlemen."

We waited for him to continue, but he didn't. He sat quietly, staring at the wall.

"Do you know for whom these three art dealers act as intermediaries?" I asked.

"No."

"Did you look and couldn't find anything or didn't you look?"

"I didn't look. I don't care."

Vinnie came into the room with a large white coffee mug and a plate. He placed both in front of Caelan, who immediately inspected the mug. He turned his attention to the grapes on the plate. "Green grapes."

"They're seedless too." Vinnie shrugged as if he didn't care. In the time I'd known Vinnie, I'd learned that he was a man who cared deeply. Despite his genuine dislike for Caelan, he was concerned. The relaxation in his shoulders and around his mouth when Caelan pushed two grapes into his mouth confirmed it.

"We'll look into that as soon as supermodel comes back." Manny looked at Colin. "Do you also think the art was being used as a currency?"

"It would make sense," Colin said. "We know that a lot of weapons and drugs have been paid for with a stolen masterpiece. That's why Maurice and I have such a good business relationship. There's no loyalty amongst these guys. They'll pay with a good forgery before they pay with the masterpiece. Whenever Maurice has one of these works, he contacts me to authenticate it. If some head of an organised crime syndicate receives a seven-million-euro painting for his drugs or guns, he wants to make sure that it's really worth that. If he'd been paid in cash, he would've checked every bill as well. They've been done in too many times by brilliantly counterfeited bills."

Somewhere in my subconscious, pieces of information were about to connect. I could feel it. Manny, Vinnie and Colin continued their discussion about art being used as a currency, but I wasn't giving it my full attention. I closed my eyes, blocked out everything I'd seen on SSS and started writing Mozart's Flute Concerto No.2 in D major.

When I opened my eyes, Manny was at his desk, as was Francine. She was biting her bottom lip, frowning at her computer monitor. Caelan wasn't here, I supposed he'd left. Vinnie was reading a magazine and Colin was sitting next to me, working on his laptop, a cup of steaming coffee next to him. In front of me was also a fresh cup of coffee. I took a sip to ready myself. "I have an idea how we can find Dukwicz. And bring him to us."

Chapter EIGHT

"What? How?" Manny's body language went from relaxed to highly alert in less than a second. It wasn't just him. Everyone's undivided attention was on me. "Doc! Speak. Tell us how we're going to catch that murdering bastard."

"Francine, can I have your tablet?" I held out my hand. Ten seconds later, I had the SSS site on the large screen. "We were going through this site today looking for artworks. We saw a lot of other illegal services and products on offer as well."

"I'm waiting for you to get to the part where we catch Dukwicz, Doc."

I ignored Manny's impatience. If I didn't give him a clear explanation, he complained. If I gave too much detail, he also complained. I had not been able to find a balance that pleased him. Therefore, I ignored him.

"One of the services offered on this site is assassinations. Colin showed me one where the service provider called himself a problem-solver. Nowhere did he call himself an assassin or use the words 'murder', 'kill', 'dead' or even the more euphemistic 'hit'. This was even more nuanced than that. If Colin hadn't pointed it out, I wouldn't have found it."

"Then give Frey a gold star. Just tell us how to get Dukwicz."

"I think I know where Genevieve is going with this." Francine was sitting straight, her eyes wide and full of excitement. She pointed a manicured nail at me. "But I'll let her tell it."

"I suggest we send an email to all of them, requesting their services. We'll phrase the email very carefully, aiming to entice Dukwicz to contact us."

"And why would he want to do that?" Manny asked.

"Because, for the services rendered, we're going to offer a partial payment in cash. The rest will be in the form of an antique clock."

"Brilliant!" Francine's bracelets jingled as she clapped her hands.

"Devious, Jen-girl." Vinnie nodded his approval. "You're catching on."

"Good idea, Jenny. We'll have to have a clock to offer though. If he responds, we won't be able to convince him if we don't show proof. We need a clock. A valuable clock."

"Phillip has a clock."

"No," Phillip said from the doorway. He walked in and sat down. "Genevieve, that clock is a family heirloom. It's a French Gilt Bronze Mantel Clock from around 1860. "

"We're not going to give it to him. We're just going to show it to him."

Manny tilted his head. "How much is that old thing worth?"

"It is priceless." Phillip pulled at his cuffs. A sign that he was exasperated. "To me it is priceless. But the monetary value of it is three thousand six hundred euro."

"Three thousand six hundred euro for a clock?" Manny huffed. "Crazy. But with the clock at that price and gilded and French, Dukwicz is much more likely to answer the email."

Phillip only shook his head at Manny's incorrect assumptions about the looks of the clock.

"I'll put a virus on the email." Francine was talking fast, her voice a tone higher. "The moment he replies, the virus will be activated and infect his computer. We'll have full access to him then."

"What are you gals waiting for then?" Manny pointed his chin at Francine's tablet. "Get cracking on that email."

"Not yet." I took a step towards my viewing room. "Colin and I saw two advertisements for assassination services. Since we weren't looking for that in particular, we might have missed quite a few more. We need to find all of them before we send out the email."

"I agree," Vinnie said. "You should hit these guys all at once with your email. Don't send to one, look for more and send another email three hours later. They might be in competition with each other, but for all we know, they might also communicate with each other."

I had never asked Vinnie about his past. A few stray comments from him and observing him had led me to the conclusion a long time ago that he had seen a lot of violence in his life. I wouldn't be surprised if he'd been dispensing said violence. That made him the voice of experience and expertise in this field.

"Then do it." Manny got up. "Just don't take all day. I want to go home early tonight."

Since it was only half past three, I too hoped we could do a thorough search of the site, send that email and have a quiet night at home. Phillip followed Manny into the hallway, and Colin and I returned to my viewing room. Francine was already working on her computer, again biting her lower lip, her eyes narrowed.

We had just settled into our chairs when Vinnie came into my room and pulled a chair closer. "She thinks she can work faster without my help. Since I'm the one here who knows the lingo, I'd think she would appreciate my help. But no. She wants to do this all by herself. We need to show her we're better."

I sighed. Lately Francine and Vinnie were in constant competition with each other. "This is not a competition, Vinnie. There's no rivalry."

"Don't care. We're going to beat her." He pushed his chair closer to the desk, closer to the monitors. "Let's do this."

Two hours later we had scoured the entire online store. Firstly, we went through it again, looking for obvious advertisements. Then we entered numerous keywords Vinnie had suggested—words I would never have associated with offering to murder someone. 'Neutralisation', 'wetwork', 'elimination' and 'liquidation' rendered a few unexpected results that even included sexual fetishes. The keyword search added another two service providers to our list. All in all, we had four names.

"Did you find anything new?" Francine came in, waving her tablet. "I found three more."

"We got four. Four, Francine." Vinnie stretched his arms, then rested his hands on his head. Confident.

"How many are new?" She lifted an eyebrow.

"Two. But we found them with my keywords."

"You're such a child. At least I didn't run to Mommy and Daddy for help. I found these three on my own."

Colin laughed and shook his head. I didn't understand Francine's reference to seeking parental help, but decided to ask her about it the next time we had lunch. "What other names did you find?"

"They're not really names. These are handles. L2OSAAYA, Dys13 and SM66OET."

"We also have L2OSAAYA and SM66OET. Only YERR2031 is new." I wrote down the new handle and looked at my notepad. "Including the first two Colin and I found this morning, we now have five people offering assassination services. How horrid."

"Yeah, it is." Francine leaned her hip against my desk, smiling when I glared at her. "Shall we write that email?"

Vinnie decided to have an input in the wording and what could have been a ten-minute task turned into a debate, an argument, nuanced insults and a five-sentence email thirty-seven minutes later.

"I wonder." Francine tapped her index and middle fingers on her lips. "I think we need to make this more real. Vin, do you also think we need someone to kill?"

I jerked back in my chair, away from Francine. "This is fictional. We are setting a trap. We are not going to put someone's life in danger by putting five assassins' focus on that person."

"Relax, girlfriend. I'm just thinking that they might check into our validity to make sure we're not cops trying to set them up. I have a wicked online persona that's been dormant for a few months. We'll bring him back to life and make him angry enough to want murder. Yes. That'll work. DREAD123 will be pissed off because... because... Oh, my God! I have it. We'll kill Edward Taylor!"

I crossed my arms tightly, my hands in fists. "No. How could you even suggest this? You are not to put Colin's life in danger at any time. What if those assassins are smart enough to track Edward Taylor back to Colin? Do you want to be responsible for Colin's death?"

"Jenny." Colin shifted closer and put his hands on my shoulders. Only then did I realise I'd started rocking in my chair. I stared at Colin, trying to focus on Mozart, but finding it hard. "Breathe. Take a deep breath, Jenny."

I shook my head, but took a shaky breath nonetheless. Three breaths later, I was able to write a line of Mozart's Piano Sonata No.11 in A major.

"Honey, I'm sorry." Francine's voice was soft and filled with contrition. "I didn't mean to upset you so."

"If you think logically about this, you'll know Francine would never do something to harm me. Or any of us." Colin waited for me to study his face. "You know I'm right."

I swallowed hard. "It doesn't mean I like the idea."

"But it is actually a good idea." He raised one hand. "Just hear me out first. If we do this right, we could kill off Edward Taylor and get Interpol off my back as well."

"Don't you first want to know why Interpol is investigating you?"

"Yes and no." His smile was sweet. He knew I hated this answer. "Yes, because I want to know who's behind this. No, because I actually don't care. I don't have to kill Edward Taylor. I just have to retire him. No one will ever see or hear from him again and eventually those Interpol bozos will lose interest."

"They might not lose interest so soon, dude. If any of them are like the old man..." Vinnie shrugged. "That would suck."

"So let's do this right," Francine said. "We can have Edward Taylor killed and end Interpol's game."

"We should talk to Manny first." My suggestion elicited many and loud responses. "I will not be part of this if Manny doesn't know."

"Know what?" Manny asked from the open glass door. As one we turned. Manny's hands rested on his hips, his thumbs pointing to the back. Argumentative. His firmly planted feet, frown, thinned lips were all indicative of his mood. "Know what, Doc?"

"They're going to get Colin murdered."

"What?"

Francine pushed away from where she was leaning and placed herself between myself and Manny. "Let me explain. We found five assassins on SSS. We were busy writing the email when we came up with a brilliant idea."

"It was you." I leaned to the side to look at Manny. "I didn't have anything to do with that idea."

Manny looked at me for a second before returning his stern gaze to Francine. "What idea?"

"To kill Edward Taylor." She started speaking faster. "In order to make the email more authentic and not make it look like we're dumb policemen trying to entrap them, I thought we should use one of my baddie online identities. He would be pissed off with Edward Taylor for saying a painting he wanted to use as payment is a forgery. The painting is worth millions, and he wants Edward Taylor dead because he lost the deal of a lifetime. I can do this so that it leaves a small but findable online trace. We can demand a photo of the dead Edward Taylor as proof of services rendered and strategically leak it. Then we make sure those Interpol idiots see it and they'll stop investigating Colin."

For a few seconds Manny just stared at Francine. Then he shook his head. "I really hope you plan to do this much more eloquently than you've just explained to me."

Francine's nose crinkled. "I know. It came out sounding silly, but I think it's a good plan."

"It needs work."

"You agree?" Francine grabbed Manny's hand and wouldn't let go when he pulled it back. "Oh, you wonderful man. I could kiss you right now."

A deep red crept up Manny's cheeks. He wrenched his hand out of her grip and stepped around Francine. "Do you have a problem with this plan, Doc?"

"She's scared it's going to put my life in danger," Colin said. "Jenny, think about this. Who knows that I'm Edward Taylor?"

"I was able to figure it out." That was why Colin had broken into my apartment two years ago.

"Yes, but you're a genius." He nodded at the monitors. "None of these guys is smart enough to make any connection between the seventeenth-century English poets and the carefully created identities who point out forged artworks."

"You can't be sure of that."

"True. But even you will have to agree that the likelihood of that is remote." He lowered his chin and raised his eyebrows. "Right?"

I considered it for a few seconds. "I still don't like the idea."

"Which is a good thing," Manny said. "That means you'll make sure we don't mess this up. And Doc?"

I looked up from where I was studying the email we'd formulated, re-evaluating the five sentences.

"Thank you for being the only sensible one in this group and insisting on telling me."

"We're a team. Everyone should know everything." I returned my attention to the five sentences, consciously not allowing Manny's smug tone, Vinnie's sarcasm and the argument that ensued to affect me.

"Will this work?" I interrupted Francine patting Manny on his cheek, making him even angrier. They looked at me and then at the monitor I was pointing at. I'd changed a few words and added another two sentences.

"Jen-girl, you're brilliant."

"I know."

"No, seriously, girlfriend. This is good." Francine dropped her hands from Manny's shoulders and turned fully to face the monitors. "You got the tone just right. It almost sounds petulant. How did you do this?"

"I mentally amalgamated your tones and attitudes and put it into words."

"Whose? Mine?" Francine slapped her hand against her chest.

"All of you." I waved my hand in their direction. "I imagined this was what you were talking about. It should sound authentic and you were arguing. It was easy to take it from there."

Their expressions were an interesting read. They exhibited combinations of amusement, indignation and admiration.

"Let's send it off then." Manny looked at his watch. "If I leave soon, it will be the first time this month I'll be home before seven."

"Wait." I looked away from Manny's scowl. "Francine needs to have her part in place before we can send the emails. She needs to put a virus in the email."

"Oh, pooh. It'll take me less than a New York minute to get all of that set up."

"How can a New York minute be different from any other minute?"

"An expression, girlfriend." Francine pulled Colin out of his chair and sat down next to me. "I'll need your brain to make this fool- and fail-proof. You boys can leave us alone."

They didn't. The men stayed while we used the online profile Francine had talked about to create an account in SSS. Fortunately, Tor and SSS had been created to make tracing someone almost impossible. Francine insisted it wasn't completely impossible, but even though there were over two million people using Tor, not many of those people had the hacking skills necessary to find someone's digital footprints.

"Now for that little virus," she said when we decided it was safe to send the emails. "I believe this is how the FBI arrested Dread Pirate Roberts. Of course, they wouldn't give away their secret how they got into Silk Road. Some say their experts found a back door in Tor that got them in. And that ol' Dread Pirate wasn't the smartest of programmers and they managed to find a weakness in his computer code and hacked into the site. Personally I think they sent him a nice little gift with one of their emails when they got him to order a hit on a delivery man."

"A Trojan horse." I knew this was the commonly used term for specific types of computer viruses, but I was referring to the original tale.

"Yes." Francine continued to type strings of code on my computer. My skills were above average, but this surpassed everything I knew about computers. "I need a photo of Phillip's clock."

"He emailed it to you," Manny said. "He wasn't happy about it."

"Nothing's going to happen to it." Francine opened her inbox on my computer and downloaded the photo. "I'm just putting it up here to sweeten the pot."

"How many of these clocks are still in circulation?" I asked.

"Phillip said they're not so exclusive as to create a problem. Yes, missy, I thought of this."

"You're calling me 'missy' and your nonverbal cues are telling me you're angry with me. Why?"

"I'm not angry with you, Doc."

"Do you know that men also suffer from menopause?" Vinnie's sincere expression was false. "They call it manapause. Maybe they should call it Mannypause. See what I did there? See?"

Manny turned his back on Vinnie, his lips in a thin line. "Phillip is taking the clock to another location as an added security measure."

"Good for him." With a final, and dramatic, tap on the enter key, Francine looked at me and smiled. "Done! Now we just have to wait for Dukwicz to step into our web."

"Do we have to do the waiting here, supermodel?" Manny's feet were pointing at the door. He was ready to leave.

"No. I'll get an alert the moment someone opens our email and another alert the moment he hits the reply button."

"We should arrest anyone who opens or answers this frigging email." Manny walked to the door. "Advertising assassination services. What next?"

"Doc G! Doc G!" Nikki's voice came from down the hallway, most likely from the elevator. Her panic had me out of my chair, moving into the team room. Everyone followed. Nikki ran into the room, almost colliding with Vinnie. He caught her and steadied her, but her focus was on me. "He's gone. He's gone."

"Who?"

"Michael."

"The young man who was studying with you in my apartment?"

"Yes." She waved her pink smartphone at me. "He's gone."

"Punk, you need to take a deep breath and start at the beginning. Jen-girl is not the only one who's confused at the moment." Vinnie gave her a sideways hug and looked down at her. "When you're ready."

Nikki took a deep breath. "Rebecca and I were shopping when I got this very strange message from Michael. I called him back, but he didn't answer. He always answers. I tried again and again and again, and still nothing. He's gone."

"Nikki." Manny's tone was gentle, but reproving. "Just because someone is not answering your calls doesn't mean he's missing. Maybe his phone's battery died."

"And you know what happened with Pascal." Vinnie gave her another sideways hug. "I'm sure he's fine, just pissed off that his phone died."

Nikki looked from Manny to Vinnie, tears gathering in her eyes. "You don't believe me. Doc G, please believe me."

I had an uncomfortable tightening around my chest seeing her tears and hearing the pleading tone in her voice. "Come to my room."

Without waiting, I walked back into my viewing room, hoping only Nikki would follow, but everyone did. I pointed to the chair next to mine and waited until she was seated. "Tell me everything. Including the information you're hiding."

"I don't want to get Michael into trouble."

"If he's missing like you're saying, he's already in trouble. Talk."

"Michael, Rebecca and I have been talking to each other every day for the last six months or so. Every day, Doc G. This morning Rebecca and I couldn't get hold of Michael. We know that he was going to meet with—"

"Don't even think of lying." I pointed at her face. "Your eyes, mouth, hand and a few other things are telling me you're going to. Who was he going to meet?"

She stared at me with big eyes. "Our visual literacy professor. He was going to meet Professor Vega after our study session last night."

"So he likes older women." Francine shrugged. "What's so bad about that?"

"Professor Vega is a man."

"So he likes older men." Francine shrugged again. "What's so bad about that?"

"The professor is married and it's against university policy. It is so not allowed."

Rules and moral dilemmas were not important now. "Do you think the professor did something to Michael?"

"No. We had visual literacy class this morning. Professor Vega asked us where Michael was. The professor said they were supposed to meet last night for an 'extra lesson'"—she put the last two words in air quotes, something she did often to indicate irony—"and he didn't show up. He also wasn't in class. He always comes to class."

"Punk—"

"Don't even say it, Vinnie. Michael doesn't do drugs, he doesn't sleep around, he doesn't party like crazy. He's like me."

"A punk who doesn't listen?" Vinnie stepped closer. "I was going to ask you when was the last time you spoke to him."

"Oh. Sorry. I spoke to him last night at the library when we finished studying. Rebecca and I went home after teasing him about his affair with Professor Vega." Nikki sniffed. "Rebecca and I were the first ones to make friends with Michael. He's always been a loner. As far as I know we're his only friends. Prof Vega is a fling that started only a few weeks ago."

I thought about everything she'd said so far. "What message did you receive in the shop that caused you to panic?"

"He left me this." She tapped on her smartphone and held it towards me so I could listen.

My immediate impression upon hearing the young male voice was that he was intoxicated. His speech was slurred and he sounded incoherent. I had to strain to hear his words. "Nikkidee, help. They have… Auct… Traders… been othe… Traff… help."

"That kid is high." Manny tilted his head. "Nikki, are you sure this is Michael? Did he phone you from his phone?"

"Yes. He has two phones. One he uses a lot because his grant pays the bills. The other one he only uses when the first one's battery dies because he's texting too much. He phoned me from the second phone."

"I'm sorry, Nikki." Manny looked truly contrite. "The police won't take this as evidence. If you take this to them and claim your friend is gone, they'll tell you to wait another day before you report him missing."

"That's why I'm not taking this to the police." She gave her phone to me. "I'm bringing it to you. You have to help him, Doc G. This is not like before. I can really feel something is wrong."

I thought about her previous behaviour. "Have you been to Michael's flat?"

She swallowed. "Yes?"

"You're not sure?"

"No, I'm sure. I just don't want you all to shout at me. Rebecca and I went to his place to look for him. We have a key, so we went inside." She sighed. "Everything looked fine. There was nothing out of place."

"But you have a bad feeling?" Vinnie asked.

She nodded.

"I think we should give your friend until the morning to surface." Manny's smile was gentle. "He's a young man. He might be doing… young man things."

"He's not like that." Her voice was strained. Manny continued to look at her until her shoulders dropped. But then she lifted her chin. "If I can't reach him tomorrow, you have to promise that you'll look for him."

Not only Manny agreed. Vinnie and Colin equally committed to finding Michael if indeed he was missing. They continued to comfort her, but my attention was on Nikki's phone. I scrolled down the SMS history between her and Michael. They spent an inordinate amount of time communicating in this manner. Many of the conversations were joined by Rebecca. It didn't take long to see the depth of their friendship. I was pleased that Nikki had friends her own age group. People who accepted her as she was. I handed her phone back to her, pondering the language used in the many messages.

"Thanks, Doc G." She quietly added, "For believing me."

I didn't know how to react to it, so I merely nodded. "I'm going home. We should all go home."

"Good plan." Colin handed me my handbag. "Vin will cook for us. Nikki can serve us ice cream if she wants to help Vin make some food."

I wanted to argue that scooping ice cream from a container was not making food, but decided against it. The mood in my viewing room had lifted and it pleased me. We'd had a productive day and a possible way to find Dukwicz. As I turned off my computers, I hoped Vinnie was going to make his Aunt Theresa's gnocchi. I also hoped Michael was enjoying a good party somewhere. Not scared and lost like the sound of his voice on that message.

Chapter NINE

I opened another window for the article on the Silk Road arrests. I'd been in my viewing room for the last three hours reading as much material as I could on Tor and Silk Road. There was surprisingly little on Sher Shah Suri. I had only found one article and it hadn't given me any more insight into this online marketplace.

Apart from the obvious illegal use of Tor, I found it to be a well-developed browser, even though it was considerably slower than the usual browsers I used. Francine had explained that the encrypted connections through relays on the network were the reason for the slow access. Had I not been prepared for the time it took to open a site, I might have lost my patience a long time ago. As a reprieve from surfing around Tor, I was now using my normal browser, reading another article.

It had been a peaceful morning so far. I was alone, enjoying the lack of bickering and constant interruptions. From previous experience, I knew that it would be another two hours before the enjoyment turned into longing. The latter irritated me. I didn't want to be used to, take pleasure in and sometimes even need the exasperating exchanges between my friends. I had just clicked on the link to another article about the arrests of illegal arms traders on Tor when my peaceful morning ended.

I hadn't closed the glass doors separating my viewing room from the team room. Therefore, Francine and Manny's loud argument reached me before they entered the team room.

Francine marched in and threw her red leather handbag on Manny's desk. "Eight minutes, handsome. It took us eight minutes to get here. I don't know what your problem is."

Vinnie was sitting at the round table. The newspaper he'd been reading was hanging loosely in his hands, a smile starting to lift the corners of his mouth as he watched Manny. The older man stopped at his desk and dropped four large shopping bags to the floor. He glared at Francine's handbag and dropped it next to the shopping bags. "My problem is that I was stupid enough to give in to your incessant nagging."

"My incessant nagging? I only asked you three times, Mister Cantankerous. Three times is not nagging." She fell into her chair, flipped her hair over her shoulder and tapped away on her computer. I got up and stood in the doorway, fascinated by their body language.

"It is when your asking is done while sexually harassing me."

"In your dreams." She spat out the words, not once looking away from her computer. "Least you can do is explain to Genevieve why we're arguing."

Manny turned to me and pointed first at his legs, then at his torso. He wasn't wearing his usual clothes. The light brown pants fitted him well, were tailored and clearly much better quality than the dull grey and brown pants he favoured. His shirt was also not two sizes too large and wrinkled. This one was beige, styled to display Manny's wide shoulders and flat stomach, making him look fitter than I'd ever seen him look.

"See this? She made me wear this off the hanger. Who wears stuff off the hanger? You would've washed it first, wouldn't you, Doc?"

His nonverbal cues indicated he was asking a rhetorical question. I didn't respond, but felt my eyes widen in the realisation why Francine and Manny hadn't been in the office when I arrived this morning. "You went shopping with Francine? Why?"

"Because he looks like a thrift-shop mannequin. And I'm not talking about one of those cool thrift shops either." She looked up from her computer. "So, what do you think about my makeover skills?"

"I think the old man looks real purdy." Vinnie pouted and winked at Manny.

"Fuck off, criminal." Manny walked to Francine's desk and waved his index finger at her. "And you. You better stop talking and get that email, supermodel."

"What email?" I wasn't particularly interested in their shopping experience.

"Supermodel got a response to your request for a killer." He glared at her. "And that is why I didn't want to go shopping."

"And as I said to you a million times, we could shop and be back here in ten minutes the moment I got an alert that I'd received an email." She lifted one eyebrow. "It took us only eight minutes to get back. What difference do you think those eight minutes would have made?"

"It wasn't the time." I'd come to that conclusion watching them. "Manny didn't want to go shopping."

"Ya think?" Francine was tapping her foot, her tone sharp. "I had to—"

"The email, supermodel!"

"Oh. Yes." She shrugged. "It's a dud."

"What does that mean?" I asked.

"This killer-idiot wants us to sell the clock and give him the cash. He says he already has a watch and doesn't need a cuckoo clock."

I walked over to her desk, stood behind her and read the email. "This is not Dukwicz. He knows his timepieces. He would never have called this French Gilt Bronze Mantel clock a cuckoo clock."

"And you don't think he could pretend not to know in case he suspects we're trying to flush him out?"

"Nope." Vinnie put down the newspaper and sat up. "Dukwicz is really not that smart. He's a great soldier, brilliant at breaking into places, good at killing, but not at strategy."

"He's been bloody good at evading capture and arrest. Doesn't that make him good at strategy?"

I shook my head. "I agree with Vinnie. His behaviour has shown that he's a soldier, following and executing orders. In my experience with him, I would not expect manipulation from him. Not smart and subtle manipulation."

"So why isn't he answering our email? We need to catch that bastard."

"Keep your new knickers on, handsome," Francine said. "We'll get him. You have to give these killers a chance to read their emails. It's only been sixteen hours. Not everyone checks their emails every five minutes."

"You bought him knickers?" Vinnie's voice was louder than usual, his top lip curled in disgust.

"Of course not." Manny's neck and cheeks turned red.

"Of course I did." Francine winked at Manny. "Sexy black boxers."

I wondered why Francine would buy Manny underwear. And why he would lie about it. I shook my head in irritation. These people had no ability to stay on topic. "Francine, I want to go onto the Interpol site and look around, but I don't want anyone to know that I've been there or where I've looked. Can you—"

"Ooh! Of course I can set you up. Give me five minutes and you'll be an invisible ghost in Interpol." She clapped her hands. "Oh, goodie."

"What the hell, Doc?"

I looked at Manny, waiting for a question.

"Missy?" The red hue on his cheeks was no longer from embarrassment. "Why the hell do you want to sneak around the Interpol site?"

"I want to find out who's looking into Edward Taylor. And why."

"Where is the thief?" Manny looked around the team room. I didn't know why he did that. Colin was clearly not here.

"Colin went to meet Maurice Dupin. He wants to find out how Interpol, or Laurence Gasquet for that matter, knew that he was going to meet Maurice Dupin the day before yesterday."

"The idiot is meeting Dupin wearing his disguise? Going as Edward Taylor? Has he completely lost his mind?"

Fear caused my throat muscles to constrict, creating a feeling of being strangled. I rubbed my throat. "He promised me not to get caught."

"Oh? He promised?" Manny sat down heavily in his chair. "Well, then everything will be just dandy."

"Are you being sarcastic? Why?"

"Because, missy, Frey should've told me so I could watch his back." Manny was angry, but it was born from concern.

"He'll be fine, old man." Vinnie picked up his newspaper and turned his head to show the small white earpiece in his ear. "I've got him on the line and I'm listening in."

"Are you recording that?"

"Yup. Francine set us up."

"Sometimes we can be quite smart, handsome." Francine looked at me. "You're also set up, girlfriend. Go and find us some dirt."

"Dirt?"

"Secrets, gossip, stuff we can use to get those guys off Colin's case."

I nodded and returned to my viewing room. I pressed the button on the keypad next to the glass door to close and seal it, hoping to keep Manny out. It didn't work. He keyed in his code and stepped through the open door.

"Talk to me, Doc." Without invitation, he sat down in the chair next to mine—the chair that I'd come to think of as Colin's. "Are you following a hunch or some fact you already know?"

I walked to my desk and sat down. My chair had been placed in the exact centre of the desk, the ten monitors spaced equally in front of me. Colin's chair was close to mine since I didn't mind his closeness. With Manny in it, I felt panic setting in. "Please move."

"You and your bloody fifty-centimetre rule," Manny grumbled as he pushed the chair to the side. "Is that good enough for you?"

"Thank you." I could breathe again.

"The Interpol site, missy?"

"I don't have hunches and currently I don't have anything factual. This is why I want to research the agents involved in Colin's case." I wanted to know if they suspected that Colin was Edward Taylor. Worrying about this had caused a restless night with little sleep.

"Okay. Let's get to it."

I knew my face evidenced my surprise.

"Doc, I'm just as suspicious as you are about this sudden

interest in Edward Taylor. I also want to know where this comes from."

I nodded and without another word opened Interpol's personnel files. "Who is in the unit looking into Edward Taylor?"

"Judith Jooste, André Breton, Paul Hugo and Jacques Boucher. Those were the names I was given."

I typed in the first name and clicked on Judith Jooste's file, but stopped reading when Manny got up. "I think it will be faster if we split this up. I'll get supermodel to set my computer up like yours. You can check out Jooste and Breton. I'll do Hugo and Boucher."

"What will you be looking for?" I had planned to do a thorough search into each person's professional and personal life.

"Everything, Doc. From their favourite toy as a baby, to their first kiss, to where they park their car, to their latest case."

"I don't think their baby toy or first kiss might... Oh. You were overstating. Yes, I also plan to be very detailed in my search."

"Just not too detailed, Doc. I really don't need to know their favourite baby toy. We don't want to waste too much time on this, okay?"

I nodded and Manny left. The door closed and sealed behind him, leaving me in blissful silence. Soon I lost myself in my quest to learn everything I could about Judith Jooste and André Breton. It made for interesting reading.

"Time to eat, Jenny." Colin's hand on my shoulder brought me out of my work.

"You're back."

"And I brought Chinese." He smiled and held out his hand. I took it and tried to move, but my legs were numb. Once again I'd pulled my legs up onto the chair and stayed in one position for too long.

"I'm going to need a minute." I lowered my legs to the floor, wincing. I hated the pins and needles that were about to accompany the renewed blood circulation. "Please don't fight with me again about this. I try to keep my feet on the floor, but when I'm absorbed, it becomes an unconscious movement."

"And that's why they should've checked on you earlier."

I didn't want to have this conversation again. "How did your meeting go with Maurice?"

"He didn't show up." Colin held out his hand again as I stood up, but I ignored it.

"Frey! Get your arse in here and report."

Colin leaned closer to me and whispered, "He's hungry and pissed off that I told him to wait for you before he can eat."

We joined the others at the round table, everyone with a carton of Chinese food in front of them. There was only one restaurant I would accept takeout food from, never having been disappointed in the quality of the dishes. No surprise visit to the restaurant had ever shown anything other than a pristine establishment run by a despotic little Chinese woman.

We ate in silence for a few seconds. Manny broke the silence between large bites. "I'm waiting, Frey."

"Maurice Dupin didn't show." Colin put down his chopsticks. "I was there two hours before we were supposed to meet to make sure it wasn't another setup. There were no law enforcement agents anywhere. Then I waited in another building, watching the café we had arranged to meet in. He never came. I phoned him ten minutes after our meeting time and didn't get an answer."

"Did you try his gallery?"

"Of course I did, Millard. Eventually, I went home, put on another disguise and went to the gallery to make sure he wasn't there. He hadn't come in at all today. His assistant also couldn't get a hold of him. He wasn't at home either."

"Hmm." Manny finished chewing. "What do you make of it?"

"I don't know. You say he hasn't been arrested again, so I have no idea where he could be."

"I checked all the hospitals and other police stations as soon as Colin phoned," Francine said. "Also nothing. Unless he's admitted somewhere under another name."

"Cell phone?" Manny asked.

"Checked that. Both numbers Colin gave me are currently disconnected."

"Let's not jump to conclusions yet. We'll give him the rest of the day to contact Frey before we get worried." Manny was already worried. It was in the *orbicularis oculi* muscles around his eyes and the *depressor anguli oris* muscles around his mouth. "While you've been playing dress-up, Doc and I have been looking at the team investigating you. Did you find anything suspicious, Doc?"

"Not with André Breton. He had an average childhood, was employed by Interpol seven years ago, after eight years serving in the local police force. He excelled at his job in the cyber-crimes division, and when he applied to Interpol, they accepted him immediately. He's not had any complaints against him, works well in the teams he's been assigned to and has a high case closure rate."

"Judith Jooste?"

"She has a family connection in law enforcement. Her father and two uncles are high-ranking officials in the Netherlands. According to her file, she's worked extra hard to prove that she deserves her position on her own merit. She has five commendations for extraordinary performance of her duties."

Manny's brows raised. "How old is she?"

"Thirty-four."

"That's really young for five commendations."

"She also has a criminology degree from Harvard and a postgraduate degree in art history. She's been with the agency since her graduation. But she's had complaints lodged against her."

Manny's reaction confused me. He looked pleased. "What complaints?"

"She has a temper and is stubborn. She's also acted against the orders of her superiors."

"My kind of girl." Vinnie smiled as he heaped more food onto his fork. He didn't like eating with chopsticks.

"What about Paul Hugo and Jacques Boucher?" I asked.

"Boucher doesn't count any more. He died. Hugo is as clean as a whistle."

"I've read that saying before, but it doesn't make sense." Most metaphors didn't make sense to me. "A whistle is really dirty. It has saliva in it causing numerous bacteria to grow, and can spread viruses as well."

Francine dropped her chop sticks. "Really? While I'm eating? Come on, girlfriend!"

"How sure are you Hugo is clean?" I asked, having learned that describing people as clean or dirty had nothing to do with hygiene.

"His file says so. Clean driving records, clean university records, clean employment records. Clean, clean, clean. Then I checked Breton. He's also clean. Too clean."

"Why don't you believe this?" I pointed at his mouth.

"When your top lip raises like that, you are disgusted as well as doubtful. Why?"

Manny looked at Vinnie. "Do you know any good, really good, cop without any citations?"

"I don't know cops." Vinnie laughed when Manny's expression changed. "Sure. I know cops, but the cops I know are not good cops. The good ones are hardasses. And no, they usually toe the line."

"I don't understand." I frowned. "How is it a good thing to break the rules?"

"Tell me, Doc. What did Jooste get reprimanded for?"

"The first time was for insubordination. She lost her temper with the local police captain when his officers didn't properly preserve a crime scene. I read the report and I agree that her behaviour, especially her language, was unprofessional."

"What was the result of the bad policing? What case did they lose?"

My eyes widened as soon as Manny asked his first question. I began to understand his reasoning. "Interpol was pursuing a serial killer who travelled a lot. Because of the local police's negligence, they couldn't use the DNA found at the scene and had to let the suspect go. Two more girls were murdered before they eventually arrested him."

"And the other complaints against her?"

I thought about it for a few seconds. "All similar in nature. Okay. I concede your point. In the one case, she continued looking into a stolen credit card complaint even though she'd been ordered off it. That led her to uncover one of the largest credit card fraud scams in France."

"Smart girl."

"If we work on these qualities, someone who has no complaints or citations is not a good law enforcement officer? It doesn't make sense."

"That would be too much of a generalisation, Doc. Many cops never do anything spectacular. They keep their heads down and simply do as they're told, never saying or doing anything controversial. They will also have a clean, albeit boring, record. But we are looking at Interpol agents. They should be out of the ordinary."

"Which means they should have at least a comment about their temper or stubbornness," Colin said.

"It is said that the seven most common traits found in law enforcement officers are that they are pragmatic, conservative, suspicious, prone to isolation, prejudiced, cynical and action-oriented. An investigator has those qualities, but is inquisitive to the point of being meddlesome and impertinent."

"Like someone we know," Manny said.

I shrugged, dismissing his lifted eyebrow. "We are all investigators here. I think we all share these personality traits."

"But I bet not many are as rational and stubborn as you, Doc. And I mean that as a compliment."

"Oh." How did we manage to digress so often? I cleared my throat. "Does this mean we are suspecting André Breton and Paul Hugo because they have clean records? Do they have something to do with Colin's arrest?"

"They were the men who arrested Frey... er... Edward Taylor."

"Then we should definitely suspect them." Vinnie's grip on his knife and fork tightened.

"No, criminal. It only means that we're paying attention to them."

"And Judith Jooste?" I asked.

"I'm paying special attention to her, in case we need more help."

"What about Laurence Gasquet?"

"What about him?" Manny leaned forward. "Did you look him up?"

"Yes." I realised Manny expected me to elaborate when a frown pulled his eyebrows together. "Apart from the basic knowledge you already have, Laurence Gasquet has a connection to Breton, Hugo and Boucher. They've worked together on a few cases, with Gasquet as a consultant. Mostly, he does what you said—investigations into corporate cases. His personal life is much more interesting."

"Please tell me you found a scandal." Francine rubbed her hands together, but stopped suddenly when her tablet pinged. She got up and went to her desk, still looking at me.

"His parents were involved in a scandal, if that is what you would like. When he was sixteen, his mother shot and killed his father after suffering years of abuse. She's still incarcerated in Italy, where they'd been on holiday when it happened. Laurence Gasquet didn't return to Bristol where they'd been living. His father was originally from Strasbourg, so he returned here. He lost a year of schooling, but eventually graduated and went to university."

"Where did he stay during that time?"

"His father's old neighbour was a generous elderly man who took care of Laurence Gasquet until he came of age. I couldn't find the name of the neighbour, but he must be in his nineties now or deceased."

"What about Laurence Gasquet's financials?"

"I didn't have time to look into that yet. I was looking at his assets when Colin interrupted me."

"You're welcome, love."

I glanced at Colin, noticed his smile, thought about it and winced. "You did interrupt me, but I don't mind."

"I know." He took my hand and squeezed it.

"His assets?" Manny exhaled loudly through his nose. "When you're done snogging."

"We're not snogging." I pulled my hand from Colin's. "Laurence Gasquet owns a large house in the city, an apartment in Bristol, a yacht and seven cars. Why does anyone want seven cars? You can only drive one at a time."

"He might be collecting," Colin said. "What kind of cars?"

"Luxury cars, not collector pieces. His assets are worth a few million."

"Could he have bought this with his income?"

"I don't know yet," I said. "He inherited the Bristol apartment and half a million pounds when his father died. I'll have to have a better look at his finances to form a real opinion. Do you think he's the one who's after Colin?"

"Not after me." Colin shook his head. "After Edward Taylor. I would also like to know if it's him or one of these Interpol goons."

"Tell me you love me. Tell me, tell me, tell me." Francine's excitement had us all looking from her to her computer and back.

"What did you find, supermodel?"

"Tell me you love me."

"Supermodel!"

"Spoilsport." She sniffed dramatically before clicking a few times with the computer mouse. The large screen against the wall came to life, showing an email. "Dukwicz contacted us. See how interested he is in the clock?"

I read his email aloud. "'I want clock. Don't care if anyone offered their services. You can keep cash. Just clock. If it's fake, I'll come after you. If it's real, you have deal. I'm on a job at the moment. Will contact you again in three days. I will need all personal details of hit and photo.'"

My chest tightened when the impact of the last sentence registered. I didn't like this plan. I didn't want Colin to be a target at all. Not even if it was one of his false identities. I chose to focus on Dukwicz's omission of definite and indefinite articles. His spoken English was accented, but not as bad as his written English.

"Do you have access to his computer?" Colin asked, no stress noticeable in his voice or on his face.

"Oh, yeah, baby."

We watched the screen as Francine accessed Dukwicz's computer. His desktop background was of a decapitated body. It looked real. I covered my mouth with my hand and closed my eyes.

A familiar hand covered my other hand that was fisted on my lap. Colin pried my hand open and intertwined our fingers. I clung onto the feeling of safety holding his hand gave me and tried to reason with myself. Still I couldn't build up enough courage to look at the assassin's computer.

Manny and Vinnie were giving Francine directions where to look, their tones grave. No matter what rationalisation I used, I could not face the screen. Trusting the others to find key information, I mentally started writing the Allegro of Mozart's Serenade No.13 in G major, known to the layman as Eine kleine Nachtmusik. By the third line, my breathing eased. When I reached the seventh line, I felt comfortable opening my eyes behind my hand. That was when Colin's body stiffened next to mine.

"Fuck." His shocked whisper was followed by loud expletives filling the team room. Dread made it feel as if my stomach had dropped to the ground. It took all my willpower not to hide in the safety of Mozart. Instead, I lowered my hand.

Chapter TEN

What I was looking at didn't make sense at first. I squinted, not willing to believe the obvious. "An auction?"

"My God." Francine's voice was hoarse from shock. "Are they auctioning this young man?"

We were looking at video footage of a young man standing in a room, empty but for a steel chair against the crisp cream wall. He was dressed only in sweat pants, his torso and feet bare. To the left of the screen was a list of letters and numbers, nothing that had any meaning to me. On the right-hand side, bids were being placed on different items.

"Is this live?" Manny asked.

"No. This is a recording," Francine said.

"Doc, what can you tell me about this kid?"

I studied his body language a few more seconds. "He looks to be in good health. His skin tone doesn't indicate distress or illness. See how he tries to hold his arms close to his torso? People do that when they're scared. What is strange here is that there is not a lot of tension in his body. Yet it seems like he's trying to pull into himself, trying to be less of a target."

"A target for what?"

"I don't know." I tilted my head. "Francine, can you zoom in on his face?"

"Give me a sec."

Ten seconds later, the young man's face filled most of the screen. The flood of information registering in my mind was overwhelming. I chose to analyse the least emotional observation first. "He's drugged."

"I'm not surprised," Manny said. "These traffickers get their victims addicted as soon as possible. Makes them more willing to do what's necessary."

"I don't think he's under the influence of a typical narcotic." I pointed at the face on the screen. "He's not perspiring excessively, there are no rapid eye movements, rigid muscles or any other symptoms you find with street drugs."

"Then why do you say he's drugged?" Francine asked.

"His expression. Assuming he's not there of his own volition, I would expect to see much more fear in his micro-expressions. If he was truly nervous, his shoulders would reach his ears and his arms would be wrapped tightly around his torso. He would blink much more frequently, swallow more, his lips would be pressed tightly together—there is a long list of cues he is not exhibiting. At least not as strongly as this situation warrants. He could be on some kind of calming or relaxing drug."

"I can't see any signs of torture or rough handling." Colin narrowed his eyes. "Francine, can you stay zoomed in on him, but check the rest of his body?"

We watched as Francine moved the focus from the top of the young man's body to his bare feet. He had the typical physique of a man in his late teens, early twenties—fully developed, but not filled out yet.

"No torture." Colin leaned back in his chair, his frown deep. "At least nothing we can see."

"Maybe he isn't scared, just uncomfortable," Vinnie said. "Maybe he wants to be there."

"Most definitely not." I shook my head vigorously. "He was kidnapped."

Manny looked away from the screen, staring at me. "How do you know that, Doc?"

I got up and went to Francine's desk. "May I use your tablet?"

"Sure. Do you want it to go up on the screen?" She paused the video.

"Yes." It took me only a few seconds to find the article I was looking for. "Three days ago, Nikki asked me to look into the possible kidnapping of her classmate. She referred to this case. This young man, Matthieu Jean, disappeared ten days ago. The police had determined it was an abduction." I highlighted a paragraph in the article. "They were able to find security video footage from a nearby bank that showed the student being forced into a vehicle."

"How do you know this is him?" Manny asked.

I clicked to the next page of the article. Two photos filled the screen. One photo was a studio portrait, the kind taken for school yearbooks. The other was of him sitting in front of a computer, unaware of the photographer and completely absorbed by what he was looking at.

"Holy hell." Manny rubbed his hands over his face. "We have to find this kid. Supermodel, do you have any computer voodoo you can do to find out where this was taken?"

"Let me check the metadata." She changed windows. We were looking at the paused image of Matthieu being auctioned. The window split, another smaller window filling the bottom third of the screen. Lines and lines of code appeared as Francine did what she was best at. "Hmm. This video was recorded off a Tor site. We won't be able to trace its origins, but at least we know it was recorded six days ago at ten in the morning."

"Which doesn't mean that footage was live at ten," I said.

"Bloody hell. We don't know anything."

"That is not true." I pointed at the screen. "We know that this young man appeared in this video which seems to be an auction."

"It gives us squat, Doc. We don't even know what they're auctioning him off for. Sex? Slave labour? What?"

"You should be more optimistic and encouraging." I recalled the teamwork books I'd read last year. "Your attitude is not conducive to good morale and enjoyable work environment."

"And yours is?" Manny glared at me.

I considered his question for a few seconds. When I looked back at Manny, the *supratrochlear* artery on his forehead was pronounced, his jaw tight.

"Maybe we should finish watching the video." This young man's life took precedence over our disagreements. Although I couldn't help adding, "And you should adopt a more positive attitude."

"Okay, here we go," Francine said before Manny could respond. She'd changed windows and once again we were looking at Matthieu blinking slowly at the camera.

On the right-hand side, the bids were increasing. I stared at the different items being auctioned. Why would this young man be sold for different things? There were six main items, three of which were reaching very high prices. I looked at the left-hand side of the screen and immediately made the connection. I got up and stood in front of the screen to point out my observations.

"Look at these letters and numbers." I pointed at the left-hand side of the screen. "It lists Ca, Pn, Ne1, Ne2, He and eight other items. I don't know what they are yet, but look at the bids. The six items that have the most bids are Ca, Pn, Ne1, Ne2 and He."

"Maybe they're sexual fetishes," Vinnie said. "Maybe it's code for some BDSM something."

"How little you know, Vin." One corner of Francine's mouth lifted in a half-smirk. "Those services can be bought for much cheaper than what these guys are bidding."

Manny turned slowly to Francine, his eyes narrow. "You sound very sure about this, supermodel."

"Oh, handsome." Her voice was husky and soft. I'd only heard her use this tone with Manny. "Wouldn't you just love to know what I know about this?"

"Not really." His gruff answer belied his micro-expressions.

"He wants to know," I said. "But it's not important now. We need to find out what these letters represent. See this?" I pointed at the listing of letters on the left-hand side. "I think these numbers describe the letters. If I can decode this, we'll know what they are auctioning and also the details of each item."

"Do that, Doc. We need that info as soon as possible." Manny rubbed the back of his neck as if trying to relax a knot. "There is nothing in that bloody room to tell us where this kid is. If he's still alive."

"Assuming he was auctioned on the day Dukwicz recorded this video, it means that he was kidnapped ten days before and kept in good health for four days." Colin frowned. "Usually kidnappers don't take good care of their hostages."

Eighteen months ago, Colin had been abducted and brutally tortured for six days. It had taken him months to recover physically and mentally from that experience. I didn't know if I'd recovered from my kidnapping a year ago. It had been a traumatic event.

"Oh, oh, oh!" Francine bounced in her chair. "I found another auction for the same kid. Look."

Another video filled the screen. Matthieu Jean was standing in the same room. There was a significant difference in his body language. He seemed much more aware, his arms tightly wound around his torso in a full self-hug. He exhibited all the nonverbal cues of fear I'd mentioned before. "He's no longer under the influence of the drug they gave him. This must be a few hours after the last auction or before it."

"What are they auctioning now?" Francine's top lip lifted, her tone adding to her disgust.

"Not the same as the previous auction." I pointed at the left-hand side of the screen again. "Some of these numbers are the same as the previous descriptions, but it's only for one item."

The single item being bid on confirmed my observation.

"None of this makes sense." Manny turned to me. "Doc, you have to do your Mozart thingie and figure these codes out. That should help us find him. Supermodel, send those videos to me so I can email them to our human trafficking unit. They need to know about this."

"Why would people sell other people?" Francine asked softly. "Look at him. He's so young. Even if he finds a way to escape or if we find him, this will affect him for the rest of his life, possibly completely screwing him up."

"In Europe alone there are an estimated twenty-three thousand victims of human trafficking and it's getting worse." I'd been doing some more reading on this topic. It was a most disquieting subject. "Officials say that the real figure is higher, up in the hundreds of thousands of victims. Sixty-two percent of the victims are trafficked for sexual exploitation, ninety-six percent of whom are female. Twenty-five percent are forced into labour in different industries."

"It's disgusting," Francine said.

"It's worse than that. In India you can buy a baby for forty-five dollars, but a buffalo will cost you three hundred and fifty dollars."

"Are you fucking kidding me?" Vinnie forcefully cleared his throat.

"No." I had found myself reaching for Mozart when I'd read those statistics. "In Mozambique, you can buy a girl for two dollars, in Malaysia you can buy a wife for around six thousand dollars. A Roma child bride can be sold for as much as two hundred and seventy thousand dollars."

"Please stop." Francine had tears in her eyes. "I can't listen to any more of this."

"You're going to have to suck it up, supermodel." Manny's tone was gentle. "This kid needs our help. It doesn't matter if he's still alive or not. We have to figure out how he was lured into this auction."

"Drugs?" Vinnie asked.

"Possibly," Manny said. "There was a survey done nine months ago across the EU states to determine the effect of drug use on students and its direct relationship to their social lives and employment prospects. I might go dig out those stats."

We continued watching the auction. It didn't take long for the bidding to be closed.

"This sickens me." Vinnie got up. "I need to go punch something."

I watched him leave, worried about him. "Is he going to be okay?"

"He'll most likely go work out with GIPN again," Colin said. "Climbing walls, shooting stuff up and running around empty warehouses, pretending to save people seems to agree with Vin."

"He's betraying us." Francine's smile contradicted her words. "I seriously can't believe how much time he's spending with Daniel."

At first I had also been surprised that Vinnie had accepted the invitation from the emergency response unit's leader. Daniel had challenged Vinnie to train with the team. After the first training session, Vinnie had come home tired and dirty, but exhilarated. The other team members had immediately ignored Vinnie's criminal history and had accepted him into their unique dynamic. I found it fascinating that so much of their continuous training was violent in nature, yet they were rehearsing for a peaceful, non-lethal outcome. I hoped it would help him calm down.

"Let the criminal go to his cop buddies. Maybe they'll have a good influence on him." Manny got up. "Doc, you need to figure out how we're going to reply to Dukwicz. We need to set a very smart trap for him. Frey, help her with that. Supermodel, get everything you can from Dukwicz's computer and email me a report. In English. Normal English. With words that I understand."

Francine winked at him. "Can I use words with more than two syllables?"

"No." His micro-smile was so brief it would have been easy to miss. "I'm going to speak to my contacts at Interpol about Matthieu's kidnapping and these videos. Maybe they know something that they haven't shared publicly. Phone me if you find anything important."

Manny left, ignoring Francine calling after him that she would phone him when she found the designer shoes she'd been looking for. I shook my head. Sometimes it seemed as if Francine didn't have any internal censorship. Without another word, I went into my viewing room. Bits of information were floating around my mind, seeking connections. Were all the events of the last four days connected? How did Caelan fit into this?

"Are you seriously asking?" The surprise in Colin's voice made me look up. He was sitting next to me, his eyebrows raised and his lips slightly parted. I hadn't noticed him following me into my room. Nor had I intended to vocalise my questions.

"Yes. I find this too coincidental. Three days ago, Caelan comes to our office with information about forged masterpieces being sold on a secret internet. That conveniently leads us to Dukwicz."

"There's nothing convenient about this, Jenny. You were the one who came up with the idea of luring Dukwicz—"

"Caelan is highly intelligent. He could've come with the ruse of these artworks, hoping that we'd see the services…" I stopped in horror and bit down on the insides of my lips. I was speculating. I hated when Manny or Francine speculated. "I need to think before I say anything else. I need to organise my thoughts. I'm not going to be like Francine and verbalise without censoring about some ridiculous conspiracy theory."

"Hey! I heard that!" When the glass door wasn't closed, Francine and anyone else in the team room could hear what was being said in my room. I heard footsteps and then she stood in the door, her hands on her hips. "I'll have you know that I don't verbalise without censoring about some ridiculous conspiracy theory. My theories are never ridiculous."

"Identity chips in pets are being used by the government to spy on and track citizens?" I failed to keep the scorn from my face and voice. "You don't think that is ridiculous?"

"Not if it's true." Her blinking rate increased. It happened every time she wasn't able to justify an outrageous statement.

I rolled my eyes and was immediately annoyed at myself. Not until Francine's and later Nikki's appearance in my life had I resorted to such juvenile gestures. I turned my attention to Colin. "Do you think there is a connection between Maurice Dupin, the Courbet paintings and Caelan?"

Colin thought about this. "I don't know. Caelan is a difficult person to get a read from. Do you find it easy to read him?"

"No. I would have to spend much more time with him to identify his different cues. I'm working on generalisations when I say that autistic people don't lie. Most people with ASD don't see the need to tell an untruth, which makes us terrible liars and unsuccessful manipulators. That does not mean someone on the spectrum does not lie or does not manipulate. Caelan is intelligent enough to do both."

"But you don't think he's lying or manipulating."

"I didn't say that."

"You're thinking it."

"You don't know what I'm thinking." I crossed my arms. "What a preposterous presumption to make."

"Okay, so you don't think Caelan is behind this and you don't think Dukwicz is behind this."

Francine interrupted Colin with a snort. "Oh, I know Dukwicz isn't behind this. His computer has such pedestrian security, it's actually laughable."

"How does his security give you absolute knowledge?" I asked.

"This might not be factual, girlfriend, but I'm thinking logically here. Someone who uses Tor and sells his services on SSS is someone who wants to stay under the radar. Um... undetected. That person would be paranoid about his internet footprint, his computer security. He would never store anything incriminating on a computer that can be hacked."

She lifted one hand and started counting with her manicured fingers. "Firstly, he saved those videos on his computer. Stupid mistake. Secondly, it was disgustingly easy to hack his computer. I had expected at least some firewalls or something. There was only the basic security a shop computer comes equipped with. Nothing more. Thirdly, Vinnie said earlier Dukwicz is not good at strategy. And fourthly, he's an ass."

I sighed. "Discounting your last point, your logic is sound. What else did you find on his computer?"

"Nothing yet. I… um…"

"Joined in our conversation because you couldn't help yourself?" Colin chuckled. "You better get back at it before Millard has a cow."

"Manny can't have a cow. What a strange thing to say. He doesn't own land big enough to keep one."

Colin laughed and kissed me on my cheek. "It's an expression, love."

"Oh." I didn't want to waste time trying to understand yet another expression that made no sense, so I opened a new window on my computer.

"What are we looking for?" Colin shifted his chair to face the monitors. "The letters and numbers?"

"No." I opened the Interpol site. Those letters and numbers had an obvious meaning. I could feel the connection hovering in the back of my head. From experience I knew that if I forced myself to find that link, it would not be forthcoming. I either had to spend an undefined amount of time allowing Mozart to soothe my mind, or I had to research an unrelated topic. "I'm going to look for more abduction cases."

"And you're still using Francine's anonymous shield. Why?"

I bit down hard and pressed my lips together.

"Jenny?" He cupped my cheek and gently turned my face until I looked at him. "What's up?"

"I'm concerned about this investigation into Edward Taylor." The words tumbled out before I could stop them. "In case someone in Interpol suspects you or might be able to make the connection between you and Edward Taylor, I would rather do all my research in such a way that nothing connects."

"You think the investigation into Edward Taylor has something to do with the kidnappings?"

"No. I don't know what to think. All these things happening in the last four days? I don't want to take the chance they are connected…"

"And put my life in danger," he finished softly. He leaned forward until our noses touched. "I love you too."

"You need to find Maurice Dupin. And you need to find Michael is well. Nikki still hasn't heard from him."

Colin leaned back. I loved him for many reasons. One of those was that he never expected an emotional declaration from me. But at this moment, I loved him even more for not exhibiting any cues of hurt when I immediately reverted back to work. "Shit, Jenny. Do you think he's really been kidnapped? That Nikki was right?"

"I don't know. That is why I want you to look for him. Go to his flat or do what you usually do."

He smiled. "What I usually do? You mean you want me to break into his place?"

I swallowed. I couldn't answer him. Never in my life had I imagined condoning breaking and entering.

Colin chuckled, got up and took his car keys from his pocket. "I'll go do what I usually do. Just be ready to go home at six. We're not staying here all night."

I didn't answer him, my mind already on the different keywords I was going to use to search for cases similar to Matthieu's. It disturbed me greatly that someone had the arrogance, the cruelty to take away the free will and freedom of this young man who had been trying to build a future for himself. Soon I lost myself in the search, taking care to follow Francine's instructions. I wanted my search to remain undetected.

Three hours later, I stretched my back muscles and reached for my coffee mug. It was empty. I swivelled my chair to get up and make my way to the kitchen, but stayed seated when Colin came in. The tightness in his shoulders, the tension around his mouth and the concern around his eyes caused my shoulders to drop. "You didn't find them, did you?"

"No. I can't get a hold of Maurice anywhere. And Michael is nowhere to be found. His neighbours didn't even know he lived in that flat." He sat down next to me. "My God, Jenny. His neighbours are mostly students, his age. They showed no interest in his wellbeing at all. It's a disgrace."

"Young people are notoriously self-centred. Nikki did tell us that she and Rebecca were his first and only friends. Do you think we should be worried about Michael?"

Colin intertwined his fingers and rested his hands on the top of his head. "I don't know. I think we should continue looking for him, but maybe not tell Nikki. Not yet."

"Why not? I'm not lying to her."

"I don't want you to lie to her. I just don't want to cause unnecessary worries." He tilted his head back towards the team room. "Where's Francine?"

"In her basement. She mumbled something about 'too much' and 'so much' and that she had to make sure about something. She didn't make sense."

"Yeah, she gets like that. Did you find something?"

"Sadly, yes." I had truly hoped that my suspicions would be unfounded and my search a waste of time. "I've only searched for missing young people in and around Strasbourg and have found three that fit a specific profile. Two young men and one young woman."

"Tell me first about the specific profile. How did you get it?"

"I looked at the background information on Matthieu, as little as it was. Then I searched for young people aged between eighteen and twenty-three, with no active social life, excelling at university, but not noticed by anyone. Matthieu had a Facebook profile, but it has no information publicly available. His university has a strong social networking site and the students are very active on it. Not him. He has minimal information on it and only two photos of a puppy." I was getting sidetracked by the details. "I used his profile as a baseline and eliminated the missing persons who have active social lives and have family and friends looking for them."

"Until a few months ago, Michael also fit that profile."

"But now he has Nikki and Rebecca as friends. And we are looking for him. Nobody is looking for these three kids." I pointed at the monitor. "The investigator's comments were that they most likely discontinued their studies and moved away."

"It's easy to assume that someone would drop out of university to travel or find a job and live it up."

"I'm going to start another search, but with broader geographical perimeters. There might be many more young people who fit this profile."

"No." Colin sat up and grabbed my hands to prevent me from reaching my keyboard. "We're going home. It's already twenty past six and Vinnie has made dinner."

"Did he punch something? Is he in a better mood?"

"He sounded cheery when I spoke to him. Nikki is helping him in the kitchen and you know how that makes him."

"Gentle."

"Come on." Colin got up and pulled my hands. "We can get back to this tomorrow morning."

I didn't like leaving in the middle of a search. Experience had taught me, though, that I could never work hard enough or fast enough. I switched off my computers, hoping that an evening at home would aid in making the connections still hovering in the back of my mind.

Chapter ELEVEN

"I don't want to be here. We should be at the office."

"It's twenty minutes to eight in the morning, Jenny. I should still be sleeping." Colin yawned and stretched his neck to one side. "But here I am with you at our favourite café. Oh, the sacrifices I make."

"If being here is a sacrifice, why did you force me to come?" I studied his expression to correctly interpret his last statement. Whenever Colin was tired or sleepy, he reverted to forms of speech that could be euphemistic. Or not.

Colin chuckled. "I was being ironic, love. Sitting here in the early-morning sun, in my favourite place, about to eat my favourite breakfast with my favourite girl is really no hardship."

When I had come out of the shower this morning, Colin had declared that we had to come to the historic district of Strasbourg for breakfast. He had reasoned that he deserved a Saturday morning breakfast even though it was not going to be leisurely or at a later hour. If he had to spend the whole weekend working, at least he deserved some compensation.

I'd relented only when he'd agreed to have me in the viewing room no later than nine o'clock. He'd jumped out of bed, showered and was dressed in record time. Then he wasted ten minutes looking for his watch. He really liked the one I'd given him for Christmas. When I'd pointed out, a third time, that he had another six watches, he'd grinned at me and took the one he'd told me he'd bought in Venice.

I loved Strasbourg's old town. Nestled on the island formed

by two arms of the River Ill, its picturesque ambience never failed to enchant me. It was an interesting blend of the city's historic past, the German influence on the architecture as visible as the French. The Gothic cathedral was the central point for me and my favourite building. A close second were the crooked half-timbered houses. Their imperfection added a happy charm to the scenery.

All the streets and little alleyways had restaurants, cafés, pubs and shops that kept the area bustling late into the evenings. But early mornings were my preferred time in the old town. People were only just getting up, leaving the streets uncrowded and giving me the opportunity to relax and absorb the ambience.

Our waitress brought our coffee, but only looked and spoke to Colin. The body language of all the staff here clearly communicated their discomfort with me. The first time we'd come here was with Vinnie. I had refused to order anything from a kitchen I could not see. Vinnie and Colin had ordered brunch, laughing when I cited the bacteria found in the average restaurant kitchen. The following week, Colin had arranged for me to see the kitchen. I'd approved and we frequented it at the weekends. In the summer months like now, we'd stop by more than once a week.

I also enjoyed sitting quietly with Colin, watching people, analysing their body language. It never failed to amuse and amaze me how much I learned about people's relationships by watching their interactions. Our breakfasts arrived and again the waitress avoided speaking to and looking at me.

"Please tell me you're not thinking about work." Colin took a bite of his omelette as soon as the waitress turned away. "We'll be there soon. Right now you should focus on—"

"I wasn't thinking about work."

"Oh. Good." He slid his chair a bit closer. "What were you thinking about?"

I took another bite of my croissant and looked at the people walking past us. It was still too early for most tourists, but the day had started rather hot and already tourists were walking through the streets in flip-flops, shorts and tank tops. "I was thinking about people's fear of that which they don't know."

"Hm-mm."

A young couple walked past us, hand in hand. The man's physique evidenced hours spent in the gym on a daily basis. The young woman was toned, tanned and groomed. Her summer pants fitted perfectly and the tight t-shirt allowed glimpses of her midriff. Her long brown hair shone in the sun, completing the picture of a healthy young woman. This was a picture-perfect couple. The only imperfections on the man were the two tattoos on the man's left bicep, if one were to regard those as imperfections.

As they walked away from us, I noticed another imperfection. The woman pushed her hand through her hair, pulling her t-shirt up and revealing a long scar on her right side, running diagonally from her back around her side down to her hip. The surgery she'd had could not have been recent. The scar was no longer pink or raised. I tilted my head to the side and stared at her scar while everything and everyone else around me receded into the background.

The connection that had been just beyond reach for the last fourteen hours burst through my consciousness. I gasped, the horror of this insight pulling me away from reality. Dark edges entered my peripheral vision, creeping closer to put me into a total shutdown.

"Jenny?" Colin was sitting closer to me, rubbing my arm, his tone gentle, calm. "Love? God, you're pale. What's wrong?"

I took a shuddering breath and grabbed his hand. "I need to get to my viewing room. Now."

"Okay." He called our waitress over and pulled out his wallet. The darkness was creeping closer and I fought it the only way I knew how. I closed my eyes and mentally pulled up a clean music sheet. In order not to completely shut down, I concentrated on Colin's voice while I slowly drew the G-clef. I took pleasure in creating the curls before I started with the F-clef. As I mentally drew the first flat, Colin took both my shoulders in his hands.

"Jenny?"

I carefully wrote the other flat and the first bar of Mozart's Piano Concerto No.27 in B flat major before I felt ready to open my eyes.

"Ready to go?"

I nodded and got up stiffly. Part of why I loved this part of the city was the lack of traffic. The streets were mostly empty, which meant it would be a five-minute walk before we reached Colin's car. He took my hand in a firm grip and allowed me to set the pace. It was hard to focus on walking when all I wanted was to crawl into the safety of Mozart.

"Can you talk about it?"

I shook my head.

"Can you talk at all?"

The slight humour in his voice brought some lightness in my chest. Colin's calm acceptance of the shutdowns and meltdowns I experienced helped me get through them much faster. The lack of stress or fear of malice and rejection was liberating. I focussed on an advertising board at the end of the street and took a deep breath. I held it for a few seconds before I slowly exhaled. "I don't want to talk now."

"Got it." We reached the SUV and were on the road within seconds. Colin fiddled with the sound system controls on the steering wheel. A second later a Mozart concerto filled the cabin. "This okay?"

I nodded, closed my eyes and relaxed into the soothing sounds of the fresh-sounding composition for flute and harp. Slowly the tightness in my throat and chest that accompanied such moments of panic subsided. I opened my eyes at the sound of a phone ringing. Colin had his smartphone on speaker and the call was answered almost immediately. It was Manny. "What's wrong, Frey?"

"Can't I just phone you for an early-morning chat?"

Annoyed breathing came through the phone. "Frey."

Colin chuckled. "Jenny's got some insight into something. We're going in to the office now."

"What insight?"

"Don't know yet. She's working through it."

"Ah." Manny dragged out the sound. After working with me for two years, he'd interpreted this euphemism Colin had used. "I'm on my way in now. I'll meet you in the office."

Without any kind of farewell, the call ended. Their conversation had taken my mind off the horror of my conclusion and my control slid back into place. A few minutes later, we reached Rousseau & Rousseau. Since this was a Saturday, Colin easily found parking and soon we walked into the team room.

"Whatcha got, Doc?" Manny got up from his desk.

I shook my head and walked into my viewing room. I made sure to close the glass door behind me, but it opened again as I sat down. Fortunately, neither man asked any questions. I turned on my computer and waited impatiently for the machine to take the forty seconds it needed to boot up.

Behind me, Colin was telling Manny about the three kidnapped students I'd found yesterday. Manny started asking

Colin questions, but my computer was ready. I entered the keywords into my preferred search engine and got sixty-six million results in a thirty-third of a second. I clicked on the link to a more reputable site and groaned loudly.

"I was right. I don't want to be right."

"Right about what, Jenny?" Colin sat down next to me.

"The auction was for Matthieu's organs."

"Bloody hell, Doc." Manny pulled the third chair in my room to my other side and sat down. "Explain."

I stared at the monitor, not able to take my eyes off the screen. A deep breath later, I opened the auction video with the letters and numbers on the monitor next to the one with the search results. "Look at the medical terms for organs. The root word for liver is hepato-, for heart is cardio-, for kidney is nephro-, for lungs is pneumo- or pulmo-. Now look at the items being auctioned. First on the list was Ca, second Pn. I think we can safely infer that Ne1 and Ne2 were the two kidneys."

"Holy shit."

"Give me a minute." I took my notepad and one of the three pens next to it and wrote down the numbers that were written under Matthieu's profile. It didn't take me long to decrypt the inferior attempt at a code. "Those numbers are his height, weight, age, blood group, and HIV status."

"Then I assume the numbers next to the letters must be some kind of test result for each organ?" Colin asked.

I used the same decoding method for those numbers. It only took two minutes. Another quick search on the internet and I had confirmation. "Full results for a liver function test require readings on the total protein in the blood, platelet count, albumin levels, bilirubin, alanine transaminase—"

"We can see that, Doc." Manny looked pointedly at the medical page I was reading from. "There are nine tests described in disgusting detail, and next to Matthieu's liver code are nine different numbers. Those must be the test results."

"So these savages can see if the liver is healthy enough to buy." Colin's top lip curled, his breathing harsh from anger.

"I can't believe people would do that to each other." Francine's whisper drew our attention to the door. She was staring at the monitors, her hand pressed over her suprasternal notch.

"Believe it, supermodel. Every year people from developed countries illegally buy the organs of people from undeveloped countries. The industry is worth over a billion dollars. In the US and other countries, the demand for lungs, kidneys and livers far outweighs the supply. Here in Europe, the asking price for a lung is over three hundred thousand dollars."

"I've read that the average price paid by a kidney buyer is a hundred and fifty thousand dollars. The person whose kidney is removed receives on average five thousand dollars." I remember the horror that had filled me when I'd read that article.

"This case is making me doubt the future of humanity." Francine's voice trembled. "We should allow the computers to take over. Or the aliens."

"Really? You're going with your stupid conspiracy theories? Don't you have something useful for us or are you just going to stand there and look pretty, supermodel?" Manny was baiting Francine, but I'd seen the concern on his face.

It worked. Francine flipped her long hair over her shoulder and straightened. She slowly wiped her palms down the sides of her fitted cream dress. "You think I'm pretty? Pah! What a stupid question. Of course you think I'm gorgeous."

"Only in your dreams, supermodel."

"Manny." She walked to him and tapped on his shoulder with a manicured purple nail. "You protest too much. If you didn't find me so irresistible, you wouldn't have worn the clothes we bought yesterday."

"Wearing new clothes has nothing to do with..." Manny slapped her hand away, his cheeks turning red. "Get away from me. Go stand over there and tell us if you found something useful."

She laughed and gave him an exaggerated wink. "I knew this shirt would look good on you."

Manny was wearing dark brown pants and a tailored striped shirt. Despite his stubble and disapproving frown, he looked elegant. He lowered his brow and glared at Francine. "Do you have something for us, supermodel?"

"Sadly, I do." The laughter left her face and she reached for my keyboard. "May I?"

"No. You are all crowding me. We can do this in the team room."

She froze, then pulled her hands back slowly. "No probs, girlfriend. Let's go."

A minute later we were seated at the round table and Francine was tapping on her tablet. "I went through Dukwicz's computer and couldn't find any other auction videos. There was nothing else of interest on his computer itself, but his history makes for fabulous fodder. My God, the man watches a lot of porn."

"Supermodel..."

"He does! But that's not really important. Just interesting." She finished tapping and looked up at the screen against the wall. "I followed his digital footprint to see what he'd been looking at on the internet. I found the site where the auction took place."

"Why the bleeding hell didn't you start with that?" Manny leaned forward, his eyes on the screen. "Can we trace this? Can we find these bastards?"

"No." She splayed her fingers, tightened them into a fist and splayed them again. It felt like my whole body was in a tight knot. Francine likely experienced the same. "I tried, but this is the success of Tor. Routing it through so many different layers makes it extremely improbable to find the original IP address. But it's not impossible. I'm not giving up. I'm going to find a way to get a virus in there to give me access."

"I know you will." The sincerity in his acknowledgement relieved some of the tightness around Francine's eyes and mouth. Manny nodded to her tablet. "What are we looking at?"

On the screen was a large digital clock, counting down from forty-seven hours and fifteen minutes.

"This is the auction site. All evidence from Matthieu's abduction has been removed. This is all there is. Since I have full access to Dukwicz's email now, I checked it for anything to tell me what the countdown is for." She tapped again and another window opened on the screen. "This email came to him with details of another auction in two days."

It was disappointing to read the email. There was no added information to give any indication of the person who had sent it. It was simply an announcement of a date and time. And a row of numbers at the bottom. I rushed to my viewing room, grabbed my notepad and pen and came back. Nobody spoke while I noted down the numbers and decoded it with the simplistic encryption used for the organs.

As soon as I'd written all the words on my notepad, the familiar tightness closed in around my chest again. I threw my notepad on the table, closed my eyes and focussed on Mozart's

Minuet in C major. Despite my knowledge of criminal psychology, I didn't want to believe that humans could be this barbaric.

"What does it say, Frey?"

Paper rustled. Colin had picked up my notepad. He grunted. "Four specimens in complete health. Details go up an hour before start."

"Dear God," Francine said. "What now?"

After a deep breath and another two bars of the Minuet, I opened my eyes. "What about the second auction? We've determined that the first auction was for Matthieu's organs. In this email, they are referring to health, which leads me to assume this will also be for organs. What part of Matthieu did they sell in the second auction? Was it sex? What?"

It was quiet in the team room.

"Did Dukwicz get an email about a second auction?" I asked.

"No. Wait. He got one that was weird." Again she tapped on her tablet until another email filled the screen. "This one says, 'You're up on the eighth. Four for four.'"

"What the hell does that mean?" Manny looked at me.

I thought about this for a minute. "I don't know."

"Supermodel? Any speculation?" Manny had to be desperate to ask Francine for one of her outrageous theories. She only shook her head. "Can you at least find Dukwicz? You have access to his computer now. Surely you can locate him."

"As soon as the virus got into this computer, I—"

"Plain English," Manny said.

"I copied his computer. Everything that was on his computer, I now have. I did this in case he went offline and I couldn't switch it on remotely. And that's exactly what's happened. Either he disconnected from the internet, he's out of wireless range, the computer's battery went flat or he took the battery out. For the last eight hours I haven't had any access to his computer. I did track his previous wireless connections and he's currently in Strasbourg."

"He's here?" Fear raised the pitch of my voice.

"I already told Vinnie." Francine blinked rapidly, her face a shade paler. She was also scared. "He told Daniel and they're working on a plan of action."

"What kind of plan of action?" Manny asked.

"For protection, he said. He should be back soon and can tell you himself."

I resented the fear that paralysed my muscles. Dukwicz had been a part of my life for the last year. Every interaction I'd had with him had been violent and traumatic. To know that he was in such close proximity took away the sense of safety I'd been experiencing for the last few months. Had I been deluding myself? Had I allowed time to create sufficient distance to convince myself the threat was not so great?

I got up, my movements stilted. "I need to work. Leave me alone."

Hoping they would respect my acute need to lose myself in a few hours of research, I walked to my viewing room, closed the door and sat down in the silent, soundproof room. I didn't know how long I just sat there, but eventually I turned to my computer, chose the Mozart playlist I'd created especially to enhance my concentration and opened the search engine.

Chapter TWELVE

"Doctor Lenard! Doctor Lenard!" Caelan's shrill shouts jerked me out of my latest discovery. I turned with a frown to the glass door that was supposed to be sealed. I'd been in front of my computer for the last five hours and had only taken a short break for lunch. When I'd returned to my room, I'd made a point of closing the glass door to ensure soundproof silence. Now the door was slightly ajar, allowing Caelan's voice to reach me. "There were two volcanic eruptions in the continental USA during the twentieth century! Doctor Lenard!"

A soft snort behind me caught my attention. I wasn't surprised to find Nikki on the floor between two filing cabinets. I'd been completely absorbed in looking for more possible kidnapping victims and going through every second of the auction videos. The videos hadn't brought much more information. I had studied Matthieu's body language, the numbers and the bids in detail, hoping for some clues. Nothing new had come up, so I'd returned to looking for missing students who fitted the profile.

I wondered how long Nikki had been sitting there, drawing. "Why are you here?"

"Vinnie wouldn't let me go into the city, go to the library, stay at home or go to the movies." She hugged her sketchpad to her chest. "He didn't even tell me why. When I refused, the crazy man threw me over his shoulder and forcibly brought me here."

"He couldn't have thrown you over his shoulder. That would mean you'd have cleared his shoulder and landed on the floor behind him."

She burst out laughing, the tension in her body easing. "You know, you're right. I never thought about it like that. Hmm. That makes it a really silly saying."

"Doctor Lenard! Zana twenty-two Dactor thirty-one seventy-eight!"

"You can't just go in there, Caelan." Tim tried to infuse calm into his voice, but all I heard was exasperation. Phillip's assistant had proven himself in the last year to be a reliable asset to the company. However, it sounded like this current situation was challenging his skills.

"Doctor Lenard! Zana twenty-two Dactor thirty-one seventy-eight! Your people are incompetent! The most powerful tornadoes occur in the US!"

"Is that Caelan? What's he talking about?" Nikki leaned forward to look around the cabinet. "And why is he here?"

"Yes, it's Caelan." I sighed. "I don't know what he's talking about. I hope Francine will stop him."

Whenever a connection was looming in my mind, I felt restless, discomfited. A feeling that was now overwhelming me. Something had registered in the last five minutes that I needed to consciously process and analyse. I turned back to face the monitors, but Caelan continued to intrude. When he wasn't calling for me or stating facts, he was repeating the odd-sounding phrase.

Francine's murmurs blended with Tim's in an unsuccessful attempt to reason with the young man. He was relentless in his demands and repetitions. Then, as if someone had switched on a light, I felt it. The connection clicked in my mind. I jumped up and walked into the team room. Caelan was standing in the corner, on the far side of the round table, bouncing his back off the wall. Tim was standing in the doorway, his body language and expression communicating his confusion and discomfort. Francine was sitting at her desk, eyes wide.

"I couldn't stop him, Doctor Lenard." Tim swallowed. "I don't know what to do with him."

"It's okay, Tim," Francine said. "Genevieve will handle him."

"Oh, thank God. I'm so out of here." He didn't wait another second and fled down the hallway, favouring his right.

"Glaciers store twenty-five percent of the Earth's fresh water! Zana twenty-two Dactor thirty-one seventy-eight! Incompetent people!" Caelan was becoming more agitated, bouncing harder against the wall. I sat down at the table, far enough from Caelan not to crowd him. I spent a few moments considering my approach and sighed.

"Caelan, take a deep breath. Focus on your breathing." I kept my tone firm, but gentle. "Take a deep breath and slowly exhale."

"Zana twenty-two Dactor thirty-one seventy-eight! Doctor Lenard! Another painting. The average snowflake is made up of a hundred and eighty billion molecules of water!"

My approach wasn't working. I hated the feeling of helplessness that filled my mind.

"What the hell is going on here?" Manny walked in, but kept his tone and movements unconfrontational.

"Caelan is upset about something," Francine said unnecessarily.

"Do something, Doc." Manny had to raise his voice to be heard above Caelan's screaming. "My eardrums are going to burst."

"Eardrums! Zana twenty-two Dactor thirty-one seventy-eight! Eardrums!"

"Caelan." I spoke a bit louder, my tone no longer gentle. "I'm not going to listen to you if you keep screaming. I have a question for you, but will not ask until you are calm."

For two minutes he continued to recite random geographical facts and odd phrases, gradually lowering his voice until it was a monotone mutter. He was still bouncing off the wall, but with much less vigour, clearly making an effort to gain control. "Doctor Lenard. Doctor Lenard."

"Yes, Caelan?"

"Zana twenty-two Dactor thirty-one seventy-eight."

"Yes, I know. Where did you see that?"

"What the hell are they talking about?" Manny asked softly behind me.

"I don't know," Francine whispered back.

"Caelan and I can both hear you." Neurotypical people could be so ridiculous in their behaviour sometimes. "Caelan, do you want to tell them or should I?"

"Doctor Lenard. Doctor Lenard."

"I'll tell them what I know, but then you must calm down sufficiently to tell me where you saw that. Agreed?"

"Yes. Yes. Yes. Yes. Yes." He bounced softly against the wall with each chanted word.

I turned around to face Manny and Francine. He was leaning against her desk, his arms folded. Francine mirrored his body language, arms also folded and her head tilted at the same angle. Nikki had made herself comfortable on the floor next to Francine's desk. Her sketchpad was open and she was drawing, her tongue protruding from between her lips. Something had inspired her.

"Francine, can you bring up the auction video?" I asked. "I want to show you the bids."

She gave a quick nod, her fingers already tapping and swiping on her tablet's touch screen. A few seconds later the video filled the screen. I cleared my throat. It was hard to look at the right-hand side of the screen, knowing each of those coded headings represented one of Matthieu's organs. I pointed to the very bottom right corner of the screen.

"Can you zoom in on that?"

She did and the tiny lettering revealed itself.

"Z22D3178. Not quite the full thingie the kid is shouting at us, but close enough. What does this mean, Doc?"

"I don't know." I looked at Francine. "Do you know?"

Her smile lifted her cheeks. "I can speculate."

"No, thanks, supermodel. Rather tell me why that would be at the bottom of a website."

"It's an ID?" She zoomed out. "I can't see it anywhere else on this page."

For a few seconds we watched in silence as the bids rose for each organ. I'd gone through this before, but it still deeply disturbed me. Using the simplistic code used everywhere else, I tried it on our new discovery. "It is not coded. Unlike the organs and descriptions, Zana22Dactor3178 doesn't translate into anything that makes sense."

"Can you decode the bids and tell us how much they paid for the organs?" Manny asked.

I'd already done that when I'd gone over the footage. "The one bidder paid two hundred and fifty thousand dollars for a kidney."

"Holy bloody hell!"

"Doctor Lenard. Doctor Lenard." Caelan started bouncing again at Manny's outburst.

"Sorry, lad." Manny pressed his fists against his eyes. "Now I have to watch what I say."

"Two hundred and fifty thousand dollars?" Francine's eyes were wide, her mouth slack. "That... that's just wrong."

"Kidneys? What kidneys?" Caelan asked. He took a few deep breaths and walked around the table, appearing more in control of his movements. He noticed Nikki, stopped and pointed at her. "Who's she?"

Nikki got up, her eyes narrowing on Caelan. She took in his attire and I noticed the compassion on her face. "I'm Nikki."

"My name is Caelan. I'm helping Doctor Lenard and her team." Caelan talked to Nikki's shoulder, pushing out his chest.

She glanced at her shoulder, a slight frown forming between her eyebrows when she looked back and Caelan was still staring at her shoulder. "Hi, Caelan."

"You must be my girlfriend. I need a girlfriend. Francine said she'll help me find one, but you're pretty enough. You are my girlfriend."

Vinnie's muscle tension increased and Manny's top lip curled, but Nikki burst out laughing. She looked at me, her eyes shiny. "He's cute. Can we keep him?"

"No." My answer might have been too sharp, judging by the way Nikki flinched. I swallowed the horrifying thought of Caelan moving into my apartment and tried to smile. It didn't work. "You cannot keep people. They're not an object or a pet that you have ownership over."

"Like selling people at an auction?" Nikki nodded at the screen.

"First kidneys, now people." Caelan sighed loudly. "Aren't you listening to me? I'm talking about art. Not kidneys. Not people. Art."

"Is that where you saw this handle?" I asked. "Did you see Zana22Dactor3178 sell a painting online?"

"Yes. I don't think this was a forgery. Colin needs to look at it. Where is he? Colin would know best. He needs to be here."

"He's looking for—"

"—a friend who can help us find these artworks." Francine jumped out of her chair, staring intently at me. She was trying to communicate her reason for interrupting me by tilting her head and moving one eyebrow. It took me only a moment to analyse the direction her head was pointed to. Nikki. Francine didn't want me to say that Colin had renewed his search for Michael. We still didn't have confirmation that he was missing, but Colin and Francine had insisted their guts were telling them something was wrong. I didn't feel comfortable lying to Nikki even if it was to protect her from worrying.

Nikki stepped closer to my side. The micro-expressions flashing across her face revealed she was reaching conclusions and finding them most disturbing. "I know you don't want me to know what you guys are dealing with every day, but I saw what you were researching. Who is this?" She pointed at the screen.

"Matthieu Jean."

"The student I told you about? The guy from Paris?" She took another step closer to me, our arms touching. I hated the distress I was seeing on her face. Whenever she was unhappy, she needed more physical contact than usual. I didn't move, not even when she leaned against me. "It's him, isn't it?"

"Yes." It was hard discerning how much to tell her.

"They were auctioning his organs?" Her voice rose, her face losing colour. "Oh, God. That's horrible. And you found all those other students. How many? Who would do this? Why would anyone do this?"

"Nikki." The soft tone communicated Manny's compassion and a warning.

She straightened her shoulders, but didn't move away from me. "I know you only allow me to hang around because I never say anything or ask anything, but this is horrible. What if this happens to me? Oh, my God! Is this why Vinnie forcibly brought me here? Am I in danger?"

"What do you mean forcibly?" Manny stood up. "What the hell did that criminal do?"

"Hell. Hell. Hell. Hell." Caelan retreated to the door, bouncing gently against the doorframe and muttering.

Manny pressed the heels of his palms against his eyes again and groaned. "Doc, deal with this before I…"

I waited for him to finish his sentence, but he didn't. He dropped his hands, resumed leaning against Francine's desk and glared at Nikki. I sighed. "Vinnie wanted Nikki to come here, because Dukwicz is in the city. She argued with him and he—"

"Threw me over his shoulder and carried me to the car." She grinned when she used the illogical expression. "He didn't hurt me. You know he wouldn't hurt me."

"He bloody better not."

"Bloody. Bloody. Bloody." Caelan was only whispering, but appeared to be affected by everything Manny was saying.

"Doc." Manny threw one hand out towards Caelan. "Please."

I didn't know what he expected me to do and wished for Phillip's calming presence. "Caelan, would you mind sitting at the table? We could use your help."

"You need my help. You are not finding the art."

"What art?" Colin asked from behind Caelan. He was standing in the doorway, his expression grim. He still hadn't located Maurice Dupin or Michael.

Caelan turned, the tension in his body slightly relaxing. "You're here. You must find the art."

"At the table." I pointed to the chair closest to Caelan, my tone uncompromising. "Now. Sit down and tell us what you know."

Caelan sat down meekly. The cough coming from Manny sounded more like a laugh, but it was the shock on Colin's face that had me wondering if I was handling this incorrectly. He walked in, kissed me on my cheek and leaned in close to my ear. "Impressive."

I found this situation hard to deal with, tempted to give in to the urge to rush back to my room and seal the door. "Caelan, would you be willing to work with Francine?"

"She must teach me how to get a girlfriend."

"After you help us, kiddo." Francine tapped her nails on her desk. "If you control yourself and don't share anymore geographical facts, you and I might make a formidable team. We can see if we can find Zana22Dactor3178. Maybe put a virus in his computer so we can snoop around."

"I don't need to know any of this." Manny got up and walked to my viewing room. "Supermodel and the kid can work in here. Doc, we need to talk."

Without waiting for agreement from anyone, Manny walked into my room. Francine looked at Caelan, her expression cautious, but not unwelcoming.

"Will you be okay here?" Colin asked.

"Me?" Francine placed her hand over her sternum. "Of course I'll be okay. I have a smart kid who's going to help me sneak around the internet."

Caelan stared at her shoulder. "What about Colin? What about the art?"

"I'll look at that soon. First, I have to talk to Je… Doctor Lenard while you're helping Francine, okay?"

"But you will look at the art?"

"Yes, I will."

"When?"

"Later, kiddo." Francine waved him over. "Bring that chair and come sit next to me. When Colin is ready to look at the art, he will. Let's try and give them Zana22Dactor3178 before that happens."

"When?" The stubborn lift of his jaw indicated no willingness to relent.

"It will be no longer than an hour." It was more than enough time to give Manny and Colin a report on my findings.

Caelan responded by picking up his chair and sitting next to Francine. I looked at them for a few seconds before going to my team room. Colin followed me and soon we were seated in front of the ten monitors. Nikki sat down on the floor between the filing cabinets, her eyes wide and her sketchpad forgotten.

It was most unconventional for her to have any knowledge of our investigations, but it had become the norm. Nikki's criminal father had had her sitting in on his meetings from a very young age. She'd learned about discretion and the dangers of accidentally mentioning something from a man who had evaded capture for decades.

Ideally, she should have had a childhood free of that responsibility, but she hadn't. As a new adult, she was mature beyond her years and had proven herself to be trustworthy and wise. Since the victims we were looking at were all her age, she might be able to give us valuable input. That was the only reason I didn't mind her taking her usual place in my viewing room.

"What have you got for us, Doc?"

"I looked for more students. The profile was the same as before: young people aged eighteen to twenty-three, not living at home, without any family or not close to their family at all, socially inactive or maladjusted. I went as far back as six months."

"Why six months?" Manny asked.

"That is how long SSS has been in operation. I'm working on an assumption that whomever is behind the auctions has only been doing it on SSS. I first looked in France and found ten students. The first three were all young men." I pointed at the top left monitor. "Christopher Leesa was reported missing by his university six months ago when he missed a payment. He is a first-year British student with dual citizenship, studying computer engineering in Lille. His only relative was his grandmother who died a year ago."

I pointed to the next monitor. "Jean Haden was reported missing by his landlord in Marseille when he didn't pay his rent nine months ago and couldn't be contacted. He's an orphan, his studies paid by a government grant. Stacey Bouzane from Paris was reported missing by her next-door neighbour. Stacey had the neighbour's computer in her flat and was supposed to fix it for her. When she didn't return it, the neighbour was at first angry, but later concerned.

"None of the cases have an exact date of disappearance. The universities, landlords and neighbours who reported them missing had no knowledge of their daily lives or activities. There also weren't friends who could say when they'd last seen them. Sandino Eandi, Robin Ames, Joni Édouard and Bradford Charon. These are more missing students I found. Seven young men and three women in France."

"Some of them don't have French names," Manny said.

"That is another trend I saw. As far as I could determine, all these young people were international students, displaced. Being far away from home made them easier targets."

"We have a lot of international students at university." Nikki's shoulders lifted towards her ears when we turned around to look at her. She blinked a few times, then lowered her shoulders and lifted her chin. "The local students don't really like them, unless they have a lot of money. Generally, they fit into two categories: those who go wild, and those who do nothing but study."

"I'm interested in the ones who do nothing but study." These were the type of students now on my monitors. "Do they integrate? Socialise with the other students?"

"No. They keep to themselves." Her face paled a shade. "Like Michael."

It was clear Nikki needed reassurance. I couldn't give it to her without lying, so I stayed on topic. "I found four students in Belgium. Elise Brenner, Lara Miller, K.A. Raya and Sheryl Bergel. In Germany I found five students. Teresa Christensen, Deborah Norling, Arthur Aguire, Trish Cox and Travis West."

"Again the non-German-sounding names," Manny said.

"Not everyone in Germany is called Hans or Gretel. Could you be any more ignorant?" Colin shook his head in disapproval. "The borders in Europe has been open for decades now. You might not be able to wrap your head around it, but people from different cultures do get married."

"I'm a Brit living in France, Frey. Of course I know what a melting pot the major European cities have become. I just find it interesting that none of these names are typically French or typically German."

"Again." Colin lifted both shoulders. "What is typically French? Dubois?"

"This is an inane argument." And I could see they were prepared to continue indefinitely. "The three students I found in Spain are all foreign students. Lori Rheiner is a second-year biochemistry student originally from Leeds. Megan McLay is from Scotland, in her last year studying art, and Cynthia Beaumont is originally from France, but got a scholarship to study business economics in Madrid."

"Are you telling me all of these students are from another country?" Manny leaned back in his chair. "Doc, are you sure about this search? What about young people who aren't students? What about homeless kids? Wouldn't they be good targets for organ dealers?"

"I chose these parameters because I needed something to work from. Twenty-two young people mysteriously disappearing in a six-month period is a lot. That is a student almost every week."

"Or it's very little," Colin said. "If each body can be sold in two auctions, totalling up to more than three-quarters of a million dollars, then I can't see the reason for someone to limit his income by only kidnapping and butchering a kid a week."

Nikki gasped and Colin's face immediately displayed contrition. He turned around and looked at Nikki for a few seconds. "This case is not good, Nix. I would feel so much better if you weren't here."

"I'm not leaving." She swallowed a few times, building up courage. "I think you're lying to me. I saw the looks you and Francine gave Doc G. There's something more to this and it involves me, doesn't it?"

"We don't know yet. There are a lot of things happening at the moment and we want to make sure everyone is safe."

"Doc G?" Nikki waited until I looked at her. "You will tell me if this affects me directly, right? You won't lie to me?"

I swivelled my chair completely so I was facing Nikki directly. "Colin, Manny, Francine and Vinnie don't want you to worry about things that might not be a problem."

"What do *you* want?"

I wanted her to never have seen violence, never have known criminals, never have been exposed to this brutal side of life. The idealism and irrationality of what I wanted irritated me. "I want you to be strong and wise."

"Argh. That doesn't tell me anything." She folded her arms. "You didn't answer my first question."

"I will not lie to you. The moment we have any confirmation, I'll talk to you and trust that you will be strong and wise."

Her chin started to quiver, but she stopped it by pressing her lips together. She glanced at Manny and Colin before looking back at me. "Okay. I can do that."

"Thank you."

"Good girl." Manny cleared his throat. "Doc, did you get all of this on the Interpol database?"

"And a few newspaper articles. Not all of these cases have been registered with Interpol." It simultaneously made me angry and sad. "It seems like the police didn't care enough about the missing young people to spend any time looking for them."

"Sometimes an adult, which they all are, wants to disappear." Manny waved a hand at the monitors. "Some of these kids might have decided that studying is too much work and they no longer wanted to do it. They'd rather live next to the sea somewhere, pour drinks in a bar and live carefree."

I knew he was right. It didn't alleviate my frustration with the system though. "We must find these people."

"We will, Doc."

"Okay. That's it!" A loud crash followed Francine's exclamation. Manny and Colin were first through the door to the team room. I was right behind them.

Both Manny and Colin stopped a few steps into the room and leaned back. Manny's nostrils flared a second before he slapped his hand over his mouth and nose. A potent smell of flatulence hung in the air.

"Look." Francine stood two metres away from Caelan, her chair overturned. "It's bad enough that you smell like the inside of a barf-bag, but did you have to do that?"

Caelan's face was expressionless, but he started rocking and shaking his head. "I don't smell like the inside of a barf-bag."

The anger on Francine's face was instantly replaced by contrition at Caelan's softly spoken words. She righted her chair and sat down. "Honey, you really smell bad. And passing wind is not going to win you any friends."

"I'm sorry," he whispered. "Does that mean you're not going to teach me how to get a girlfriend?"

Francine let out a surprised laugh. "No, sweetie. I'll still teach you. As a matter of fact, we can start with your first lesson right now."

Caelan inhaled sharply, his eyes moving from Francine's one shoulder to the other. "Now? Really?"

"Yes, really. Lesson number one. No girl is going to want to be near you when you smell like a bum sleeping under a garbage dumpster." Francine's tone and expression were kind, softening the words. Not that Caelan would register those subtleties. He'd only hear the stark truth. "Your clothes are dirty and look like you've worn them for the last three years. Your hair is in desperate need of a cut. You're not rocking that afro at all. Your nails are long and gross. Sweetie, you are gross. And I say this with a lot of love in my heart."

"So much for breaking it to him softly," Colin said quietly.

Caelan stared at the wall behind Francine, shaking his head.

He appeared to do this whenever he was considering something. "I don't have soap."

"That's an easy problem to solve," Francine said.

"I don't like smelly soap. All soap smells. I don't want soap that smells."

"There is the coolest organic shop about three blocks from here." Nikki walked past me, pressing her fingers against her lips, a gesture we employed when we realised we'd erred. "No, I think it's four blocks. Maybe five. Oh! It doesn't matter. This shop has soap that has no smell at all and it makes your skin really soft."

"Is it white?" Caelan asked. "I like white soap."

"The one I bought was kind of transparent. We'll have to ask them if they have white soap." Her eyes flashed open. "Ooh! I have a rad idea. Let's go shopping. I'll take you to the soap place first and then we'll go buy you some clothes. Doc G, can I have your credit card?"

I barely managed to stop my panicked refusal by biting down on the insides of my lips. Nikki's trust in me had to be one of the most challenging issues I'd had to deal with. Her request had come without any guise, her expression open and excited. I wasn't worried that she would spend too much money. In the year that she'd stayed with us, she'd proven herself competent with finances. When her father had died, he'd left her a considerable estate, all of which would only be available to her upon her twenty-fifth birthday. Until then, a trust fund paid for her studies and provided her with a very small stipend.

I trusted her with my money. It was my carefully-planned budget that was going to change if I handed her my credit card. The change in my monthly spending plan weighed heavily on me as I studied her guilelessness. This was about more than just my credit card and I knew this. I cleared my throat three times before I felt ready to speak. "Please bring my handbag."

"Yay!" Nikki ran to my viewing room and was back a few seconds later, handing me my handbag as if it was fragile. I closed my eyes, took a deep breath and took my credit card from my wallet and gave it to her. She turned it over a few times, then pressed it against her heart. "Any limit?"

I couldn't speak. The distress of my pedantic budget changing was pressing hard enough on me to consider grabbing my card out of Nikki's hand. I shook my head.

"No limit? Doc G, you're the best." She stepped closer. "I'm going to hug you."

She threw her arms around me and hugged me tightly. I gingerly put my arms around her and patted her on her back.

After a second, she lifted her head and put her lips against my ear. "I love you."

I froze. Tears formed in my eyes and I blinked them away, my arms dropping to my sides. I knew how much those three words would mean to Nikki, yet I couldn't get my mouth to form them.

A few months ago she'd declared her love for everyone in the household and frequently told us how much we meant to her. Apart from myself, everybody else expressed their love for her, often in a light-hearted manner.

Nikki released me from her embrace and stepped back. Intense relief flooded me when I couldn't detect any hurt or offence on her face. She wasn't expecting anything else from me. Her smile was beautiful and genuine when she turned to Caelan. "Come. Let's go shopping."

Chapter THIRTEEN

For the second time today I found myself in a place I didn't want to be. I was standing in the men's clothing section, my arms folded tightly around my torso. Caelan's response to Nikki's invitation had been strong and unexpected. He'd grabbed onto the idea of shopping with surprising ferocity, but had refused to even leave his chair without my agreement to accompany them.

Vinnie hadn't liked the shopping proposal at all, not with the recent discovery of Dukwicz being in Salzburg. Manny and Colin had agreed with him. Francine had lamented her inability to join us, getting excited about the prospect of shopping. But she had too much work. I also had too much work. I didn't want to be standing between men's pyjamas watching Nikki playfully banter with Caelan. She was incredibly successful at getting his agreement to her choices in pants, shirts, socks and other clothing.

Manny and Vinnie's resistance to the idea had brought realisation followed by regret to Nikki's eyes which had affected me. By then Caelan had already latched onto the idea and no amount of reasoning had been able to dissuade him from his desire to go shopping with me. When it had become clear that no more work would be done until I went shopping with Caelan, Vinnie and Manny had insisted we go to a shopping centre. Their reasoning that it was safer and easier to contain did not add to my sense of comfort or safety.

I wanted to be in the soundproof safety of my viewing room. Instead I stood here, observing the two members of

GIPN aiding Vinnie in providing security. Daniel and Pink had joined us within fifteen minutes of Vinnie phoning them. That had been the first time Colin had relaxed about the shopping suggestion. He trusted Daniel's and Pink's ability to assist Vinnie in keeping us safe.

The two GIPN men's fast appearance in our offices led me to suspect they been in close proximity. Currently Daniel was standing next to the ties, Pink next to the men's underwear. They were alert, screening every person who came close to us. Since Caelan had showed signs of a meltdown when I had insisted on staying in the office, Colin volunteered to remain behind and help Francine.

Nikki had promised that the shopping spree would take no longer than an hour. It had already been forty-seven minutes and Pink was carrying four large shopping bags. In one was a smaller paper bag with seven bars of fragrance-free soap. There were also seven pairs of socks, seven pairs of underwear and seven t-shirts. Nikki and Caelan were busy choosing his seventh pair of pants.

"What do you think, Doc G? This green one or this green one?" Nikki held up two pairs of pants, the colours differing slightly. She shook the one in her left hand. "I'm liking this one more. I goes well with half of the t-shirts we've bought."

"All the t-shirts you've bought are white, Nikki."

She giggled. "I know."

"I want another pair of blue pants." Caelan pointed to a rack behind Nikki.

"No." Nikki shook her finger at him. "You already have two pairs of blue jeans and a pair of blue pants. You need variety."

"Why?"

I took a step back, allowing Nikki to answer that question. They walked towards the blue jeans, Caelan getting more animated in his desire for another pair of blue pants. Nikki's patience and kindness towards the young man caused a warm sensation in my chest. She looked happy and carefree as she rolled her eyes and started a different line of reasoning with Caelan.

The effect she had on people was fascinating. Within minutes of meeting her, both Daniel's and Pink's expressions had mimicked Vinnie's. Affection, tolerance and amusement alternated with the suspicious looks they gave everyone else. I didn't have to look far to see Vinnie. He wasn't looking at Nikki and Caelan. Instead he was watching me. He gave an exaggerated eye roll, nodding his head towards the two young people and lifted his shoulders in a hyperbolic sigh.

I knew he didn't mind Nikki's enthusiasm. It was clear on his face. After an exaggerated wink, he turned back to survey the shop behind me. On the other side of the store, a two-year-old started screaming in a typical tantrum. I shuddered at the thought of having to deal with that kind of auditory assault on a daily basis. People who procreated had my admiration. Observation and academic knowledge informed me that parenting was not an easy life-long task.

"Excuse me, ma'am?"

I turned towards the soft voice. A shop assistant stood a bit behind me, her uniform immaculate, her hair in a soft bun, her smile social. She was in her mid-twenties and stared at me as if she'd never seen another woman before. When she didn't say anything else, I lifted one eyebrow. "Yes?"

"Are you Doctor Lenard?"

I frowned. "Yes."

Her smile turned from social to real. "It's such a pleasure to meet you. I didn't know people like you existed."

"People like me?"

Vinnie took a step towards me, but I shook my head. Nothing in this woman's body language alerted me to any kind of aggression. She was curious and in awe. It caught my interest.

"Experts in body language. The man said you helped solve crimes just by analysing what people do with their hands and faces. Is that true?"

I barely heard the last part of her excited babbling. Cold entered my limbs and I took a shuddering breath. "What man? Who told you about me?"

"Oh, the big man who was here a few minutes ago." She looked towards the open doors leading into the mall. "He said that you changed his life. You solved a crime that had affected him. He went on and on about how amazing you were."

My mouth was dry. My fingers tingled from the adrenaline rushing through my body. I tried to ask one of the many questions that were rushing through my mind, but I couldn't get my mouth to obey my mind. I was frozen. I couldn't even call Vinnie.

"He was so deeply touched to see you again, he asked me to give you this." She held out her hand. "He said that you knew him and would be so happy to see him again. But he didn't want to impose while you were shopping with your family. Isn't that just too nice for words? He said he knew that your husband was leaving soon and that you would be very sad.

"I told him that you've just been standing to the side letting your children shop. I was sure you wouldn't mind the company. You don't mind, do you? See, I told him so. He should've given this to you himself. But he didn't want to. He said that you would know this meant he was grateful to you for giving him the opportunity to achieve his goals. Here, take it. Don't you want this? The man said it had great value to him." She pushed her hand closer, looking pointedly at the items she was holding out to me.

I stared at the watch resting on her open palm. Darkness surrounded me and I fought to keep it at bay. But Colin's watch kept pulling the darkness closer. This was the watch I had given Colin for Christmas. The watch Colin had been looking for this morning while I'd waited impatiently for him.

An announcement sounded over the shop's sound system. The shop assistant pressed Colin's watch and a folded piece of paper into my hand. "Ooh, I have to go. Busy, busy, busy. By the way, the man said that his name was Du.. Duk... Duk-something. Ooh, I really have to go. Was so cool meeting you."

I didn't pay attention as she left. All that existed in my world at present were the two items in my hand. The watch was warm from her body temperature and felt like it was burning through my skin. Dukwicz had been here. He had followed us.

He had also been in my apartment. In my bedroom. He had gone through the drawer in my bedroom where Colin kept his watches. I found it most disconcerting that the watch he had chosen was a gift I'd given to Colin. Had he known that too? How much time had he spent in my apartment? He had to have been there the evening before while we'd still been in the office, working.

I managed to get my fingers to open the piece of paper. The handwriting analysis I would leave for later, but the aggressive strokes in the letters were impossible to miss. "*Doctor Lenard. I warn you. Buy something black. You need it soon. Got job to eliminate your boyfriend. It will give me happy. You and the kid I leave for later. Boyfriend soon. D.*"

I knew I was going to shut down. The darkness was too close now. Too safe. This man, this international assassin, had threatened the one person I'd allowed to break through all my emotional shields. I felt the hard floor under me and realise that my legs had folded under me. I was sitting on a dirty shop floor, clutching Colin's watch in one hand and crushing the note in the other.

"Doc G? Doc G!" Nikki's voice came closer. "Oh, my God. Vinnie! Pink! Vinnie!"

I tried to focus on Nikki hand touching my arm then quickly moving away again after a quick apology. It didn't keep the darkness away. I forced myself to listen to the tightness in her voice as she babbled. Still the darkness overwhelmed.

"I'm phoning Colin. He'll be here soon. Just hold on, Doc G. We'll get you out of here soon. Just hold on."

I heard Vinnie ordering Colin to get here, then trying to calm a distraught Nikki. I lifted my hand towards the sound of Vinnie's voice, hearing my own keening. His angry swearing somehow soothed me and I wished Vinnie would pry the items from my fingers. He didn't. He told Colin to get here sooner.

When Nikki spoke again, her voice was thick with tears and close by. It sounded like she was sitting next to me. Instead of focussing on Mozart to calm myself and bring myself back, I found myself distracted by the need to comfort her. She sounded so lost, so young. I fought off the darkness. I couldn't let her be alone. The realisation that she was sitting next to me, not knowing that I loved her devastated me. My keening became louder.

I should've told her when the opportunity had been there. She had given me her uncensored emotions, shared with me the depth of her feelings. I had not had enough courage to reciprocate. I did love her. I loved the lightness she brought into every single conversation. I loved the uninhibited manner with which she attacked life. I loved that she wasn't scared of her own emotions and that she wasn't scared to express them. She was braver than I would ever be.

In the background I heard sirens and shop assistants ushering people out of the store. Nikki never left my side. She spoke to me, telling me that Colin was coming and he would make everything better. That I was going to be okay.

Only when I heard Colin's voice did I allow myself to give in to Mozart's Piano Sonata No.11 in A major. He would take care of Nikki. He would make sure she didn't sound so scared.

Chapter **FOURTEEN**

"Nikki." I waited until she looked at me. "None of this is your fault."

It had taken an hour for me to return to reality and for us to return to Rousseau & Rousseau. Nikki had refused to leave, even when Colin had arrived. Vinnie had somehow managed to convince Caelan to return to the office with one of the GIPN members to help Francine. When I'd come to, Nikki had been crying. Vinnie had been angry.

He'd been against leaving the office from the beginning and was now in the conference room with Daniel, the leader of the GIPN team, to discuss protection for whenever we did have to leave. We would all have bodyguards until Dukwicz was found.

Colin was sitting next to me in my viewing room, looking at Nikki. She was on the floor between the two filing cabinets, her back straight, her body tense.

"I always push. I shouldn't push. I should listen to you. You told me we shouldn't go shopping. Everyone told me we shouldn't go shopping." She looked up from her hands. "I'm sorry, Doc G."

"We all learned a lesson, Nix." Even though Colin had been calm and in full control of the situation, there were still tension lines visible around his mouth.

As I looked at Nikki worrying a cuticle, all I could think of was my overwhelming concern in the shop. My heart felt as if it was pounding against my sternum and my breathing was uneven. I wrote a few lines of Mozart's Piano Sonata No.11 in A major and took a bracing breath. "Nikki?"

She looked up, her eyes sad. "Yeah?"

"I love you."

Colin inhaled sharply, but I continued looked at Nikki. Her eyes filled with tears and she scrambled to her feet. Two seconds later, I was enveloped in a tight embrace, warm tears dampening my shoulder. I swallowed against the need to push her away and scrub her tears off my skin. I hugged her back. After a long moment, she straightened and artlessly wiped her cheeks with the backs of her hands. "You're the best, Doc G."

This emotional moment overwhelmed me. The pride and deep affection visible on Colin's face as he looked at me, then at Nikki, added to my desire to escape. I was terrified that I would say or do something that would negate what I'd just declared. I felt ill-equipped for moments such as these. Ideally I would avoid them, but I never wanted Nikki to feel rejected.

"Yo! Sailors!" Francine's strange address from the team room broke the moment and filled me with immense relief. "Get your hardy-har-har butts in here. We have something!"

Nikki giggled, the intensity of the last hour instantly lessening. Francine called us again and we got up. Nikki walked into the team room, but Colin held me back. He turned me to face him and waited until I looked at him.

"Thank you."

"For what?" My voice cracked.

"For giving Nikki a gift bigger than you can ever imagine."

He was wrong. I could imagine it. For the first nine years of my life, I'd longed to hear those words from my parents. When I'd realised they would never be spoken, I'd blocked that desire. I didn't expect the young woman teasing Caelan in the team room to enter my life and remind me how valuable those words were. Especially coming from someone we looked up to.

"Are you two coming or not?" Francine's impatient tone draw me from my thoughts. I gave Colin a small, genuine smile. He kissed me on my nose and followed me into the team room.

"Tell them what you told me, Caelan." Francine had been working with Caelan when Colin and I had returned to the office. Caelan hadn't even looked up from the computer when we'd walked to my viewing room. "Go on. Tell them."

Colin and I were standing in front of Francine's desk. Manny was also in the team room, seated at the round table, his body language distancing himself from us. I wondered if he did that to make Caelan feel more at ease. I suspected Manny would take offense if I asked him.

Caelan stopped rubbing the hem of his t-shirt. "Fifteen months ago, I saw an artwork sold on Silk Road. It was *A Bay with Cliffs* by Gustave Courbet. The highest sea cliff is in Kalaupapa, Hawaii and is one thousand and ten metres high. I thought it was interesting that someone would sell art in a place where criminals hang out. Then I wondered if they were criminals, so I looked for more artwork. There is a lot of crap being sold. A lot of it. Those pieces are easy to find. The more interesting pieces were the ones not so easy to find."

Manny grunted and slid down the chair into a low slouch. His brow was lowered in frustration, one arm folded across his chest, the other hand in a fist, pressing against his mouth. He was trying to prevent himself from speaking. Knowing him, he was most likely trying to control his many impatient questions and orders. Caelan was oblivious to this.

"I saw a pattern quite quickly. On the second day of every month, a Courbet painting would go up for sale. They were not crap paintings. At first they were put up on Silk Road, but then it was shut down. As soon as SSS launched, I found a

Courbet painting on the second day of that month. I didn't know if they were real or forgeries. That was when I decided to get someone who would know." He glared at Colin's shoulder. "You were supposed to help me and tell me if these paintings are real or forgeries. But no. You haven't even looked at the paintings."

"How was I supposed to look at the paintings when you've been the one playing games?" Colin shrugged. "You seem more interested in manipulating us than in solving a mystery."

"It's not a mystery. It's a crime!" Caelan wrapped his arms around his waist and lowered his chin until it was almost touching his chest. "I thought you wouldn't listen to me unless I had something to make you listen."

I wondered about this adolescent's life experience. Had people been treating him so badly that he considered manipulation the only way to get and keep someone's attention?

"I suggest we start over then," Phillip said from the door. "Here we treat each other with respect. No matter who you are. You don't have to scream or kick my assistant to gain anyone's attention. I would greatly appreciate it if you would simply ask next time."

Caelan was quiet for a long time. We waited in silence and I wondered if Tim was injured or merely bruised. Caelan raised his chin a bit and looked at my shoulder. "Are you listening to me?"

"We all are."

"Okay. I'll try to ask next time."

"That's great," Colin said. "Now maybe you can tell me about those paintings you've seen."

"It was Courbet's *Desperate Man, The Stone Breaker, The Waterfall in the Jura, The Bather, The Sleeping Spinner, The Wrestlers.*" Caelan named another eight paintings in a monotone. "And *Full Standing Figure of a Man*. I thought they were the original paintings. A forger would need to see the originals to make such good forgeries."

"Hmm." The *frontalis* muscles drew Colin's eyebrows up. "Yes, you might be right. To paint an acceptable forgery, you need to see the direction and thickness of the brush strokes, the correct colouring, the right shading. From a photo that's almost impossible."

"Tell them the rest, Caelan." Francine was sitting back in her chair, looking like she was enjoying herself immensely. "What did you find yesterday?"

"I looked for all the paintings that went up on the second of every month. It's all the same seller. Zana22Dactor3178."

Francine clicked with her computer mouse and looked pointedly at the screen behind us. "Look what we found."

Colin and I turned around. On the screen was an SSS storefront. Like so many others I'd looked at in the last two days, several products were displayed with a description and price. There were photos of small bronze sculptures, watercolour paintings and sketches. All of them looked amateurish.

"What's so special about this, supermodel?"

"This is Zana22Dactor3178's shop." She clicked on a product and another window opened. "This lovely watercolour painting of three roses is a lure. As soon as I clicked on a product the first time I visited this storefront, a pop-up window opened asking me to become a member of Zana22Dactor3178's VIP section. Like the super-smart woman that I am, I didn't subscribe to anything."

"Why not?" Manny asked.

"Oh, my darling grumpy bear." Francine fluttered her eyelids dramatically. "I'm not the only one who uses Trojan horses to get into people's computers. The moment ol' ZD has my email address, he can get into my computer. Well, he can try."

"Does this story have a happy ending, supermodel?" His sharp tone caused Caelan to start rocking in his chair. Manny sighed heavily.

"Of course there is. Caelan and I hacked the auction website." She smiled at Caelan. "ZD's profile on SSS has a link to his website. Any guesses which website it is? Huh?"

"The auction website," I said.

"That's right, my lovely bestest friend." She clicked again and the screen changed to show the clock counting down. "Now your average visitor will only ever see this. Or the auction video whenever ZD puts it up. But we're not average, are we, Caelan?"

"Francine totally hacked into the website," he said. "You should see the things we found there."

"We make a good team, Caelan," Francine said.

"Then be my girlfriend." He winked at her shoulder, the gesture exaggerated and unpractised.

"The answer is still no, kiddo." She clicked once more and the clock was replaced with a gallery of paintings. "Here are more than thirty Courbet paintings."

"Oh, my." Phillip sat down heavily next to Manny. The sudden tension in Colin's muscles caught my attention. His eyes had narrowed and he was leaning towards the screen, studying it intently.

"What is it?" Before I could stop myself, I moved a bit closer to him until our arms touched.

"Maurice showed me one of these paintings." He took a shuddering breath and looked at Manny. "When I met with him three days ago."

"The day you were arrested?" Manny asked.

"Yes. Maurice showed me Courbet's *Nude Reclining Woman* he wanted me to authenticate. We were chatting about the value of it were it the original when he told me the owner had said he had more such paintings. Apparently, he'd told Maurice he would ask us to authenticate five more if he were satisfied with our service. I thought how strange it was and was about to ask Maurice about it when those Interpol idiots stormed in."

"Which painting is it?" Manny squinted at the screen. "They all look the same to me."

Colin and Phillip both glared at Manny. Phillip spoke first. "Second row, third painting from the left."

"It's the one with the naked woman, Millard." Contempt made Colin's voice hard.

"Aha. Okay. Hmm." Manny repeated these meaningless interjections a few times, his eyes narrowed.

"I prefer the paintings with landscapes. People paintings don't interest me," Caelan said, looking at Colin's shoulder. "You should check how much the people paintings are."

"They're called portraits," Phillip said. "Where on earth did these paintings come from?"

"More importantly, who the blo…" Manny grunted. "Who is this ZeeDee seven million idiot? If we can get him, we might get some answers about the paintings."

"It's Zana22Dactor3178." Caelan paused. "Why don't you say 'bloody'? I say 'fuck' all the time. Bloody is not a swear word. I'm not a kid."

Nikki's snort drew our attention to the door. "Don't even try to understand this, Caelan. I've been through this with them. They think swearing in front of young people will injure our delicate ears."

Caelan touched his ears. "I don't have delicate ears. I don't mind swearing. I like it. It helps me when I'm angry." He glanced at Manny's shoulder. "I don't like it when other people are angry."

Nikki walked to Manny, stopped behind him and leaned with her elbows on his shoulders, her chin resting on the top of his head. "Manny always sounds angry. He's like a grumpy bear, but he's totally harmless."

"Get off me, lass." Manny patted her elbows, pushed them, patted, then pushed until she stood up. He looked at Caelan until the young man focussed on Manny's shoulder. "Nikki's safety, your safety, everyone's safety is my first concern. I don't have time for bullshite emotions when people are in danger."

Caelan focussed on the ceiling and muttered under his breath. His eyes narrowed slightly before he jumped out of his chair. "I'm going home. I will find more to help you. You listen."

"Hey, Caelan!" Nikki's call stopped him halfway into the hallway. He turned around and looked at her shoulder. "I like your duds."

The *zygomaticus* muscles pulled the corners of his mouth up into the first smile I'd seen on his face. Without another word, he turned towards the elevators and walked out of sight.

"What are duds?" I asked Colin quietly.

"Clothes, love. He's wearing the new clothes he bought with Nikki."

Regret made my chest feel heavy. How had I not noticed Caelan's clean clothes? I tried so hard to be aware of those around me, but time after time I failed.

"I don't get that kid." Manny slumped deeper into his chair. "Why did he run off like that?"

"To find more information to help us. That is what he said." I didn't see anything in Caelan's nonverbal cues to indicate otherwise.

"He's really, really, really strange." Nikki sat down next to Manny. "But I like him. He's cute."

Vinnie walked into the team room, his large form making the room feel smaller. Any more people and I would feel compelled to retreat to the safety and emptiness of my viewing room. Vinnie glanced around the room and sat down in his usual chair at the table. "Where's the kid running off to? When I came out the conference room, he nearly ran me over trying to get to the elevator. Did you scare him, old man?"

"He's going home." The increased tension around Manny's mouth indicated offense. "Where the hell have you been, criminal?"

"Aw, look at you sweet-talking me." Vinnie put his hands behind his head and stretched his legs out, communicating his confidence. "Did you miss me?"

"Like a haemorrhoid. Now tell me where you were."

"I walked Daniel out." He looked at me. "We won't have a repeat of what happened today, Jen-girl."

"You can't guarantee that."

"I can fuc… I can try my best to guarantee that."

Manny rubbed his hand over his face. "How the bleeding hell did Dukwicz know where you were, Doc?"

"I don't know." This had been the one question foremost in my mind. "In the note he said he got a job to kill my boyfriend."

"Since I know for a fact you're not romantically involved with anyone else, it has to be me." Colin crossed his arms. Defensive. "I simply can't see how Dukwicz could have made the connection between Edward Taylor and me."

"There is an alternative option." I didn't like the thought of it. "Someone else hired him to kill you. Colin Frey."

Colin was shaking his head before I'd even finished my sentence. "The only reason they would look for me, would be through the work I do as my aliases."

"Kubanov wanted you," I said softly.

Colin sighed. "You're right. We have to consider all possibilities. I just find it highly unlikely."

"Dukwicz was in my apartment. He took your watch."

"In our apartment. And he still has my watch. The one he gave you is a terrible fake of the one you bought me. It's cheap plastic." Colin shook his head. "I still don't believe he knows I'm Edward Taylor."

"But if by some miraculous way he does, how on God's green earth did he find that out?" Manny asked.

It was quiet in the room for a few seconds.

"I hate to be the one saying this,"—the expression on Francine's face confirmed it—"but could it be one of the GIPN guys?"

"I asked Daniel that same question," Vinnie said. "He convinced me it's impossible."

"This speculation is not productive." I knew they were capable of creating different theories and arguing about it for the next hour.

"I agree, Doc. It would just be really nice to know where Dukwicz is getting his info from." Manny frowned when his eyes rested on Colin's back. Colin had moved closer to the screen and was staring intently at the paintings. He was not paying attention to Vinnie discussing security measures.

"I didn't know about this one." His words were barely audible above the bantering.

"Which one?" I asked.

"This site selling art." He shook his head, the *corrugator supercilii* muscles pulling his brows low. "These paintings are worth millions. Why didn't I know about this place?"

"Does it mean you know about all the others?" It was a logical deduction. All attention was now on our conversation. Nikki took her sketchpad, sat down on the floor and started drawing.

"You better be talking about this place selling art and not organs, Frey. If you knew about a place cutting people into pieces and selling them off, you'd better have reported it a long time ago."

Colin huffed dismissively. "Calm down, Millard. I'm talking about these obviously lucrative and obviously illegal sales of masterpieces."

"Ah, the delicate line you walk between being a thief and a... a whatever you are." Manny had found it very hard to accept that Colin was employed by Interpol. Outside of our team, only four people knew he was retrieving objects for the international law enforcement agency. "So tell me, why is Interpol so interested in Edward Taylor?"

Colin took a step closer to Manny. "What do you know, Millard?"

"I met Laurence Gasquet today." There was no mistaking the derision on Manny's face. "Cagey. Very cagey."

"What does that mean?" I didn't want to make the mistake of assuming what I thought it meant.

"He answered every question like a politician would, Doc. I didn't get one straight answer from him."

"What did you get from him?" Colin asked.

"He said some confidential informant, whose identity he was not willing to divulge, has been feeding him info on Edward Taylor. Gasquet sat on it for a while before he went to his mates at Interpol. They decided to look into it and that's how the official investigation was opened. It was also this supposed CI who told Gasquet that you were going to meet with Maurice Dupin three days ago. Of course, Gasquet was an upstanding citizen and told his Interpol guys about this."

"And I was arrested."

"You have to think harder, Frey. Who did you piss off?"

Colin's smile was mocking. "Seriously? The list is long and you take up the top four places."

"But I'm no longer trying to arrest your thieving arse." Manny leaned forward, resting his elbows on his knees. "Think. This unit is swamped with cases. Why would they waste their time with a nobody like Edward Taylor?"

"When did the confidential informant first contact Laurence Gasquet?" I asked.

"Ah, this is where I didn't get a straight answer. From what I could gather, it's more than a year ago."

"That long?" Colin's frown deepened.

"What does Interpol know about Edward Taylor?" When I'd looked at the electronic file, there was very little information.

"That was another battle. They didn't want to share their precious information with me. Eventually they admitted to knowing very little. They suspect that Edward Taylor is a false identity, but can't confirm it. Apparently, Edward Taylor has a full electronic history, making him appear legit and less likely to set off alarms."

A quick glance between Colin and Francine made me wonder if she was responsible for all his pseudonyms.

"How many times did you work as Edward Taylor in the last year?" I asked.

"Two… no, three times. The last time was yesterday when I went to look for Maurice. The time before that when we were arrested."

"And the first time?"

"Also with Maurice. Also to authenticate a painting. That one was for his gallery and everything was above board."

"What about last year? The year before?"

Colin's eyes shifted to the left, remembering. Two seconds later, his eyes flashed wide open. "I… Edward Taylor reported a painting to Interpol about nineteen months ago."

"When? What? Where? Why?" Manny sat up.

"It was also a job for Maurice. He had a painting that the owner wanted appraised. It was interesting that the owner didn't want to authenticate the painting and I told Maurice so. I didn't care what the owner wanted. I first made sure the painting was real before I put a monetary value to it.

"The problem was twofold. Firstly, it was a forgery of Courbet's *Chateau of Blonay*. It was the first of these Courbet forgeries I saw. The second issue I had with this piece was that the original's provenance is being fought over in court by a family claiming many artworks looted by the Nazis from their family collection have still not been returned. Maurice knows my stance on war-looted paintings. I will have nothing to do with them. Not even a forgery. I left and immediately reported the forgery to Interpol."

"Did you ever follow up on the investigation?" Manny asked.

"No. A week or so later I was kidnapped and tortured by a Russian psychopath." The *depressor anguli oris* muscles turned the corners of Colin's mouth down. It had been a difficult time for Colin, but also for Vinnie, who'd flown to Russia to rescue Colin. It had taken six months of intense physiotherapy for

Colin to walk normally again, but he still bore the deep scars on his right leg from that time.

"Kubanov. Hope he's rotting in hell." Vinnie mimed spitting on the floor, his features tight.

"The question now is whether there is a connection between the first Courbet you saw, all the Courbets sold on the dark net, Maurice Dupin, the owner, Laurence Gasquet, your arrest, these paintings on ZeeDee seven million's site and the organ auctions. Doc?"

"It's Zana22Dactor3178." I knew it was senseless to expect Manny to get names right, yet I couldn't stop myself. I sighed and focussed on his question. "I don't have enough data to make any connection."

"But you think there is?"

I ignored Francine's enthusiastic question. She exhibited that tone and expression whenever she came up with another implausible conspiracy theory. "I need more data. You're expecting me to give viable conclusions based on a few conjectures. It is outrageous."

"Like building a whole puzzle with only a few pieces." Nikki pulled her shoulders up when we looked at her. "What? It's a good comparison."

"Nikki is right. Very astute of you." It was an accurate analogy. "I need more pieces. Colin, tell me more about the owner of the forged *Chateau of Blonay*. Did you ever meet him?"

"Actually, I did." Again, his eyes shifted to the left and up. A visual memory. "His apartment was a disgusting example of a hoarder gone bad. Maurice had asked me to come around to his gallery for the first meeting. Usually Maurice has the painting there for me to authenticate and appraise. Not that time. He only had a photo. I told him, he knew better than to give me a badly-lit photo. I needed to see the painting. A week later he'd managed to convince the owner to let us see the piece, but the owner refused to let it leave his apartment. So we went there."

"Do you remember where it is?" Manny asked.

"Yup. I'll give you the address. A middle-class neighbourhood, none of the buildings in the area spectacular. But this man's place was... I don't think he'd thrown anything away in decades. Rows and rows of books, ornaments, newspapers, magazines. Anything you can think of."

A shudder went through me at the image Colin was creating. Being non-neurotypical, I understood that each person's neuro-patterns were unique. Some people's neuro-patterns were of such complexity it compelled them to wash their hands every ten minutes, never throw anything away, only eat green foods and numerous other interesting differences. My compulsions were mostly manageable, but it was easy for me to surrender to the obsessive need to organise everything in threes or check my apartment's locks seven times before being satisfied they were truly locked. Most days I was stronger than these needs. Some days I wasn't.

"He introduced himself as Monsieur Emile Rimbaud. He wasn't happy that we'd come to his apartment, but he showed me the painting. He was in his late eighties and had no kids or other family. He needed to sell the painting to pay some medical bills. He talked about a young neighbour who could've helped him, but he didn't want to take advantage of the boy. He wanted the money to pay his own bills. A proud old man."

"You're talking about him in the past tense," I said. "Is he deceased?"

"I don't know. He looked very fragile when I was there, so I suppose that's why I'm thinking of him as dead. For all we know, he's still alive and kicking."

"The painting?" Phillip asked softly.

"Oh, it was a brilliant forgery. I haven't seen many like that. What especially caught my attention was that it seemed old. At least forty, fifty years old. I told Monsieur Rimbaud it was a forgery and I was not going to put my... Edward Taylor's name to it. He was very upset about it and got even angrier when I offered to organise social services to help him." Colin stopped for a moment, his expression pensive. "Hmm. He seemed overly protective of his apartment. I thought it was just because he was a pack rat and didn't want anyone to remove anything. Maybe there were more paintings than just the one Courbet."

"How did you report it to Interpol?" Manny asked.

"Just gave it to my usual contact. Told him they could maybe go in under the guise of a social check, gas leak check, tax audit or something of that sort. I hadn't thought about this again until now. Being kidnapped and catching Kubanov kind of took over my life for a few months."

"Doc, will you check into that investigation?" The corners of Manny's mouth pulled down. "Use supermodel's invisible cloak to make sure no one knows you're snooping. I hate that we can't even trust our own."

"Aw, you can trust me, old man." Vinnie laughed when Manny lifted his middle finger.

I decided not to ask about Francine's invisible cloak. As it was, my mind was reeling with all the loose ends and questions. I didn't want to get into a debate about the physical impossibility of invisibility. "Francine, is there a way you can get into Zana22Dactor3178's computer like you did Dukwicz's?"

"There's always a way, girlfriend. I must warn you though that he's much harder to trace than Dukwicz. Once we had the handle Dukwicz used on SSS, it was easy to trace his online movement on Tor and the normal internet. The killer isn't the brightest bulb in the pack, let me tell you. He used the same handle everywhere. Amateur." She rolled her eyes. "ZD, on the other hand, can't be found anywhere else on the interwebs. Not that such a teensy setback would stop me. I'll find him, by hook or by crook."

I nodded absently. Already I was thinking about the many questions I had about Emile Rimbaud, hoping that my research would render answers.

Chapter FIFTEEN

"I got him." Francine's triumphant whisper pulled my attention away from my research. I glanced at the computer's clock. It was twenty-five minutes to six. I'd been looking around the Interpol website for the last three hours. Colin had left, once again to look for Maurice and Michael. He'd disguised himself as an elderly professor and had conceded to having Pink accompany him. Manny had gone to a meeting he hadn't wanted to tell us about. Vinnie had not left his usual seat in the team room. Last time I'd glanced that way, he'd been reading a hunting magazine. "Genevieve, get your cute little butt in here!"

Nikki giggled behind me. She was still on the floor, but no longer sketching. The pad and pencils were spread on the floor around her and I swallowed my complaint. She always tidied up. At the moment, she had her tablet on her lap, likely watching videos or one of the many other time-wasting activities she and her friends enjoyed. I got up stiffly and went to the team room.

"Took your merry time, girlfriend." Francine was bouncing in her chair. "I got him."

"So you said." I stopped next to her and looked at her computer screen. "Who is this 'he' you are talking about? Zana22Dactor3178?"

Her shoulders dropped a bit. "No. Not yet. He's a wily one, but I'll get him. I'm talking about Dukwicz. He switched on his computer five minutes ago and sent me an email three minutes ago."

"What's happening?" Colin came in, kissed me on my cheek and looked at Francine. "You look very pleased with yourself."

"I have Dukwicz."

"What do you mean, you have him?" It was at times infuriating when Francine became too excited for sensible conversation. "Do you know where he is? Have you phoned Manny or Daniel to go arrest him?"

"Uh, no. After he sent me the email, he turned his computer off again. For the three minutes it was on, I was able to trace him to a moving vehicle going through the city centre. I assume he was in a taxi. Sending emails while driving would be really stupid."

"You have him?" Frequently, I had to keep her on topic.

Her smile was genuine and warm. I valued her friendship, especially since she didn't take offence at my frankness. "Yes, I do. He wants the cash payment up front as a deposit."

"Who wants what as a deposit?" Manny came in and put an old-fashioned cake tin on the table. Francine jumped up and was at the table in three long steps. She struggled with the lid until it squeaked off. Her eyes widened and her mouth dropped open.

"You brought me Brigadeiro." Francine had told me numerous times about the chocolate bonbons that she used to buy in the Brazilian village where she'd grown up. Her nonverbal cues when she recalled those days and the taste of this delicacy revealed how much she enjoyed and missed them.

There had to be at least thirty bonbons in the tin. I didn't think she was going to share. It looked like she had to drag her eyes away from the contents of the tin to look at Manny. "I want to marry you and have your babies."

A deep red blush discoloured Manny's neck and cheeks. "If you talk such nonsense, I'll give the Brigadiers to… I'll give them to the kid."

"Pah! He only eats green foods. And you'd never be that cruel. You adore me." A soft expression replaced the teasing around her eyes. "Thank you, handsome."

"Hmph. Now tell me about this deposit."

Francine closed the cake tin, patted it gently and returned to her computer. "Dukwicz sent me an email, wanting a ten-thousand-euro deposit to do the job."

Manny whistled softly. "Ten thousand euros? Isn't that a bit much for killing someone?"

"Not if you want it done properly." Vinnie put his magazine down. "To brutally murder someone is easy. To make it look like an accident or natural causes requires a lot more work."

"Well, I'm not paying that money." Manny sat down in the chair closest to him.

"Millard." Colin pressed his hand against his chest. "I'm deeply touched that you don't want to pay someone to kill me."

"Don't tempt me, Frey. I'll do it for free." There was no malice in his threat. Still, I didn't like this line of conversation. Dukwicz's presence in the shop, his note threatening Colin were still too fresh.

"How does this mean you have him?" I asked Francine.

"He gave me his banking details. I'm going to deposit the ten grand and then I'm going to go through every single transaction in his account."

"Do you need to deposit the money to do that?"

"No, but if I pay the money, he won't become suspicious. I just needed his banking details to get into his financial history. This way, it will give us more time to locate him."

"Take the money from my Dutch account," Colin said.

"You have ten grand just lying around that you're willing to throw willy-nilly at your own assassination?" Manny's voice rose as he spoke.

"Did you just say willy-nilly?" Francine laughed. "You're the cutest thing ever."

I was watching this exchange with fascination. Manny didn't display nearly as much contempt and suspicion as he tried to convey. Colin's nonchalance about the ten thousand euro and the subsequent regret he displayed when he'd realised how much he'd revealed were noteworthy. Unconsciously, he trusted everyone in the room, including Manny, enough to reveal that not only did Francine have access to his accounts, he didn't consider ten thousand euro to be a significant amount.

Vinnie's lack of reaction to any of this implied that he too carried knowledge that I didn't. I'd never considered inquiring about Colin's finances. I realised now that I'd avoided thinking about it, uncomfortable with what that knowledge might reveal about him. I lived on a strict budget and planned big expenditures in advance. Since I was financially independent, my apartment was fully paid for and I had savings to ensure I didn't have to work for four years, I spent little time concerning myself with financial issues.

Despite having combined the two neighbouring apartments, I still carried the financial responsibility for my part. I'd never asked about Colin and Vinnie's financial arrangements, nor had I thought to. I realised that since Vinnie had taken over cooking most of our meals, I'd seldom bought any groceries. Even my favourite cleaning products never seemed to need replenishing. How could I not have noticed this? Three months ago, Colin had taken my car in for a service and had not given me the bill. What else had he been paying for?

"How much money do you have?" The words left my mouth before I could stop myself.

"You're only interested in my money now? No longer in my looks? My charm?"

I took a step away from him, horrified that he would think something like that. Only when I studied his face and noticed the lifted eyebrow and slight smile did I realise the light-heartedness of the question. It made me angry. "Don't tease me about something like this. I don't care about your mo… I do care. I care about how legal it is."

Both Colin and Manny laughed. I took a deep breath of relief when I didn't detect any offense.

"I have a lot of money, love. When we don't have such a large audience, I'll tell you where it all comes from." He paused. "Hmm. Francine, when you have time, please give Jenny access to all my accounts."

The surprise on Francine's face was almost immediately replaced by a soft smile. "Done."

"You can't do that." My throat tightened. "I can't have access to your money. I have my own money."

Colin put his hand on my forearm and lowered his head until we were at eye level. "I want to do this. We can talk about it later, okay?"

I followed his pointed look and saw everyone, including Nikki, watching us. I truly wanted to pursue this topic, but agreed that this was not the appropriate time. I nodded tightly.

"Okay, I just sent Dukwicz the money." Francine leaned back in her chair. "Now we need to send him some info on Edward Taylor."

"I don't like it." I pulled my arm away from Colin's touch. "You shouldn't be put in danger like this. We haven't established that Dukwicz doesn't know you are Edward Taylor. I don't like this."

"I agree with Jen-girl." The corners of Vinnie's mouth turned down. "Dude, you shouldn't be without protection until we find this asswipe."

I could see Colin was ready to argue. I put my hand on his arm and knew he took notice. "Please. For me. Please don't be a stereotype and attempt to prove your manhood or bravery by doing something not worthy of your intellect."

He put his hand over mine and squeezed. "Would you feel comfortable if I promise to only leave when absolutely necessary and always in disguise?"

I thought about this. Colin's disguises were exceptional. I doubt Dukwicz, or anyone else, would easily recognise him. "As long as Pink or Daniel accompanies you. But only if it is really necessary."

He lifted my hand to his lips and places a gentle kiss on my knuckles. "There is no way I'm going to endanger what I have now, love."

"Would you two stop doing that?" Manny shifted in his chair. "Supermodel, make sure that Dukwicz is convinced we still want Taylor dead. Don't give him too much info, just enough to confirm what he already suspects. If he suspects that Frey is Taylor."

Vinnie grunted. "Just email him that you know Edward Taylor is an art expert."

"Okay, but why do I want him dead?"

Vinnie thought about this for a moment. "We can't make this art-related in case Dukwicz makes the connection and thinks it's a trap."

"Tell him Edward Taylor stole your boyfriend." Nikki's smile was mischievous. "What? A man can steal a woman's man. Francine could say that she came home early one day to find her boyfriend in bed with Edward Taylor doing the wild monkey dance. Obviously, she's very angry and no one steals what is hers. She could sound like one of those crazy, clingy, stalkerish girlfriends."

The more she spoke, the more she became animated, clearly liking her story. Vinnie and Francine showed nonverbal cues of approval as opposed to Manny. He was horrified.

"I… I just… How…" He shook his head and slumped deeper into his chair.

"I love this backstory. What do you think, Vin?"

He nodded, grinning at Manny's discomfort. "It's brilliant, punk."

"But we can't use it. We've already established that the persona who contacted him was one of Francine's online baddies who wants revenge because Edward Taylor caused him to lose money." I felt silly using Francine's description of this pseudonym.

Nikki pouted. "That sucks. I like my story more."

"Our original reason for wanting Edward Taylor dead is more believable." Francine lifted one shoulder. "Sorry, Nikki."

"Just remember to demand proof of death," Vinnie said. "He must send you a photo."

Intellectually, I agreed with Colin that this was a sensible method to engage Dukwicz. Emotionally, I found it deeply distressing, no matter how I rationalised it. It took a lot of control to maintain quiet and not interfere while Francine worked on her computer.

"Done. Okay, now I need some time to go through Dukwicz's account."

"Doc, what did you find out about Emile Rimbaud's investigation?"

It took me a few seconds to let go of the deep discomfort about Colin willingly putting himself in danger. I focussed on my breathing and then on Manny's question. "A case file was opened the same week Colin said he'd reported it to Interpol. There was no movement on it for three days. On the fourth day, Interpol sent agents to the apartment pretending to be building inspectors. They reported that Monsieur Rimbaud had been extremely suspicious of their presence, but since all their paperwork was legitimate, he let them in and they went through the apartment. Emile Rimbaud became agitated when they wanted to enter his bedroom. When they opened the bedroom door, he had a heart attack.

"They called emergency services and did CPR while waiting for the ambulance. Unfortunately, he died in the hospital a few hours later. They went through the apartment, but their initial search didn't deliver any more paintings. The next day André Breton and Paul Hugo insisted on taking over the case, claiming that their unit was better equipped for looking into that case. It was given to them and four days later they closed it."

"What was their reason?" Manny asked.

"The alleged perpetrator was deceased, there were no other paintings found in Monsieur Rimbaud's apartment, and their unit was too busy with other cases of more importance."

"Too busy, huh?" Manny's top lip curled slightly. "One has to wonder why they insisted on having the case, only to dump it after not investigating."

It was a good question, one I'd asked myself when I'd come across this information. "I've been looking for a connection between Monsieur Rimbaud and André Breton and Paul Hugo. I've only started and have not been able to find anything."

"Doc, run it down for me. How do you think these things are connected?"

"Without speculating, I can't say."

"Please. Speculate." His facial expression did not communicate it as a request. When he issued an order like this, I knew he would insist until I relented.

"There are many missing pieces, but we have a few connections, even if they are rather nebulous. Dukwicz is connected to Zana22Dactor3178 through the auction video on Dukwicz's computer. On Zana22Dactor3178's website are paintings that Edward Taylor has been asked to authenticate—Courbet paintings. These works are connected to Maurice Dupin, who had contacted Edward Taylor about the authentication. The last authentication had led to Edward Taylor's arrest, which in turn led us to Emile Rimbaud and his connections to Judith Jooste, André Breton, Paul Hugo and possibly Jacques Boucher."

"My head is spinning." Francine pouted. "There are all these connections, but nothing makes sense."

"I'm searching for someone who knew Monsieur Rimbaud. Maybe they could give us more information about him and where he got the Courbet forgery that Colin saw in his apartment."

"I'll look into that, Doc. You can make the connections when I get us more info on this old man." Manny waited until I agreed with a sigh. "Okay, now tell me what you found on Breton and Hugo. You did look into them, didn't you?"

"Yes, I did. Breton is good with computers and anything technology-related. Hugo has the psychology background and is the team member who builds profiles of their targets or suspects. Before Judith joined the team, they were partnered with Jacques Boucher. He was a mathematician and solved many crimes through calculating odds, working out probabilities, using chaos theory and the like."

I would've loved to have the opportunity to work with someone of Boucher's calibre. I'd looked up his credentials— he'd been one of the top mathematicians in Germany before Interpol recruited him to work with this unit. Mathematics gave me great pleasure. Not as much as Mozart, but it calmed my mind whenever I worked on a complex problem. The logic, the predictability of the results soothed me.

"But then he died," Manny said.

"Yes. Jacques Boucher died in a car accident. The vehicle's brakes failed as he travelled through a mountain pass."

"Whoa!" Vinnie threw his magazine on the table. "That sends up all kinds of red flags, dinnit?"

"It does," Manny said. "Who investigated the accident?"

"The local police." There had been a frustratingly limited amount of information available. "The newspaper reports agreed with the last note on his personnel file. There was no evidence of foul play, so they ruled it an accident and closed the case."

"No way!" Vinnie frowned. "That's totally foul play."

"We are only suspicious of this now because of the context we are working in." I'd found that context always lent a different perspective to whatever or whomever one was researching. "The crime laboratory reports on the car didn't raise any doubts. The brakes had been old and worn. Nothing was… Nothing seemed like it had been tampered with."

It was quiet in the team room.

"We need to find out what Boucher was working on before his death. That accident could have had something to do with who or what he was investigating."

"I already looked into his cases. Those I saw were nothing noteworthy." I didn't have sufficient rationale for what I was about to say, but I'd been thinking about it for the last few hours. "We need to speak to Judith Jooste."

"The newest addition to the art crimes unit?" Manny raised his eyebrows. "Why do you want to involve someone who has such close ties to people of interest in this case?"

"You were the one who said we should keep her in mind. All because she had complaints against her."

"I know what I said, Doc. I'm asking you why *you* want to speak to her."

"I've looked at her files. She was recruited out of the Netherlands' AIVD, their General Intelligence and Security Service." It was the unit dealing in counterterrorism, counterintelligence, and all extremist movements. "Her work is meticulous, detailed and her reports are extremely well-written."

"Seriously?" Francine snorted. "You want to trust this woman because she writes well?"

I pulled my shoulders back, my chin lifting slightly. "Of course not. It is what her writing reveals that makes me willing to take that risk."

"So now you're a palm-reader too, Doc?"

"If you're referring to reading handwriting, it would be a graphologist." I found Manny's misnomers most irksome. "And no. I'm not reading her handwriting. It was all on her electronic reports. In a few instances her reports did not co-ordinate one hundred percent with her teammates'. She included details that made their reports look biased and incomplete. Her reports also reveal an analytical mind and someone who is detail-oriented, looking for anomalies in the data."

"You think she might know something about Breton and Hugo?" Colin correctly anticipated my line of thought. "Maybe she knows something about Boucher's death?"

I nodded. "A few weeks ago, Judith requested all of Jacques Boucher's files for the six months preceding his death. I could find nothing in their present caseload to require looking into past cases. It made me wonder why she requested them."

"Hmm. She might be on to something." Manny thought for a moment and then nodded. "We have to speak to her. Preferably somewhere away from Breton and Hugo."

Vinnie jumped up. "Let's go visit her at home. It's only a four-hour drive to Lyon. We'll catch her before she goes to bed."

"You shouldn't go." I ignored his frown. "You'll intimidate her and she'll respond by withdrawing. We won't get her co-operation when you go while in this mood."

"Hey." Vinnie put his hands on his hips. "I can be charming."

His frown turned into an offended scowl when numerous snorts and laughs filled the room.

"Doc and I will go."

Manny was still speaking when Colin moved imperceptibly to put his shoulder in front of mine. An unconscious movement to put himself between me and Manny. "Jenny is not going alone. Not after today."

"She won't be alone, Frey. I'll be with her."

"And you're going to protect her with what, your scowl?"

The muscle tension in both men increased. From experience, I knew this had potential to become a lengthy argument. "Do you have a disguise nearby?"

Colin's eyes widened. "Brilliant idea. I have one in the car. Vin can get it for me. I'll be ready in less than ten minutes."

Manny grunted. "This is turning into a circus."

"You need protection. All of you. Pink has been really good blending in." Vinnie lifted an eyebrow at Colin. "Dude, do you think we should ask him to go along? I have some things I need to do here."

I approved. "Pink won't scare Judith."

Vinnie's smile was genuine. "Thanks, Jen-girl."

"Whatever for?"

"Acknowledging my superpower. You know, the one that makes all people tremble in fear of me." The twitching around his mouth alerted me to teasing. We didn't have time for that.

"Can Pink meet us here in ten minutes?"

"He'll be here." Vinnie took his smartphone from one of the many pockets in his pants and walked out the team room.

"And I'm coming with." Colin lowered his brow as he addressed Manny.

Nikki looked at Colin, then at Manny. "Not to be like offensive or anything, but you and Doc aren't really the best in social skills. Colin is a natural. He'll know how to get this Judith woman to talk."

Nikki was only partially correct. Colin's social skills were indeed natural and more polished than mine and Manny's. But I'd seen Manny interview suspects. He would appear completely harmless, sometimes even bleary. It made people feel in control around him, often with the result of them revealing more than they'd intended.

I, on the other hand, had no natural social skills. From childhood I'd worked very hard at understanding and later on mimicking social interaction. If needed, I could be socially appropriate, my education aiding me in even being manipulative. But it was a conscious competence, always laborious and tiring.

Manny's lips pulled into a thin line. "Fine. But I'm taking the lead, Frey."

"Uh, guys? You won't have to go to Lyon," Francine said.

"Judith is here in Strasbourg. She came with Breton and Hugo three days ago and seems to still be here. Hold on a sec."

We stood in silence for almost two minutes. It was much more than 'a sec'.

"Our girl is living with her aunt. I'll send the address to your phones. And before you ask, handsome, I activated the GPS on her phone. She's at her aunt's house at the moment. If she moves, I'll phone and let you know."

"Pink will be here in five minutes." Vinnie walked into the room, putting his smartphone in another side pocket.

"Oh. Oh, my." Francine looked like she'd won a prize. "I'm going to put you all on a mini-high with this."

"Stop pointing at the computer and tell us, supermodel." Manny put his hands on his hips. "We want to get moving before Jooste goes out clubbing or something."

"I'm in Dukwicz's bank account and it's giving me sexy shivers." She stopped to shake her shoulders in an exaggerated attempt to prove her point, all the while reading whatever was on her computer monitor. "Scandals, darlings. Delicious scandals. There are a few cash transfers by people who are smart and don't want to leave an electronic footprint. But then there are these beauties. I'm looking at three transfers that will cause ripples throughout France. I don't think Dukwicz is selling property, so I'm working on the assumption that all these transfers are for assassinations."

A delighted smile lifted her cheeks as she worked on her computer. After a few seconds, she sat back with an even wider smile. "One of these transfers is from an account I just traced to one of the richest men in France. Another transfer was direct from the account of Marc Delile's wife."

"And he is?" Manny asked after Francine paused and didn't continue.

"You know, sometimes I think you're living under a rock, handsome. Marc Delile was a politician notorious for his womanising. Last year some time, he was accused of rape and was about to appear in court when he died from a bee sting. He was majorly allergic to bees. There was speculation how lucky his wife had been that he no longer had to spend hundreds of thousands on the court case, defending himself in what he called a concerted effort by his enemies to bring him down.

"Apparently, he'd already spent a chunk of his savings on all his women, and the rest on his high-flying lawyer. He would've had to sell one of their properties if he'd wanted that legal firm to continue representing him in that trial." Francine sighed happily. "It was such a luscious scandal at the time."

"So you're thinking the wife paid Dukwicz to off this politician?" Manny rubbed his hands over his face. "Holy Mary. If you're right, this is going to ruffle some big feathers."

"Well, she made a transfer of twenty thousand euro to Dukwicz's account a few days before her husband died. Then she transferred twenty-five thousand the day after his death. Ooh, this is my birthday, Christmas, Hanukkah and Halloween all wrapped in one."

"Just keep digging, supermodel. If we're going to make cases out of these, we'll have to present real evidence. Not aliens on a stick."

"You brought me Brigadeiro." She pressed both hands against her cheeks. "I'll give you a rock-solid case, handsome."

Manny stared at her for a few moments, then shook his head tiredly. He turned to Colin. "You have ten minutes to powder your nose, Frey."

While Colin was putting on his disguise, I used the time to close all the open folders on my computer. In a bit less than nine minutes, a middle-aged man limped into my viewing room. He was wearing a suit a size too large and a shirt that had once been white. The tie had to date from two decades ago. His dark brown eyes were the exact colour as the hair that hadn't yet turned gray. Again, it was only Colin's lips that gave away his true identity. I was impressed.

"Do you approve?"

I swallowed and nodded. "I still don't like this."

Manny appeared in the doorway. "Come on, you two. Let's see if we can catch Judith at her aunt's home."

"Are you carrying, old man?" Concern pulled Vinnie's brow in and down. I had no idea what Vinnie was asking, but Manny lifted his shirt to show a leather holster holding a handgun. Vinnie looked at Colin. "Dude?"

"In here." He nodded towards my cabinets. "I'll get it now."

"You have a gun in my room?" My voice raised a pitch. "Why would you have a gun in my room?"

"I hope it's registered, Frey."

Colin ignored Manny. He stared at me with one raised eyebrow for a few seconds. "The same reason I have a weapon in our bedroom, Jenny."

I closed my eyes and mentally wrote three bars of Mozart's Horn Concerto No.2 in E-flat minor and opened my eyes. Colin was walking into the team room, pulling his oversized jacket over the bulge in his back.

His confidence and the comfort with which he carried the concealed weapon went a long way to ease my mind. I abhorred weapons and everything they represented, but Dukwicz had made his intensions very clear. Manny grunted instructions to Vinnie to keep Nikki occupied and Francine safe before following us to the elevator. I wondered if Judith would be willing to trust us, listen to us, speak to us.

Chapter SIXTEEN

We turned into a tree-lined street in the suburbs of Strasbourg. It was one of those areas with spacious homes nestled in large gardens set in quiet streets. Some houses were almost on the street, others were deep into the garden, walls and lush vegetation providing privacy. This very popular suburb for upper-middle-class professionals was near enough to the city centre to ensure a short commute to work while still living in a greener and less built-up area.

Manny had agreed to go in Colin's SUV. It was a more comfortable vehicle than Manny's older sedan. And cleaner. Colin was at the steering wheel. Manny was slouching on the backseat, Pink next to him, leaning against the door. Not once in the last twenty minutes had Colin and Manny argued or baited each other. I was looking out at the picturesque street we were driving through. Cesária Évora's melodic voice was the only sound filling the spacious interior of the car.

We slowed down and I glanced at Colin. I found it rather disconcerting how well he was disguised, how well he acted as a middle-aged man. Manny had merely mumbled about wasting time, but had said nothing about Colin's new look.

It was easy for me to understand the necessity Colin had for not revealing his identity. It was hard bracing myself not to only accept, but also pretend along with the lie. I'd spent the drive mentally preparing myself not to address Colin at all in case I called him by his name—his real name and not the one of some seventeenth-century poet.

Colin turned the SUV into a neat gravel driveway and drove to the side of the large two-story home. Under three tall shade trees, a Ford Fiesta was parked in front of a brightly coloured sign inviting guests to 'please park here'. The dark blue Ford's registration number confirmed that it was Judith's vehicle. Colin parked next to it and turned off the car.

"Doc, do your face-reader thing while I handle the introductions."

Colin looked in the rear-view mirror and lifted one eyebrow. "You sure you want to start this by pissing her off? We need her to work with us, Millard."

"Bugger off, Frey." Manny got out of the car and slammed the door. Pink also got out, but leaned against the car as if nothing interested him. I knew he was aware of every movement and sound in close proximity.

I took my handbag, got out and took a moment to look around. The garden was lush and beautifully designed. Flat, round stones laid a path through the manicured lawn to the front door. To the left, in front of the house, a cream marquee provided shade for wicker chairs arranged around two low coffee tables. It looked like the perfect place for guests to spend lazy evenings, sipping wine.

As soon as we started walking towards the front door, I saw the difference in Colin's posture. His shoulders were no longer straight with confidence. He'd hunched over and favoured the side of his limp as he studied the house. I was amazed at how he transformed himself into someone clearly considering this magnificently maintained house and garden as beneath him.

I was about to comment on it when a huge dog ran around the side of the house, straight towards us. It was widely believed that we reacted to danger either with a flight or a fight response. That was wrong. The third response was how I found myself watching the dog running towards me. Frozen in fear.

I had never had a pet. My knowledge of domestic animals was purely academic. As a child, my parents had never allowed such frivolity as pets. As an adult I'd never even considered having an animal in my pristine apartment. The female dog coming towards me was proof why it had been a good decision. Her paws were muddy as was her nose, leading to the conclusion that she'd been digging in the ground. Her long hair was the type that would shed and attach itself to any material it came in contact with. The thought that people lived with animal hair on their clothes, furniture, carpets and, worst of all, bedding induced as much panic as this dog not slowing down.

It was only my expertise in human nonverbal communication that prevented me from completely shutting down in the face of this unknown danger. The dog exhibited no signs of aggression or imminent attack. She stopped a few feet away from us, her muscle tension leading me to the conclusion that if confronted she would run away rather than attack.

"What a gorgeous Saint Bernard." The moment Manny held out his hand, palm down, the dog's muscle tension increased and she lifted her lip—not enough to show teeth, but it was enough for me to recognise the warning.

Colin laughed softly. "Go figure. A female who doesn't like you, Millard. So hard to believe."

I had not moved from my position and found myself even more frozen when the dog walked to me, not taking her eyes off Manny. She stopped next to me, leaned against my leg and wagged her tail. Dogs carried bacteria like campylobacter, salmonella and numerous others that caused hundreds of thousands of people to yearly contract diseases from toxoplasmosis to hookworm. I couldn't begin to imagine how many unsavoury bacteria this animal was transferring to my light linen pants. Already I was thinking about throwing these pants out as soon as I got home and cleansing myself under a hot shower. With disinfectant soap.

"She likes you, Jenny." Not even the gentle smile in Colin's voice succeeded in getting me to look away from the threat against my leg. "It's a compliment."

I knew that. Animals were honest in their observations about the environment around them. The average human lied approximately three times every ten minutes. These need not be great untruths. An adaptation of a personal opinion, a slight embellishment qualified.

We'd had to adopt this behaviour to be perceived as polite while in social settings. Animals had the luxury of not having to tolerate small talk, social smiles and polite lies. Before I could calm myself enough to ask Colin to remove this animal from my side, the dog pushed her head under my hand.

I jerked my hand away and tucked both hands in my armpits. Those bacteria were now on my hand. Panic lowered over my shoulders like a heavy cloak and I focussed on visualising the disinfectant gel I kept in Colin's SUV. As soon as it was safe, I would get it and use it generously.

"Aw, she just wants some love, Jenny. You should pat her head. She won't bite." Colin moved closer, but immediately leaned back when the dog stilled, her gaze on him assessing. "Hmm. It seems she only likes you. She has good instincts."

"That is true," a strange voice with a soft Dutch accent said. A tall woman stood a few metres away from us. I hadn't heard her approach, my concern focussed on the dog now rubbing her head against my thigh. As a specimen, she was a beautiful and obviously well-cared-for dog. Her pelt was shiny and groomed.

I'd only needed a glance to recognise the woman. Judith Jooste looked much like the photos I'd seen of her. Her medium-length hair was neatly styled even though she was dressed in shorts and a t-shirt with 'These puppies are real' written across her chest. What the photos didn't convey was the intensity of her expression while she studied us. Her eyes widened for a millisecond in recognition when she looked at Manny, but then narrowed as she first took in Colin, then me. The muscles around her eyes and mouth softened when she saw the dog bumping my thigh with her head.

"Dogs see right through people's bullshit. You can't get a dog to believe a bad person is good." She looked at Manny. "What are you doing here, Mister Millard?"

"Ah. You know who I am." Manny hunched his shoulders fractionally more.

"Of course I do." She pointed her chin to me. It was clear she was wary of our presence. "Who are they?"

"My colleagues. Doctor Genevieve Lenard and—"

"William Strode," Colin said with a strong American accent. Judith turned her attention to him and didn't see Manny lift his eyes skyward, shaking his head.

I was becoming marginally more comfortable with the animal pressed up against me. She was still not showing any signs of aggression, but I continued to look at her every few seconds just to make sure. I wished human life was as uncomplicated as the animal kingdom. At least then I wouldn't have to be part of Colin's new lie. He held out his hand and shook Judith's. "Pleased to meet you."

"Yeah, we're not sure about that yet." She looked at her dog, then to me. "Mister Strode was right. You should pat her. Maxie doesn't take to strangers at all. I'm really surprised she's so open to you. Go ahead. Pet her."

I did not expect to see the change in her expression when she looked at me. With the men she'd shown distrust, but when she assessed me, I saw acceptance and trust. That change had only come after she'd seen Maxie's trust towards me. Interesting.

The meagre information I'd garnered on Judith, combined with the last five minutes, confirmed what I'd assumed about her. Manny might see the need for subterfuge and Colin the need for false identities and charm. In Judith I saw the appreciation for truth. I relaxed a bit. "I don't know how to pet a dog. I've never had one."

Judith's bottom jaw went slack and she stared at me for a few seconds. "That is just sad. They're man's best friend. I love my Maxie."

I reminded myself that the disinfectant gel was only a few metres away and forced my hands from under my arms. I slowly lowered my index finger and touched the top of Maxie's head. My other fingers were tightly tucked into a fist and I only allowed the very tip of my finger to make contact. The moment I did, Maxie looked up and pressed her head harder against my thigh.

"She's asking for more." Judith laughed. "Come on. Let's sit and I'll show you how to pet a dog."

She walked to the wicker chairs next to us, sat down and slapped softly on her thigh. "Maxie. Come here, sweetie."

The dog seemed reluctant to leave my side, but then walked to Judith, looking over her shoulder at me. I wrote two bars of Mozart's Symphony No.40 in G minor and walked to the chair next to Judith's. Despite this new and disconcerting experience, I was aware of Colin and Manny. They were leaning back and away, distancing themselves from this bond of trust that was forming. They knew Judith was trusting me because of her dog's behaviour. If we were to get answers to our questions, I was going to have to do the asking.

Judith held the sides of Maxie's head in both hands, her fingers lost in the hair. She was rubbing behind the dog's ears until Maxie swayed. "Ooh, you like that, don't you?"

I sat down slowly. In this position, the dog was eye level with us. It was not a position of comfort for me, and it took a lot of control not to jump up and put myself behind the chair. Maxie pulled her head out of Judith's grasp, took two steps and sat down on my right foot. I swallowed at the panic tightening my throat and watched in horror as the dog rested her head on my lap.

"Aw." Judith sat deeper into her chair, an affectionate smile softening her features. I also noticed the micro-expressions of disbelief. "She really likes you. Scratch her ears, pat her back, rub her belly, she likes it all. A real glutton for attention."

I wrote another bar of the symphony and rested my palm between Maxie's ears. Her hair was soft under my hand—soft and warm. "Did you know humans contract gastroenteritis from the bacteria around their pet dog's mouth? Dogs lick themselves all the time around their genitals and anus. The bacteria is transferred to the hairs on their muzzles. If the animals are indoors, they transfer the bacteria everywhere, or if they lick you, it's on you. Their hair also catches a lot of microbes when they are outside, which they then transfer to the inside of your home."

"I didn't know that." Judith frowned. "That makes me want to clean my house."

"You should." People didn't know how many dangerous bacteria lurked in their homes. I acknowledged the argument that we needed exposure to germs to build immunity, but I didn't have to like it.

Maxie's eyes closed and her head became heavier on my lap. She wiggled a bit, shifting position on my foot, and let out a contented sigh. To my surprise I was enjoying this experience. I touched her ears, marvelling at their velvety texture.

"Why are you here?" Judith asked quietly.

"We need your help." I looked away from Maxie's long eyelashes and took a moment to study Judith. Colin and Manny sat down in chairs facing ours. They were quiet. Observing. As was Judith. At this moment, I realised the importance of what I was not seeing. Calculation, aggression, posturing and deceit were completely absent in her nonverbal cues. I decided to trust her. "We are investigating a complex case and your team members have come up in the search."

"Breton and Hugo?" She moved her hands from the armrests to her lap, her left hand holding her right wrist. She was closing up. "In what capacity?"

"Doc?" Manny was in his usual slouching position, but his eyes were alert, his expression questioning. "Are you sure about this?"

Judith leaned back in her chair and crossed her arms tightly across her chest. "What's going on here?"

Maxie must have heard the change in her owner's voice. Her muscle tension increased and she opened her eyes, looking at Manny. I patted her head. "We don't know exactly what is going on. That is why we are here. We hope you can help us. We are investigating black-market sales of organs."

"And you think Breton and Hugo have something to do with that? Oh, my God."

"We don't know what we're thinking yet." Manny straightened a bit in his chair. "The person we're looking into has very strong connections to Breton and Hugo, and we're wondering if there might be more than just friendship."

"You're talking about Laurence Gasquet." Judith's lips thinned. "That man is bad news. I've only met him twice, but my perp-radar started screaming both times."

"What is a perp-radar?" I'd never heard of any such equipment.

"She's talking about her subconscious reaction to him." Colin smiled. "She had a gut feeling that he's a bad guy, a perpetrator."

His teasing was made worse with the strong American accent. I bit down on the insides of my lips to refrain from berating him yet again about gut feelings.

Judith narrowed her eyes, evaluating me again. Or maybe re-evaluating. Maxie relaxed against my legs, her weight strangely comforting. I pushed my fingers through the thick hair in her neck and massaged her lightly. "Why did you request Jacques Boucher's files two weeks ago?"

Judith's reaction was similar to when I first saw Maxie. She didn't move a muscle, didn't even breathe for a few seconds. Then she rubbed the corners of her mouth. "Jacques Boucher was a great agent. I was filling his shoes and wanted to learn from reading his case files."

"You're lying." I lifted Maxie's ear, enjoying its softness. "I don't know if you don't think Jacques Boucher was good at his job or if you were lying about your motivation for getting his files. Ah, it is about your motivation."

"Doc Face-reader here is one of the best body language experts in the world, Judith." Manny looked smug. "You won't get one past her."

Judith closed her eyes. Blocking us out. "I don't know you."

"We also don't know you." I shrugged, but Judith didn't see. She'd placed her hands over her eyes, strengthening her blocking. I ordered my thoughts, trying to find the right words to reach her. "This case is sensitive. We are dealing with students who are being kidnapped, their organs sold in online auctions. These young people have no families and are not very social. When they are taken, they are not missed. Your history tells me you care deeply about people, about protecting the innocent. We are trusting you to help us."

Judith dropped her hand back on her lap with a sigh. "You might be trusting me, but those two aren't."

Manny lifted both hands. "Hey, if Doc trusts you, it's good enough for me."

"What he said." Colin pointed his thumb at Manny. Their lie was well told, but not perfect. It was clear to me Manny didn't like that I'd revealed so much of our case to Judith.

"Okay," she said after a few moments. "I kept hearing how great Boucher was. At first, I only checked out his online case notes. Then my motivation was really to learn from him. In his last three cases, I noticed a difference. His notes were not the same as before. The change was subtle, but it was there."

"How was it different?" The profile I'd created on her did not include her openness to improving herself. Her employment history showed a woman who was accomplished, with the potential for greatness. She had not allowed her successes to turn into arrogance and her mind to be closed to new methods, new thinking and ultimately improvement and growth. I greatly respected that.

"He was not disclosing as much detail in the last cases as before. In his previous case notes, he would add impressions of the people or the situation. These were not part of the official report, but these kinds of side notes are extremely helpful if ever that suspect is investigated again or that case comes up again. The last three cases were dry, factual notes. So I started wondering why he was leaving things out. These files are accessible by most Interpol agents. Other law enforcement agencies could get access to them if they put in a request."

"And you thought he might have made old-school notes and left them in his paper files." Manny's single nod conveyed approval.

"Did he?" I asked.

She uttered a sound of disgust. "No. Before I could get those files, Breton and Hugo dragged me here to arrest some art criminal. They've had a hard-on for him for the last few months."

The changes in Colin and Manny's facial muscles were so small they would easily have been missed. Fortunately, neither said or asked anything. Judith was speaking to us, but her body language was still closed. She would withdraw her co-operation the moment she felt uncomfortable.

"Our caseload is insane," she continued. "I don't know why they're wasting so much time on this alleged art trader. Shouldn't it be your job?"

"Why our job?" Manny asked.

For the first time, Judith looked at Manny for an extended period. "I looked you up when you made sure that art trader wasn't formally charged. You have a fancy-smancy job investigating art and insurance crimes here in Strasbourg. I don't quite understand how you can be employed by Interpol, but work here. You should be in Paris or in Lyon, not here. Maybe I should ask for a job like yours."

"Have you resigned?" I asked. "Or do you plan to resign?"

"Can you read faces or minds?" She didn't look happy about either.

"I read all nonverbal cues."

"So you're a walking talking lie detector."

"Our body language reveals much more than just our lies."
I stopped myself. Talking about my field of study frequently
led to a monologue many people found boring. "Why resign?"

"I didn't resign. I've asked for a transfer. I don't want to
work with those two much longer."

"Help us and I'll put in a word for you." Manny made the
promise sound unimportant, but I knew the value of what he'd
just committed to. "Go back to Lyon, get those files and bring
them to us."

Judith took a long while to consider this. When she
straightened her shoulders and relaxed her hands on her lap, I
knew we had her co-operation. "I was going to go to his home
and ask his wife if he'd left any notes there."

"Good thinking," Manny said. "Bring whatever you can
find and we'll check it out together."

"You'll clear everything at the office so I won't have any
problems?"

"Sure." Manny touched his jacket pocket where he kept his
smartphone. "I'll organise the clearance. See if you can be back
by tomorrow afternoon at the latest."

Judith smiled. "My aunt would be happy. She loves it when
Maxie and I come to stay. That gives her an excuse not to take
any guests. I don't even know why she has this guest house.
She hates having guests other than us."

Maxie moved and I gently touched the bridge of her nose.
It was well-known that animals had a calming effect on people.
From experience, I could now agree. Although I still planned
to throw away my outfit and take a lengthy hot shower, the
summer heat notwithstanding.

"Do you know which were the very last notes Jacques
Boucher made?" I asked as something important tried to
connect in my mind. "Did you check the electronic date
stamps to see when he made his last entry?"

"I didn't even think of it," she said. "I'll check that out when I get to the office."

"Don't worry," Colin said. "We've got that covered. Just bring us those files."

Judith leaned back into her chair, staring at the roof of the marquee. "There was something, but it might be nothing."

"Never assume that," I said. "Frequently, it is the seemingly most insignificant detail that solves a case."

"True that." She sat up. "In his second last case, he mentioned a survey that needed to be double-checked. I didn't find any other references to that survey and didn't think anything of it."

"What survey is that?" I didn't like the hollow feeling in my stomach.

"It was the DFW survey."

"Bloody hell!" Manny pressed his knuckles against his eyes. "That's the survey I talked about the other day. The Drugs, Friends and Work survey checking what students' social and work lives are like and if and when they use drugs. Doc, we need to have a closer look at that survey."

"Okay, seriously. What is going on?" The wariness around her eyes was replaced by alarm. "If you want my help, you're going to have to tell me."

"Bring us the files and we'll fill you in on everything."

"No. I want to know now."

As before, Maxie lifted her head to glare at Manny. I patted her head and she lowered it onto my lap, her eyes not leaving Manny.

A ringtone singing about reasons for being happy came from my handbag. Colin had changed that ringtone a while ago for Nikki's profile and it suited her. I apologised and lifted my handbag from next to my chair.

I looked at my hands and saw the shiny layer of oily dirt covering the surface of my palms. I didn't want to touch the inside of my handbag or my phone with these hands, but there wasn't time to rush to the SUV and clean my hands. Nikki had proven herself to be mature on so many levels, including her phone calls. She never phoned me unless there was a legitimate reason. Taking into account the case we were working at the moment and the fact that Colin still had not found Michael, I took a deep breath and put my hand into my bag to find my phone.

Chapter SEVENTEEN

"Is there a problem, Nikki?" I tried to prevent my hand from touching my face or hair, but I was going to need that hot shower soon.

"Doc G, I think Steve has also been taken."

I couldn't immediately recall who Steve was, but there was a more pressing concern. "Why are you whispering?"

"I don't want Francine to hear me. Her crazy stories have been getting crazier by the minute. If she hears this, she'll—"

"Where are you?" I interrupted.

"In your viewing room."

"Is the door closed and sealed?"

"Yes."

"That makes the viewing room soundproof. Francine won't hear you."

"Oh. Yes. Of course." Her groan was familiar. She called it her 'blonde moments' when she did something that embarrassed her. I didn't know why she would think blonde people were more inclined to doing something imprudent.

"Why do you think Steve has been kidnapped?"

"What the hell?" Manny sat up in his chair. "Doc, put that thing on speakerphone."

I blinked at him a few times, wondering if Nikki would consider it a breach of trust.

"Now, missy!" The unmistakeable command in his voice had Maxie lifting her lip at him and shifting even closer to me. I turned on the speakerphone and held the phone towards Manny.

"Nikki, who's this Steve kid?"

"Oh, hi." She cleared her throat as if to speak to an audience. "Rebecca studies with Steve Robinson for her literature credits. He's like super smart, but also super quiet. They were supposed to meet today for their usual weekly study session, but he didn't show."

"Maybe he has a hangover," Manny suggested.

"He doesn't drink. Steve is like a total vegan teetotaller." The tension in her voice was increasing with every word. "It's just that he's, like, you know, the profile of the others. Should we go look for him?"

"No!" Colin, Manny and I answered her as one in varied levels of loudness.

"Where's the criminal?" Manny asked.

"Vin's in the team room. He's been phoning contacts, asking if anyone knew about auctioning people. I can't believe people can be this horrid."

"Get him on the phone." Manny leaned closer to the device in my hand. "Now, Nikki."

She mumbled something that sounded like 'Yes, Colonel,' but said, "On my way."

Manny looked at Judith, who had been watching us with alertness. "Whether you wanted to or not, you're now in this. You better not screw us over. These kids need your help."

"Whaddap, old man?" Vinnie's voice boomed over the phone and I almost dropped it.

"Didn't Nikki tell you?"

"Nope. She just hopped in here saying you wanted to speak to me." There was a slight pause. "What were you supposed to tell me, punk?"

Another short pause ended with an audible sigh. "I think Steve has been kidnapped."

"And you phoned the old man?"

"I didn't." Her voice rose in indignation. "I phoned Doc G. Manny made her put me on speakerphone."

I sighed. Working with people was extremely taxing. I didn't want this to become a full-blown argument, ending in a lot of screaming and slammed doors. I brought the phone closer to my mouth. "Nikki, you are an astute young woman. Are you sure your concern for Steve is not borne from the unfolding events, that you might be drawing incorrect conclusions?"

"I thought about this like really hard before I phoned you. Steve has never been late for a single study session with Rebecca. It's sometimes his only social contact in a week. He's like a really nice guy, Doc G." Her voice gained a thickness associated with tears. She cleared her throat. "Rebecca went to his apartment when he didn't show at the library, and he wasn't there. He never goes anywhere. He does all his shopping online and gets it delivered to his apartment. His only outings are to the library to study with Rebecca."

"He sounds agoraphobic."

"No, no. He isn't scared of spiders." A slapping sound made me wonder if she had slapped her forehead again. "Sorry, you weren't talking about arachnophobia."

A sudden concern made me pull the phone even closer. "Where is Rebecca?"

"Um… I asked her to come here. I hope that's okay. I didn't want her to disappear as well. I promise we'll be, like, totally quiet."

"Good thinking, punk," Vinnie said. "You'll both be safe here."

I could no longer bear sitting in this beautiful garden with Maxie resting her head on my lap, watching me unblinkingly. "Nikki, I'm leaving now. I'll be in the office soon and we'll find Michael and Steve."

"Oh, my God! Michael! We need to find him too, Doc G."

Regret was like a belt tightening around my chest. I had just added to Nikki's distress with my thoughtless comment. I stared at the phone, not knowing how to remedy what I'd done. Colin got up and took the phone from my hand. He winked at me, tapped the screen and walked towards his SUV, talking to Nikki in a calming tone. He would know what to say to her.

"I'll be back tomorrow afternoon with the files." The wariness on Judith's face had been replaced by determination. Nikki's anxiety must have also affected her. "When I get back you can catch me up on the case. But then I expect to be given the full picture."

Maxie nudged my hand for more attention. It was all becoming too much for me to process. I needed to be in my office. I needed to be clean. I needed to observe Nikki and assure myself that she was handling this emotional situation adequately. With the tip of my index finger, I pushed Maxie's head off my lap and looked at Judith. "Can you show me to your washroom, please?"

Five minutes later, it took an almost insurmountable amount of willpower to leave the neat, white washroom to join Colin at the SUV. I'd washed my hands under scorching hot water, then my forearms, and had to write another three bars of Mozart's Symphony No.40 in G minor to stop there. The desperation to be clean of Maxie's hair and germs was fast overwhelming me. At the SUV, everyone had already said their farewells and soon we were on the way back to the office.

"I need to shower. Take me home first." I pulled my linen pants away from my legs, the thought of dust and other dirt from Maxie's pelt reaching my skin inducing panic. "I won't be long. I can't work if I'm contaminated."

Pink snorted and Colin took his eyes off the road to stare at me in surprise. "You're not contaminated, Jenny. It's just a bit of doggie-love."

"There is no such thing. And if there were, I wouldn't want it all over me. Take me home."

"If being clean is going to help you find those kids, Doc, then we'd better go to your apartment first." Manny leaned to the side to catch Colin's eye in the rear-view mirror. "Get supermodel on the horn for us, will you?"

The rest of the twenty-minute journey to my apartment was in conversation with Francine and Vinnie. New keywords for searches were decided on and different approaches to the case discussed. When Francine started sharing her absurdly improbable theories, I closed my eyes and allowed Mozart to calm my mind. With all the data that was coming in, there was a lingering connection that stayed out of reach. Much to my frustration.

When I walked into Rousseau & Rousseau an hour later, I felt refreshed in body and mind. My linen pants and blouse were sealed in two plastic bags and in the rubbish bin in the kitchen. My skin was still tingling from the hot shower, and I was comfortable in my jeans, t shirt and sandals. Colin was still in disguise and was walking beside me. Pink was in the conference room.

As soon as we entered the team room, Nikki jumped up from where she was sitting on the floor and ran to me. I braced myself, knowing what was coming and how important it was to her.

She threw her arms around me and tucked her face into my neck. Her breathing was erratic, her muscle tension worrisome. I switched on the Mozart Symphony I'd been mentally writing and put my arms around her. She responded by holding me even tighter, a shudder shaking her slim body.

We stood like that for more than a minute until she slowly relaxed in my arms. Dealing with this young woman's need for me and the distressing physical closeness was stretching my control to its limits. Therefore, I chose to ignore the silence in the room as everyone watched us.

Nikki's arms relaxed around me and she lifted her head to look at me. "Thank you." She stepped away from me and straightened her shoulders. "You remember Rebecca, right?"

I looked at the young woman sitting at the table. In front of her were a small tub of ice cream, hamburger wrappers and an empty orange juice bottle. She got up and smiled. It was a social smile. She played with her watch, caught herself and gripped one hand with the other. "Hi, Doc G."

"Hello, Rebecca." I glanced at Vinnie. "Is he making you nervous?"

"What? Him? No!"

Nikki bumped me with her shoulder. "You are."

"Oh." I understood that. I made many people nervous. I shrugged. "You don't have to be nervous here, Rebecca. You're safe."

"I know," she said softly.

"Do your parents know you're with us?"

"My parents?" She looked at Nikki, a frown pulling her eyebrows together.

"Rebecca's parents live in Toulouse, Doc G." Nikki left my side to stand next to Rebecca. "She's at the university on scholarship and doing so much better than me. Her parents have a small farm outside the city where they grow strawberries. Rebecca is the first in their family to go to university."

"Your parents must be very proud," Phillip said from the door. I wasn't surprised to see him in the office at this hour. I was, however, surprised at the pride he exhibited for Rebecca's achievements.

"They are. That's why I don't want them to worry." She played with her watch again. "I didn't tell them about the kidnapped student in Paris or Michael or Steve. I just hope this will go away soon, so I can phone them."

"Why can't you phone them now?" I asked.

Rebecca made a sound of disbelief. "My mom will immediately know something's wrong. It's like she has some supernatural Spidey sense. I'm sure she would be able to diagnose me with appendicitis just from hearing me say 'hello'."

"Your mother most likely knows the different levels of tension and frequencies in your voice. I can say with confidence that she does not have a Spidey sense, since nothing like that exists."

Everyone laughed and I realised I'd misinterpreted something Rebecca had said. At least the tension in the room was no longer so clearly expressed in everyone's body language.

"Ladies, why don't you come with me and I'll set you up in the conference room." Phillip lowered his voice as if telling Nikki and Rebecca a secret. "We have a state-of-the-art multimedia system and I'm sure Tim can get a movie or two to play on it. If you want, we can send him for some popcorn as well."

Both young women relaxed and smiled. Phillip led them out of the room and down the hall, discussing the different films they could choose from. The girls were talking about a romantic comedy and I suppressed a shudder. To worsen it, they insisted on the largest popcorn Tim could get them. It was at that part of the conversation that I turned to Francine. "What did you find out about this survey?"

"'Hi, Francine.' 'Oh! Hi, girlfriend. How are you?' 'I'm well, how are you, Francine, my best friend?' 'I'm fantastic, thank you for asking.'" Francine sometimes went into such a monologue when I was extraordinarily brusque. There was no sign of anger or hurt on her face, only amusement. As usual. "'So what do you have for me, my bestest friend?' 'Oh, you won't believe what I found, bestie. This survey was done via internet. It involved more than four hundred universities across all the EU member states, and over six hundred thousand students. Cool, huh?'"

I made sure she was looking at me so she would see my sincere expression when I said, "Thank you."

"No biggie. But there's so much more. The main aim of this survey is to determine the susceptibility of students to succumb to excessive alcohol consumption and drug use. It is the largest such study ever done. They also want to know if the students would progress from drugs to a life of crime, even petty crimes like theft, plagiarism, buying exam papers, hacking into the university servers and changing their grades. Stuff like that.

"The survey has found that international or displaced students are the ones with the most ambition, the least likely to give in to peer pressure and the most likely to succeed. Their families usually sacrifice a lot to give them a better future. They see the value in what's being given to them and don't want to waste such a once-in-a-lifetime opportunity. The same counts for students coming from disadvantaged backgrounds and studying on grants. They're working especially hard to get themselves out of the lives they've been born into."

"How long did this study last?" I asked.

"Oh, it's still ongoing. It's now been five years, but they're constantly updating their data. Since most courses are four years long, they closed the first group a year ago. This year will be their second graduating group. I get the sense that they might be following-up even after graduation."

"Is the study anonymous?"

"Yes, but only on the surface. The students aren't required to give their names, but they have to log in with their student IDs, which is as good as giving their names. They are also asked to volunteer their email addresses for follow-up. Like most young people in today's digital age, these sweet little angels are all far too open and generous with their personal details. More than eighty percent gave their email addresses."

I didn't want to ask my next question. I took a deep breath. "Did any of the twenty-two missing students give their email addresses?"

"All of them." All light-heartedness disappeared as Francine's lips thinned.

"Michael and Steve?"

Francine nodded stiffly.

"Holy frigging hell. I did not see that one coming." Manny rubbed his hands hard over his face. "Okay, so now we know where this arsehole is harvesting his victims from. Do we know who's been looking at those contact details?"

"The pool is too big," Francine said. "The survey was outsourced. That means the people working for the company who did the survey, plus loads of Interpol employees and probably a few others have had access to this data. I'm sorry, handsome, but it's really impossible to determine anything by looking at whoever accessed that info."

"Which company did the survey?" I asked.

"GDD Security Industries. I checked them out and they came out clean. There was nothing spectacular about them." She stopped when she noticed Manny staring at her. They continued looking at each other until Francine threw her hands in the air. "Fine. I'll look deeper into them. But only because you asked so nicely. I better dig up some juicy scandal."

Vinnie had been observing everything from the far side of the round table. He exhibited special enjoyment every time Francine irritated Manny. I turned towards him. "Nikki said you'd been phoning around to find out if anyone knows anything about the kidnappings. Did you get any useful information?"

"Actually, I'd been asking to buy some... well, some company, someone to have fun with. And I'm not talking about paying per hour." He tried to maintain a look of apathy, but I noticed the micro-expressions of disgust. It mirrored the expressions of everyone else in the room. "It is not as uncommon as one would think. I reckoned that if someone could sell me a sex slave, they might know where I could buy body parts. Most of the people I spoke to suggested I just go and choose someone off the street and take her home."

"That's... That's..." Francine wrapped her arms tightly around her waist. "I don't have words for that level of low, scumbag, mud-sucking, cruel—"

"I agree, supermodel."

"I insisted that I wanted someone clean." Vinnie shrugged when he saw my raised eyebrows. "I remembered all the health and medical details about Matthieu on the auction site and used them to narrow the search down to something that might bring us closer to that ZD asswipe."

"Did you get something useful?" Colin asked.

"Two people told me they'll phone me back, but I'm not holding my breath."

I knew very little about Vinnie's childhood and still had not found the appropriate moment to ask him about the large disfiguring scar running down the side of his face. The few times he'd been without a shirt, I'd looked at that scar continuing down his torso and wondered who could have done that to him.

He had always been quite open about his criminal past, which gave him the many contacts he still had. He worked hard maintaining the trust and favour of many notorious criminals. From a few hints, I'd come to the conclusion that Interpol had full knowledge of his work and these relationships. I knew he would be able to help me with the new idea that had burst into my mind.

"Vinnie, I'm going to need your help to work through some data."

Vinnie's eyes widened in surprise. "Sure, Jen-girl. I don't know if or how I can help, but I'll try. I'm not all that smart."

"That's a lie. You have a slightly above average IQ, but your ability to assess information and reach viable conclusions is far above average."

"Wow." Vinnie's chest puffed out. "Y'all hear that? I'm a genius."

"I didn't say th…" I sighed. The look I gave him had him chuckling as he followed me into my viewing room.

"Jenny." Colin walked up to me, his expression sombre. "I'm going to try again to find Maurice. It's been three days and I'm very concerned. He's not one to disappear or get caught by surprise. I'm also going to see if I can find anything else about Michael and Steve."

I lifted my hand to touch him, then dropped it. "I don't want you to go. You know what Dukwicz said."

"I know, love. But no one else is looking for these people. And I'm in disguise. I'll be very careful." He took my hand and kissed my knuckles. "Also, Pink is coming along again."

It was hard to let go of his hand and watch him leave the room. Vinnie had taken Colin's chair next to mine and waited for me to join him. I needed to do something to take my mind from the intense worry about Colin's safety. A minute later I had my computer running and I opened to the second auction site. That was when I realised my skills were too limited. "Francine?"

"Yes, hon?"

"Could you come in here and help us?"

"Of course." A chair creaked and her bracelets jingled as she walked into my room. "What do you need?"

"Sit down. This might take a while."

"Yes, ma'am." She pulled the third chair closer and sat on my other side. Both of them kept a comfortable distance so that I didn't feel crowded. I appreciated it. "Ooh. You're back on the auction site. What are we doing?"

"I want to go into each bidder's profile and look at their history." I turned to Vinnie. "You must see if anything in those profiles reminds you of someone of your acquaintance."

"Like what?" he asked.

I turned back to Francine. "Could you go to the first person's profile?"

"Sure thing." She pulled my keyboard and mouse closer and started working. I breathed through my need to grab back my equipment and arrange it in its carefully chosen places. It took a few minutes before Francine nodded. "Hmm. For someone crawling around the dark net, he's not very secretive. His profile doesn't give us any identity, but it shows us that he has a shop on SSS. We can see what he's selling and also what he's recommending."

"What do you want me to look for, Jen-girl?" Vinnie was squinting at the monitors. "This dude is selling some hardcore ammo."

"You know the business of your acquaintances, right?"

"Right." His facial muscles relaxed. "Aha. You want me to look at these profiles and see if I can put a name to the selection of products on offer—same as what they sell on the street. Smart. Very smart. You're the real genius, Jen-girl."

"Just look at this profile."

"Yes, ma'am." He winked at Francine, then became serious. To the casual observer, he would look disinterested— lounging in the chair, his head tilted to one side, looking at each page without much change in his expression. I knew he was focussed, analysing each item offered and building a profile. When the corners of his mouth turned down and he shook his head, I knew he hadn't connected the first bidder to anyone he knew.

It took us three hours to meticulously work through eleven profiles. I felt sickened by the weapons, sex, pornography and many other illicit products and services for sale. Francine and Vinnie had stopped bantering more than an hour ago. We were quietly working through the ninth profile when Vinnie tensed. "Go back to the previous page."

Francine glanced at Vinnie before she did as he'd asked. I stared at the items, trying to see what Vinnie might have recognised. On the page were hunting rifles, ammunition in quantities I was sure were illegal, telescopes and night vision equipment.

"Do you know who this might be?" I asked. "Does he have a hunting business?"

Vinnie's *masseter* muscles tightened, his jaw stiff when he breathed heavily through his nose. He took out his smartphone, swiped a few times and put it against his ear.

"Frank, you ugly bastard, how are you?" Vinnie leaned forward and stared at the carpet between his feet. "Oh, you know, I've been around… Yup… Haha, no, I'm not going to date your sister. Your mother, well, that's another… Yes, you're a motherfucking SOB too… Hmm. Man, I was jonesing for some fun and thought of Jonas. Is he still hosting his games?… No? Damn, that's a pity. I was in the mood for a good hunt, ya know… Oh, really?… That's fucking A, man… Yeah, yeah, I will. You too. And tell your mom I say hi… Yeah, fuck you too."

He finished the call and dropped his head into his hands. After a few seconds, I couldn't stand it anymore. "Vinnie?"

He heaved a deep sigh and sat up. "Francine, go to deerheadlights dot onion."

Vinnie's movements had become jerky from the tension in his muscles. On the centre monitor a website opened on a home page that immediately caused my *corrugator supercilii* muscles to pull my brows together. It had the same analogue clock as the auction website. This one was set for four hours after the auction. Francine moved the cursor over the clock and a drop-down menu appeared.

"Oh, my God." Francine's whisper was loud in the room. She clicked on a subpage, which opened to a gallery of videos. Dark panic entered my peripheral vision as I looked at the still frames from each video. I didn't have to watch them to know what they were. They were evidence of the worst of humanity.

Chapter EIGHTEEN

"Manny!" There was a note of hysteria in Francine's voice as she turned to the door and called again.

The sound of running preceded Manny as he rushed into my viewing room. His facial muscles were tight with concern. And fear. "What's wrong?"

Francine pointed at the monitors displaying a gallery of videos. Vinnie had crossed his arms, his hands in tight fists. I had to focus on their nonverbal cues if I was going to keep the darkness at bay.

"Is this what I think it is?" Manny stepped closer. "One of you better bloody answer me soon."

His angry order had an oddly calming effect on us. Vinnie told him about our search through the profiles of bidders for the second auction. "Jen-girl's plan worked. When I saw these guns, ammo and gear, I thought of Jonas. He used to organise hunting trips, but not the kind of hunting trips normal people go on."

"Normal people don't hunt innocent animals and take pleasure in it, Vin. It's barbaric." Francine's skin was returning to its normal colour. She seemed more composed, unlike me.

"It's in our nature to hunt." I grabbed onto the topic to take my mind off the monitor for a few seconds. "Nowadays we no longer need to hunt down our food. As a species we've become quite lazy in our comfortable, civilised living. Not that it should be considered a negative aspect of our development. Knowing that we can get our meals or the ingredients for our meals from a shop allows us to focus on a higher level of growth."

"Doc." Manny's tone was gentle, his expression the same.

I pulled my legs onto the chair and wrapped my arms around my knees. I nodded tightly for them to continue. I didn't want to derail the conversation any more. I hated when they did it. Now I was doing the very same thing.

Vinnie put his hand on the armrest of my chair, not touching me but offering comfort. I stared at his hand and nodded again. He cleared his throat. "When I knew Jonas four, five years ago, he was organising hunting trips for individuals who wanted to hunt people. He got his prey from the streets. They were mostly military vets who were homeless and traumatised from their tours in Iraq and elsewhere. They couldn't get back into civilian life. He reckoned these guys made better prey, because they knew how to evade the enemy. It made for a better, more challenging hunting experience."

"Fucking hell." Manny's eyes were wide.

"Here's the kicker though. During the time I was hanging out with Hawk, Jonas and Dukwicz were friendly. I saw them chatting a few times in Hawk's warehouse."

Hawk was Nikki's late father—a criminal Dukwicz had killed. He had then tried to frame Colin for the murder. Despite his professional life, Hawk had been Vinnie's friend.

"Were Jonas and Dukwicz close friends?" My voice was hoarse from tension.

"No, they were only friendly. I don't think they ever spent time together outside of the job."

"And you think this Jonas has hooked up with Dukwicz to auction these kids for hunting?" Manny asked.

"Think about it. They are needed for their organs. The only reason doctors won't accept your organs is if you have HIV. That gives these bastards the opportunity to chase the kids around some warehouse or some forest and wound them in strategic places, not damaging any organs. Until they kill them."

"They won't kill them." I couldn't believe I was having this conversation. "They would keep the young people alive to preserve the organs for as long as possible. This means ZD is profiting twice from kidnapping socially isolated young people. Selling their organs and having them hunted down. This is very disturbing."

"That's being polite about it, girlfriend." Francine's nostrils flared, her lips thinning. "ZD and whichever other buttwipe is doing this are sick, truly sick in their souls."

I hugged my knees tighter. I had nothing to add to Francine's unprofessional assessment. She was right. We were quiet for a few seconds, nobody's expressions communicating positive emotions.

"I don't think any of us want to watch the videos, but they might give us some idea of where these kids were hunted," Manny said quietly.

I looked at the gallery of videos. At the bottom of the page it indicated that there were another three pages of videos. This one had ten videos, which led me to believe there had to be between thirty and forty videos on this site. Was that how many young people had been hunted down and then carved up? Manny was right. I didn't want to watch this twisted brutality, but knew there could be valuable information in it.

I took three deep breaths and lowered my legs to the floor. I'd had decades to master the art of dissociation. Now might be the most appropriate time ever to attempt viewing the footage objectively. Being honest with myself, I didn't think it was possible. "Francine, can you find the most recent video?"

"Let me see." She clicked on the first two rows of videos

before she returned to the very first one. "The metadata on this shows that it was taken seven days ago."

Vinnie muttered a few swearwords. "We need stiff drinks for this."

"It will impair your ability to see nuances and other key factors. Although I also feel the need for alcoholic courage." I tried to smile, but wasn't able to. I could anticipate the body language I was about to witness on these videos. It was not going to give me any pleasure to observe.

Francine clicked on the video and a view of a densely wooded area filled the screen. It was a beautiful area, in full summer bloom. The many trees casting the ground in shade made it impossible to determine the time of day. If this had been taken recently and locally, the summer days starting at half past five in the morning and ending at half past nine in the evenings would further complicate determining the time.

"Let the games begin," a male voice said, sounding very close to the camera. I shuddered at the arousal in his tone. Further thought on this deviance was drawn away by movement coming from the left of the screen. A man was running away from the camera. When he turned his head, all four of us gasped.

"Oh, my God." Francine's hand flew to her throat, covering her suprasternal notch.

"Matthieu Jean," I said unnecessarily. We'd all recognised the young man who was cradling his right arm against his chest. With the exception of the sneakers, he was dressed only in sweatpants—like in the auction video. I imagined the addition of footwear was to lengthen the hunt. Someone with damaged feet couldn't run fast or long enough.

"Run, Forrest! Run!" the voice shouted and laughed when Matthieu stumbled. The footage started bobbing as the hunter followed Matthieu through the woods.

The movement came to a sudden halt. Before I could register the barrel of a rifle entering the screen, a loud shot sounded through my viewing room. I jumped in my chair and pulled my legs up to hug against my chest. I forced the Mozart Symphony into my mind to keep myself from giving in to the tempting warm safety of a shutdown.

"Fuck!" Vinnie had both his fists resting on his head, pressing into his skull.

Matthieu stumbled, his uninjured hand letting go of his arm and holding his side.

"They must be shooting with rubber bullets," Vinnie said through his teeth. "The wound is not bleeding."

When Matthieu lifted his hand, the skin on his side was a deep red and it was clear he was feeling the pain. His speed had diminished and he was favouring the side where he'd been shot. I hated seeing his shoulders lowering, his head hanging. Those were signs of resignation. I didn't want him to give up running, fighting for his life.

Another shot sounded through the system. This time Matthieu's hand went to his hamstring. He didn't stop moving, but was dragging his leg. As his injuries and fatigue were worsening, his desire to run was lessening.

"Come on." The hunter sounded disappointed. "Give me at least another ten minutes. A good ten minutes."

Matthieu gave him twenty. It was an agonising twenty minutes, watching Matthieu fall, get up, stumble over fallen trees, running behind thicker tree trunks for protection and getting shot over and over again. The hunter's breathing didn't even increase over the microphone. He continued to bait Matthieu, laughing cruelly when Matthieu begged him to stop, to let him go home.

"It's time," a new voice said. It was a deep male voice, but had spoken too softly to recognise. Again, the camera stopped moving. The barrel appearing was not the same one that had been used to shoot rubber bullets at Matthieu the previous seven times. The hunter took aim and I cringed in anticipation of the sound. It was a softer pop. Whatever the hunter shot Matthieu with hit the young man in his back. Had it been a real bullet, it would have been a heart shot.

Matthieu managed to take another three steps before he dropped to the ground as if dead. The video's sound exploded in distorted whoops of celebration as the hunter ran to Matthieu. The camera was moved down to focus on the bruised and scratched body lying on the ground. When the hunter's brown boot came into view and rested on Matthieu's back, I closed my eyes. This atrocity was inhuman.

"We have an hour to get him to base," the second voice on the video said. "Let's get…"

The video ended abruptly, filling my viewing room with silence.

"They're worse than animals," Colin said hoarsely from behind us. He was standing in the doorway, his hands deep in his trouser pockets. He was wearing his own clothes again. He slowly moved his eyes from the video and looked at me. The *orbicularis oculi* muscles contracted around his eyes, his concern evident. He walked to me and cupped my face. "Are you okay?"

"No." I only managed a whisper.

He leaned over and kissed me lightly on my forehead. He straightened, his posture more aggressive. "Vin?"

"Dude, they're using the second auction to fucking bid on hunting down these kids." For the next minute, Vinnie swore colourfully. Knowing that it was a coping method for him, and also a way to release his anger, I didn't comment.

"We need to find these bastards," Manny said. "This cannot continue. We're living in bloody France, for Pete's sake. This is supposed to be civilised Europe."

"And we know how much slavery there is in France alone." Again facts helped me focus. I breathed deeply a few times. "What is our next step? How are we going to find them?"

"I will see if I can get into this site and find its location," Francine said. "I'm still waiting for ZD to respond to my email. He's smart. I've not been able to hack into his website yet, but I will. I'll find a backdoor into his sick little world and we'll put the full apocalypse on his ass."

"Well, since the clock is literally ticking, we'd better get to work." Manny looked at me. "Doc, someone needs to watch these videos and find some clues here. Are you up for it?"

With great conscious effort, I lowered my legs to the floor and straightened my shoulders. "I'll see what I can find in the footage."

"Frey, help her with that." He walked towards the door. "People, we're not going to be sleeping soon. That clock is someone's life. God help us all, I don't want to see another video like the one I've just seen. Not if we can prevent it."

A ringtone coming from Colin's pocket stopped Manny's progress. Colin took out his phone and narrowed his eyes at the screen before he swiped it. "Yes?"

The sudden frown of sorrow lowering Colin's brow had me studying him closer. He was listening intently. After a few seconds, his face lost colour, his sorrow increased. Someone had died. Someone he'd known. He ended the call after requesting updates as they came in.

"Who?" I asked when he didn't speak.

"Maurice." He briefly pressed the heels of his hands against his eyes. I almost flinched at his stark expression when he looked at me. "I can't believe this. I looked everywhere for him, then I called in a few favours. I didn't want to raise any suspicion, but I wanted to check the hospitals and morgues for someone fitting his description."

"They found him," Manny said.

"In a morgue. He was found in a back alley somewhere. My contact says the police think he was dumped there. His injuries look like they come from two incidents. The one that killed him was most likely from being hit by a car. He has all the classic injuries from blunt-force trauma caused by a moving vehicle. But he also has seventeen unexplained bruises all over his body." Colin stared at the monitors. "From the description, it sounds like it could be the same kind of injuries Matthieu got from being shot with rubber bullets."

"He was also hunted?" Vinnie asked.

I had trouble aligning this with the other data of the case. "He doesn't fit the profile. He's too old and he's socially active."

"True, but he was the one who got us arrested." Colin paused. "He's quite central in this case. He's connected to my arrest as well as the paintings, which are connected to the Tor site and ZD's auction site. I knew Maurice for eight years. He was an artist at heart. A greedy artist, but an artist. He was only interested in selling art, whether it was above board or not. I wonder if he didn't maybe see how he was being used by this client, made some connection and asked questions to the wrong person."

"Hell." Manny looked at the monitors and shook his head. "This needs to end."

"Um… excuse me?" Tim was standing behind Manny in the team room. I was surprised to see him here. It was close to midnight and I had never seen Tim stay this late after hours.

He must have gone home, because he was dressed much more informally in calf-length pants and a brightly coloured shirt. "There's a man in the conference room asking to meet with you, Colonel Millard."

Vinnie jumped up from the chair. "You put a strange man in the conference room with Nikki and Rebecca?"

Tim rolled his eyes. He didn't move or change his body language, despite being faced by two aggressive alpha males. "No. As you know, we have more than one conference room. He's in the small conference room and he isn't a complete stranger. He introduced himself."

"Who the holy hell wants to speak to me in the middle of the night?"

"He said his name is Laurence Gasquet and that you know him."

"He's here?" Manny turned to Francine. "Is that room rigged to record video?"

"I'll have it recording before you get there."

"Good. Let's hope he gives us something useful." Manny followed Tim out the room, suggesting that Tim should ask for a salary increase so he could buy new pants. No one should wear their childhood pants they'd outgrown.

"Okay, darlings." Francine stood up, a bit slower than usual. She was tired, but I suspected it was more from the emotional cost of this case than a lack of sleep. "I have loads of work to do. If anyone needs me, I'll be in my basement."

"Wait." Colin reached into his pants pocket. "I have something for you."

He took out a cell phone and gave it to Francine.

"Whose is this?"

"Maurice's. I broke into his loft apartment when I couldn't find him anywhere. Someone's already been through it, but they missed the safe built in under the sofa. I thought you might get something off it."

"Done. Was there anything else of interest in that safe?"

"A few documents and contracts, but nothing that might help us here."

"Okay, I'll get on this now."

"We need to watch the other videos." I empathised with Vinnie's swearing and Colin's groan. "We don't have a choice. It might give us insight into who is organising this, which might help us find the location."

"And hopefully Michael and Steve," Colin said.

Vinnie cursed again before he sat in the chair Francine had vacated. "Let's do this, Jen-girl."

The next six hours were possibly the most difficult in my life. My well-honed skill of dissociation failed me. There were thirty-eight videos, of which thirteen were of young women. Their terror—male and female—their facial expressions and desperate pleas to stay alive kept the darkness of a full shutdown hovering at the edges of my peripheral vision at all times.

As much as I wanted to, I didn't turn off the sound. It was important to listen to the voices in case we could identify one of the hunters. The second voice I'd heard on the video of Matthieu was in every other video. The first six videos revealed nothing about the hunters or the second voice. It was at the end of the seventh video when I heard it. The second voice's accent had slipped.

"Dukwicz." The name came out as a breathless whisper.

"Son of a bitch." Vinnie leaned forward and glared at the monitor. "You're right, Jen-girl."

"Can't say I'm surprised," Colin said. "He's been in and out of this case from the beginning."

The next video confirmed his identity. Dukwicz was the guide, sometimes suggesting a better route to cut off the 'prey', as he called them. Mostly, he was quiet throughout the hunts. Only at the very end would he make sure the shot was well-placed and that they were quick about getting the young person back to 'base'.

Twenty-eight of the thirty-eight videos were taken at night in eerie green shadows. Despite the many videos, it remained impossible to determine the location. Each hunt started at a different place and followed a unique path through the woods. Lacking the necessary knowledge, I could only identify three different trees commonly found all across Europe.

"I feel sick to my stomach," Vinnie said as we finished watching the last video. I agreed. I didn't know how many Mozart concertos, symphonies and possibly operas I was going to have to work through to clear the images burned into my memory.

"But how are we going to find out their involvement?" Vinnie pointed at the monitor.

"Whose involvement?" My mind had drifted to choosing the best Mozart composition to start dealing with this.

"Breton and Hugo." Colin pointed his chin towards the door. "And Laurence Gasquet."

"We need more data on them." More than the glowing personnel files Interpol had on them. "Francine is busy enough. Vinnie, could you find out if there are any rumours about them in your circles?"

"Sure can do, Jen-girl." He got up and took his phone from his pocket. "Let me start making calls."

"We should look at news archives," Colin said. "Despite Google's agreement to remove details if a person requests it, most newspapers keep all their articles archived and available."

He'd suggested the exact line of research I had thought to follow. We started with the larger news agencies and worked our way down to the smaller, more local newspapers. It didn't take very long.

"How is it possible that neither name is mentioned anywhere?" Colin raised both hands, palms up.

"They were mentioned twice."

"Yeah, in cases of absolutely no interest and because they were such good agents." His tone and facial expression unmistakeably contradicted the compliment.

I wondered if Manny, Vinnie and Francine had been more successful. Not once in the last twelve hours had I forgotten about the analogue clocks on the two auction sites. We were running out of time. No amount of rationalisation would be able to prevent me from being overwhelmed by guilt if we failed to stop the auctions and save the life of the next victim.

"Where's the criminal?" Manny asked from the door. His newly acquired outfit was rumpled, the stubble on his chin thicker and the shadows around his eyes darker.

"I don't know," I said. "What did you learn from Laurence Gasquet?"

"That he's an arsehole." Manny rubbed his face. "Get the criminal and supermodel in here. We need to debrief, regroup and speed up. We only have four hours until the next auction."

Chapter NINETEEN

"You sure this is enough food?" Vinnie scratched his head as he looked at the two serving plates and three bread baskets in the centre of the round table. One basket was heaped with fresh croissants, another with different types of bread rolls and the third with pastries. One serving plate had an overflowing selection of fruits, the other of tubs of yogurt.

Tim put down a second pot of coffee and frowned. "I can always get more."

"That will not be necessary, Tim. Thank you." Phillip reached for the coffeepot and started pouring for everyone except Manny, who had his milky tea in front of him. "You've outdone yourself so early in the morning."

I agreed. At seven minutes past six, I was surprised that Tim had been able to find so many freshly baked goods. Tim had disappeared for a few hours and had returned dressed in his office attire, carrying bags of shopping. Phillip came in a few minutes after him, looking fresh and rested. As usual.

Francine had also changed her outfit, looking as if she'd also had a shower. I wondered what other alterations had been made to her basement. Despite the dark circles under her eyes, which she had tried to camouflage with makeup, she was the only other person who looked rested. I hadn't spared the time to look at myself in the mirror. A wise choice if I recalled previous all-night investigations.

"Okay, people." Manny put a croissant and a sweet pastry on his plate. "We have less than four hours before the first auction starts. Let's pool our info."

"Did you discover anything useful from your conversation with Laurence Gasquet?" I forced myself to take a few strawberries and a natural yogurt. This case had affected my appetite.

"Well, I know Gasquet really wants to get Edward Taylor out of the way."

"What does that mean?" I asked. "Does he want to kill Colin's pseudonym?"

Manny broke the croissant in half. "The way he was talking about Taylor, I got the impression he wanted him dead, not arrested."

"Why?" Colin raised both shoulders. "I have no idea who this man is. What have I ever done to him?"

"He didn't say," Manny answered. "But he did suggest that there is an underground website selling illegal art that he suspects you are running. Not that he actually said that. It was all roundabout-like."

"Maybe we should look at the recording." I turned to Colin. "You can look at this man, his mannerisms and his speech. Maybe you have met him before, but he was disguised. Maybe it was many years ago."

"Sure. If I've met him, I'll remember his face."

Francine pushed a whole strawberry into her mouth, somehow making the action look very sexual. She wiped her fingers on a serviette and picked her tablet up from next to her plate. I wondered if she slept with it under her pillow like Nikki did with her smartphone. A second later the large screen came to life, giving us a full-colour downward view of the smaller conference room.

"Fast-forward through the first few minutes, supermodel. It was small talk." Manny took a cookie and dipped it in his tea.

I shuddered. The thought of crumbs floating to the bottom of the cup, creating a disgusting sediment, appalled me.

I looked at the screen, determined to focus on something I understood. Francine had set the speed at three times faster and I watched as Manny shook Gasquet's hand in a cartoon-like manner. They sat down across from each other. Manny was slouching in the chair, his hands pushed deep into his pockets.

Gasquet rested one ankle on his other knee, hooked an arm around the back of the chair and puffed out his chest. He was posturing. His hair was completely shaved off in what I suspected was an attempt to hide a receding hairline. Even seated it was easy to see how tall he was.

"Stop." I had seen one of Manny's hands fist in his pocket. I wanted to know what had caused that. "Go back a few seconds."

Francine took us back and played the video at normal speed. Gasquet's voice was measured, as if he didn't care. "It's just a pet project for me. Taylor has been running around France creating chaos for too long."

Onscreen, Manny's hand fisted in his pocket. "How long is too long?"

"My CI brought him to my attention a year ago. I suspect he's been at this for a lot longer."

"At what exactly?" Manny sounded bored and sceptical.

"Oh, my source is telling me that Taylor is into much more than just selling forged and stolen works of art."

"Stop," I said again. Francine did and everyone looked at me. "He's lying. Look at his eye movement, his blinking rate and the way he lifted one shoulder. People are able to control certain nonverbal cues when they lie, but not all of them at once. Very few accomplished liars have control over the feet, legs, arms, hands and facial features when they're lying. Even then, there are micro-expressions that only Botox can eliminate."

In a previous case, I'd seen a suspect use Botox to outwit me. He hadn't been successful. I'd had the rest of his body to read.

"We know he's lying, Doc. Frey is an arsehole, but he's not what Gasquet is accusing him of."

"Love you too, Millard." Colin raised his coffee mug to Manny before taking a sip.

I squinted, but Gasquet was sitting too far from the camera to confirm what I thought I'd seen. "Does Laurence Gasquet have complete heterochromia?"

"I don't know, Doc. He didn't sneeze once." Manny grunted. "What the hell is heterochronus?"

"Heterochromia is when each eye is a different colour."

"Ah. Yes. His left eye is green and his right eye is blue. Why is that important?"

I thought about this. "It isn't. It's just interesting."

We continued watching the video. Manny exhibited anger at many of the accusations Gasquet made, the only evidence of that his fist. At times it flexed, at others it pressed hard against his thigh. Since that part of his body was not in Gasquet's line of sight, I doubted the other man had noticed Manny's growing ire.

A lot of the conversation sounded like a marketing interview. Gasquet told Manny about all the successes of his security business and how he had all the resources at the tips of his fingers to catch Edward Taylor. Manny impressed me with his ability to deflect questions about our case. He successfully created the impression that we were equally interested in Edward Taylor and his illegal activities. This lie was believable since they were meeting in a high-end insurance company, known for investigations into forged art.

Throughout the fourteen-minute video, Colin watched quietly. Studying and analysing Gasquet's body language distracted me sufficiently to bring back my appetite. In addition to the yogurt and strawberries, I also had a banana and a muffin. The meeting finished and Francine stopped the video.

"Do you know him, Frey?"

Colin shook his head. "Never seen him before."

"Then how does he know you?"

Colin shrugged. "Gasquet is smooth—too smooth. He's too relaxed, too confident, too everything. He's off."

"The idiot thinks he's fooling everyone." Manny threw his napkin on the table. "His arrogance is going to be his downfall. Where do you think he got that sketch of you in disguise as Edward Taylor?"

At the nine-minute mark, Gasquet had said his CI had given him a sketch of Edward Taylor. Gasquet hadn't had the file with him, but had promised to email the sketch to Manny. He'd lied.

"Another question I don't have an answer for, Millard."

"I found you by going through hundreds of newspaper articles reporting the revealing of forged artwork, or the discovery of works thought lost in war or a heist." It had taken me days to read through all those articles. "Edward Taylor was in only one article and there was a photo of you. Well, not you. Edward Taylor."

"Good lord, Jenny. That photo was published… what? Six years ago?"

"Eight." I had found numerous seventeenth-century poets active over a period of eleven years, finding lost art. "It is a possibility that Gasquet saw the same photo and is calling that his sketch."

"What about his CI, Doc? This person has been giving him all this information on Taylor."

"It's not a CI." I remembered the look on Gasquet's face when he'd talked about his CI. "It is someone he knows. Someone he cares for."

"Which means I want to know everything about Gasquet. How many pairs of socks he owns, his favourite ice cream, what toothpaste he uses. Supermodel—"

"I'll get on it as soon as we're done here."

Something Colin had said previously came back to me. "You said you haven't used this disguise often. That should make it easier for you to think of who you met while in this disguise."

"Hmm. Let's see. Maurice is the one who saw this disguise first. It was only with him and his clients."

"Who were the clients?"

"René Faye, a real snake of a man." He counted on his fingers. "Martin Ferré, a brilliant artist who never got a lucky break and went into forgeries—really great forgeries. Armand Goll, who died eight years ago. Alain Labrie and Emile Rimbaud—"

"Emile Rimbaud." Manny tapped with his index finger on the table. "What are the odds of him showing up again?"

"The odds are favourable. Colin mentioned him before, when we spoke about his appearances as Edward Taylor in the last two years." What a silly observation. I organised my plate, cutlery and cup to be neatly aligned. "We need to find the connection between Monsieur Rimbaud and Laurence Gasquet. Or between Monsieur Rimbaud and Breton and Hugo."

For a few moments no one spoke. "Doc, what else did you see in that video? Not about me, but about Gasquet."

"He lied about the one-year timeline. It wasn't a year ago when he received that supposed sketch. It could be before or after that. I don't know. He also lied about his interest in Edward Taylor. It isn't about catching an art criminal. I don't know what his true motivation is, but that is not it. He also exhibited classic markers for narcissistic personality disorder. He sees himself as superior, despite his accomplishments, and expects constant adoration and admiration from others. From his boasting it was clear to deduce he is obsessed with being perceived as powerful, influential, intelligent and successful. You were right in saying that his arrogance will be his downfall. It blinded him to your lies. He believed them."

"I didn't lie, Doc. I just didn't tell him the whole truth."

I was thankful when Francine waved to get our attention. I'd had too many arguments already about the difference between a lie and an omission of truth.

"Okay. My turn." Her chin was lifted, her shoulders pushed back. "I got into ZD's website email. It's hugely encrypted, but I beat it. I got in. He's had that website for the last eighteen months. I looked back as far as I could, but didn't find one single personal thing. All the emails were communication with the winners of the auctions. In those emails, he requested a cell phone number. He said he'd SMS further instructions to them. Half of those idiots gave him traceable numbers."

"Brilliant." Manny's smile wasn't friendly. "We can prosecute them."

"Totally." Francine winked at him. "Just for granola and giggles, I checked out a few numbers and have names, addresses, everything. Why are they using Tor if they're not careful everywhere else? Never mind. The other half gave him numbers to untraceable disposable phones. I checked the traceable phones and co-ordinated them with the dates of the emails to look for ZD's phone. All I found was another untraceable number."

"He also used a burner phone," Vinnie said.

"How many emails have you read?" I asked. "How far into his email history?"

"I read the last eight months or so, but I'm not going to stop. If handsome hadn't dragged me in here for these wicked pastries, I'd still be working on that. Hopefully ZD mentioned something, somewhere that we might use to locate him."

"And we only have"—Manny looked at his watch—"three hours and twenty-five minutes left."

"That really doesn't leave much time." Phillip pushed away his plate. "Can't you ask for more help?"

"I've been ordered not to," Manny said. "I spoke to the Secretary-General at Interpol. I gave him a brief outline of what's going on, including the investigation into Edward Taylor."

"Is he one of the few who knows?" Phillip knew Colin's work for Interpol was known only by a few of the very top Interpol personnel.

"Yes. And he's also one of the few I would trust with a case like this. He's given me orders not to get any assistance from within Interpol. Not if Breton and Hugo are involved. He's aware of how favourably they're viewed and how well they're connected. And he wants me to give him a full debriefing over a secured line."

"I'll set it up in the conference room," Francine said. "The small one. The girls are still sleeping in the big one."

"You saw them?" I felt like cringing at forgetting about Nikki and Rebecca.

"I did. They had a Vin Diesel movie marathon last night and are recovering from it now."

"What is a Vin Diesel?"

Everyone laughed.

"Not a what, love. A who." Colin kissed my cheek. "He's an actor who mostly plays in action and science fiction movies."

"And he's gorgeous." Francine drew out the last word while pressing both palms against her chest. "Wouldn't mind getting me some of that."

"Where are they sleeping?" I wasn't interested in actors.

"Who? Oh, the girls." Francine lowered her hands. "Tim organised inflatable mattresses for them. It looks like a pyjama party in there. And smells like a movie theatre."

I shuddered, but was glad Nikki and her friend were comfortable. I returned my attention to the case at hand and asked Manny, "Did you tell the Secretary-General about Breton and Hugo's connection to Gasquet, Dukwicz and ZD?"

"I didn't go into details. We were on a secure line, but I don't trust these things anymore." Manny had had many arguments with Francine about smartphone security. Clearly she'd been winning those arguments. "That's why he wants a full debrief."

"Have you thought about contacting Daniel?" Vinnie asked. The bread basket closest to him was empty. He reached for the platter of pastries.

"I was going to ask you to do it since you're all buddy-buddy with them now."

"Will do. They should be on standby in case we locate Dukwicz and have the chance to get those kids out."

"I have loads of emails to work through." Francine got up. "What are you going to do now, girlfriend?"

"Sorry to interrupt, but there's another visitor in the small conference room." Tim stood at the door, a mug of coffee in his hand. "She said she came as soon as she could."

"Who are you talking about?" Manny got up.

"She said her name is Opal Luedke and that she came as early as possible."

"Ah." The tension in Manny's face lessened. "Doc, I think you should come with for this."

"Who's Opal Luedke?" Colin put his arm out to prevent me from getting up.

"Bloody hell. It feels like I haven't slept in a week." Manny rubbed his hand over his face. "I don't remember what I told you. After I spoke to Gasquet, I looked for someone who knew Emile Rimbaud. It was actually quite easy. Madame Luedke was old man Rimbaud's neighbour for almost forty years. She confirmed that he didn't have any family and agreed to come in and answer a few questions. Doc, I could really use your sharp eye."

I pushed Colin's arm away and stood up. He joined me. "I'm going with."

"Could you instead look for some more connections between those works of art?" I was surprised by his protective attitude.

"She's in her sixties, Frey. I'm sure she's not going to do anything to us." Manny shrugged. "And I'm there."

Colin snorted. "Like that's supposed to comfort me."

"You are comforted. You relaxed when Manny said it, so there's no need to agitate him."

Vinnie snorted and Francine laughed. Colin was not pleased with me. I walked past him and followed Manny to the small conference room. The woman sitting at the table sipping tea did not look to be in her sixties. Her dark hair was short and spiky, her complexion smooth. Only around her eyes were a few laughter lines, giving away her general humour.

"Madame Luedke." Manny's French was slightly accented, but perfect. He stepped closer and held out his hand. "Manfred Millard. Thank you for coming in."

"Oh, please." She waved both hands at Manny before shaking his right hand. "My English is still fabulous after a lifetime in this snobbish country. And please call me Opal. Even my grandkids call me Opal. Who are you, honey?"

I took a step back when she turned to me. This vivacious woman seemed too eager to touch me. Observing her nonverbal cues assured me that her intentions were simple friendliness. Her colourful skirt, top and the strings of beads around her neck fitted the hued personality I was witnessing. I forced myself to step towards her, but didn't hold out my hand. "I'm Genevieve Lenard."

"An English Genevieve." She leaned a little closer as if to impart very important information. "Personally, I prefer the English pronunciation. Makes the name much sexier."

I could see how people could easily like this woman. She was open, friendly and seemed to be without any artifice. I thought how well she and Francine would get along. Manny sat down across from Opal and I joined him.

"Thank you for coming in so early, Mada... Opal. This is of importance to us, so I really appreciate it." It was clear that Manny also liked this woman. He wasn't slouching as much as usual.

Opal took another sip of her tea. "Now tell me how I can help an insurance company in an emergency."

"We have a few questions about Emile Rimbaud."

"So you said over the phone. What do you want to know about that old hoarder?" She winked at me. "I swear to all that is holy, that man collected more junk in the last twenty years of his life than most people could in an entire lifetime."

"How well did you know Monsieur Rimbaud?" I asked, feeling comfortable enough to not mind interacting with this woman.

"We were neighbours for forty-two years. We knew about all the skeletons in each other's closets. And he had a big one." Her eyes crinkled when she noticed our interest. "You want gossip? Ooh, how delightful! Since he's pushing up daisies—the goddess bless his soul—I don't mind dishing."

"Please do." Manny's voice held a tone of amusement. I wondered if he also saw the resemblance to Francine.

Especially when Opal clapped her hands. "I love a good gossip session. Oh, where do I start? My Robert and I got that flat from Robert's parents as a wedding gift. You see, I got married quite young, not like the wiser young people today. But Robert was the love of my life, so it was a good choice. Anyway. Robbie was a doctor and working all kinds of crazy hours. One evening I had problems with the plumbing and that was how I met Emile. But he was totally useless with any kind of work involving tools. It was his lovely Adam who helped me."

"Who was Adam?" Manny asked.

"Adam Marot was Emile's partner. Mind you, no one ever knew they were gay. It was only after about two years of friendship that they told me what I'd already known. You two are too young to remember those days. You see, homosexuality was not something anyone wanted to be associated with. Emile didn't have any family, but his work as a city engineer was quite prestigious. He didn't want to lose his job and Adam understood."

"What did Adam do?"

A soft smile lifted her cheeks. "He was an artist through and through. He had the soul of a poet and painted the most amazing artworks. I still have two paintings that he made for me as birthday gifts. Such a kind soul. Emile was devastated when Adam died."

"What kind of paintings did Adam paint?" I couldn't keep the excitement from my voice.

"He was such a brilliant artist, yet he never painted his own stuff. He travelled the world, looking for original Courbets so he could copy them."

"Excuse me?" Manny leaned forward. "He painted Gustave Courbet paintings?"

"Yes. I think he must have painted more than fifty of the originals." She took another sip of her tea. "You see, Adam came from a very rich family. When he told them he was gay, they gave him two million francs and told him to never darken their door again. Adam liked living modestly with Emile. All he wanted to do was find original Courbets and paint them. That was what he used his money for. Too sad that money couldn't buy him a cure for cancer."

"When did he die?"

"It was Christmas Eve 1992. It was the saddest day in our lives, but it was so much worse for Emile. You see, Adam and Emile became each other's family. And in a way Robert and I were also part of that family, but they were each other's nucleus. Even when they took that child in, they were the strongest unit I'd seen."

"What child?" Manny was leaning forward again.

"I can never remember how that boy came to live on his own when he wasn't even eighteen. I do remember Emile and Adam having a seventeenth birthday party for him in 1975. It was three days before the birth of my youngest. You see, Robert and I never planned that youngest. She was quite a surprise to us, but what a delight she is. Today she is a neurosurgeon. Would you like to see photos?"

"Maybe later, Opal." Manny had difficulty remaining passive in his interest. I wondered if he felt half the excitement I did. My mind was racing with all the new connections. "Tell us more about this young boy. Do you remember his name?"

"Of course I do. Renzo was a huge part of Adam and Emile's lives. When he moved into the flat next to theirs, they took him in as if he was their own son. You see, they helped him get back to school and graduate. When he joined the military, they were as proud and as worried as if they were his biological fathers. Renzo was devastated when Adam died. He made sure Emile was well taken care of."

She sighed sadly. "But I think a big part of Emile died when Adam died. That was when he started hoarding. He refused to throw any of Adam's things out and wouldn't let Renzo even throw out newspapers."

"Do you know Renzo's surname?"

She tilted her head to the side, her eyes shifting up and to the left. "Oh, my. For the life of me. Oh dear. I think that might be a sign of aging. But he really loved Emile and Adam. He would visit with Emile for hours until his death. That was another sad day for us all."

I thought of the video we had watched earlier. "Can you describe him?"

"Of course, honey." She waved one hand in the air. "A really strapping tall man. He must be in his fifties now, but the last time I saw him, he was still as tall as a tree. What always got me was his eyes though. You see, there is something very interesting about people with one blue and one green eye."

Chapter **TWENTY**

"Oh, my God!" The shock on Francine's face resembled Manny's when Opal had told us about the heterochromia. He had rushed out of the small conference room and had come back with a screenshot of the interview video with Gasquet. She had positively identified him as Renzo, a name he'd used when he had been younger.

We were in the team room and Manny had just finished briefing everyone on the meeting with Opal Luedke. Francine was the only one sitting. I saw the same restlessness in Manny, Vinnie and Colin that I was feeling.

My mind was still reeling with all the smaller bits of information we'd collected thus far falling into place. I mentally played Mozart's Piano Concerto No. 20 in D minor and allowed the subdued sounds to soothe my mind as it sifted through everything we'd learned so far.

"So, Laurence Gasquet is kinda like Emile's godson?" Francine asked.

"Yes, and we had the bastard here."

"Aren't you going to arrest him?" Vinnie asked. "We should send Daniel's team out to find him."

"And on what grounds are we going to arrest him? Being a narcissist? We need concrete evidence to send out the troops." Manny rubbed his hand over his face. "Doc, we need more proof. We need paper trails, we need clear connections between Gasquet and this."

I looked at the large screen in the team room when he shook his index finger at it. On the screen was the clock counting down the minutes to the auction. There were two hours, seven minutes and thirty-nine seconds left. I swallowed at the tightness around my throat.

"What happened to all those paintings?" Colin asked. "I've seen three—no, four, if we're including the one from the day I was arrested. And Caelan saw fifteen at auction. That makes nineteen paintings. Madame Luedke said she saw more than fifty, right?"

"Apart from the one you saw in his apartment, the other paintings were put up for sale only after Monsieur Rimbaud died." I rubbed my temples. "Zana22Dactor3178 was the one putting those paintings up for sale. Can it be that Gasquet is ZD?"

"Of course!" Francine sat up and started working on her computer. "If I have more specific parameters, I can get much better search results."

Even though this was a logical inference, I knew there was something missing. What exactly it was, I could not point out. I settled back into the Piano Concerto playing in my mind. There were still so many links to clarify.

"You didn't answer my question, Millard," Colin said. "Where are the other paintings?"

"Opal doesn't know." Manny had asked her four times to try harder to remember if Adam had had a studio and if so where it had been. She had been telling the truth when she'd said she didn't know.

"She did say that Monsieur Rimbaud used to have different paintings hanging in his apartment at various times." I'd found that interesting. "It sounded like he would hang new paintings every few months. She also said he had his favourites, and the one he liked the least was Courbet's *Nude Reclining Woman*."

Colin's eyes widened. "The painting he wanted Maurice to sell, the one in his apartment."

"Doc here doesn't like to speculate, but I'm thinking that when he became desperate for money, he decided to sell the painting he liked least."

"Why would he be desperate for money?" Vinnie asked.

"Opal said that she only found out about this after he had died." I'd observed true sorrow when she'd told us that. "Apparently, the old man had cancer that had spread all through his body. If that heart attack hadn't killed him, he would have died within a year. She also thought that he didn't want to tell Gasquet how sick he was because Gasquet took Adam's death so hard."

"Yeah, and he took Monsieur Rimbaud's death so hard that he started selling those paintings. What a big heart." Vinnie's tone and facial expression revealed his sarcasm.

"I also consider selling Adam's paintings so soon after Monsieur Rimbaud's death quite callous. But it fits in with the typical self-interest of a narcissist." The more I learned about Laurence Gasquet, the less I respected him as a human.

"So what are you doing about Gasquet, old man?" Vinnie got up. He looked ready to leave.

Manny lifted one eyebrow. "Stand down, criminal. I've already spoken to your pal, Daniel. He's got his GIPN team on standby. The moment we have something that would get us a warrant for Gasquet's arrest, they're on it."

I pointed at Manny's face. "You're being calculating. What are you planning?"

"Being smart, Doc. I plan to be smart about this. Let's assume Gasquet is ZD and we arrest him now. The auctions won't take place. The problem is that he's been working in and with law enforcement his whole life. I don't think he'll tell us where the kids are. Our priority should be to find the kids."

"Michael and Steve," Francine said softly, not looking up from her computer.

"Assuming that they were taken, yes. I would prefer to stop this thing before the organ auction starts in"—Manny looked at the screen—"an hour and fifty-five minutes. But we do have some leeway."

"An extra four hours." The relief I felt was not enough to lessen the tightness around my throat. "If they stay true to form, the hunting auction will take place four hours after the organ auctions."

"And if we have enough to take them down, we can do this right and save the students' lives." Manny took a deep breath. "We need to get this right. I want to make sure these bastards are locked up and the key is thrown away."

"Francine?" I waited until she looked up. "Did you find any more information on Gasquet?"

"I'm looking for it now. What I have so far is an elaboration of what we already know, but nothing new."

"Look in his financials. See if you can find any connections between Gasquet, Breton and Hugo, other than what we already have. Look in their financials as well." People didn't realise how much their financial data revealed about their personal lives. I was hoping one or more of them had been negligent at some point, giving us something that could lead to a breakthrough.

"I'll send you what I get as I get it. I've already emailed you Dukwicz's financials. I got that two hours ago, but haven't been able to go through it yet."

"I'll analyse that."

"I'll look in on the girls, then I'll join you." Colin walked to the door, stopped, turned around and pointed his finger at me. "And don't you dare feel guilty about being focussed on this case. If Michael and Steve are out there, Nikki would prefer you ignored her and helped them."

I gave him a smile that I knew didn't reach my eyes. Rationally, I agreed with him, but it didn't erase the discomfort I felt. Nor the illogical personal responsibility I felt towards Michael and Steve. Without another word I went to my viewing room.

When Colin joined me fifteen minutes later, I was going through Dukwicz's financial history of four months ago. Colin placed a mug of coffee on the coaster next to my keyboard and sat down. "What have you got?"

"Weekly payments from some company that I can't trace." I highlighted a transfer. "The amounts differ every time, but they are paid two days after the auctions. Hmm. Give me a minute."

Francine had uploaded the entirety of Dukwicz's computer content into a cloud folder. She'd found more videos and had placed them in an individual folder. I opened it and clicked on a chosen video. I had no interest in watching another young person being auctioned. It was too difficult to observe the terror in their eyes during the second auction when the sedative I assumed they had been given had worked through their system.

I took the video to the very end and left it on the first monitor. I repeated this process with three more videos until I'd confirmed my suspicion. I sank deeper into my chair with a sigh. "These are payments for the hunting auctions. On the seventh of February this young man was sold to some hunter for forty thousand euros. On the ninth, Dukwicz received a payment of twenty thousand euro."

"Shit. He's getting fifty percent commission for this?" Disgust was thick in Colin's voice.

The next three cases confirmed it. Two days after each auction, Dukwicz received a payment of half the value of the final bid. Violence, torture, brutality were not new to the human race. From the beginning of recorded history, humans had proved themselves to be inventive in ways to make each other suffer. Knowing this didn't soften the horror I felt working on this case.

We spent the next forty minutes working through Dukwicz's financial history, looking for ways to connect him to Gasquet, or even Breton and Hugo. If there was a connection, it wasn't obvious. I would need more information.

"Where are we, Doc?" Manny asked from the door separating my room from the team room.

I frowned. "We are in Rousseau & Rousseau."

"Oh, hell." Manny pressed the palms of his hands against his eyes. When he looked at me, I noticed extreme fatigue and worry lining his eyes. "What I meant was, where are we on this case?"

"Dukwicz started receiving regular payments from an untraceable source five months ago."

"Before that I think all his money came from his hits." Colin knew I wasn't comfortable with the assumption. I did, however, think it had merit. "Taking into consideration that SSS and the apparent hunting and organ auctions only started six months ago, this makes sense. He must have hooked up with Gasquet and taken this side of the business."

"Have you found any evidence linking Dukwicz to Gasquet?"

My shoulders slumped. "No. Not yet."

"Well, we've run out of time." Manny looked behind him to the screen in the team room. I saw in Manny the same helplessness I felt. I hated that feeling and wished there was more I could do, more information I could find. "They've put up the details about the auctions."

I got up and walked into the team room, my eyes locked on the screen. It was divided into four, and each quarter was filled with numbers—the crude code. I walked back to my room, grabbed my notepad and a pencil and returned. Sitting at the round table, I deciphered the information about the four young people within ten minutes.

"Doc?" Manny was standing behind Francine, his hand resting on the back of her chair. "What have you got?"

"Three males, one female." My voice cracked and I cleared my throat. "From the description of two of the males, I deduce they are Michael and Steve."

"Holy hell." Manny looked at Colin. "Do we tell them?"

"Tell who?" I asked.

"Nikki and Rebecca."

"Tell us what?" Nikki asked. She was standing in the doorway, holding a tray with coffee and cookies. She walked into the room, put the tray on the table and turned to me. "Tell me what, Doc?"

Colin shook his head as he came to sit next to me. When I looked at Nikki, I focussed on the intelligence and toughness I knew she possessed. "Are you going to be wise and strong?"

"Jenny?" The concern in Colin's voice was justified. But I'd promised Nikki honesty.

She sat down slowly in the chair closest to me, her eyes searching my face. "Is Michael dead?"

"No." I swallowed the 'not yet'. "I think both Michael and Steve might be up for auction."

Nikki's eyes were wide in her pale face. "Find them, Doc G. Please find them."

"Go to Rebecca. The fewer distractions I have, the sooner we can hope to find them."

She stared at me intensely for another three seconds before nodding and leaving the room. I dropped my face in my hands and focussed on my breathing. It was quiet in the team room and when I looked up, everyone's expressions were grave. From nowhere, anger filled me. Anger at the feeling of hopelessness, at Gasquet, at Dukwicz, at the human psyche allowing for such illnesses to enter and thrive in our beings.

I stood up, pushing with my hands on the table. "We have another fifty minutes before this auction commences. Let's use it."

"I'm still looking for more on Gasquet," Francine said. "Someone has scrubbed his internet history. This person has to be very good to leave only enough to create a digital footprint, but nothing revealing."

"It could be André Breton." It fitted perfectly. "He was well-respected in the cyber-crimes division before he joined Hugo and Boucher. He could've changed all their digital data."

"Maybe." Francine shrugged.

"Where's the criminal?" Manny asked.

"He joined Daniel," Francine said. "He couldn't sit around doing nothing. He wanted to be in on the action when we take these guys down."

I hoped Vinnie's faith would not be misplaced.

Colin's phone rang, breaking into the fragile atmosphere. His eyes widened briefly when he looked at the screen. He answered the call and listened in silence for a few minutes, only making encouraging noises. Everyone in the team room was watching his face, me included. From the brief appearance of sadness followed by anger, I was wondering if the call was about Maurice's autopsy. When he ended the call, his anger was clearly visible.

"They hunted him. The bastards hunted Maurice." His jaw was tight, his nostrils flared.

"Was that the morgue?" Manny asked. "What did they say?"

"Maurice died from injuries sustained by the car hitting him. They had CCTV footage of the man dumping him in the backstreet and have already arrested him. Apparently, Maurice had just run out into the road, asking for help, but this idiot saw him too late and ran him over. It could've been vehicular manslaughter, but now that guy is up on all kinds of murder charges. He didn't want his wife to know he wasn't at work like he'd told her and that was why he didn't report it and why he dumped Maurice's body."

"Why did you say Maurice was hunted?" I put my hand on the armrest of Colin's chair. He grabbed and held onto my hand with both of his.

"They found peri-mortem injuries that were positively identified as coming from high-impact projectiles like rubber bullets." Colin's hands tightened even more around mine. "He'd outrun them. They had chased him through that forest and he'd outrun them."

"Most likely because of his triathlon training," I said.

"Every time we met, he told me about the latest race he'd finished. He was good at it, too. His favourite was cross-country running." Colin shook his head. "Then he got killed by a fucking speeding car."

"Do the police know on which road this guy hit Maurice?" Francine asked. "That could help us narrow possible locations."

Colin's laugh had a broken quality to it. "He's too scared of his wife to say. If he reveals where he was, she'll know who he was with and it would cost him a lot of money in divorce settlements."

"Has he lawyered up?" Manny asked.

"Yup. Now he doesn't have to say anything to anyone."

"Bastard."

"I looked at Maurice's phone." Francine's change of topic caught me off guard. It took a moment to recall that Colin had retrieved a cell phone from a secret safe in Maurice's apartment.

"Did you find something, supermodel?"

"Phone calls to an untraceable burner phone. Neither of those two phones has been switched on in days. I'm sorry, Colin."

"It was worth trying." He glared at the screen. "Those kids are students. Most likely all of them are nerdy. They're not athletes. They're not going to outrun Dukwicz and whichever sick fuck is hunting them. Come on, Jenny. Let's see if we can get anything else from Dukwicz's financials."

He didn't let go of my hand as he got up and pulled me to follow him. We went into my viewing room and followed up every transaction paid into Dukwicz's account. When ten o'clock arrived, we still had nothing concrete, nothing that could lead us to the location of the auctions.

"They're on." Francine's whisper carried enough emotion to catch our attention. Colin and I joined her and Manny, all four of us staring at the screen. The divided screen with the coded medical information of the four victims was replaced by a young man standing in the same room I'd seen on all the videos. He was also dressed only in tracksuit pants. His back was turned to the camera, his spine and bony shoulder blades visible.

As if on order, he slowly turned around, exhibiting the same intoxication as the others. The moment his features were turned to the camera, blackness rushed at me. An involuntary keen escaped me and I pushed both fists against my mouth. On the screen, Michael continued to turn towards the camera until he came to a swaying stop. He slowly blinked and swallowed a few times.

This young man had been in my home, found my idiosyncrasies amusing and made Nikki laugh. I could not allow panic to overwhelm me and prevent me from finding him. I forced Mozart's beautiful Violin Concerto No. 1 in B flat major into my mind and returned my attention to my surroundings. Manny was on the phone ordering someone to 'keep the girls in the conference room'.

"Doc, you're with us?"

"Of course. I'm here." My answer brought a micro-expression of relief to his face.

"Good. Now tell me what you think." He moved to the side to take my focus away from the screen. Away from Michael. "Should we watch this and see if we can learn anything new? Or should we be doing something else?"

I considered this. "I see no reason why this auction would be any different from the other auctions they've done. Apart from the identities of the victims, we've learned nothing from those auctions. I suggest we keep an eye on the auction, but continue to search for a way to find out where they are."

"And stop them before the second auction." Francine typed hard on her keyboard and clicked a few times with the mouse. The screen split in two, the auction a smaller window in the top right-hand corner. "Let's work with what we've got."

"Financials," I said. "What did you find on Breton and Hugo?"

"Oh, I found dirt, girlfriend." She rubbed her hands together. "Both have overseas accounts registered under dummy corporations. These accounts are each a few million strong. I bet they didn't get that from being good Interpol agents."

"A few million what?" Manny asked.

"Dollars. Both have around two and a half million dollars stashed away there. Unfortunately, I didn't find anything that connects them to Gasquet's financials."

"How far back did you look?"

"Two years. It seems like our timeline starts around nineteen months ago when Monsieur Rimbaud first approached Maurice and then Colin got involved."

"Could you compare any major transactions into or out of Breton and Hugo's accounts? We might find payments from the same person or place."

For a minute, the only sound in the team room was Francine's typing and clicking. A few final clicks and three side-to-side documents filled the screen. "There's nothing else. Just this payment they received from GDD Security Industries eighteen months ago. It is listed as a bonus payout to shareholders."

"GDD Security Industries?" Manny sat down. "Where have I heard that before?"

Another connection clicked. "It's the company responsible for the DWD survey."

"Holy bloody hell!" Manny jumped up. "The bleeding survey that interviewed all the auctioned kids?"

"How many payments from GDD?" I asked.

"It was only that once."

"What other information do you have on them?"

Francine's brow pulled in and down. "Shit, I forgot to get more on them. Give me a minute."

"Doc, tell me if you agree with my theory. ZD is Gasquet. He became mates with Breton and Hugo when he helped them with a case in a consultant capacity. This had to be before Monsieur Rimbaud died."

"Their first official case together was three years ago." I had read their Interpol files. "But their paths had crossed before while Gasquet was still with Interpol."

"So they've known each other a long time. Then Monsieur Rimbaud gets sick, but doesn't want to tell Gasquet. He tries to sell a painting, but dies from a heart attack when it brings Interpol to his door. Somehow Gasquet finds out about the role Maurice and Edward Taylor played in the death of this man who'd cared for him and decides to take revenge. Hmm… where do SSS and the auctions fit in?"

"According to Caelan the first Courbet painting was put up on Silk Road after Monsieur Rimbaud's death," Colin said. "What's the bet Gasquet didn't know the value of any of those paintings until he found out about the event that had triggered Monsieur Rimbaud's heart attack? A man like Gasquet could never have enough power. I think he gets off on the illegal aspect of all of this."

"It doesn't completely fit the profile of a narcissist." I was still bothered by a few conflicting facts. "A narcissist wants to be the centre of attention and wants people to acknowledge how powerful he is. ZD's online behaviour does not support that. I know that we have very strong evidence suggesting that Gasquet is ZD, but at the moment it is still circumstantial."

"What are you saying, Doc?"

"We don't have the complete picture yet." I liked Nikki's analogy. "We're missing some pieces."

"Here's another piece for you." Francine nodded towards the screen. "Laurence Gasquet is one of the major shareholders of GDD Security Industries."

"That connects him to Breton and Hugo, and connects the three of them to the kidnappings." Manny slammed his fist into his other palm. "Getting closer. We're getting them."

"Where are all those students?" It was a question that had been in the back of my mind. "No bodies have been recovered. I looked for reports of bodies missing organs, but I haven't found one single such case. Not within the parameters we are working."

"Let's shelve that question for now, Doc." Manny looked at the top right-hand corner of the screen. "Right now we need to find out where Michael, Steve and the other two are."

"They can't be far from Strasbourg," Colin said. "Before the guy who killed Maurice called his lawyer, he said that it was a quick visit. He always went home to his wife, even if it was in the early-morning hours."

"That eliminates Breton's and Hugo's homes in Lyon. That's a four-hour drive from here. What other properties do they have?"

"None," Francine and I said together. She waved her hand at me to continue.

"If they own any other property, it is not registered in their names and has not been declared. Gasquet has his house here in Strasbourg and the apartment in Bristol."

"I'll get Daniel to check out his house." Manny took his smartphone from his pocket.

"It doesn't make sense to have the students in the city," Colin said. "It would attract attention to move them so many times. Firstly, when they're kidnapped and then to take them to some remote location to be hunted. I think they're being held outside the city, but not too far away."

"We need more information." Despite my deep dislike for repetition, I couldn't say this enough times. "The more data we have, the easier it would be to find them."

"I might be able to help with that," a familiar voice said from the door. Judith Jooste was standing next to Tim, a suitcase on wheels next to her.

Chapter TWENTY-ONE

"You made good time." Manny looked at his watch. "We expected you this afternoon."

"I got a lift with a buddy of mine who owns a helicopter service." She tilted the suitcase and rolled it into the room. "Much faster and less stressful than driving four hours there and four back. It also gave me more time to get as much paperwork as possible."

Manny lifted both eyebrows, looking at the large suitcase. "That's a lot of paperwork."

"Um… If all is well here?" Tim took a step back, into the hallway.

Manny nodded once.

"Thank you for escorting me." Judith gave Tim a warm smile.

"No problem. I was only following orders." On his last two words, he glared at the back of Manny's head before winking at Judith. "I'll make fresh coffee."

Despite the exhaustion from not having slept in the last twenty-nine hours, I didn't think coffee would be a good idea. Not for me. Adrenaline was causing me to feel queasy. Although, thinking about it, I didn't know whether the queasiness was the adrenaline from rushing to find these students or the knowledge that Michael would be auctioned as hunting prey in another four hours.

"Doctor Lenard." Judith smiled a greeting to me before holding out her right hand to Colin. "I'm Judith Jooste."

It took me a millisecond to remember that Judith had never met Colin. She'd met William Strode. Colin displayed no discomfort, no surprise and no deception when he shook her hand.

"Colin." He nodded towards the suitcase. "Right now we can do with all the extra help and information you can give."

"Hi!" Francine waved from behind her desk. "I'm Francine."

"She's our IT expert." Manny glanced at the suitcase again. "What have you got for us?"

"All of Boucher's notes that he kept at home." Judith put the suitcase on its side, crouched next to it and unzipped the large case. "I also have the official case files I requested, but I think we might find more in his personal notes."

"His wife co-operated?" Manny asked.

Judith looked up from the case. "She believes someone killed her husband. According to her, Boucher was pedantic about the upkeep of his cars. He would never have allowed his car's brakes, or anything else for that matter, to become so worn that they would fail him. She said that she's questioned the police reports, asked for further investigation, but no one would listen to her. They all think she's just a grieving widow."

"Did Boucher ever talk to her about his cases?" Colin walked closer, crouched on the other side of the case and helped Judith unpack numerous folders and notebooks onto the round table.

"Sometimes he brought notes home and worked on them in his study, she said. He didn't talk about it, but he did brood a lot. He would sit in his study and spend hours going over his notes, especially if he had a particularly difficult case. But that didn't happen too often."

"What about the months before his death?" I asked.

"She said there was definitely something bothering him. He spent more time than usual in his study, and some days came home very late because he'd been researching something."

"And of course she doesn't know what he was working on, right?" Manny asked.

"Nope. But she was very happy to give me all his files. Made me promise that I was going to find the people responsible for her husband's death. She also seemed keen on cleaning out his study. It didn't look like it had been touched since he died." Judith shook her head. "Sad, really."

The round table was covered in piles of folders, papers and notebooks that looked well paged through. I clenched my teeth at the disarray on the table. "Is there some sort of order in all of these documents?"

Judith frowned at the table. "No. I just grabbed everything I could and rushed back. I haven't looked at a single file yet."

"You should look at the Interpol files first," I said. "You know what the electronic files said and can compare it to his case notes. If there are any differences you'll notice them."

"Good idea."

"Okay, Doc. What do we do?"

"Not me." Francine waved her hands in front of her. "I'm working on trying to find a way to locate these bastards. If I can get into that live feed, we might be able to stop this auction or prevent the hunting auction."

Judith's head shot up. "What hunting auction?"

"They're first auctioning these students' organs." I pointed at the screen against the wall. The second organ auction seemed near its end. I didn't want to look too closely at the prices paid for the young man's body parts. "In another three hours and forty minutes they will auction each of these students to be prey to some sick individual who enjoys hunting innocent, defenceless human beings."

Judith stared at me, her mouth agape. Then she turned to Manny. "What is she talking about?"

While Manny gave her an impressively concise summary of the case, I started putting some order to the papers on the table. I put all the notebooks on one pile. There were four large notebooks, seven smaller ones and ten very small notebooks that I suspected Boucher had carried around in his pocket. I made another pile with the loose papers that didn't seem to belong anywhere. The folders I separated into two piles. One for the Interpol files and one for Boucher's personal files.

Despite the disorganised state of these documents, Boucher appeared to have been quite meticulous in the private records he'd kept. On each folder was a name and a date. Inside these folders numerous pages of information were neatly attached with notes in the margins. The first page in the folder I was looking at was a photocopied page of a newspaper article about the budding ski industry in the smaller hills outside Strasbourg. The article didn't catch my attention as much as the fact that the notes were written in some kind of code. Every folder I opened had coded notes on the documents.

It took Manny four minutes to finish his condensed summary. "That's the skeleton. We need to go through these files to see if Boucher had any idea where these kids might be."

"How did you determine which were the last cases Boucher paid attention to?" I asked. "I looked at the cases your team is investigating and I didn't see anything of interest in the last three cases before Boucher's death."

Judith took a long time to look away from the screen. When she did, her lips were thinned. She blinked a few times, refocussing. "At any one time we have between three and twenty cases open. Some cases take a week to close, others take years of intense investigation. Boucher kept a log on his computer of the cases they were working on. Every week he changed the priority of those cases and saved it as a new file. The three cases that caught my attention were in the last six or seven cases the unit took on before Boucher died. I noticed the first asterisk in one of the documents saved five weeks before his death."

"How did you get access to his computer?" Francine was clearly listening while she was working on her computer. "Don't the big guys lock someone's computer away as soon as they are no longer with the agency?"

Judith's smile was secretive. "I learned very early in my career how important friends can be in this business. Especially friends of the IT variety. That was my first stop when I started this job. I made sure that I gave the IT guys something of value."

"Something that would prove you're trustworthy and worth doing extra work for." That was one of the reasons I would never be able to work in an average corporate setup. Not only did I lack those skills, I had no interest in the calculating approach to potential friends this required.

"Yes. It worked. The IT guys gave me Boucher's computer for a day so that I could"—she lifted both hands and just like Nikki made finger quotes in the air—"learn from Boucher."

"Devious." Francine winked. "I like you."

Judith's smile widened. "Thanks. Having the computer didn't really give me much. The most I got were the weekly lists he saved. But it did make me look at those three files."

I followed her index finger pointing at the three Interpol files carefully laid on top of each other. "Tell me about the cases."

"In a nutshell? The first one that got an asterisk was an ID theft case. It was cut short to look into Edward Taylor. When I checked out Boucher's report on this case, it had considerably less information than his other cases. He was really quite detailed in his other reports. This one was just the basics."

"Did you see anything suspicious about the case?" Manny asked.

"Apart from it being put on the back burner to investigate Edward Taylor? No. It was the second case that made me suspicious. It was abandoned after a week. In that week very little investigation was actually done."

"What kind of case?"

Judith glanced at the screen. "An art student at a Lille university was reported missing a few days before a major exhibition. He was some kind of prodigy. His university called in the report six months ago."

The adrenaline rushing through my body made me feel cold. "Are you talking about Christopher Leesa?"

Her eyes widened in surprise. "You know about him?"

"He's one of the many students Doc found missing across Europe."

"I know I didn't find all the missing students." I stopped myself from rubbing my arms in a self-soothing gesture. "I found twenty-two names. We found thirty-eight videos showing students being hunted. I don't have names for all of them."

"My God." There was no sound in her shocked exclamation, just a rush of air. "What are we dealing with?"

"Monsters." Francine's top lip curled, her voice hard.

"What about this case?" Colin asked. "Was there anything apart from the asterisk that's interesting?"

"No. I was hoping to find something in Boucher's notes." Judith lifted one of the files on the table. "If not in the case file, maybe the notes from his house."

"The last case?" I asked.

"It was an anonymous tip about someone offering assassination services. The case was opened a few days before Boucher died and went cold after his death. I asked Breton and Hugo about this and they said only Boucher ever spoke to this informant. Since they had no idea how to get hold of this person or where to even start investigating this alleged crime, they dumped the case."

"Dukwicz," Colin said.

"We can't be sure it is him." We had no evidence.

Colin shrugged. "Taken into context, I think we can be sure it's him. For all we know Boucher was the so-called informant."

"That is outrageous conjecture." I didn't want to waste any time on theories. The auction on the screen had concluded. I didn't recognise the second young man, had never met him, but felt irrationally responsible for what he was experiencing. "Judith, look through the Interpol files and report if you find any additional information. We will start looking through these folders. We need to find notes Boucher might have made relating to these cases, to Breton and Hugo, to Gasquet, to Dukwicz or to anything related to the kidnappings."

No one questioned my directive. Judith took the three official files and sat on the chair Vinnie usually used. Manny joined us at the table and the room became quiet, only the rustling of papers and Francine's tapping on her computer audible.

When Judith sighed heavily for a third time, I looked up. She was biting her bottom lip, a deep frown pulling her eyebrows in and down.

"What's wrong? Have you found something?" I hoped so.

"Nothing. The Leesa case doesn't make sense." She lifted a folder and shook it. "This has reports from Breton, Hugo and Boucher. Breton and Hugo's reports give exactly the same spiel. Most of their reports are a lot of blah, blah, blah. And then they state that Leesa isn't missing. In their opinion as investigators who have seen many such cases, they reckon Christopher Leesa dropped out of university and is working somewhere warm, most likely in a bar in Greece. Can you believe it? They actually wrote that here! Their reasoning is that he's a social misfit and wanted to go someplace where he could start over."

While Manny and Judith discussed the lexicon used in the report and its possible interpretations, I wondered about Breton and Hugo's involvement in the kidnappings. I also thought it sounded as if they had closed this case in this manner to draw away any suspicion. Were *they* kidnapping the students? Were they using their positions in Interpol to ensure no investigation into these kidnappings? What were their roles?

"Doctor Lenard! I'm here! Doctor Lenard!" Caelan appeared in the doorway, Tim slightly behind him. Phillip's assistant looked at me with his eyebrows and shoulders raised. Caelan's hair was short, in places cropped tight against his skull. I wondered if he'd cut it himself. He no longer smelled bad, was wearing a pair of blue jeans and a white t-shirt and appeared relaxed. The lack of inappropriate geographical facts confirmed that he wasn't distressed. "I want a girlfriend."

Francine made a distinctly unfeminine sound and Manny scowled at Caelan.

"Have you got any useful information for us, lad?"

Caelan frowned. "In 1932, the winter was so cold that Niagara Falls froze completely solid."

He stepped into the room and Tim shifted behind him, clearly waiting for something.

"What is the problem, Tim?" I needed to understand his discomfort.

"Is this okay? Can he stay?"

I looked at the pile of disorganised documents on the table and made a decision. "Yes, Caelan might just be able to help us."

"I want a girlfriend." Caelan walked up to Judith and studied her, his eyes finally settling on her shoulder. "Who are you? You're kind of pretty. A bit old, but pretty. Will you be my girlfriend?"

Judith's eyes widened, her bottom jaw going slack.

"That's not how you're going to get a girlfriend, kiddo." Francine rapped her knuckles on her desk to get his attention. "You better listen to Doctor Lenard and help us. We really need you."

"Will you teach me then how to have a girlfriend?"

"You're like a dog with a bone." Francine shook her head. "Yes, I said I'll teach you."

"Do you really have nothing useful to add to this case, lad?"

"No. Doctor Lenard said I didn't have to give you anything. So I Google Earthed."

"You what now?" Manny turned to Francine when Caelan ignored him. "What's he talking about?"

"Google has mapped out the whole planet, handsome."

"Yes, I know Google Maps."

"Well, it's pretty much the same thing. You can really travel the world with this. There are satellite images of the rural areas and street views of most cities and towns."

Judith was quietly observing this interaction, leaning away from Caelan. He had surprised her and she wasn't comfortable.

I understood that. More importantly, I wanted this inane conversation to stop so we could return to finding these students. "Caelan, will you help us?"

He thought about that for a few seconds, then he straightened and looked at my shoulder. "What can I do?"

"We have a lot of documents here and we are looking for specific information. How good are you at concentrated searches?"

"The best." He glanced at Francine. "Maybe not the best, but almost the best."

I didn't need to speak to Caelan as I did to neurotypical people. It made explaining what we were looking for much easier. I could be specific without having to give context and lengthy explanations. It felt good.

Caelan took the chair furthest from Manny and opened a notebook. "This is written in code. Oh, this is so amateur."

"What is?" Manny asked.

"Boucher used a modular arithmetic shift cypher." I'd recognised it immediately. It was simplistic and easily decipherable.

Manny grabbed a folder, opened it and frowned. "Bloody hell, Doc. Please don't even explain to me what it is. Just tell me you can uncode this."

"Uncode isn't a word." I took a deep breath. "It is easy enough to decrypt. Each number represents a letter."

I took one of Boucher's notebooks and opened it to the first page. Within three minutes I'd worked out the code and had written the numbers and their corresponding letters on the sheet of paper. "You can use this to decrypt his notes. I suggest we be as thorough as possible not to miss a potential clue."

"It's going to take weeks, Doc."

I looked at Caelan. "No, it won't."

He was paging through the notebook, dragging his finger down each page before moving on to the next. I was impressed with how easily his mind was translating the numbers to letters, giving him the notes Boucher had made.

Manny and Colin looked at each other, both exhibiting apprehension and dread. Colin was the first to take a deep breath and pick up a notebook. "I think we should each have a copy of the cypher."

"I'll get it." Manny grabbed the paper I'd written the code on and made three copies. Caelan didn't even look up when Manny placed a sheet in front of him. He had memorised the code and was already one third of the way through his notebook. Manny sat down and stared at the documents on the table. "I think Judith and I will go through the folders with notes that we can read. You people can uncode that mathematical insanity."

I thought it a prudent suggestion. Colin had opened a notebook and was already working through the first page. He was much slower than Caelan, but was making good progress. I took the notebook I had worked on and went through it at around the same speed as Caelan.

Two hours later, the three of us had worked through more than two thirds of Boucher's notebooks. Manny and Judith had gone through the documents they could, left the team room and returned with fresh coffee and muffins.

I didn't care for food or beverages. My attention was divided between working through the notebooks and what was taking place on the screen. An hour ago, the last young person's organ auction had concluded. It had been Nikki's other friend, Steve. He had not raised as much money as Michael, but it had still been a very profitable auction.

We didn't talk about what was happening on the screen. Everyone's eyes constantly strayed to it, now displaying the hunting auction's page. The same large clock was counting down to the start of the auction and we were only twenty-seven minutes away.

Francine had left for her basement, hoping to have more success locating the live feed. Picking up another notebook, I was not feeling very optimistic.

"Um... I think I might have something." Colin leaned closer to the notebook he was working on. "This is frying my brain, but I think this might be about these last cases."

All movement stopped in the team room. The tension in everyone's bodies had been increasing in the last two hours. Therefore, the hope on Judith's face didn't surprise me. Colin pushed the notebook towards me. "I think you'd better read this. It would take me much longer."

The first sentence confirmed Colin's observation. "He's talking about Christopher Leesa's case."

"Read it out, Doc."

I nodded. "'Leesa case stopped too fast. Why? Neighbours, schoolmates say CL is ambitious, studious, boring. Not adventurous. Caseload not fuller than usual. Why rush? Why use that excuse to stop? No one to complain. Why are B and H defensive about this when asked? Doesn't add up.'"

"B and H would be Breton and Hugo." Manny spoke as if to himself. I had thought the abbreviations to be self-explanatory. "What else does it say, Doc?"

I read for another fifteen minutes, none of what I was reading pertinent to our case. Boucher had dated each of his entries. Four days after the entry about the Leesa case, my eyes widened as I read Boucher's note. "'Why stop that investigation? Rimbaud had a Courbet forgery.'"

"Oh, my God. He's talking about the old man." Francine was sitting at her desk again. I hadn't seen her return. "Did I miss how he became interested in that case?"

"Nope." Manny stretched his neck. "His notes are questions about cases, a lot of free thinking, but so far not much that's helpful."

I looked up and the blood drained from my face. "The auction has started."

"Holy Mother of all." Manny got up and rubbed his hand hard over his face. "Supermodel, where the bleeding hell are they?"

Francine's shoulders slumped, her head lowering. "I can't get through the routing and encryption. Maybe after a few days with some extra help, but... I'm sorry, Manny."

"Just keep trying, supermodel."

The first person auctioned to be hunted was Michael. I wondered if this was going to be in the same order as the organ auction. Michael's body language was different from the previous auction. As with Matthieu and all the others, he was no longer under some pharmaceutical influence. He knew his life was in grave danger. Fear was in every movement of his face and his body. Most predators loved watching the fear, the fight for survival, no matter how pointless it might be.

Already the bidding was picking up speed. Selling Michael to the highest-bidding hunter wouldn't take more than ten minutes. I looked around the screen for any clues, anything different from the videos on Dukwicz's computer.

It was on the top right-hand corner. They didn't even bother to write it in code. Clear for all to see, the announcement went in and out of focus as I tried to maintain control and not give in to the blackness rushing at me.

"The hunting will start in two hours." I was surprised my voice was audible.

"What are you talking about, Doc?"

"Look at the top of the screen."

"Aw, hell!" Manny walked to my viewing room, came back, walked away again and stopped in front of the screen. "Two hours. Shit."

I couldn't watch anymore. I hated feeling so powerless. There had to be something in these documents that could help us find the key that would lead us to the students. I continued reading Boucher's notes. Colin moved closer and was looking at the notebook as well, most likely slowly decrypting. There were a lot more questions about cases that Breton and Hugo hadn't investigated properly, or that they'd outright dismissed.

His next entry was questioning the friendship between Breton, Hugo and Gasquet. How did Breton and Hugo fit into Gasquet's relationship with Emile Rimbaud?

Three sentences later, I gasped and reread the last sentence. The connection was so obvious, yet so well hidden it didn't surprise me that we hadn't seen it before.

"Jenny?" Colin touched my forearm. "What is it?"

"The folder. I need to find that folder." I got up and started looking through the folders on the table. No one spoke, the room quiet except for my frantic search. I found what I was looking for in the third folder. My breathing was erratic, my hearting pounding in my chest. I took out the photocopied newspaper article and held it in the air. "I know where they are. I know where Michael, Steve and the other two are."

Chapter TWENTY-TWO

Manny stepped closer to me, took his phone from his pocket and swiped the screen. "Where are they, Doc?"

I paged through the rest of the folder until I found the correct document. I scanned it before giving it to Manny. "Here."

"Where is it?" Colin asked.

"It's in the mountains southeast of the city." I was angry with myself for not pursuing this line of investigation earlier. "The article is about the ski industry in the smaller mountains around Strasbourg and how the local property owners were divided in their views. Some liked the increase of tourists. Others didn't. I only scanned the first paragraph, so I don't know how the rest of the article continues. It was Boucher's note in the margin that gave me the connection."

Judith leaned closer to Manny to look at the article. "It's coded."

"It is only one word." I took a deep breath. Why had I not looked into this earlier? "'Inheritance'."

"Okay?" Judith lifted both shoulders.

"The certificate in this folder is proof of ownership for a large piece of land." I lifted the folder that I got the article from. "It is registered in Adam Marot's name."

"Oh, my God. He was Monsieur Rimbaud's lover who died twenty years ago." Francine's eyes were wide. "Give me a moment."

As soon as she started working on her computer, Manny tapped on the screen of his phone. "We need to get the team there."

He put the phone on the table and ringing came through the speakerphone. It rang only twice before Vinnie's voice boomed through the room. "Whaddup, old man?"

"We've got them." Manny lifted the proof of ownership document. "Get in the helicopter and start heading southeast. I'll get supermodel to send you the co-ordinates now."

"Are they still alive?"

Manny glanced at the screen. "They're busy auctioning the second kid. The hunting is going to start in less than two hours. You better move your arses."

"I've seen those vids. We need to narrow down the search, old man. We can't go running around the woods, wasting precious time."

"I'll keep you updated. Just get out there now."

"On it."

Manny swiped the screen to end the call and sighed. Judith tapped with her index finger on the photocopied article in front of her. "This article is from twenty years ago. Boucher must have gone through the newspaper archives looking for information on Monsieur Rimbaud. This article has a quotation from Adam Marot who did not appreciate the tourists coming onto his land, hiking in the summer and looking for places to ski in the winter. He wanted to keep his piece of land as protected as possible, because it served as his inspiration and also a place where he and his housemate, Emile Rimbaud, went to get away from the city."

"Adam bequeathed that piece of land to Gasquet." Francine leaned back in her chair. "I have the change of ownership documents here. It was in his name until nineteen months ago."

"When Rimbaud died," Colin said.

"He transferred the ownership to one of his dummy companies' names." She sneered. "The same company that made payments into Breton's and Hugo's accounts."

"Send those co-ordinates to the criminal. They need to get there."

"Already done." She straightened, her lips thinned. "Vinnie was right. We need to send them to the right place. That piece of land is more than two hundred and fifty hectares of mountainous terrain. They won't find the students if they don't know exactly where to go."

"Doc, how sure are you that they're there?"

"I'm not." And I hated it. "It is just the most obvious conclusion taking into consideration everything we've learned about this case so far."

"Genevieve is right." Francine nodded at the screen. She'd brought up a satellite map, showing mountains and valleys. The image zoomed in until we were looking at an area that seemed completely green. There was not a building in sight. "This is Adam's piece of land. It's far from the nearest village, there are no major roads nearby and if there's a building, it's obscured by all the trees."

"What videos?" Caelan asked. He'd been quietly listening to us, his arms tightly wrapped around his torso.

"What are you talking about?" Colin asked.

"The big guy said that he'd seen videos. What videos?"

"Um… I don't think he should be looking at those videos." Francine shifted in her chair, her expression concerned. I shared that concern.

"What's on the videos?" Caelan's voice raised a fraction.

I took a moment to consider what I knew about Caelan. It was a risk, but too many lives were in danger. "It shows young people being hunted in the woods."

"Show me."

"Now, wait just a moment there, lad." Manny looked at me, communicating a warning. "Why would you want to see that? It's not horror movie night."

"I can help."

I thought so too. "Tell him how you'll be able to help."

"I know the area. I've been there a lot."

"You know the mountains?" Judith's tone mirrored the doubt exhibited on her face.

"Yes. I go there often. I was there yesterday."

Manny's muscle tension increased. "Explain yourself, laddie."

Caelan closed his eyes, blocking out Manny. I was not surprised at his reaction to the harsh demand in Manny's tone. I sighed, knowing that I was going to have to intervene. "Caelan can correct me if I'm wrong, but I'm sure he wasn't there in person. He travelled that area using Google Earth. Did you, Caelan? You like exploring different geographical areas, right?"

He opened one eye and looked at my shoulder. "I don't have a car or a passport, so I travel the only way I can."

"If you watch these videos, you might be able to tell us exactly where the students are." It was a method I'd never considered.

"Lad, these videos are not easy to watch. Are you sure you're up for it?"

"I'm up for it. Show me."

I had hoped to never have to watch that footage again. Seeing terrified young people running for their lives while sick individuals hunted them had been traumatic for me. But finding Michael and the others took precedence.

Francine printed out a large map of the piece of land in which we suspected the hunt would take place. Judith helped clear the table and placed the printout in front of Caelan. It took us an hour and forty minutes to go through thirty of the videos, focussing solely on the surroundings, not on the hunting.

Since very few of the hunts started at the same place, we had to work through every recording individually. Caelan impressed us all with his ability to locate small paths through the wooded areas and point out which mountain they were facing. The night-time recordings were more difficult because of the lessened visibility, but even then he was able to point out locations.

It wasn't long before a pattern emerged. Many humans wished to be unpredictable, to present themselves as different, interesting. Yet inherently, we preferred routine. We liked the predictability of the known and avoided the unsettling unknown. Dukwicz presented a pattern.

He favoured seven different places, the exact starting points mere metres from each other. The density of the vegetation, the time of day and changing shadows had made each place look individual to my untrained eye. But as Caelan pointed out these places time after time, I saw the similarities in the areas.

Manny's phone rang, interrupting a particularly brutal hunt of a female student. Francine paused the footage and Manny answered, again placing the phone in the centre of the table. "Millard."

"Have you got a tighter location for us?" Vinnie's voice was lowered. "We're on the northeast end of this property, but we need directions."

"We're working on it," Manny said.

I leaned closer to the phone. "We've isolated seven possible starting points. We'll send you the co-ordinates so you can prepare."

Francine nodded when I looked at her and tapped on her tablet's screen.

"Thanks, Jen-girl. We're on standby. Daniel has called in backup. They'll search the rest of the property for a building or someplace they're are working from. They should be here in ten minutes or so." He paused and cleared his throat. "How long until the hunt starts?"

The hunting auctions had taken less than fifty minutes to conclude. Since then another large digital clock had been counting down the minutes. I blinked a few times and swallowed. "Nine minutes."

"I know no one here wants to say it, so I'm going to." Colin's mouth and eyes were tense, his expression almost angry. "We're going to have to wait until the first video comes up before we can send you to the right location, Vin. Caelan has been helping us and I reckon we'll know exactly where they're starting as soon as the feed goes live."

"Aw, hell." Manny fell back into his chair and pressed the heels of his hands against his eyes.

"Shit, dude. That sucks."

"I'm fast. I'm good." Caelan stared at the phone. "I'll give you their location when I see the video."

"You do that, kid. We're all counting on you." It was the first time I didn't hear annoyance in Vinnie's tone when he was speaking to Caelan.

The call ended and we sat in silence for a few seconds.

"We should move to your room, girlfriend." Francine got up and tilted her head to my viewing room.

"Why?" I didn't want all these people in my room. Already the team room felt crowded.

"You have more monitors. I have access to the GIPN team's vest cams. We can keep an eye on the hunting footage as well as where Daniel, Vinnie and the others are."

"I don't want to know how you got that access." Manny got up and walked to my viewing room.

It became clear that I didn't have an option in this and I followed them. Francine was already sitting in the chair next to mine, working on my computer and opening different windows on each monitor. Manny and Judith stood in front of the antique-looking cabinets. Caelan was behind me as Colin and I walked into my room.

We sat down and Caelan walked to the other side of Francine and stood there, rocking slightly. No one spoke. Split across the four monitors in the centre, the digital clock of the hunting site counted down from six minutes and twenty-two seconds. The surrounding monitors displayed live footage from the cameras attached to each GIPN team member's vest.

It was a few minutes before four in the afternoon. Summer in France meant that the sun was still high, giving us a good view of the team's surroundings. I counted three SUVs parked deep in the woods. The team members were talking quietly, the tension visible in all their bodies.

A shot of adrenaline went through me when I saw Vinnie on the second top monitor. Each monitor displayed the date, time, camera number and team member's name. That was how I knew Vinnie was speaking to Daniel. Vinnie nodded and took his phone from one of the many side pockets in his black cargo pants. He swiped the screen and lifted the device to his ear.

I jerked in surprise when Colin's phone rang. He answered it, looking at the monitor. "Vin."

"Dude. Have you got something for us?" Vinnie's voice was clear over the system. The equipment GIPN used was of superior quality.

"Not yet. We're in Jenny's room and watching you guys on her monitors."

Vinnie looked startled for a millisecond, then looked directly into the camera on Daniel's vest. "Cool. It'll be good to have extra eyes on this."

"I think we should keep an open line."

"Good idea." Vinnie opened another pocket on his pants and took out a cordless earpiece. In his left ear was an earpiece I assumed was from the GIPN team. He put his phone earpiece in his right ear and put the phone back in a pocket. "We're good to go."

"One minute," Francine said softly. "When this is done, I'm finding a way to bypass all Tor security. This will not happen again."

Determination hardened her face. This case had shown us many weaknesses in our abilities. I didn't have time to ponder on this any longer. The clock turned into a paper target and the centre exploded in a bad attempt at special effects, sending fake blood splatter all over the screen.

Colin touched my arm, his hand warm. "Breathe, Jenny."

I took a shuddering breath, but stopped when woods filled the four centre monitors. The next second a young man ran away from the camera into the shadows the tall trees provided.

"Where are they, lad?"

Caelan stared at the monitors, his breathing erratic. "I don't know. I don't know. Siberia contains around twenty percent of the world's forests."

"Oh, hell. Doc, work with him."

I couldn't. I could barely hold on to my own control as I recognised the young man running through the woods. Michael was wearing the same type of running shoes as I'd seen on the other students. He also displayed all the same nonverbal cues of fear. This young man was Nikki's friend, called her Nikkidee and tolerated her teasing. I liked him.

"Doc!"

"Jenny, we need you." Colin squeezed my arm and I nodded.

I didn't take my eyes from the monitor. "Caelan, don't look at the person running. You said you prefer looking at landscapes. Look at the landscape. Tell me what you see."

"Trees. Shadows to the right. He's running—" The barrel of a gun came into view, the sound of the shot loud in the room. Michael stumbled, his hand grasping his shoulder. "Neptune is the coldest planet!"

Caelan keened, his eyes tightly shut. I was equally tempted to give in to the darkness that was closing in on me. But Michael needed us. "Caelan. Where are they? Where is Michael?"

He shook his head, rocking back and forth. He mumbled something and I thought he was in a complete shutdown. When he repeated himself over and over again, relief stole my breath.

"They are in the southwest corner." I took the printed map Francine had brought and pointed to the exact location. "It was the second location Caelan identified. He said that tree looked like the letter B."

"Vin, did you get that?" Colin's voice held urgency.

"We're on our way. It's going to take us about five minutes."

"Please stay alive." Francine clutched her hands in front of her in a praying gesture. "They're coming, Michael. Just stay alive."

Michael was running fast. Faster than most of the other students I'd seen. He leapt over fallen logs, zig-zagging the whole time, making himself a difficult target. The breathing coming from the hunter was increasing as he followed Michael. He made just as much noise racing through the woods as Michael. It would make them easier to find. I hoped Dukwicz and the hunter were so focussed on the hunt they would not hear Vinnie and the team until Michael was safe.

Caelan's keening stilled, but he was still rocking. He shuffled closer and I glanced at him. He was looking at the screen, biting his bottom lip, his face pale. He moved a bit closer and put a shaky index finger on the map. "They're here. Moving north."

Colin immediately relayed the co-ordinates to Vinnie. The vest cams showed them still in the vehicles, racing along a dirt road. The visibility from the last vehicle was very low because of the dust being kicked up by the SUVs in front, but the driver didn't slow down.

Another shot sounded through the room and I jerked. On the centre monitors, Michael was holding his side, a deep red circle developed on the skin under his hand. It slowed him down, but he continued running, moving more erratically than before. I pulled my legs onto the chair and hugged them hard against my chest.

Caelan retreated until his back was against the wall and he slid down into a sitting position, similar to mine. But he was no longer looking at the monitors. He dropped his head onto his knees and bounced his back off the wall.

"They're there." Francine pointed at the top monitor. "Look. Daniel can see them."

A shudder went through my body as two men jogged past Daniel. Their body language indicated their attention to be totally focussed on Michael. The tallest man was easy to recognise. I had been looking for him for the last six months.

He'd been in my bedroom. He'd terrorised me in the shop. Dukwicz was wearing camouflage pants and a dark green t shirt, a rifle slung over his shoulder.

The other man was shorter, stockier. He was running at a comfortable pace, not racing after Michael. The short moment I had to look at his face was enough to see his enjoyment. He was having fun chasing an innocent student through the woods, shooting him with rubber bullets.

I looked at the monitor displaying Vinnie's vest cam. He was not near Dukwicz and the hunter. He seemed to be running much faster than anyone, as if wanting to reach a certain point before the others. His running slowed and his breathing became more audible. "Dude, have you got eyes?"

"They're still making their way north, Vin. I don't have a visual on Michael."

The next moment, Michael ran into the view of Vinnie's camera. He saw Vinnie and his eyes stretched with fear. He tried to swerve away from Vinnie, but didn't make it in time. Vinnie caught him and held on. I didn't know if Michael had met Vinnie. If he had, he'd obviously not recognised him. The stark fear on Michael's face told me he expected to die at Vinnie's hand.

"Calm down, kid. I'm here to help."

The struggle was up close, giving us only glimpses of Michael wrestling for freedom. Vinnie grabbed both Michael's hands and pulled him in so close, the camera only showed the young man's shoulder. "I'm Nikki's friend. We need to get you out of here before—"

A loud shot rang out and Vinnie grunted. He pushed Michael away from him with a loud, "Run!" The camera shuddered and slowly moved downwards, briefly showing

Michael running as fast as he could. The image jerked when Vinnie landed on the ground. He grunted again. "Son of a…"

"Well, well, well. Aren't you just making my day fun." The familiar accented voice brought ice-cold fear into my chest. Black boots came into view and kicked Vinnie's chest. "Hurts like a motherfucker, doesn't it? Your back is going to have a huge bruise thanks to that Kevlar vest. Not that you'd see it. You know, I've never had a problem shooting someone in the back. But for the kill shot, I think I'll look you in the eye."

Vinnie turned enough for the camera to show Dukwicz looking down, his weapon trained on Vinnie. It was a powerful handgun, not a weapon for shooting tranquilising darts or rubber bullets. The darkness came closer and I focussed on Dukwicz's body language.

From this angle, Dukwicz looked taller, even more vicious than I remembered. He rested his boot heavily on Vinnie's hand and bent down to take Vinnie's weapon. "Is that delightful doctor also here?"

"Fuck you." Vinnie sounded weak. In pain.

Dukwicz kicked Vinnie again, aiming for his stomach. Vinnie grunted loudly, the camera shaking. "Why do you people always have to fuck everything up for me?"

Vinnie didn't say anything. I wasn't breathing, moving, not even blinking. I could not watch my friend die. We were supposed to save the students. We were supposed to capture Dukwicz, the hunter, Gasquet, Breton and Hugo. *This* was not supposed to happen. I couldn't take my eyes off the monitors to see if Michael was safe, or if someone was going to come to Vinnie's aid.

I couldn't imagine why Vinnie wasn't fighting back. Was he that badly injured? His breathing sounded even. Harsh, but even. Dukwicz lifted his rifle to his shoulder and aimed above the camera at Vinnie's head. "Killing you might be the highlight of my career. It will also make you number three hundred and fifty. Such a nice round number."

The camera shook and a violent flurry of movement ensued. It was impossible to see what was happening. My chest ached and I hardly breathed as I searched the footage for a clue to Vinnie's safety. There was too much movement and Vinnie's arm obscured the view a few times. When the movement and camera stilled, Vinnie was sitting on top of Dukwicz's chest.

The camera moved with Vinnie's body as he punched Dukwicz, breaking his nose. Already, Dukwicz had a bright red bruise on his jaw and his eyebrow was split. Vinnie didn't stop. The camera moved again as he raised his fist, but the image jerked to a halt.

"Enough, Vinnie. You've got him. He's secure." Daniel came into sight, holding out his hand. Vinnie took it and stood up. Three of Daniel's team members had their weapons aimed at Dukwicz. One of them holstered his gun and took out zip ties to cuff Dukwicz.

"No, wait." Vinnie moved closer to Dukwicz. He grabbed Dukwicz's left hand and twisted it until the man under him yelled out. Only then did Vinnie take Colin's watch from Dukwicz's wrist. "Motherfucking bastard."

Vinnie straightened and the GIPM team member fastened the zip ties around Dukwicz's wrists. They looked a bit tight.

"Where's Michael?" Vinnie turned to the direction Michael had run. Only trees filled the monitor. He turned back to Daniel.

"Pink has him. He's secure." Daniel slapped Vinnie on the shoulder, but frowned when Vinnie groaned. "What happened?"

"Nothing. A bruise." He paused. "What about the other kids?"

"The Beta team found the hideout. We have the three students. The one male is very traumatised, but they all seem to be physically unharmed." The smile lifting Daniel's mouth wasn't friendly. "We got Breton, Hugo and two others."

"Gasquet?"

"Not there."

"Fuck!"

"Don't worry. He's on every law enforcement's radar. He won't be able to move around freely in Europe."

Vinnie's eyes widened suddenly. He looked into Daniel's camera. "You guys still there?"

"Yes." Colin cleared his throat when the word came out hoarse. "Yes, Vin. We're here."

"Come home, Vinnie." Francine's voice was thick with tears.

"Be there are soon as I can." He blinked a few times. Concern contracted the muscles around his eyes and mouth. "Jen-girl?"

Irrationally, I nodded at the monitors.

"She's here, Vin."

"Is she okay?"

Colin looked at me and said softly, "She will be."

Chapter **TWENTY-THREE**

I stepped out of my bedroom and was met with a loud argument.

"I'm not putting lemon garlic on a steak. Get out of my kitchen, you evil woman."

"I tell you, it will bring out the steak-ey flavour if you add a few spoons of this to your marinade." Francine held out a small shaker. Vinnie took it and put it on the highest shelf. Francine stretched to reach it, but he blocked her. Still reaching up, she turned to Vinnie and put her arms around his neck. After a second, he pulled her close and gave her a tight hug. She slapped him lightly on his shoulder. "You scared me, you big lug."

"You scared everyone, Vin." Colin got up from the sofa and walked to me, studying me. "Feeling better?"

"Much. Thank you." I had just spent an hour lying in my bathtub, mentally writing Mozart's Fugue in G minor. The two hours after Dukwicz's capture had been spent first calming Caelan and getting him to allow Tim, Nikki and Rebecca to take him home. Eventually Phillip had joined them to make sure Caelan had enough food and that everyone was safe.

Francine and I had searched for alternative locations where Gasquet could have gone, but had found nothing. Manny had been the one to order us all to go home and rest. The students had been taken to hospital for evaluation and there had been nothing more we could do.

Nikki had looked at me once and had gone to Colin for a hug. As soon as we'd arrived at my apartment, I'd locked the reinforced door of my bathroom and surrendered to the harmony of Mozart's composition to restore calm and control in my mind. I couldn't remember ever feeling so drained. Paradoxically, Vinnie and Francine's argument energised me.

He let her go and turned to me. "Thank you for finding those kids, Jen-girl."

"We all did our part." I walked closer and stopped in front of him. I studied the scarred face of a man who had seen much violence in his life. Yet he argued with Francine about spices and gave her comforting hugs. I lifted my hand until it was two centimetres from his sternum. He just stood there silently, giving me the time to find the right words, the right gesture. I slowly rested my hand on his chest, over his heart. "I am so proud to call you my friend."

"Aw, Jen-girl." Vinnie took my hand in his and pressed it hard against his chest.

I pulled my hand out of his and took a step away from him. "Does your back hurt?"

"Like a son of a bitch." He turned around and pulled his shirt up. A bruise larger than my hand covered the upper left side of his muscular back.

Colin whistled softly. "That looks painful. Is anything broken?"

"Don't think so." Vinnie dropped his shirt and faced us again. "It doesn't feel like any ribs are broken."

"Did you have a doctor or someone check you out?" Francine asked.

"For what?" Vinnie lifted one shoulder. "To tell me not to sleep on my back for a few days? Nah. This isn't my first rodeo, girl. I know what a broken rib feels like, so I'm pretty sure I don't have any of those."

I looked around my apartment. "Where's Nikki?"

"She's with Rebecca in her room. They're listening to music." Colin's smile was relaxed. "Nikki was a real trouper—really strong."

"I know she's strong." Stronger than me. I had barely held on to my control until we came home. Even now I was fighting the blackness that still hovered around the periphery of my vision. The toll this case had taken on each of us was higher than ever before.

The doorbell rang, immediately followed by impatient knocking. Colin shook his head and walked to the front door. "That will be Millard. He said he'd be around."

"He's just coming for the dinner." Vinnie turned to the stove. "He'd better be hungry. I'm making enough food to feed an army."

Colin checked first before opening the door. Manny walked in and pointed with his thumb over his shoulder. "Look who I brought with."

Michael walked in behind Manny, still pale, but with his head held high. He stepped past Manny and walked straight to Vinnie, stopping in front of him. It took him three tries before he could speak. When he did his voice shook. "Thank you. No. Thank you is not enough. I don't know what to say. I don't have the words."

Vinnie looked down at the young man, his face soft. "I know. And you're welcome."

Michael turned to me. "Thanks for finding me."

I nodded, uncomfortable with the strong emotions overwhelming me. A happy shout from the other side of the apartment saved me.

"Michael! You're here." Nikki ran towards us and threw her arms around Michael. He groaned loudly and she lifted her arms. "Did I hurt you? Oh, my God. Did they hurt you? Are you okay? Do you need to go to the doctor? Doc G, we need to take him to the hospital."

"I'm okay, Nikkidee."

"I just brought him from the hospital." Manny sat down at the dining room table. The dark circles under his eyes were not the only indication of his exhaustion. "Apart from a few bruises, he's okay."

"Are you?" Nikki leaned in and looked deep into Michael's eyes. "Are you really okay?"

He put his hands on her shoulders and nodded slowly. "I'm alive. I'll be okay. Actually, I'm… um… I'm hungry."

He looked so embarrassed about it that Nikki burst out laughing and gave him another hug, which made him groan again and made her apologise again. Rebecca joined us and gave Michael a quick hug. Vinnie organised the young people to help him prepare two different kinds of salads. When Francine offered her assistance, he bared his teeth and banned her from the kitchen. She joined us at the dining room table. Colin had pulled his chair close to mine, his arm around the back of my chair.

"Where is Judith?" I asked.

"She went back to Lyon. This is a huge cluster—" Manny looked towards the kitchen and the young people laughing with Vinnie. "It's a big mess. The other two members of her team are gone and she needs to be debriefed."

"What's going to happen to Breton and Hugo?" Francine asked.

Manny snorted. "Hugo is such a big sissy. He's already started spilling all the secrets. Apparently, he and Breton went to visit Gasquet on the farm after Emile Rimbaud died. Even though Adam had given Gasquet the farm, he had left the house the same way Adam and Rimbaud had decorated it for those times Rimbaud went there.

"Breton and Hugo were going to help Gasquet clear out the house and make it a weekend getaway. That was when they discovered all Adam's paintings. Gasquet hadn't known about any of it. But once he knew, he fought so hard to get Rimbaud's case closed and forgotten. He refused to believe that Rimbaud and Adam could be guilty of anything illegal. By the sounds of it, he really idolised them."

"Discovering that Adam had painted so many forgeries and that Monsieur Rimbaud had tried to sell one of those to pay for his medical bills had to be disillusioning." And very difficult for a man who'd had such a hard childhood.

"I reckon that was the trigger that turned him into such a psycho." Manny slouched deeper into the chair.

"He didn't turn into something. It was already there. This was only a catalyst that brought his dark behaviour to the fore." It happened more often than we knew.

"Okay, so what was the deal with Breton and Hugo?" Colin asked.

"Oh, Hugo wanted to report those paintings immediately. He said that Gasquet really put the squeeze on him to keep quiet. That was when he received the first payment. From there it just went south. Gasquet got them to open an account on SSS." Manny lifted his index finger. "Ah, he said the three of them worked together as Zana-whatever-D."

"Zana22Dactor3178," Francine said.

"Yeah. That. It was the handle they used for all their illegal activities. And when Hugo started spilling... It seems like there have been quite a lot of illegal activities. He said that he just got in deeper and deeper and eventually didn't know how to get out of it."

"That's a bullshit excuse," Colin said through his teeth.

"I fully agree, Frey. He wouldn't have been selling students for spare parts if he wasn't already crooked in some way."

"Huh. So ZD was actually three men." Francine nodded slowly. "Makes sense. They had enough expertise to pool together. No wonder it worked well for such a long time."

"How did they go from selling forged Courbet paintings to kidnapping students and selling them in auctions?" That was a leap in behaviour I didn't understand.

"Hugo blamed it on Gasquet. He said one of Gasquet's legit clients had a kid who needed a kidney, but the waiting list was too long. He came to Gasquet in confidence, asking if he knew a way to find a kidney for his child. At first Gasquet refused, but the client offered a quarter of a million dollars."

"That's a huge temptation," Colin said. "And a bigger payday than trying to sell a forged Courbet painting."

"Which makes it no surprise that the bastard agreed. Hugo said that was how Gasquet came up with the idea."

"How does Dukwicz fit into all of this?" I asked.

"Ah." Manny's smile was not friendly. "Apparently Gasquet has many friends in low places. Not only did his clients request him to find organs, but someone requested this kind of hunting. His lower than low contacts gave him Dukwicz and the rest we know."

I thought about this for a few seconds. The realisation of our carelessness made me feel cold. "Did Dukwicz get CCTV footage from the police station of the day Colin, or to be more correct Edward Taylor, was arrested? He could have seen me with Colin and would have drawn a very logical conclusion."

"Shit, Jenny." Colin shook his head, his eyes wide.

Manny looked apologetic. "That's indeed what happened, Doc. Like I said, Hugo spilled his guts. Including telling us about aiding and abetting an international assassin."

"Who is now in maximum security," Vinnie said from the kitchen.

The doorbell rang again. Manny and Colin looked at each other and walked to the front door side by side. Colin looked through the peephole, straightened and opened the door.

"I'm hungry and I want a girlfriend." Caelan walked into my apartment and immediately looked at Francine's shoulder. "You promised me a girlfriend. I want one."

"I didn't promise you a girlfriend, kiddo." Francine was smiling, the tension caused by our discussion gone. "I promised to teach you how to get one. Big difference."

"Teach me now."

"Do you need a girlfriend now or do you need to eat now?"

Caelan thought about this and turned to the kitchen. "Eat. But only green food. I'm not eating that."

Vinnie narrowed his eyes on Caelan before turning his look to Nikki. She lifted both shoulders. "Sorry. I should've told you I invited him. He looked so lonely when we took him home. I told him that he's welcome to join us for dinner."

"You said there would be green food." Caelan frowned at her shoulder. "Did you lie to me?"

"Hold on there, kiddo." Vinnie stepped in front of Nikki. "There's green food here. I'll make you green food. Don't go around accusing people of lying."

"He didn't accuse me." Nikki tried to push Vinnie out of the way, but didn't budge him. "He asked a question."

"Sounded like an accusation to me," Vinnie mumbled. "And you better dig through the fridge for green food, little punk. You invited him with promises. You better keep those promises."

My apartment was overflowing with people. Bantering, insults, laughter and teasing that should confuse and frustrate me made me feel safe and at home. I leaned back in my chair and felt Colin's arm around my shoulders. I shifted to lean against his chest.

The resilience of Vinnie, Nikki and Michael fascinated me. I felt like I was never going to recover from the horror of this case. Looking at them laughing, listening to Francine teasing Manny in her sexy voice and him growling back at her gave me hope.

I would never have normal in my life. I didn't want normal in my life. But I had the safety of strong friends.

~ ~ ~ ~ ~

Be first to find out when Genevieve's next adventure will be published.
Sign up for the newsletter at http://estelleryan.com/contact.html

~ ~ ~ ~ ~

Listen to the Mozart pieces,
look at the paintings from this book
and read more about Tor, the 2012 haul and Bitcoin at:
http://estelleryan.com/the-courbet-connection.html

The Gauguin Connection
First in the Genevieve Lenard series

Murdered artists. Masterful forgeries. Art crime at its worst.

A straightforward murder investigation quickly turns into a quagmire of stolen Eurocorps weapons, a money-laundering charity, forged art and high-ranking EU officials abusing their power.

As an insurance investigator and world renowned expert in nonverbal communication, Dr Genevieve Lenard faces the daily challenge of living a successful, independent life. Particularly because she has to deal with her high functioning Autism. Nothing—not her studies, her high IQ or her astounding analytical skills—prepared her for the changes about to take place in her life.

It started as a favour to help her boss' acerbic friend look into the murder of a young artist, but soon it proves to be far more complex. Forced out of her predictable routines, safe environment and limited social interaction, Genevieve is thrown into exploring the meaning of friendship, expanding her social definitions, and for the first time in her life be part of a team in a race to stop more artists from being murdered.

The Gauguin Connection *is available as paperback and ebook.*

The Dante Connection
Second in the Genevieve Lenard series

Art theft. Coded messages. A high-level threat.

Despite her initial disbelief, Doctor Genevieve Lenard discovers that she is the key that connects stolen works of art, ciphers and sinister threats.

Betrayed by the people who called themselves her friends, Genevieve throws herself into her insurance investigation job with autistic single-mindedness. When hacker Francine appears beaten and bloodied on her doorstep, begging for her help, Genevieve is forced to get past the hurt of her friends' abandonment and team up with them to find the perpetrators. Little does she know that it will take her on a journey through not one, but two twisted minds to discover the true target of their mysterious messages. It will take all her personal strength and knowledge as a nonverbal communications expert to overcome fears that could cost not only her life, but the lives of many others.

The Dante Connection *available as paperback and ebook.*

The Braque Connection
Third in the Genevieve Lenard series

Forged masterpieces. Hidden messages. A desperate swan song.

World-renowned nonverbal communication expert Doctor Genevieve Lenard wakes up drugged in an unknown location after being kidnapped. As someone with high-functioning autism, this pushes the limits of her coping skills.

For the last year, Russian philanthropist and psychopath Tomasz Kubanov has been studying Genevieve just as she and her team have been studying him. Now forged paintings and mysterious murders are surfacing around her team, with evidence pointing to one of them as the killer.

Genevieve knows Kubanov is behind these senseless acts of violence. What she doesn't understand are the inconsistencies between his actions and the cryptic messages he sends. Something has triggered his unpredictable behaviour, something that might result in many more deaths, including those she cares for. Because this time, Kubanov has nothing to lose.

The Braque Connection *is available as paperback and ebook.*

The Flick Connection
Third in the Genevieve Lenard series

A murdered politician. An unsolved art heist. An international conspiracy.

A cryptic online message leads nonverbal communications expert Doctor Genevieve Lenard to the body of a brutally murdered politician. Despite being ordered not to investigate, Genevieve and her team look into this vicious crime. More online messages follow, leading them down a path lined with corruption, a sadistic assassin, an oil scandal and one of the biggest heists in history—the still unsolved 1990 Boston museum art theft worth $500m.

The deeper they delve, the more evidence they unearth of a conspiracy implicating someone close to them, someone they hold in high regard. With a deadline looming, Genevieve has to cope with past and present dangers, an attack on one of her team members and her own limitations if she is to expose the real threat and protect those in her inner circle.

The Flinck Connection *is available as paperback and ebook.*

Find out more about Estelle and her books at
www.estelleryan.com
Or visit her Facebook page to chat with her:
www.facebook.com/EstelleRyanAuthor